Praise for *Majestic Descending*

"Fluent prose, smooth pacing, and an engaging protagonist make this narrative shine. The whodunit payoff is a real corker." —*Mystery Scene*

"The sinking of the *Majestic* is exciting." —*Publishers Weekly*

"Pure fun . . . The trial scenes are nail-biters and the action set-pieces are first-rate. Like all great trips, it offers excitement, adventure, humor, and even a splash of romance. . . . *Majestic Descending* is first class all the way." —J. A. Konrath, author of *Whiskey Sour* and *Bloody Mary*

"One of the year's top ten books." —*The Strand Magazine*

"Mitchell Graham is a new voice in the thriller scene. His novel *Majestic Descending* begins his career with a healthy bang." —David Hagberg, author of *Soldier of God*

"A powerful, enthralling, and believable thriller." —*Midwest Book Review*

MAJESTIC
DESCENDING

MITCHELL GRAHAM

TOR®

A TOM DOHERTY ASSOCIATES BOOK
NEW YORK

This is a work of fiction. All of the characters, organizations, and events portrayed in this novel are either products of the author's imagination or are used fictitiously.

MAJESTIC DESCENDING

A Tor Book
Published by Tom Doherty Associates, LLC
175 Fifth Avenue
New York, NY 10010

www.tor-forge.com

Tor® is a registered trademark of Tom Doherty Associates, LLC.

ISBN-13: 978-0-7653-5774-8
ISBN-10: 0-7653-5774-7

First Edition: June 2007
First Mass Market Edition: June 2008

Printed in the United States of America

0 9 8 7 6 5 4 3 2 1

To my son, Douglas,
who makes me proud every day

ACKNOWLEDGMENTS

I humbly and gratefully acknowledge the help, contributions, support, and advice of my editor and friend, Jack Dann, a brilliant author in his own right. Thanks also to Denis Wong, Norma Hoffman, and Claire Eddy, who made me think about quality rather than quantity. Last, but by no means least, my sincere thanks must go to Deborah Gross and Robbie Johnson who acted as first readers and who (patiently) offered their suggestions throughout the laborious process of crafting this novel.

MAJESTIC DESCENDING

PROLOGUE

Maybe she was dead.

She had a vague recollection of falling. It seemed to take forever to fall. Then came the darkness, silent, black and impenetrable. She had no idea where she was. In the distance she could see a light. Somewhere in the back of her mind she recalled hearing stories about light and about people moving toward it, but she couldn't recall what they said now. Tentatively, Katherine tried moving her fingers and toes. It was no use. She felt nothing. The absence of sensation was both disconcerting and frightening. No pain . . . no cold . . . no heat—nothing at all. Perhaps this was how death was supposed to feel.

She glanced at the horizon as the light began to fade and the silence closed in on her once again. It was disappointing because she had begun looking forward to the light. It was the only change in a world of endless black. She felt weightless now, as though she were drifting high above the ground on soft currents of air. Perhaps she was the only person left in the world. Time passed—first one day and then another. In the distance the light came and went. There was no pattern to it. On the third day a change took place; murmuring voices floated up to her on the wind. They were indistinct and it was difficult to catch all the words, but someone was definitely speaking.

"Where did they find her?" a man asked.

"At the bottom of the gorge, poor kid. She was half in the water, half out. Do you think she'll make it, Doc?"

There was a pause.

"It's hard to say," answered the doctor. "How long was she out there?"

"Maybe four days," the deputy replied. "Her room-mate came to the station to file a missing person report. When Patterson told her we would look into it, she pitched a fit and insisted we start a search immediately. It's a good thing we did. We were about to give up when one of the dogs picked up her scent. According to the paramedics a few more hours and it wouldn't have made a difference."

Before the doctor could respond a nurse entered the hospital room. Both men stepped aside while she checked an IV tube running into a vein on the girl's left forearm. The nurse frowned and tapped it twice to dispel a tiny air bubble near the base. Satisfied, she noted the time and placed an entry on her chart.

"Has there been any change in her condition, doctor?" she asked quietly. "Her roommate's been sleeping in the lobby for two days and she won't leave."

"Not really. I'll go out and speak with her when I'm done."

"I'm sure she'd appreciate that."

The doctor took a deep breath and looked at the girl lying on the bed. He shook his head slightly.

"By all rights she should be dead. I can't believe that bastard cut off one of her fingers. But this one's a fighter, which will help." He then turned to the deputy. "Did your people catch him?"

"What was left," said the deputy. "The cabin was on fire by the time we got there. He burned himself and the other girls alive."

"Dear God," said the doctor.

The nurse put a hand to her mouth to stifle a gasp.

The deputy continued. "Interesting thing is we found

two sets of footprints on the ground. Both belonged to her, but they were going in opposite directions."

"I don't understand," said the doctor.

"We're thinking she went back and tried to get the others out before Jenks torched the place. Tell you the truth, Doc, if we had taken him alive there wasn't much chance he'd have made it to trial. The sheriff's daughter was the first and they never found her head."

The nurse came around the side of the bed and smoothed Katherine's hair into place. Her oldest daughter had just started Ohio State and was about the same age as this girl. The whole campus, the whole community, was in an uproar over the grisly murders. It was as though a monster had descended on Columbus, Ohio. She didn't want to hear any more of the details. She placed a comforting hand on Katherine's shoulder and left the room.

"Richard Jenks was a piece of work," said the doctor. "I can't say I'm sorry—*what the hell?*"

Without warning a piercing alarm on the monitor above Katherine's head went off. At the same time the readouts showing her vital signs suddenly became erratic.

The doctor reacted immediately and punched a button on the intercom.

"*Code Blue! Code Blue!* I need a defibrillator in 306 *STAT—repeat STAT!*"

"What the hell's happening?" asked the deputy.

"Her pulse just went off the chart. Blood pressure's spiking . . . respiration is up. She's having a seizure."

"Oh, Christ." Instinctively, the deputy reached out and took Katherine's hand. "You hang in there, little lady. Help is on the way."

THE MENTION of the cabin is what did it. All at once it came flooding back to her. The screams exploded in her head, the endless, endless screams—hers and the other girls'. Jenks's breath was so close to her face she could smell it, horrible and sickly sweet. And the whispers in the dark . . . whispers of what he planned to do . . . what God told him to do.

The cabin wasn't the *only* place—it was just where he first took them. She knew that as surely as she knew anything. There was a house. Other images began to flash into Katherine's mind. They were all locked in separate cells in a basement. All the while Jenks kept up his whispering. A rotting smell hung in the air, gagging her. By the second day she was certain she would go insane if she didn't get away from it. No, the cabin wasn't the only place. Desperately she tried to clear her brain. The house was old and badly in need of paint. She'd only caught glimpses of it through the fog of drugs Jenks had given her, but it was large and it had a porch. Another image snapped into her mind now, one that caused her entire body to convulse. There were heads mounted on the wall—human heads, heads of girls the same age as she was. Jenks called it his trophy room. The smell of formaldehyde returned to her with terrible clarity.

She saw the trophy room only once more. She was running for her life in blind panic then. Jenks had made a mistake. He was too arrogant, too full of himself to think anyone would fight back. When he came into her cell to feed her, to whisper again about what he planned to do, he didn't see the broken water glass lying beside her cot. The moment he let down his guard she rammed the largest shard into his thigh. He screamed. Katherine burst past him into a dimly lit corridor and started running. She had no idea which way to go. Up the stairs, down a hallway, through the horrible room and out into the night. Jenks came after her dragging his injured leg behind him, the broken glass still embedded in his thigh.

* * *

"Doc . . . *Doc!*" yelled the deputy, as he felt Katherine's fingers close around his wrist. She began pulling him down. "I think she's trying to say something."

But the doctor was in the hallway shouting for the orderlies to hurry with the defibrillator.

Confused and clearly out of his depth, the deputy tried to calm the girl.

"It okay. It's okay," he said, patting her gently on the forearm.

But the girl continued to pull with a strength that surprised him.

"You'll be fine," he said. "Just try and take it easy. Help is coming. I promise."

When her eyes suddenly opened it startled him and the deputy tried to pull away. The girl wouldn't let go. If anything her grip tightened and she pulled harder on his arm until he brought his ear close to her lips.

"There are others," she whispered.

The recent breakthrough in our ability to grow brain stem cells under controlled laboratory conditions must rank as one of the greatest medical achievements of the last century. I can envision a time in the near future when diseases once thought to be incurable will be specters of the past.

Michael Braithwaite, M.D.
Letter to the *New England Journal of Medicine*
October 9, 2003

ONE

Atlanta
May 2006

When Katherine Adams's telephone rang at seven-twenty in the morning, she opened one sleepy eye and looked at it with a groan. She let it ring twice more before her conscience got the better of her.

"This better be good," she mumbled into the receiver, "I'm on vacation."

There was a slight hesitation on the other end of the line before her secretary, Galena Olivares replied, "You're gonna kill me, K.J., but I swear I didn't know what else to do. The answering service called about fifteen minutes ago. Sherri Wallace was served with an emergency petition to change custody this morning."

Katherine opened the other eye and pushed herself up onto one elbow.

"Are you serious?"

"I called her and explained you were on leave of absence but she's hysterical. She says they're going to take her children. Do you want to fire me now or later?"

"Later," Katherine said.

"I'm really sorry," said Galena. "I know you're crazy with leaving this afternoon, but Bert's in Houston for depositions, Jerry is on trial in Savannah, and no one else here knows squat about domestic relations except you."

"Lucky me," Katherine said, brushing the hair away from her face.

"That's what you get for being a lawyer. What can I do to help?"

Fully awake now Katherine sat up in bed.

"What time is the hearing scheduled?" she asked.

"Ten-thirty, in front of Judge Morehouse."

"Morehouse? Frank Hanes is assigned to this case. How did Arthur Morehouse get it?"

"Hanes is on vacation," Galena explained. "Morehouse is presiding and it's an emergency petition, so it went to him."

"Damn it. Dick Royal knows I'm leaving today and he pulls a stunt like this."

"*Dick*'s a good name for him. They can't make you come if you're on leave, can they, K. J.?"

Katherine swung her feet over the edge of the bed, stood up, and stretched. Her plan to sleep late, finish packing, and take a leisurely trip to Nordstrom for some last-minute items for her trip began to look more and more remote.

"No . . . they can't make me," she said slowly.

Technically, a leave of absence meant she was excused from appearing in court. There was no legal obligation to be there. It was as simple as that. The problem was the other attorney had filed an emergency proceeding which gave the judge the authority to temporarily remove Sherri's children from her home if he thought the situation warranted it. Worse, he might even place them in foster care. Katherine debated with herself for a few seconds whether to let the situation wait until she returned from vacation. She liked Sherri Wallace and couldn't imagine her doing anything that would place her children in jeopardy. The woman was a good mother. One more attempt to talk herself into leaving fell flat before she gave up. The children were the deciding factor.

"Get in touch with Sherri and tell her I'll call her in forty-five minutes."

"Will do. I'll be in the office at eight-thirty if you need me. Good luck."

* * *

RICHARD ROYAL, Katherine Adams's adversary, was a member of the "courthouse crowd." Had he been born in the South, Royal might have been known as a "good ol' boy." Unfortunately, he was born and raised in Philadelphia. Over the years he had painstakingly cultivated a Southern accent to help him fit in better, and that strategy had worked. Along with his two partners, he had managed to develop one of the more active domestic-relations practices in Atlanta. His specialty was boutique-type divorces for clients who could pay his fees.

Early on in the Wallace case Katherine concluded that for all Royal's talk about wanting to "settle things amicably," he was, to put it simply, a hardball player. "Amicable" meant settling on his client's terms.

For the past nine months Royal had frustrated every attempt at settlement they made. Each offer she submitted was either rejected as "outrageous" (in light of his client's limited financial condition) or simply ignored. Mark Wallace, Sherri's estranged husband, owned three cosmetic dentistry clinics. And the only counteroffer Katherine got back was so ridiculously low, no competent attorney would have given it more than a passing glance.

The Wallaces had two children, both girls, who were presently living with their mother. Now with the trial fast approaching, it appeared that Royal and his client had decided to raise the stakes considerably. It was probably just coincidence they chose the very day she was leaving on vacation to do so. Katherine thought about that as she turned on the shower and stepped in.

Coincidence, my foot.

FIFTEEN MINUTES later she wrapped a towel around herself and sat down in front of her magnifying mirror to put on her makeup. A quick glance at the clock showed the time was seven fifty-five. She began to calculate rapidly.

Twenty minutes to get dressed. Thirty minutes to the office, pick up the file, and another thirty minutes to get to the courthouse. . . . I can just make it.

THE FACE that regarded her in the mirror was still beautiful after forty-five years. High cheekbones and blue-gray eyes were inherited from her grandmother, and a trim figure that could still draw looks from men half her age was the result of regular workouts and good genes. Her workouts were part of her daily routine and something she adamantly refused to give up.

She kept at them throughout her marriage despite getting little or no help from her husband with the children. The heart surgeon's excuse was that he was simply too busy with his medical practice or on his way to various business meetings. Katherine never complained. She loved being with her kids and managed to sneak in enough exercise to maintain her shape by dancing in the family room for an hour each day. What she didn't know at the time was that half of the heart surgeon's "meetings" were with nurses at an apartment he and two other doctors had secretly rented for their trysts. The sordid details came out during their divorce trial.

James and Alley, Katherine's two oldest children, were now away at college at the University of Georgia. Two years apart in age, they each had their own apartment, but saw the other frequently. Zach—her baby, as she referred to him, had started high school a year earlier and was nearly as tall as she was.

High school, Katherine sighed, as she applied a small amount of eyeliner to her lower lids.

Another glance at the clock told her she was still on schedule. She picked out a charcoal gray Rena Lange suit from the closet and put it on. It was professional and stylish without being overstated. A brief wave of panic hit her as she was zipping up the skirt.

Pantyhose.

It was one of the items she had planned picking up later that day. A quick check of her stocking drawer confirmed her fears. She didn't have a decent pair to wear to court.

Then it dawned on her—*Alley.*

Katherine bounded up the stairs to the second floor of her home and into her daughter's room.

God, I hope she hasn't moved everything to her apartment yet.

Ever since her junior year in high school, Alley Adams had become something of an authority where lingerie was concerned. Katherine wasn't sure when the change had taken place or precisely how she felt about it, since some of the things Alley wore tended to be sexier than her own undergarments. When the sales clerks at Victoria's Secret started sending thank-you notes to the house, she made a mental note to have a chat with her daughter the next time they got together.

Katherine started to open the top drawer of the dresser and stopped. On the corner was a framed photograph of the two of them taken a few months earlier. A smile creased the corners of her eyes. She had no idea Alley had made a copy of it. There was nothing special about the photo, which showed them lying on a bed together watching television. Their heads were nearly touching. She studied it for a few seconds longer and then, with a twinge of guilt, slid Alley's lingerie drawer open. She found what she was looking for, a new pair of Givenchy pantyhose still in their package. Fortunately, mother and daughter both wore a size six and their tastes were similar, at least in pantyhose. Katherine removed the stockings, hiked up her skirt, and began the ritual of struggling into them.

The clock read ten after eight.

When she was through she hurried down the stairs and located a pair of black pumps that went well with her suit, grabbed her briefcase, and left the house. On the way to the office she placed a phone call to Sherri Wallace.

"Hi, Sherri, it's Katherine."

"Oh, Katherine. Thank God. I've been frantic."

"Galena gave me your message. I'm on my way to pick up your file now. What's going on?"

"Mark wants to take my kids. The sheriff served papers on me this morning. I told him you were on vacation, but he left them anyway. How can they do this?"

The words were all coming out in a rush.

"Just calm down and tell me exactly what he's alleging."

"Alleging?"

"Read me what the papers say, Sherri."

"Wait a minute."

In the background Katherine heard papers rustling as Sherri started flipping through them.

"All right . . . he says that I'm an unfit mother and that it is in the best interest of the children for custody to be changed immediately. He also says I'm not providing a good moral environment for them."

Sherri Wallace's voice cracked as she read the last part and she started to cry.

Katherine said, "Look, I know this is difficult but we don't have a lot of time. Is there anything else in the papers?"

"That's it," Sherri said, taking a deep breath. "I'm sorry."

"Don't be. Do you have any idea what he's talking about?"

"No."

"*None* at all?"

"*No,* I swear to God, Katherine. Nothing's changed."

Katherine started to tick off different possibilities in her mind. She knew Richard Royal, and was positive he hadn't filed the motion just for practice. Something was definitely amiss.

"I'll call you back in five minutes," she said. "I need to speak with the other attorney and see if he's willing to share what this is all about."

Katherine hung up and punched in Royal's number. On the second ring a receptionist answered, "Chamblis, Royal, and Bullard."

"This is Katherine Adams. Is Mr. Royal available?"

"Just a moment, ma'am, I'll check."

There was a pause as she was put on hold. Ten seconds later, Richard Royal came on the line.

"Katherine, how are you?"

"Not good, Richard."

"I know, I know," he said. "I'm sorry to do this to you, but we didn't have any choice. I agonized about waiting until you got back from your vacation, I really did, but my client is extremely upset and he directed me to proceed."

Yeah, I'll just bet you're sorry, thought Katherine. "I understand. What seems to be the problem?"

"In a nutshell, it's come to our attention that Sherri's been leading a parade of men through the house, and Mark feels . . . well . . . it's just not the type of environment he wants his girls exposed to. I mean, this woman is supposed to be setting an example for her daughters, you know?"

The longer Royal went on, the thicker his Southern accent got.

"You're telling me men have been sleeping at Sherri Wallace's house?"

"That's exactly what I'm sayin', Kathy. Mind you, I have no moral objection to a woman seeking male companionship. I mean it's the twenty-first century and all. But not in front of impressionable young girls. That's just totally unacceptable."

"I see. And you have proof of this?"

Royal chuckled. "I expect I'll be able to make out my case if that's what you're asking."

"Actually, I was asking if you intend to call any witnesses. I'd like an opportunity to speak with them prior to the hearing," said Katherine.

"Unfortunately, I don't have the file in front of me at the moment. My paralegal's putting it together right now and I've got a client in with me. I did want to take your call, though. Tell you what, Kathy, let's you and me talk for a few minutes before the judge gets on the bench and see if we can't work things out."

"My name's Katherine, *Dick*. I'll see you down there."

When Katherine hung up she realized that she had just driven two blocks past the entrance to her office. Cursing under her breath, she pulled into a convenience store parking lot, and did a U-turn.

Galena was waiting in the lobby with her file. As soon as she saw the big Mercedes pull up, she ran out to the car.

"So?" she asked, handing Katherine the file through the driver's window.

"Royal says that Sherri's had men at her house when her daughters were present."

"*What?* I don't believe it. That meek little thing? There's no way. She bends over backward for those girls."

"Let's hope she wasn't bending over backward for some man when the kids were around."

Galena's eyebrows lifted. "We're not in a good mood this morning, are we?"

"Not particularly," Katherine answered. "Do me a favor. Check the airlines and see if there's an afternoon or evening flight to Miami. I'm not sure how long the hearing will take and I might have to catch a later plane."

"No problem, boss," said Galena.

"Okay, who called this meeting?" asked a voice at the end of the car.

Katherine looked in her side-view mirror and saw the youngest member of their law firm, Jimmy D'Taglia, walking toward them. Jimmy was a born and bred New Yorker, who had graduated with honors from Fordham Law School. Hired a year earlier, the firm had been grooming him to take on some of Burt Boyd's overflow. Jimmy was a tough, aggressive kid, with one of the most pronounced New York accents Katherine had ever heard. This made him something of a novelty in Southern court-rooms, but did nothing to diminish his string of successes over the last six months. It took him about the same amount of time to stop getting lost in the city once he realized Atlanta had thirty-eight separate streets all named Peachtree.

"Hey, Jimmy," said Katherine.

"Hey, kids," he answered.

"Katherine's on her way to court," Galena explained.

Jimmy frowned. "Aren't you supposed to be on vacation?"

"That seems to be the general consensus. Turns out an attorney on the opposite side of one of my cases filed an emergency petition to change custody this morning."

"Gee, what a coincidence," said Jimmy. "He just *happens* to set it down for the day you're leaving. What a mook."

Katherine wasn't exactly sure what a "mook" was, but she got the general idea.

"Is there some kind of physical abuse involved?" Jimmy asked.

"No, nothing like that. They're claiming the mother is

sleeping around. I don't have all the specifics yet, but the whole thing sounds like a crock."

"It is," Galena assured Jimmy. "You should see this woman."

"Yeah? Who's the other lawyer?"

"Richard Royal," Katherine answered.

Jimmy shook his head and said, "The guy sounds like a—"

"A royal asshole," Galena said, finishing his thought.

Jimmy blinked and looked at her.

"Yeah . . . exactly. You sure you're not from the Bronx?"

"Venezuela, honey. They're a long way apart."

"Whatever," Jimmy replied, taking her by the elbow. "I gotta run. Listen, K. J., if I can knock out my deposition quickly, I'll come down and help. What time is the hearing?"

"Ten-thirty," said Katherine.

"Damn . . . you're on your own. Call me though and let me know what happens. If worse comes to worse, I can always have my cousin Vito kill him."

"I'll remember that," Katherine said, starting the engine. She was about to back out when Galena tapped on the window.

"I almost forgot to give you these," she said, handing Katherine a thick yellow envelope. It contained a packet of photographs.

Katherine frowned. "What's this?"

"Pictures of Zach's birthday party. You asked me to get the film developed last week, remember? I got double copies. The drugstore was having a special."

Katherine reached through the window and gave Galena's hand a squeeze. "Thanks. I don't know where my head is this morning."

"K. J., can the judge really take her kids away?"

Katherine looked up and met Galena's eyes. "If he believes her husband's story," she said quietly.

Galena thought about that for a second. "You do good by her, huh?"

"I'm sure as hell going to try."

TWO

Most of Atlanta's rush hour was gone by the time Katherine turned onto I-75. Along the way she called Sherri to fill her in on her conversation with Richard Royal. As expected, her client was taken aback by the accusation and vehemently denied it. She told Katherine the only date she had had after her separation was with a Delta Air Lines pilot named Howard Halpern. Katherine then asked the inevitable question about whether they had slept together and held her breath. When a pause followed, she knew the answer before it came.

"Yes," Sherri finally replied.

"But your daughters weren't home, were they?"

"Of course not! Jennifer was in Athens for a band competition. Half of Lincoln High School was there with her. And Lisa had a sleepover at a friend's house. Nobody was home but us, I swear."

"When was the last time you were with this man?"

"Wednesday night."

"Two days ago?" Katherine asked, incredulous.

"Mm-hm."

"All right. We'll just have to deal with it at the hearing. I should be at the parking deck in about ten minutes. What are you wearing?"

"A conservative blue dress."

"What about your shoes?"

"Uh . . . closed-toe pumps—blue."

"Not too much makeup, right?"

"Just a touch," Sherri replied. "I'd look like a ghost if I didn't wear any."

"Me too," Katherine said. "Let's meet by the elevators on the fourth floor. We can take the bridge across and talk as we go."

"Okay, good-bye."

As a trial lawyer, coincidence was something Katherine mistrusted. "*Two days,*" she repeated to herself. "Two days and Richard Royal just happens to find this guy. Amazing."

IT'S GENERALLY conceded among members of the Atlanta bar, that apart from murder trials, custody cases are perhaps the most draining a lawyer can take. Emotions inevitably run high and clients are so involved they can barely get their minds on anything else. From personal experience Katherine knew that anyone involved in a custody battle was rarely able to see things objectively.

This was especially true in her own case when her husband tried to get custody of their children. Not that he actually wanted them—they were just bargaining chips. "You give up your claim to my pension plan, and I'll drop custody." That sort of thing.

It all came down to hitting them where it hurt most and Katherine despised the tactic with all her heart. It made her furious when someone pulled it in a divorce trial, as they were trying to do now. In the beginning of her practice, she'd thought she'd become jaded, like some of the older lawyers she had met. That never happened. She loved practicing law, and detested it when people misused the process.

During the course of Sherri Wallace's case, she served the standard discovery pleadings on the other side, just as most attorneys did. One of the questions she asked Sherri's husband was whether he had any photographs of his wife. She also asked if he had any electronic recordings of her client that he intended to use at trial. In each instance, Richard Royal had responded "no" on Mark Wallace's behalf. Though she didn't trust Royal she conceded he wasn't a stupid man. If the situation *had* changed and they now intended to call in a private investigator as a witness, Royal would have been obliged to amend his answers and put her on notice.

No, she thought, *something's definitely wrong. They'll have to produce a live witness, and that can only mean one thing.*

Sherri was waiting for her by the parking deck's elevators. Katherine started to wave when she spotted her, but had to step to sideways to avoid being hit by a car that suddenly came tearing around the corner, tires squealing. It sped up to the next parking level.

The look of surprise that appeared on Sherri Wallace's face caused Katherine to turn and see what she was staring at. Through the opening in the deck on the next floor she saw a powder blue Ford Escort pull into the first empty parking space and its driver jump out.

"Oh, my God, that's Howard," said Sherri.

Katherine took her under the arm. "Let's go."

A BRIDGE connects Atlanta's superior court complex with the parking decks. Three men in blue pinstripe suits rolling heavy litigation briefcases were walking ahead of the women. Through Plexiglas windows, Katherine could see the newly renovated Underground Atlanta in the distance.

Ten years earlier all the old buildings were gutted and

replaced with a variety of bars, trendy restaurants, and souvenir shops. The city fathers hoped the project would revive the failing downtown business district and become a tourist attraction the way Faneuil Hall had done for Boston. It hadn't.

"I need you to calm down," Katherine told Sherri, feeling the tension in her client's arm. "If I'm going to defend you properly there are things I need to know."

"Okay," Sherri said, relaxing slightly.

"First off, where did you meet this guy?"

"He ran into me in the supermarket—Kroger's, I think."

"What do you mean he ran into you?"

"I mean, *literally*. He wasn't looking where he was going and he bumped his shopping cart into mine."

"How long ago was that?"

"A little over a week."

Katherine frowned at her and Sherri replied with a shrug. "He's really cute," she added.

While they were waiting for an elevator to take them down to the courthouse lobby, Howard Halpern appeared. He was athletic-looking with sandy-blond hair and a handsome face. He was dressed in a tan business suit with a white shirt and maroon tie. Katherine could see why Sherri found him attractive. Halpern waved when he saw them.

"Hey, I've been trying to call you," he said, as he came up. "The sheriff served me with a subpoena at eight o'clock last night. Then your husband's lawyer called me. What the heck is going on, Sherri?"

Instead of responding to his question, Sherri replied, "This is my lawyer, Katherine Adams. Katherine . . . Howard Halpern."

"Pleased to meet you Mr. Halpern," Katherine said, extending her hand.

"Howard," he replied. "Can either of you tell me what this is about?"

"Sherri's husband filed an emergency petition to change custody of her children. Would you mind sharing what you and his attorney talked about last night?"

"Sure," Halpern said. "The man's name was Royal, Richard Royal, but he didn't say anything about a custody hearing. He told me there was a divorce and that he was representing Sherri's husband. I already knew that because Sherri had told me the same thing. Royal said Mark, that's her husband, was driving past her home and saw us. He also wanted to know if we slept together. I told him it was none of his damn business."

"But you did sleep together, didn't you?" Katherine asked.

Howard blinked and looked at Sherri before answering. "Well, yeah. But like I said, I told him to piss off. Excuse my French."

"Did the attorney ask you anything else?"

"No . . . not really." Halpern's brows came together and he thought for a moment. "Wait, he also wanted to know if Sherri had introduced me to her daughters, but that's about it. When I told him I didn't want to speak with him, he said he'd see me in court today. That's when I started calling you," Howard said to Sherri.

"I'm sorry," said Sherri. "I was so upset after I got the papers, I didn't want to talk to anybody."

"Do I need a lawyer or anything?" Halpern asked as they got on the elevator.

"Technically, I'm not allowed to give you legal advice, but I wouldn't think so since you're here as a witness." Katherine replied. "Just tell the truth and we'll deal with the situation as best we can. What do you do for a living, Howard?"

"Howard's a pilot with Delta Air Lines," Sherry

answered, taking his hand. She smiled at him. "I'm sorry I didn't answer your calls."

"It's all right." he said, smiling back at her. "Your husband sounds like a real schmuck. They won't get anything out of me. You can count on that."

By the time they reached the courthouse lobby, something was bothering Katherine but she couldn't put her finger on it. A line of people were waiting to pass through the metal detectors. They got on at the end of the line and waited along with the others. When it was her turn, Sherri beeped twice and had to remove a silver lapel pin she was wearing. She handed the pin to a guard, who placed it in a lockbox and gave her a receipt to pick it up later.

The detectors had been installed a few years earlier at considerable taxpayer expense after a defendant in a criminal trial tried to shoot his way out of the courtroom. He'd just been convicted of driving under the influence. Regrettably, the only person killed was his attorney—supposedly by accident. At a press conference held later that week, both the judges and court administrator agreed the $2.2 million dollar expenditure for heightened security was worth every penny.

The new Fulton County Courthouse is located on Pryor Street directly across from the old courthouse, which is now reserved mostly for the clerk's office and administrative personnel. Two blocks away is the Richard B. Russell Federal Building where Katherine had worked for eight years as an Assistant United States Attorney in the major crimes division. It was there that she learned the ropes and refined her trial technique.

Though she was an excellent lawyer, going to court always filled her with ambivalence. Her divorce from the heart surgeon had come as a complete surprise—not only to their mutual friends, who thought them the perfect couple, but to Katherine herself. Now, each time she returned to the Superior Court, some part of her was always reminded of that bitter, vitriolic battle. It was ancient history, but at the time, their divorce was the talk of the courthouse with its legal bills topping $500,000. The trial ended with her badly shaken and ready for a change, any change. Four months after it was finished Burt Boyd offered her a job doing domestic-relations work for his firm and Katherine jumped at the chance. It took two years for her to make partner.

Though she vehemently denied having any agenda, she conceded a lot of her cases *did* seem to involve doctors. It wasn't that she disliked doctors. She knew a great many of them and most were good people. It was the bullies she couldn't tolerate, the ones who wanted to dominate and control no matter what the cost. Early on in Sherri's case, Katherine decided that Mark Wallace was a bully—not a coarse, physically imposing individual, but a bully nonetheless. She took an active dislike to him from the beginning. The rational part of her mind knew Wallace and Richard Jenks were different people. Jenks had been dead for over twenty-five years, but the scars he left were still very much alive. Her medication helped keep the flashbacks in check, but in her mind when she looked at Mark Wallace she could see the similarities to Jenks. It was all about imposing their will. Wallace didn't just want to win, he wanted to break Sherri.

As they waited in line Katherine reflected on her decision to leave the U.S. Attorney's Office. Not having to deal with criminal cases anymore had helped, but not as much as she thought. With divorce cases, only the players and their methods changed. There were were still predators out there. The naïve notion that right would eventually prevail evaporated six months into her new practice. Katherine quickly learned that justice often went to those who were able to afford the best lawyers. Divorce cases

tended to be notoriously expensive, and eventually the
party with greater earning capacity simply ground the
other down. A good number of these cases seemed to involve doctors in the midst of a midlife crisis.

She wasn't surprised when the faces of the four dead
women flashed into her mind again. They had been her
constant companions over the years. All of them had died
in a burning house—Richard Jenks's last victims . . . the
ones she couldn't save. Sometimes their presence was so
real it was palpable. Trials like this one often brought
them out. Katherine clenched her jaw willing them away.
She could do nothing for the dead. But Sherri Wallace
wasn't dead and she wasn't going to be a victim.

The law is about helping others—a simple concept and
one which Katherine believed in. Years earlier, when she
announced her intention to go to law school, it was in
spite of the heart surgeon, who detested attorneys and
who told her not to expect any support from him. Unde-
terred, she enrolled in night school and carried her youngest child with her to class. That decision might have
contributed to their split. She was never certain. Nevertheless, she graduated valedictorian three years later.

As they moved closer to the metal detectors, the nig-
gling feeling that had been bothering her on the way
down from the parking deck simply wouldn't go away.
She still couldn't put her finger on it and was so deep in
thought she failed to respond when another lawyer said
hello.

Eventually, the guards passed them through and they
proceeded across the lobby to yet another bank of elevators that would take them up to the courtrooms.

The first thing Burt Boyd had taught her when she
came to work for him was where the free telephones at
the courthouse were located. He also told her never to
assume a courthouse elevator could get you from the

lobby to the ninth floor in under ten minutes. With the new building's construction, everyone assumed the problem would be cured. Unfortunately, whatever malaise had reduced the old elevators to operating at a snail's pace also infected the new models. So they waited.

The elevator finally arrived and people began pushing forward. Over the years Katherine had found Atlantans as a group tended to be extremely polite. Basically, if you saw someone walking down the street you were expected to say "Good morning" or "Hello" and they would respond in kind. In the confines of the courthouse however, a great deal of that gentility seemed to disappear. Prepared for the rush, she made sure Sherri and Howard got places among the first group. A split second before the door was about to close, Katherine suddenly knew what was bothering her.

"I'll meet you both upstairs," she said, stepping back into the lobby. "Wait for me in the courtroom. If the judge calls the case, tell him I'll be there in a minute. I need to check on something."

Whatever her startled client was about to say was forever lost when the elevator door closed in her face. Katherine turned and walked rapidly toward the parking deck elevators.

Twenty-eight minutes, she said to herself, glancing up at the large clock above the entrance.

She half-ran, half-walked back across the bridge, nearly slipping twice on the slick granite floor. The second time she lost her balance, she cursed the man who invented high heels and decided that her dignity wouldn't suffer too much if she removed them. Pulling off her shoes, she trotted the rest of the way to the garage.

Howard Halpern's blue Escort was still in the same place. She jotted down the license number and headed back. Along the way she called her office from her cell phone. It was answered on the third ring by Barry Levitt, the firm's managing partner, who told her Galena was away from her desk at the moment.

"I need a favor, Barry and I need it right away."

"Sure, K. J., go ahead."

"I'm down here at Arthur Morehouse's court and they're about to hold a custody hearing on my client. I don't have much time, so listen carefully. Take down this license plate number. It's a Georgia tag, ZHG-719. I need to know who it's registered to. Get hold of Dave Maxwell. I don't care if he's in bed with one of his floozies. Tell him I needed this information ten minutes ago. Tell him anything, but get it for me."

"What's up?" Barry asked.

"Just a hunch. Now listen, I can't use my cell phone in the court, so you'll have to leave a message with the judge's secretary or his law clerk. Ask them to give it to me, okay?"

"Okay," said Levitt. "I'm on it. I'll call you back as soon as I have the information."

The next thing Katherine did was get to the phone number for Delta's corporate office from directory assistance.

"Good morning, Delta Air Lines. How may I direct your call?" an efficient sounding woman answered.

"I'd like to speak with your personnel office, please."

"Is this in reference to a job?"

"No."

"Is this a stockholder query?"

"No, I just need to speak with personnel."

"Are you filing a customer complaint, ma'am?"

No, you imbecile, just connect me! Katherine nearly shouted. "Actually, I'm trying to get a message to my husband. We've got a small emergency."

"Oh, I'm sorry. Just a moment and I'll put you through, Mrs. . . ."

"Halpern."

"Certainly, just a moment."

After a short pause a lady, who identified herself as Susan Zwicki, came on the line and said, "Good morning, Mrs. Halpern. How can I help you?"

"I'm so sorry to bother you, but Howard has a new cell phone and I don't have his number programmed into mine yet. I just got a call from his dad who said his mother took an earlier flight from Houston and she'll be getting in two hours ahead of schedule. There's just no way I can pick the kids up from school and her at the same time."

"I understand. How do you spell your last name?"

"H-a-l-p-e-r-n," Katherine answered.

The sound of a computer keyboard could be heard in the background.

"Hmm . . . that's strange. I don't see him on our list. 'Howard Halpern,' you say?"

"Yes."

Another pause.

"No, I don't see him here, and he certainly should be. If you can hang on for a moment, I'll switch you over to flight operations. I'm sure they can find him for you."

"Oh, thank you so much," Katherine said, sounding as relieved as she could.

She disconnected while she was on hold.

THREE

Judge Arthur Morehouse's courtroom was paneled in dark walnut, with the flags of the United States and the State of Georgia flanking either side of his bench. A three-foot gold medallion, embossed with Georgia's State Seal, hung on a wall behind him and gave an air of solemnity to the room. Both the jury and witness boxes were positioned to the right of the bench, and a small built-in desk for the court reporter was on the left side. Typical of most courtrooms, two long tables reserved for attorneys and their clients were set up on opposing sides of the room. They were separated from the public gallery by a waist-high railing—the bar. This was where the expression "passing the bar" came from.

Sherri Wallace's face relaxed the moment Katherine entered the court. Howard Halpern, who was seated on Sherri's left, was still holding her hand.

Richard Royal also turned when he heard the door open and nodded to her. Royal was dressed in a white cotton suit with a light blue shirt and a red tie which made him look like Gregory Peck in *To Kill a Mockingbird*. His client, Dr. Mark Wallace, gave her a momentary glance and turned back around again.

Wallace was a maxillofacial surgeon, who now specialized in cosmetic dentistry. In the five years since he entered private practice he had opened two offices in the fashionable West Paces Ferry and Dunwoody sections of Atlanta. Each clinic earned over five million dollars a year. That morning he was dressed in a navy blazer, a white shirt, and a striped tie. Next to him was his nurse, Tami Copeland, recently promoted to the position of office manager at their Dunwoody office.

Katherine recognized her teased blond hair immediately. Earlier in the case, she had taken Tami's deposition, and learned that Tami, fifteen years Mark Wallace's junior, had been divorced twice herself. During her testimony Tami firmly maintained that she and Dr. Wallace were simply business associates and nothing more. As the questioning proceeded it soon became obvious both Tami's financial circumstances and lifestyle had recently taken a substantial turn upward. She now drove a new Jaguar XK-8, and had recently purchased a condo at the Park Regency on Peachtree Road for $685,000 dollars—all on a salary of $52,000 a year. Her responses to Katherine's questions were accompanied by long-suffering sighs and exaggerated hair tosses. During the cross-examination Katherine and her regular court reporter, Wendy Elgin, each noticed that Tami's teeth were all quite perfect and a dazzling shade of white. They reminded her of Katharine Hepburn's line in *A Lion in Winter*, "She smiled to excess, but she chewed with great distinction."

Katherine studied Dr. Wallace while they were waiting for the judge to appear. At his deposition the good doctor had worn a gold Patek Philippe watch. He was now wearing a Timex with a plain black strap.

Arthur Morehouse, who would hear the case that morning, was recently appointed by the governor to fill a spot on the bench that became vacant when his predecessor unexpectedly died of a heart attack.

While Morehouse was not regarded as the sharpest tool in the shed by many Atlanta lawyers, Katherine knew him to be a diligent and thoughtful man. They had worked with each other for five years in the U.S. Attorney's office before he left to go into private practice with a small criminal defense firm. His appointment to the domestic division came as a surprise to most local attorneys because to everyone's knowledge Morehouse had never so much as handled a divorce case in his life. Many of his rulings weren't particularly brilliant: Katherine knew that. She also knew a number of lawyers felt Morehouse tended to miss the more sophisticated points of law that came up during a trial. His saving grace was that his orders were always carefully drawn and tended to come down on the side of equity wherever possible.

THE BAILIFF'S call of the case interrupted Katherine as she was instructing her client to maintain an even composure no matter what the other side said. Despite many years as a trial lawyer, a familiar nervous flutter gripped her stomach. She stopped talking and waited for the judge to speak.

"All right, people, what do we have today?"

Richard Royal got to his feet.

"Good morning, your honor. If it please the court, this is an emergency petition to change custody of the parties' two minor children from the defendant to my client, Dr. Mark Wallace."

"I was given to understand that Ms. Adams is on leave of absence for the next two weeks," Morehouse replied. "Is that correct, Ms. Adams?"

"Yes, your honor. Good morning, by the way. I just found out about this petition a couple of hours ago."

The judge turned back to Royal. "Can't this wait until she gets back, Counselor?"

"Regretfully no, your honor. I do want to say, out of deference to Ms. Adams, I would have preferred to deal with this matter when she returned from her vacation. However, this is an egregious situation involving the welfare of two little girls. If I didn't fully believe it was *exigent*, I assure you I would not have brought the petition."

The judge raised his eyebrows, leaned back in his chair, and considered Royal for a long moment.

"All right, I suppose we'd better hear what you have to say, Mr. Royal. You can call your first witness."

"Would your honor prefer to hear an opening statement?"

"I think we can dispense with that for now, Counselor."

"Very well. Then I call Mr. Howard Halpern to the stand."

After Howard gave his oath and was seated, Royal began. "Now, Mr. Halpern, you are here under subpoena, are you not?"

Halpern leaned forward and spoke into the microphone. "Yes, I am."

"Are you acquainted with the young lady seated over there?" Royal asked, pointing to Sherri Wallace.

"Yes, sir."

"Please tell the court in what capacity you know Mrs. Wallace."

"Well . . . we met about two weeks ago, and we're friends," Halpern replied, smiling at Sherri.

Very smooth, Katherine thought. She wondered whether Barry Levitt had been able to reach their investigator Dave Maxwell yet.

"Mr. Wallace, would it be correct to state that you and Ms. Wallace are *more* than just friends?"

"Not really. We're friends, like I said."

"But you *have* seen each other socially, haven't you?"

"Well, yes," Halpern replied, "but we're just friends."

Um-hm, Katherine said under her breath.

Richard Royal rubbed his forehead and turned to the judge.

"Your honor, I request that I be allowed to treat Mr. Halpern as an adverse witness."

"Why?"

"I took the opportunity to interview him last night, and the testimony he's offering now is not the same as when we spoke."

"Any objections, Counselor?" the judge asked Katherine.

"No, your honor."

Royal's switch in tactics came as no surprise to her. The longer Katherine listened to the scenario being played out, the more she was convinced it was a carefully orchestrated charade put on for the judge's benefit.

"Very well. There being no objection, you may proceed," replied Morehouse.

Royal turned back to the witness.

"Mr. Halpern, you understand that you have taken an oath to tell the truth, don't you?"

"Sure."

"It's only natural to protect a lady's honor, but—"

"Objection, your honor," Katherine said, coming to her feet. "Mr. Royal is here to ask questions. If he wants to testify, we can swear him in and he can take the stand. His statement implies facts that are not in evidence and it's improper."

The judge nodded. "Let's just stick to the facts, Mr. Royal. I'm going to sustain the objection."

"Of course, your honor," answered Royal. He turned back to Howard Halpern. "It would be correct to say that you and Ms. Wallace are something more that just friends, wouldn't it?"

"Well . . . yeah, I guess."

"And it would also be true that you and she have been intimate with each other, wouldn't it, sir?"

Halpern didn't answer right away. He looked at Sherri Wallace and turned his palms up.

"Please answer the question," Morehouse prompted.

Halpern waited another few seconds and nodded his head in acknowledgment. This produced a warning from the judge for him to respond with an audible "yes" or "no" so the court reporter could take down his testimony.

"*Yes*, your honor," Halpern replied.

"Is your answer to Mr. Royal's last question also a 'yes'?"

"It is."

Morehouse gestured for Royal to continue.

"Now Mr. Halpern, when you and Mrs. Wallace had sexual relations, was anyone else present?"

"*What? No,* of course not. That's absurd."

"I didn't mean to imply that anyone else was in the room with y'all. What I'm asking, sir, is if anyone else was at home when you two became intimate."

"Sherri's daughters were home. But we weren't running around naked. The bedroom door was closed the whole time."

"Of course. And after y'all finished your business, you stayed the night and left the following morning, didn't you, Mr. Halpern?"

"Yes, but I'm telling you we didn't do anything improper in front of the children."

While Halpern was talking, Katherine leaned over to Sherri and whispered, "I thought you told me your girls were away."

"*They were,*" Sherri hissed.

Katherine nodded. "You said, one of them was away at the university—Jennifer, I think—and Lisa was at a friend's house."

"That's right."

"Then what hell is he talking about?"

"I don't know," Sherri answered, in the same vehement whisper.

This was bad. Katherine knew Royal was going to spring something, but she didn't think it would be a direct statement that Sherri and Halpern had had sex while her daughters were at home. It felt like she'd just been hit in the stomach. The clock over the jury box read 11:15 a.m.

Based on her conversations with Delta, she was certain Halpern had lied about where he worked. A lot of men did that to pump themselves up. The question in her mind now was, *Why is he making up a story about the girls being home?*

"Sherri, who was Lisa staying with?" Katherine whispered.

"Debbie Fincher. She lives in the next subdivision."

"Do you have her number with you?"

Sherri nodded and started to take her cell phone out of her handbag.

"You can't use that in here," Katherine said. "I'm going to ask the judge for a recess. See if you can get hold of her and ask her to come down right away."

"Ms. Adams," the judge's voice cut in, "Counsel is through with the witness. Do you have any questions for him?"

Katherine took a moment to collect herself.

"I do want to question Mr. Halpern, your honor, but I'd like to reserve my cross-examination until later, if I may."

The judge looked at Richard Royal.

"That's fine with me," Royal said with a shrug. "I can go on to the next witness."

"Your honor," said Katherine, "I was also wondering if my client could be excused for a few minutes."

"I suppose that will be okay," said the judge. "Please be back as quickly as you can, ma'am."

Sherri Wallace got up and left the courtroom.

THE NEXT witness was Sherri's husband, who professed his shock and sadness at the situation. He told the court that he had nothing against Sherri and wanted only the best for her. But that under the circumstances he thought it was in their daughters' best interest to change custody to him. He testified that he was willing to hire a nanny for the girls to ensure someone would be home when they got out of school. Wallace said he didn't care what the expense was—his daughters came first. Of course, he made no mention that if custody *were* changed, it would save him $4,000 a month in child support payments—nor did his lawyer ask him about it.

If Howard Halpern was smooth, he was nothing compared to Mark Wallace, whose testimony was seamless, well-rehearsed, and delivered with all the sincerity of an actor in a television soap opera.

Several times during the questioning, Katherine stole a glance at the judge, and what she saw she didn't like. Morehouse was buying the act—hook, line, and sinker. After Royal concluded his examination, the door to Morehouse's chambers opened. His secretary, Velma Blanchard, poked her head out and whispered something to him.

"Ms. Adams, your office has left a message for you," the judge said. "You may approach the bench."

Katherine took the piece of paper Velma handed her, read it, then put it in the pocket of her suit.

"The plaintiff rests, your honor," Richard Royal announced.

KATHERINE HAD just begun questioning Dr. Wallace when Sherri re-entered the courtroom and flashed her a quick smile. It was accompanied by a slight nod of the head. For the next hour, Katherine conducted what she later referred to as an extended tap dance, or the single most boring and tedious cross-examination of her career. It ended when a heavyset woman in a blue jogging suit opened the door of the courtroom. The woman wiggled her fingers at Sherri, then sat down in the last row.

"That's all I have for this witness your honor," Katherine said.

Morehouse leaned back in his seat and looked at the clock.

"It's almost time for lunch," he said. "Do you all want to take a break, or go straight through?"

"I have no problem going straight through," Royal answered.

"Your honor, I have my cross of Mr. Halpern and two witnesses, who will only take about ten minutes each," said Katherine, "so I'd like to go straight through as well."

"All right, I can take it if you can," Morehouse said.

Out of the corner of her eye, Katherine noticed Royal and his client exchange satisfied looks with each other. Wallace's new girlfriend, Tami, continued to smile dazzlingly at anyone who looked in her direction.

FOUR

Katherine's first witness was Sherri Wallace, who admitted that she and Howard Halpern did indeed know each other, and that they had slept together. When she made the last statement, the judge glanced at her and jotted down a note on his legal pad. In response to Katherine's next question, Sherri forcefully reiterated that her daughters were *not* at home at the time. She said she didn't know why Howard had made such a statement.

Next, Katherine called Howard Halpern to the stand.

"Mr. Halpern, we met earlier, didn't we?"

"Yes, we did," he said with a pleasant smile.

"When I asked what you did for a living you told me that you worked for Delta Air Lines as a pilot, didn't you?"

"Well . . . uh, Sherri was actually the one who said—"

"But in fact you don't work for Delta, do you, Mr. Halpern?"

"No, I . . . uh—"

"You work for a company named Jasper Medical Technologies, out of Nashville, Tennessee, isn't that right?"

"Yes, I work for them. But I think there's some misunderstanding here. I mean, I never said—"

"And Dr. Wallace's clinics are one of your accounts, aren't they, Mr. Halpern?"

Richard Royal came to his feet.

"Your honor, I really must object. I appreciate Ms. Adams's zeal in representing her client, but she's not giving this man a chance to answer one question before she starts asking him the next one."

"You need to give him a chance to answer," the judge said without looking up from the notes he was making.

Katherine tucked a strand of hair behind her ear and walked back to the defendant's table. She took out the paper Judge Morehouse's secretary had given her and pretended to study it for a moment. The effect was sufficient to get everyone focusing on what she was doing.

"Mr. Halpern, when you testified earlier, why didn't you tell us you were acquainted with Dr. Wallace?"

"I don't think anybody asked me, Counselor," Halpern responded. His tone was not quite as friendly as it had been.

"I see. And you also didn't tell Sherri Wallace that you knew her husband, did you?"

"I wouldn't say we know each other, Ms. Adams. The Wallace clinics are clients of mine it's true, but that's all."

"Right," Katherine said, drawing out the word. "As I understand it, Mr. Halpern, you met Sherri Wallace in a Kroger Supermarket about two weeks ago, didn't you?"

"Yes, I did."

"But you don't live here in Atlanta, do you, sir?"

"I think he said he lives in Tennessee," the judge said, consulting his notes.

"I live just outside of Nashville," Halpern supplemented.

"Good for you," said Katherine. "Now, Mr. Halpern, would you tell the court what you were doing in a supermarket at ten o'clock on a Friday night?"

"I needed a few things to eat."

Arthur Moreland twisted around in his seat and looked at Halpern.

"Where were you staying when you met Mrs. Wallace?" he asked.

"At the Marriott, your honor."

The judge frowned and scribbled something on his pad again. Then he motioned to his bailiff, who was now leaning forward in his seat, suddenly interested in what was going on. The bailiff stepped up to where the judge was seated and Morehouse whispered something in his ear. He nodded and promptly disappeared through the door to the judge's chambers. Morehouse apologized for the interruption and told Katherine to continue.

"Mr. Halpern, you testified Sherri Wallace's daughters were home when you and she had your date," Katherine said.

"When we had *sex*," Halpern corrected.

"When you had sex. How is it you knew both girls were home? Did you meet them?"

"Your honor," Richard Royal interrupted, "Ms. Adams is asking the witness two separate questions."

"He's right," the judge said. "Let's try to ask one at a time."

"Sorry, I just get a little excited sometimes."

"Perfectly understandable," said Morehouse. "Go ahead and rephrase your question."

"Did you personally meet the Wallace girls?"

Halpern darted a look at Richard Royal, who stared back at him, poker-faced. "No, I didn't meet them."

"Then how did you know they were home, Mr. Halpern?"

"Because I heard them talking upstairs," he said, a faint smile playing about his lips.

"You heard them talking upstairs?"

"Right."

"Is it possible that what you heard was the television set or their answering machine?"

"I don't think so, Counselor."

"Would it surprise you if I told you that Jennifer Wallace was away at the University of Georgia for a high school band competition at that time. And that Lisa Wallace was sleeping at a friend's house that night?"

"It certainly would. I heard what I heard."

Katherine already knew Halpern was not going to change his story, nor was she going to get him to crack. That sort of thing only happened on television. She walked back to the defendant's table racking her brain about what else to ask. That was when she noticed the package of photos Galena had given her sticking up out of the corner of her purse.

"Would you hand me those photos, please?" Katherine asked, loud enough for everyone to hear.

Sherri blinked and looked at Katherine's purse, then retrieved the package, and gave it to her.

"May I have a second, your honor?" Katherine asked, as she took the photos out of the envelope. She began flipping through them.

Arthur Morehouse didn't respond. At the plaintiff's table, Wallace and Royal exchanged puzzled looks with each other.

"Ah, here they are," Katherine said, pulling two

photographs out of the package. She turned back to Halpern, whose eyes were now riveted on them.

"A little while ago you told us Dr. Wallace is simply a customer of yours. Isn't that correct?"

"Yes," Halpern replied cautiously.

"But that's not true, is it, Mr. Halpern?"

"I don't know what you're talking about."

"In fact, you and Dr. Wallace have spent a good deal of time with each other recently, haven't you?"

"We discussed his company purchasing a new X-ray system," Halpern stammered.

Royal was on his feet once again. "Your honor, if she's going to cross-examine the witness on those photographs, he's got a right to see them, and so do we."

"I haven't submitted them into evidence yet," Katherine said, before the judge could answer.

"We only met a few times," Halpern blurted out.

His answer nearly caused Richard Royal to go apoplectic.

"Your honor, I move to strike the witness's last statement as unresponsive to the question."

Arthur Morehouse shook his head.

"Mr. Royal, there's no jury here today. And I think I'm able to separate the wheat from the chaff, so your objection is overruled. Do you have anything else, Ms. Adams?"

"Not from this witness, your honor," Katherine said, with a dismissive gesture.

Morehouse nodded. "I take it that athletic-looking young lady who's been sitting so patiently in the back of the courtroom is your last witness?"

Katherine's heart was pounding and she took a deep breath to slow it. For the first time that morning, she began to relax. She made a deliberate effort to keep her face and voice neutral. With a glance at the plaintiff's table she noticed girlfriend Tami had suddenly stopped smiling and was looking from Mark Wallace to Richard Royal for an explanation.

"Yes, Judge, that's Debbie Fincher," Katherine replied, pulling her attention away from them.

Morehouse motioned to Debbie Fincher.

"Step up here if you would, please, ma'am."

Debbie Fincher was a plump brunette who was wearing no makeup. She looked like she had just come from the gym, as in fact she had. She got up and walked to the front of the courtroom.

"What do you expect her to testify to?" asked Morehouse.

"Ms. Fincher is here to corroborate my client's statement about her daughter sleeping at her home on Wednesday night."

"Is that what you're going to say?" Morehouse asked Debbie Fincher.

"Mm-hm, that's exactly what happened. Lisa and my daughter came home together after school and I dropped her off the next day around one-thirty after we had lunch. Oh . . . and I want to apologize for looking this way, Judge," she added, straightening her hair.

The comment caused Morehouse to start chuckling.

"It's quite all right, you look very presentable. My wife has a warm-up suit just like that."

Morehouse turned to Richard Royal, who was just getting to his feet. "Do you want her to take the stand, Counselor?"

"Uh . . . no, your honor, that won't be necessary," Royal replied.

"Ms. Adams . . . anything further from you?"

"No, your honor. The defendant rests."

While Arthur Morehouse was looking over his notes, the bailiff came back and put a piece of paper in front of him. Morehouse glanced at it, and the bailiff resumed his seat, but not before giving Howard Halpern a pointed look as he walked past him. The judge then declared a five-minute recess, picked up his legal pad, and left the bench.

The next minutes were the longest Katherine could remember. Twice she found that she was holding her breath, and twice she had to remind herself to relax and breathe. She kept watching the door to the judge's chambers. Richard Royal, on the other hand, seemed wholly unaffected by the wait, and was calmly placing his papers back in his briefcase.

Shortly after she began practicing law, Katherine learned that when a judge came out of chambers and looked at you or your client, or if he began his ruling by telling your client what a fine job you had done, it meant you were screwed: The decision was going the other way.

Finally, the door to Arthur Morehouse's chambers opened. He came back in the court, took his place on the bench—and looked directly at Richard Royal.

"All right, based on the evidence presented today, I am going to deny your petition, Mr. Royal."

Sherri Wallace grabbed Katherine's hand and squeezed so hard it almost hurt.

"I am also going to award attorney fees to the defendant. Ms. Adams, I'll give you ten days to submit your request to my office once you've returned from your vacation."

The judge then looked at Howard Halpern and Mark Wallace, who both sat there rigid and tight-lipped.

"Gentlemen, neither of you have a great deal of credibility as far as I'm concerned. To begin with, there are no refrigerators in the rooms at the Marriott, Mr. Halpern, so what you were doing shopping for food at that hour of the night is beyond me. Also, your *chance* meeting with Mrs. Wallace is highly suspicious.

"As for you, Dr. Wallace, I strongly suggest you do your best to settle this case before it comes to trial. Do I make myself clear?"

Wallace nodded while Halpern turned red in the face and looked down at his feet. As soon as the judge left the bench, Halpern got up and left the courtroom without speaking to anyone. Mark Wallace followed him, trailed by his new office manager, who lifted her chin, stuck her chest out, and walked by everyone with an exaggerated sway to her hips. Katherine and Sherri watched her for a moment, then turned to each other and mouthed, "Boob job," at the same time.

They were both giggling like schoolgirls when Richard Royal approached the defendant's table to congratulate Katherine. Sherri gave her attorney a quick hug and brushed past Royal without so much as a glance.

"Fine job, Kathy. Clients never fail to surprise you, do they?" he said, shaking his head.

"Excuse me?"

"Well, it would have been nice for ol' Dr. Wallace to let his lawyer know he and our chief witness were personally acquainted, wouldn't it?"

Pathetic, thought Katherine. "Yeah, it's too bad."

"Now listen here, I'd like to know if you're willing to produce copies of those photographs you were waving around without me having to file a formal subpoena."

"Why would you want these, Richard?"

"Because under the Civil Practice Act, I have a right to see any document in your possession that could lead to admissible evidence," Royal explained patiently. "Why don't we just cut all this dancing around and you tell me what you've got there?"

"Actually, they're pictures of my son's fourteenth birthday party. Oh . . . and here's one of my cat. Isn't he cute?"

Royal stared at the photographs for several seconds without saying anything. He locked eyes with Katherine and said in a quiet voice, "You have a nice vacation, Kathy girl. We'll talk some more when you get back."

He added a solicitous pat on her waist and turned to leave, never knowing how close he had just come to getting hit over the head with Katherine's briefcase. Fortunately, they were both spared the experience by the bailiff who approached Katherine and handed her a note.

Royal's brows came together and he looked at her for an explanation. None came. She simply shrugged and said good-bye.

FIVE

The note turned out to be another message from Katherine's office telling her that Galena had changed her flight to 4:45 p.m. which left her with a little over an hour to kill. Going home wasn't an option because of the late hour, and there hadn't been any decent shopping in downtown Atlanta for fifteen years. Nor was waiting in an airport lounge at the top of her list. She'd missed lunch earlier and Katherine suddenly realized that she was hungry. Now that the excitement was over, she felt her adrenaline draining away. The high of victory was always followed by an emptiness, like air seeping out of a balloon. She wasn't surprised when it happened. There were more than enough good feelings to fill the void.

That's one for the home team, she thought, as she stood at the top of the courthouse steps.

A warm breeze blew down Pryor Street and felt good against her face. She ran a hand through her hair, unbuttoned the top button of her blouse, and walked down the street turning right at the corner. There was a little café in Five Points she hadn't visited in years and she hoped it was still in business. They used to serve aperitifs in small crystal glasses that tasted like the fruits they came from and warmed when they went down. The café came into the view a few blocks later and she was pleased to see it. Katherine took a seat at one of the sidewalk tables and ordered a plate of shrimp and a glass of wine. She sipped the wine quietly and watched people.

Outside the café, a homeless man was pushing a shopping cart that contained what looked like all of his worldly possessions. He stopped and sat down on a bench. His expression caught Katherine's eye because he appeared confused by the mass of people passing in front of and around him. He looked at their faces, but no one looked back at him.

Briefly, he and Katherine made eye contact and he smiled at her. She nodded and looked away. One of the waiters noticed the man sitting there and went out to say something to him. She couldn't hear what was said, but the old man got up slowly and began pushing his cart again.

When the shrimp came they still had a faint sense of the sea that the wine washed away. The empty feeling gradually left her as the wine did its job, and a slight smile played at the corners of her mouth. She thought about what had happened in court and the emptiness retreated further. If the result had been bad, she would have felt depressed and in a poor frame of mind. That didn't happen. It was pleasant to sit there enjoying the day—something she hadn't done in years.

A half-hour passed and the shrimp were gone and the wine was mostly gone when Katherine asked for the bill. The waiter brought it and told her to come again. She stood up and was about to start for the door when a familiar voice stopped her.

"How did you know he was lying?" Arthur Morehouse asked. He was seated at a table with two other judges. Both acknowledged her with nods.

"I'm sorry, Judge. I didn't notice all of you sitting there."

"We have that effect on people," the judge on the right said. "It's the advantage of old age and stealth."

Katherine smiled and was about to reply when Morehouse repeated his question.

"How did you know he was lying, Ms. Adams?"

Katherine stared at Morehouse for a moment, unsure how much to reveal. Running a person's license plate was not exactly a kosher thing to do. The other judges had stopped eating and appeared to be equally interested in her answer.

"My client and I ran into Halpern on the way in from the parking deck and I noticed the license plate on his car started with a 'Z.' That meant it was a fleet vehicle. I've never heard of Delta providing cars for their employees, let alone a pilot. I also figured there's no way the captain of a jumbo jet is driving a Ford Escort."

Arthur Morehouse stuck out his lower lip and exchanged a glance with the judge on his left.

"Interesting. And from that you deduced he wasn't being truthful about his employment."

"Well . . . that and the fact that I called Delta to ask if he worked there."

Morehouse laced his fingers together and rested his chin on the back of his hands. The expression on his face was unreadable.

"So you used the information on Halpern's license plate to identify the vehicle's true owner, which turned out to be his employer. Am I correct?"

"Something like that, your honor."

"I see. And that trick with the photographs, where did you get that from?"

There was a pause before Katherine answered.

"Uh . . . a young lawyer taught it to me several years ago when I was with the U.S. Attorney's office. He actually looked a little bit like you, but if I recall correctly he had more hair."

Arthur Morehouse frowned and glanced at a mirror hanging on the wall. Except for a fringe above his ears sprinkled with gray, he was almost completely bald.

The words were no sooner out of Katherine's mouth than she regretted saying them. After several seconds passed the silence became uncomfortable. She was about to apologize when she noticed Morehouse's stomach was shaking. In fact, his whole body was quivering— with laughter, which he was having a hard time suppressing.

"I did have more hair then, didn't I?" he said, feeling his scalp.

A moment later Morehouse's face broke into a wide grin and he turned to his two companions and said, "I told you so." Then he looked at Katherine. "It's good to see you again, K. J."

"It's good to see you, too, Arthur. The way you were looking at me during my direct, I was sure you were going to rule against me."

"I was. If I thought those children were home when she brought a man into the house, that's exactly what I would have done. But all things considered, you did a good job. You still don't give witnesses a chance to answer. But you did good."

"It's just that I get caught up in the moment," Katherine said, "and Halpern was such a lying scumball."

Morehouse started laughing again and held up a hand.

"We'd better not discuss the merits of this case any further. This is getting dangerously close to an ex parte communication, Counselor."

"Sorry," Katherine replied, as the wall between judge and lawyer went back up.

"Is Mr. Royal still pretending he's a Southerner?" asked the judge on the left.

Katherine gave him a tight-lipped smile and turned the palms of her hands up.

"That boy needs to work on his accent," the judge said. "He sounds like a fellow from New York trying to do an imitation of a Southerner."

"Philadelphia," Katherine corrected.

"Whatever," said Morehouse. "I assume you got the note from your office about your secretary changing your plane reservation."

"I did, Arthur, thanks."

"Well, get a move on, girl," Morehouse said, glancing at his watch. "Don't be standing around here wasting the court's time."

Katherine smiled and said good-bye to everyone

"Have a good vacation," he called after her. "And try to settle that case when you get back."

WHILE SHE was waiting to cross the street, Katherine realized she wasn't alone. The man with the shopping cart was standing next to her. He was an old man and needed a shave. The suit he was wearing was badly rumpled. They looked at each other.

"I had a house," he said, "but I had to leave it."

"Excuse me?"

"I had a dog, and a cat, and a bird."

Katherine nodded and began walking when the light turned green. So did the man.

"I gave the bird away to a neighbor, but I couldn't find

the dog when I left. Cats are okay—they take care of themselves, but I'm worried about the dog."

Normally it wasn't her habit to talk with strangers, but something about the old man seemed so fragile, so lost.

"I'm sure he'll be all right," she said.

"He was a good dog. He lived with me for a long time."

When they reached the other side of the street, Katherine could have kept walking, because the old man was moving so slowly, but she didn't.

"Do you have any family?" she asked.

"No, no," the man replied. "Only the animals."

"I sure they'll be fine. Do you have someplace to live now?"

"There is a mission not far from here," the man said. "They let us stay for the night, but we have to leave in the morning. Cats are very independent, you know. It's the dog I'm worried about."

They continued down the street toward the parking deck where she had left her car.

"Maybe your neighbor will find him and take care of him."

"Yes, perhaps. The neighbors were nice people. I gave the bird to them. They will certainly feed her."

He said the last part more to himself than to Katherine. They were in front of the entrance to the garage now and the old man stopped when she did.

"Are you going to the mission now?" she asked.

"Later," he said, "when it's dark. We have to leave during the day. I'll rest here for a while."

Next to the garage was a building with a broad stoop and gray granite steps. The old man walked over and sat down on them.

Katherine glanced up and down the street. "You should really try to go to the mission soon," she said. "This isn't the best neighborhood."

"I'll rest for a while. I try not to concern myself, but I cannot think what will become of the dog."

Katherine wanted to say something that would ease his mind, but the words that came to her all sounded contrived. There was nothing she could do. The emptiness returned once again and leaned against the door of the garage, waiting. She took twenty dollars out of her wallet, pressed it into his palm and went inside.

SIX

Ellis Stephens watched the DNA's double-helix pattern form on his computer's monitor. His fingers were laced together, cradling his chin. Only his eyes moved as they scanned the image of a single-cell nucleus being graphically reproduced line by line. Four minutes had elapsed since the program stopped producing columns of numbers. They filled not only his screen, but the one next to him as well. An image of a cell began to form shortly after that.

On the monitor to Stephens's right was a digitally enhanced photograph of a fertilized human egg. Nine days earlier a small jolt of electricity had fused the egg and nucleus together, commencing the fertilization process. The cells on the outside combined to form a placenta, while the ones on the inside became stem cells. Slowly, painstakingly, cultured genetic matter was introduced into three of those cells. The material came from the diencephalic portion of a brain—a human brain, to be exact—one that had once belonged to a nineteen-year-old girl. The girl had been killed in an automobile accident three days earlier.

Stephens was a professor of Molecular Genetics at Columbia University. His hair was mostly gray with some remnants of brown mixed in. He wore a white lab coat that seemed entirely too large for his thin frame. A pair of old-fashioned bifocals rested on the bridge of his nose. He had a tendency to blink when he spoke.

Ten more minutes ticked by. An indicator at the bottom of the screen told him the program was now sixty percent complete. Without taking his eyes from the computer, Stephens reached to his left, found a half-finished cup of coffee and picked it up. He took a sip, then made a face, and put the cup back down. It was cold.

Compared to other laboratories at Columbia, the genetics lab was not terribly interesting to look at. Outside of a few computers, there were no exotic machines with blinking lights or spinning centrifuges. It did contain two powerful-looking microscopes that sat on workbenches in the corner along with a large whiteboard that was covered from top to bottom with equations and diagrams.

The program was ninety percent complete when Ellis checked the screen again.

Jamie Yamaguchi, a graduate student working on her PhD in microbiology, glanced up from her work when Ellis didn't respond about where they should go for lunch. She noticed his expression and came over to see what her boss was staring at. A minute later, they were joined by Keith Haynes, an associate professor in the genetics department. Haynes had been working on the project for the last two years.

The bar graph at the bottom of Ellis's screen read ninety-six percent complete.

Yamaguchi put a hand on Ellis's shoulder and stared at the computer model on the right screen, then looked back at the cell on the left which was now almost fully formed. No one spoke. When a small chime went off, signifying the program had finished running, it caused all three of them to jump. For several seconds everyone held their breath before the faint sound of the computer's hard drive came on again. The second computer followed suit. They continued churning for another thirty seconds, then the drives stopped.

Jamie gasped and squeezed Ellis's shoulder, for there on the screens were two identical models of a human brain cell with the same message flashing beneath them in red letters.

MATCH
99.99999 percent
CONFIDENCE LEVEL HIGH

"My God," Haynes whispered. "Ellis, you've done it."

At first Stephens couldn't believe his eyes. Then the three of them began hugging and dancing around the room like children. For the next three days he and his two assistants checked and rechecked the program for errors. During this period the cell they had created split again, reproducing itself six times. At the end of the fourth day, Ellis sent his report to the head of their department.

It took Dean Warren Wilkerson all of fifteen minutes to burst through the front door of the lab, excitedly offering his congratulations.

"Ellis, I . . . I . . . can't find the words," he said, shaking Stephens's hand. "This is the most extraordinary thing that's happened to us since . . . I don't know when. You'll have to publish, of course, maybe in the *New England Journal of Medicine,* or . . . or . . . the *Journal of Regenerative Medicine.* This will certainly result in a nomination for the Nobel Prize. In fact, I'm going to speak with the president of the school and the board of trustees about it today."

"Thank you, Warren," Stephens laughed. "But I must point out this was very much a team effort. Jamie and Keith should certainly receive their share of recognition, too."

"Nonsense, Ellis," Haynes protested. "It was your baby from beginning to end."

"He's right, Dr. Stephens," Jamie said. "You'll get the Nobel for sure. I'm so proud of you."

"I'll make certain Ms. Yamaguchi and Dr. Haynes are prominently mentioned," said Wilkerson. "You've all done a fine job. Simply astounding. The possibilities are so limitless they boggle the mind. I can barely imagine the things we'll be able accomplish."

Stephens smiled. "I look at it. I see the results on the screen, and I still can't believe it. I keep thinking this is all a dream and I'm going to wake up any moment to find out it's vanished."

"It's not a dream," Wilkerson said, placing a hand on Stephens's shoulder. "By the way, you all look like hell. As dean of this department, I'm going to make an executive decision. I want you all to get out of here and not come back until Monday. Go dancing, sing, get drunk, or howl at the moon if you want, but don't let me catch any of you in this lab. Those are my orders."

"Aye, aye, sir," Haynes said, saluting.

"Thanks, Dr. Wilkerson," Jamie said. "That's very sweet of you. My sister's in from Chicago for the weekend and I could use a break."

"Excellent," Wilkerson replied. "Then off with you, young lady."

Jamie gave Ellis a quick hug, grabbed her purse, and disappeared through the door. She was followed by Keith Haynes.

"That goes for you too, Ellis," said Wilkerson, wagging a finger at him.

"Just let me just pack up a few things, Warren," said Stephens, looking around the lab. "Rest sounds like a good idea. I can't remember when I slept last. Libby's probably forgotten what I look like."

Wilkerson smiled. "No more than five minutes or I'll call security and have them evict you. Stop by and see me on the way out, okay?"

WEARING A tan raincoat that looked like it had been slept in, Ellis Stephens knocked at Wilkerson's door. He was clutching a silver attaché case to his chest as though it were a child.

"Come in . . . come in," Wilkerson said, the moment he saw him.

He was on the phone and pointed to a chair in front of his desk, indicating for Stephens to sit.

"Very good, very good. Listen, I have to run. I've got a very important person in my office at the moment," he said into the receiver. "We'll see you tomorrow night."

"My wife's sister," Wilkerson explained, as he hung up. "They're throwing a surprise party for her youngest girl. She just got accepted to medical school at Johns Hopkins."

"Congratulations, Warren."

"Thank you. It's wonderful news. The whole family's all abuzz about it. But more important . . . how are *you* doing? I wasn't kidding when I said you look like hell."

Stephens made a dismissive gesture with his hand. "I'm fine. I just need a little R & R, that's all. We've been going pretty hot and heavy for the last four days."

"I don't doubt it. This is just about the most exciting thing that's happened around here for ages. Did I say that before? Anyway, what are your plans now, if you don't mind my asking?"

"Plans?"

"Yes. Ellis, *plans*." Wilkerson laughed. "You're going to be a very wealthy man in case you haven't realized it. Some company will pay a fortune for this research. You need to start giving the matter some serious thought—maybe get a financial adviser or an attorney."

Stephens blinked and stared at the dean for several seconds. "It never occurred to me to sell the process, Warren. I wouldn't mind being compensated, of course. Lord knows Libby and I could use the money. We've got two boys in college."

"Exactly."

"I suppose I'll have to think it over."

"What's there to think about?"

Stephens shook his head. "When you mentioned getting a financial planner, it threw me. I've never really thought along those lines."

"I'm sure you haven't, but it's high time you did," said Wilkerson. "If you decide to go the corporate route, I can put you in touch with a number of very fine companies. The university's worked with them in the past, and I'm sure they'd treat you well."

"Are you suggesting we sell it outright?"

"I'm not suggesting anything, except for you to get some rest and put your thinking cap on. You owe it to yourself. And for God's sake, don't sign any papers without letting our legal counsel review them."

"I won't," Stephens assured him. "I must say, this is all quite overwhelming." Stephens started to say something else then stopped and appeared to change his mind. There was a silence before he spoke again. "Warren, do you suppose the department could spare me for, say, three weeks?" he asked.

The dean's brow furrowed. "Three weeks? Sure, I imagine we could. Haynes or Berman can cover your classes. What do you have in mind?"

"Well . . . Libby's been after me to take a vacation for a while now. I read something about a cruise in the *Times* the other day—the *Ocean Majestic,* or one of those big ships. They go to Europe, do the Mediterranean, then fly you home. I think they were having a special."

"That's a fantastic idea," Wilkerson said, slapping the top of his desk for emphasis. "We were on the *Majestic* last year. We only did the Caribbean but I guarantee you'll love it. You'll probably come back ten pounds heavier, but you should definitely go. I can put you in touch with my travel agent if you want. She did a great job for us."

"Thank you, Warren. That's very kind."

Stephens thought for a few more seconds and then made up his mind. "You know, that's exactly what I'm going to do. I'll bring home the tickets and surprise Libby. She's been talking about going back to work again now that the boys are out of the house. I suppose that can wait. Do you have the name of that agent handy?"

"Right here," Wilkerson said, flipping through his Rolodex. He located the right card, jotted down a name on a piece of paper, and handed it to Stephens.

Both men stood at the same time. As they were shaking hands Stephens's face grew serious again.

"Warren, I want you to know how much I've appreciated all of your support and encouragement throughout the years; you've been a good friend. I want to talk this over with Libby before we make any decisions. You're right. A trip sounds like exactly what we need. And I do promise to think about it . . . I mean really think about it. My initial leanings have always been that a development like this should be available to anyone. I can't imagine letting some corporation charge a patient with a failing liver twenty-five thousand dollars for a new one. That would be grotesque. Can you see telling a family whose father is getting worse every year from Alzheimer's that we can reverse the process, but only if they have enough cash? I could never do something like that."

"I'm not saying you should. In fact, I'm not saying anything at all. I'm only saying sleep on it. Go on your vacation and have the time of your life. When you come back rested and refreshed we'll talk further."

"Sounds good."

"By the way, have you made a backup copy of the program yet?"

Stephens smiled and patted his briefcase.

Wilkerson wished him a good trip and asked that he remember him to his wife. Once the door closed, the dean stared at it for several seconds, then picked up the phone and made a call.

SEVEN

To Katherine's surprise two people were waiting for her when she reached her car. She hesitated until she recognized one of them was Galena; the other was Jimmy D'Taglia.

"What are you guys doing here?" she asked.

"We heard you kicked Richard Royal's fat butt," Galena said, running up and hugging her. "It took me fifteen minutes to find your car in this dump."

"How could you possibly hear that so soon?" Katherine asked. "I just left court a little while ago."

"Velma told me."

"Velma Blanchard? The judge's secretary?"

"She was giving us a play-by-play on our way down. Congrats," Jimmy said, kissing Katherine on the cheek. "Sounds like you did a hell of a job."

"But, I don't understand how—"

"Velma has a monitor on her desk in case the judge needs something. All the secretaries do," Galena explained.

"Oh . . . but what are you both doing here?"

"We brought your suitcase," said Galena. "I figured you'd be running late, so I went to your house and I finished packing for you. I'm pretty sure I included everything you'll need. Some things I had to guess about."

Katherine's jaw dropped.

"How did you get into my house?"

"You gave me the code to your alarm when you went to Washington for those depositions in the Rivera case. Remember? You wanted me to stop by and feed your cat."

"Sure I remember," Katherine said, "but you gave my key back." She looked at Galena, then at Jimmy for an explanation.

"Growing up in the Bronx carries some fringe benefits, ya know?" Jimmy told her.

"You broke in to—"

Katherine stopped herself before she shouted out the rest of the sentence. She took a deep breath, mentally counted to ten, and repeated in a whisper, *"You broke in to my house? Are you nuts?"*

"I wouldn't exactly put it in those terms," said Jimmy, "but that basically captures the spirit."

"You're unbelievable. You could both have gotten arrested. Is that my suitcase?" Katherine asked, pointing to a black bag next to Galena.

"I just told you we brought it, K. J.," Galena said. She gave Katherine a puzzled look, then turned to Jimmy, who shrugged.

Katherine put her hands over her face and shook her head.

"I can't believe you people did this, but thank you. The

next time just . . . oh, never mind," she said, putting her key in the lock.

Jimmy opened the rear door and tossed Katherine's suitcase in with a grunt. "Jeez, what'd you put in here, rocks?" he asked Galena. "Those thongs must be a lot heavier than they look."

"What?" said Katherine.

"I'll never look at another thong without thinking of you," he added.

His statement produced an indignant gasp from Galena, who slapped him on the upper arm. "You weren't supposed to look," she said.

"I'm Italian," he replied, rubbing his arm. "It's in my blood."

Katherine felt the color in her face rise by at least two shades but decided it was best to say nothing. She got in the car. Before she could start the engine, Jimmy leaned in through the open window and rested his elbows on it.

"Listen, if you ever decide you want to go for a younger man. . . ."

"Oh, for God's sake," Katherine said, "I'm old enough to be your mother."

"I know," he replied, lifting his eyebrows twice theatrically. "Older women turn me on."

"Yuck," Katherine replied, pushing his face back out.

Despite her efforts to maintain a stern expression, she couldn't manage it and started laughing. A second later they all broke up.

"Go," said Galena. "You'll be late. I called Ms. Doliver and let her know you were taking the next flight. She said it was no problem."

Katherine was still laughing when she pulled out of the garage.

EIGHT

Depending on who you speak to, Atlanta's Hartsfield airport is either the busiest or second busiest airport in the world. The title tends to shift between O'Hare in Chicago and Atlanta on a monthly basis depending on when the Department of Transportation releases its travel figures. For reasons Katherine never fully understood, Atlantans seemed to take inordinate pride in being number one, even though being the busiest airport in the world also meant it was the most crowded. Friday afternoons were particularly bad. But given that her ship was departing from Miami the next day, she had few other options. Katherine left her car in a satellite lot on Camp Creek Parkway and took their courtesy shuttle to the terminal.

At the counter an attendant examined her identification and gave Katherine's face a cursory glance. Apparently satisfied the two matched, she issued a boarding pass and said the plane would be leaving from Concourse B.

Katherine made it through the metal detectors without incident and hurried to the escalator that would take her down to the "transportation mall." The name was an invention of some advertising executive and a mystery to nearly everyone who heard it, since there weren't any shops, and it didn't bear the slightest resemblance to a mall. As soon as she reached the platform a disembodied mechanical voice announced the train would be there in two minutes.

When the airport had first opened, the voice was that of an upbeat pleasant-sounding woman who welcomed everybody to Atlanta and told them to "have a wonderful day." Unfortunately, the voice was so nice, many people chose to ignore it, particularly when it asked them not to hold the train doors open. People began missing their flights. One man actually said, "Fuck you" to the recording when it announced over the PA system, *"You are being delayed because someone has interfered with the door closing."*

Katherine half-expected the voice to respond with a cheerful *"Fuck you too, sir."* Fortunately, it didn't.

In a little under four minutes they arrived at Concourse B and another escalator whisked the future passengers back up to the departure gate. There was still time to stop at a newsstand for a book. Katherine picked out a John Grisham novel and balanced it with a magazine on antiques that she was addicted to. She tucked them safely away in her purse and started for the gate but only got a few steps before a voice called out, "K. J.!"

A tall brunette in a designer business suit got up from one of the benches in the waiting area and ran forward with her arms out.

"Beth!" Katherine yelled, waiving excitedly.

Beth Doliver and Katherine had been best friends since their freshman year at Ohio State. They began as roommates. In their second year, when the glamour of living with five hundred other girls wore off, they rented an apartment together near campus and filled it with an eclectic mix of furniture donated by their parents and the Goodwill store. Beth was Zach's godmother. She was the one who called the police when Katherine failed to return home and insisted they start a search for her. For three days Beth and forty police officers and volunteers scoured the woods outside Columbus looking for her friend. She was part of the team who found Katherine two miles from the burned-out cabin.

During Katherine's stay at the hospital, Beth slept in the same room with her on a cot the nurses brought in.

A month after Katherine's release from the hospital the flashbacks made their first appearance, horrible frightening episodes that left Katherine devastated. Beth promptly found a doctor for her.

After college, Katherine moved to Atlanta and Beth took a job as a CPA with a prestigious accounting firm in New York City. Despite the distance they remained close. When Beth's oldest child was injured in an automobile accident, Katherine was the first person she called. They managed to talk on the phone once every couple of weeks and recently had started sending e-mails back and forth. Each time they spoke it was as if the years melted away.

"I can't believe it—look at you," Beth exclaimed, holding Katherine by the shoulders. "You look wonderful." She hugged her again.

"I look like a wreck," Katherine explained. "I just came straight from court. I almost didn't make it at all."

"I heard. Congratulations on kicking that jerk's ass."

Katherine stared at her friend for a moment.

"How could you possibly . . . I just left there."

"Your secretary filled me in on the details when I called."

"*Galena,*" Katherine said, rolling her eyes upward.

Before she could say anything further, the public address system announced that Flight 257 to Fort Lauderdale was ready for boarding. Five minutes later they took their seats in the first-class cabin.

"It was really nice of Jack's company to do this," said Katherine.

"He's a sweetheart. Jack's administrative assistant told me they have enough frequent flyer points to circumnavigate the globe. When I mentioned a trip with you he just picked up the phone and told her to arrange for our tickets."

"It's good to be a CEO," Katherine observed.

For the next few minutes they caught up on what everyone in their families was doing. Beth told her about her charity work and the public relations she did for Jack's company.

"Business must be great," said Katherine. "Every time I open the paper I see their name."

Beth nodded. "Two months ago it was some medication that reduces the chance of congestive heart failure; last week it was a new allergy pill. It never ends. Now, tell me what's going on with your love life."

Before Katherine could reply a cabin attendant appeared and asked if they wanted anything to drink. Beth ordered white wine and Katherine ordered a Diet Coke.

"So that's how you keep your figure," Beth said glumly. "You haven't changed since college."

"I've changed. I just hide it better."

"I need to get back to the gym," Beth sighed. "If my hips get any wider, they'll start charging me for two seats."

Katherine slapped her lightly on the knee. "Your hips are fine. You've got a great shape."

Beth looked down and studied her hips for a moment, then asked the flight attendant to change her drink to Diet Coke.

"Okay," Beth said, snuggling into her seat and facing Katherine, "you were just about to tell me about your love life."

"There's not much to tell. I had a few dates with a college professor, but it didn't work out."

"How come?"

Katherine shrugged. "He started getting a little weird, so I broke it off."

Beth gave her a look and leaned closer to hear the explanation.

"He wanted to know if I ever let anybody tie me up, and

what I thought about spanking . . . stuff like that. I wasn't getting good vibes, so I ended it."

"Who did he want to do the spanking?"

"I never found out."

"You are the dullest person," Beth said, pushing her away. "You have to learn to relax, K. J."

"Getting tied up and spanked isn't my idea of relaxing. Now, sailing to Europe on a cruise ship . . . *that's* more my speed. I can't believe we're finally doing this, can you?"

Beth smiled. "We've only been talking about a trip together for ten years. I decided I'd better get things moving before we were both too old to enjoy it."

Katherine was about to tell her friend the spanking part was only the tip of the iceberg. The professor's comments were actually made tongue-in-cheek. It was just a convenient way to explain their breakup. Unfortunately for the professor, who wasn't really a bad person, his questions had touched on a sore spot. Trust wasn't something that came easily to her anymore, if at all, particularly following her divorce. Katherine shook her head. When you threw her night terrors and flashbacks into the mix, some men left skid marks. According to the doctors, the flashbacks might continue for the rest of her life. They were the result of what happened when she was nineteen. Medication helped control them, but it couldn't do anything about how she reacted when a man got too close. Her recent relationship ended the way all her relationships had—she pulled away.

Though her marriage had fallen apart for slightly different reasons, Katherine viewed it as another nail in the coffin. During their divorce trial, the heart surgeon, in a heated exchange with her lawyer, claimed that Katherine had driven him to having an affair with his nurse because she was emotionally closed off. His description of her as *damaged goods* didn't sit well with the jury, which was composed of four men and eight women. As a result, he was slammed with a substantial alimony award. It was the first time in her life Katherine had been called that and only she knew how close to the truth it was. *Damaged goods*, she whispered to herself, pushing the memory from her mind.

Katherine looked down at her hands and smiled.

But we still keep trying, don't we?

The pilot came on the intercom interrupting her thoughts and told everyone they were third in line for takeoff. Their flight to Fort Lauderdale would take about an hour and twenty minutes. He also said it was eighty-eight degrees there with clear skies and winds out of the southeast. When he finished speaking, the flight attendant gave her speech about making sure everyone's seat belt was securely fastened and instructed all passengers to return their trays to an upright and locked position.

In less than four minutes the jet's engines increased power sharply and the plane began moving down the runway. Katherine looked out the window and watched the earth fall away. In the distance she could see Atlanta's skyline with its gold capitol dome gleaming in the sun.

The sight brought to mind Zach's fifth-grade school trip to the little town of Dahlonega, where they had panned for gold together. She had made the same trip with each of her children. No one ever found any gold . . . except for the town's merchants who sold everything from "genuine Indian arrowheads" to homemade preserves and rock collections. By her estimate, three separate rock collections were now gathering dust somewhere in the upstairs closet.

THE FLIGHT was uneventful. Beth now lived in Scarsdale, a village about forty minutes outside New York City. Most of their talk was of the mundane variety and centered on what kinds of cases Katherine was handling. Beth filled her in on the latest happenings in New York's fashion scene. It was a marvel how easily they could slip back into their old relationship with no awkwardness.

Inevitably, the heart surgeon's name came up. Katherine told her he was now on his third or fourth marriage and his fifth home. She had lost count, since he'd married one of his wives twice.

"What's a trophy wife?" Beth asked, in response to Katherine description of the latest Mrs. Adams.

"You know . . . younger, boobier, blonder, dumber."

Katherine held out her hands in front of her chest to illustrate, nearly causing Beth's drink to go down the wrong way.

"You've met her?"

"A couple of times. But I wouldn't recognize her if she was sitting next to you."

For some reason Beth turned and looked at the person to her left. Across the aisle an overweight businessman was struggling with the air nozzle above his head. He eventually gave up and rang for the flight attendant.

THEY LANDED at Fort Lauderdale Airport with its bright turquoise and orange terminal, waited for about thirty minutes to claim their bags, then headed for Katherine's condo on Williams Island. It was one of the investments she got from her divorce settlement. Katherine insisted on keeping it because the kids liked to go there during Christmas holidays and on spring break.

Williams Island was an oasis in the middle of what was once the city of North Miami, and it literally was an island. A small bridge separated it from the "mainland," or Biscayne Boulevard as the natives called it. The Aventura Mall was a half-mile away. Ten years earlier, the residents of North Miami, tired of paying for services that never seemed to be forthcoming, had staged a peaceful revolution and formed their own city, naming it Aventura. A little over a mile square, Aventura contained some of the most luxurious condominiums on Florida's east coast.

The island consisted of seven high-rise buildings, a harbor, three sets of guard gates, and a private security force. Thanks to a creative marketing campaign, it had become home to a diverse group of wealthy foreigners, actors, and businessmen. Some of the yachts moored there were over a hundred feet long.

After dropping their luggage off, Katherine asked the valet to bring her car around and they headed for Bal Harbour. Nine times out of ten, all she ever did was walk around the mall and look in the store windows because prices bordered on the obscene.

A fair number of women she saw that evening fit nicely into the trophy-wife category. As she and Beth strolled it amazed her how many twenty-year-old girls with breast implants were walking arm in arm with men in their fifties or sixties. She assumed the relationships were symbiotic.

One place they did go to was the shop of a young man named René Ruiz to pick up a gown Katherine had been considering for several months. Trained by Valentino, Rene knew more about designing clothes for women than any man Katherine had ever met. He was one of the best-kept secrets in Miami and had a following that would walk across hot coals for one of his creations. After she gave Beth the go-ahead to book their cruise, René was the first person Katherine called.

The gown was brown velvet, with an antique lace insert that went all the way up her hip. Beth voiced her approval immediately. Though Katherine had reservations

about how much the insert would reveal, she gave in.
René added his vote as well.

I'll have to sue a lot of people to pay for this, she
thought, as they walked to the car.

NINE

The next morning, Katherine and Beth had breakfast at
the Veranda restaurant at Turnberry Isle before leaving for the ship. They sat on the patio enjoying the warm
Florida sun. In the pool a couple of children splashed
each other while their parents kept one eye on them and
one on the book or newspaper they were trying to read. It
all felt delicious. When breakfast was over they drove back
to the condo, picked up their suitcases, and headed for the
port. Before leaving, both women called home to say
good-bye to their families. Beth reached Jack at the office,
even though it was a Saturday morning, and Katherine got
the answering machines at James's and at Alley's apart-
ments. She had better luck with Zach, who told her not to
worry and to have a good time. He informed her that his father was taking him paintballing later that day with two
friends.

"What's paintballing?" Beth asked, when Katherine
hung up.

"They get dressed up like soldiers and run around the
woods shooting each other with paint. Zach's obsessed
with it, but he's supposed to be one of the best on his
team."

"They have teams?"

"It's not just kids," Katherine explained. "Men play, too.
Some of the paintball guns cost over a thousand dollars."

"I don't get it. They just hide in the woods and shoot whoever comes by? Doesn't it hurt?"

Katherine shook her head. "I hate it. He comes home with these purple bruises all over his body and they look absolutely horrible. Zach says they don't bother him. Personally, I'm dubious."

"Maybe Zach should invite his father to play," said Beth. "I wouldn't mind seeing him shot a few times."

THE CRUISE ships became visible as they drove over the causeway from Miami. Katherine had seen them many times, but never paid much attention to them. The closer she got the more overwhelming they looked. Gleaming white in the sun against a cloudless blue sky, the ships stood out like modern monoliths. This was her first cruise and it was all she could do not to gape.

"Jeez, they're huge, K. J."

Katherine nodded and kept driving.

They made a wrong turn and stopped at a security gate to ask a lady on duty where they could find the *Ocean Majestic*.

"*¿Como?*" she replied.

"*Donde esta el Majestic, por favor?*" Katherine said.

"*Ah . . . numero siete.*"

"*Gracias, Señora.*"

"*De nada. Tiene un viaje bueno.*"

Beth, who had taken French in school, listened to the exchange and grumbled, "That's what I love about Miami: It's so close to the United States. What'd she say?"

"She was telling us to have a good trip."

"Oh."

Inside the terminal another security guard checked their travel documents and told them they were supposed to be on the "purple" line. He pointed to a broad purple stripe painted on the floor which led to a counter where a cheerful-looking young lady was busy checking people in. While they were waiting, Beth lightly touched Katherine on the leg and made a small motion with her head. Katherine's brows came together, and she turned to see what her friend was looking at.

On the next line was a dark-haired man in his late forties, patiently waiting his turn. He was tall, well over six feet, Katherine guessed, and had a good physique with a handsome face. The title of the book he was carrying read *Closing Arguments*.

"He's a doll," Beth whispered.

"He's probably married."

"No wedding ring."

"Then he's probably here with his girlfriend," Katherine whispered back.

"I don't see anyone with him."

The man reached the front of the line and picked up his boarding documents. As he turned to leave, by coincidence he and Katherine made eye contact. He smiled at her and she smiled back, and then he headed for the escalator.

"Did you see that?" Beth asked, squeezing Katherine's hand. "He looked right at you."

"He was just being polite," Katherine said, pushing her hand away.

"Well, he's got a cute ass."

"Oh, for God's sake."

"Hey, I'm on vacation," Beth said, with a shrug.

Katherine didn't have a suitable reply, so she said nothing. At the counter, a hostess examined their documents and decided the photos on their passports bore a reasonable resemblance to them. They were then directed to another counter with the name ADMIRALS' CLUB above it in gold letters.

A young man stepped out as soon as he saw the women walking toward him and introduced himself as Derek.

Like the hostess, he welcomed them to the wonderful world of the *Ocean Majestic*.

"We've been expecting you," Derek said. "May I see your boarding documents, please?"

Katherine and Beth looked at each other, then handed him the thick package they'd just been given at check-in.

"Everything looks fine. If you'll follow me, I'll take you directly up to your cabins. It looks like you're on the Panorama Deck in 7385 and 7386—that's amidships."

"Is that good?" asked Katherine.

"Fantastic," Derek said. "The Neptune Pool is one deck up from you on the Sun Deck. You'll also find the gym and spa there if you're into exercise. Another big attraction is the Seafarer's Buffet, but I'm sure we won't be visiting that *too* much," he said with a wink.

"What's the Seafarer's Buffet?" asked Beth.

"Oh, my God," Derek exclaimed, placing a hand over his heart and stopping in his tracks. "It's to die for. They've got every salad known to man, and at least eight different entrées a day. You can get breakfast, lunch, and dinner there if you don't want to eat in the formal dining room. They have tons of fresh fruit and vegetables—and the desserts . . . don't get me started on the desserts."

"I guess that's why they have a gym onboard," said Katherine.

"Exactly. Is this is your first cruise?"

Katherine nodded.

"It's my second," Beth told him. "I went on one for my honeymoon, but that was fifteen years ago and the ship wasn't anything like this. This looks more like a floating building."

"That's a great way to describe it," Derek agreed. "It really is like a hotel. The Fincantieri people did an amazing job. The *Majestic* is the largest cruise ship in the world—160,000 tons and over three football fields long. We have twenty decks, which makes it taller than the Statue of Liberty. And if you're into jogging, there's a track on the Capri Deck—three times around is a mile."

Katherine's next question faded from her mind as they stepped off the elevator into an eleven-story atrium. Palm trees and exotic flowers surrounded a circular marble lobby, where a string quartet was playing Bach. A man on a grand piano accompanied them. Twenty glass elevators, all lit with white lights on the outside, sped up and down the side of the atrium carrying passengers to and from their rooms. Couches and chairs were clustered in cozy conversation groups. Many passengers were already seated, listening to the music and sipping drinks from tall colored glasses.

Derek smiled patiently, noting their reaction. "Everyone does the same thing their first time here," he said.

Beth shook her head in wonder. "This is fuckin' amazing. Listen, I don't mean to sound ungrateful, but how come we're getting the royal treatment?"

"Warwick Reed is one of our biggest clients," said Derek. "Your husband called the hotel manager personally and asked him to make sure you and Ms. Adams were treated well. That's why we've upgraded you to junior suites. The full suites were already taken or we'd have put you there."

"I didn't know Jack did that," said Beth. "What a sneak."

"Did you just say 'hotel manager'?" asked Katherine.

"I did. That's what we call the senior officer in charge of operations. Now, if you'll follow me, I'll see that you're properly settled in. Feel free to ask all the questions you want."

Beth and Katherine followed Derek to the elevators and up to the Panorama Deck. In the middle of a long corridor were two white sets of double doors trimmed in gold. Their luggage was waiting outside. Derek opened the first door, rolled Beth's suitcase inside, and put it on a rack.

Although Katherine was well-traveled, she wasn't sure what to expect from a ship's cabin, and for the second time that morning she found herself speechless. Not only did the room have a queen-size bed and a balcony, it had a full Jacuzzi-style bathtub. Until then, the only firsthand reports she'd had regarding shipboard accommodations had come from her oldest son, James, who had gone on a cruise during spring break. He and his friends slept four to a room and he described the whole experience as "cool."

On a table in front of the couch was a huge bouquet of flowers and a welcome basket filled with cheeses and a bottle of champagne. There were two cards: One was compliments of the captain; the other was from Jack, Beth's husband.

Katherine's room was a duplicate of Beth's, complete with the flowers and the cheese basket. She read the card from Jack Doliver, wishing them both a wonderful time and reminding them not to drink the water.

It's definitely good to be CEO, she thought.

Derek said good-bye and handed Katherine his business card, telling her to call him if she needed anything. He also said she and Beth were invited to a cocktail party later that evening after they set sail.

The term "set sail" sounded odd since there wasn't anything on the ship remotely resembling a sail, but she got the message. Once Derek was gone, Katherine opened her suitcase and began unpacking. She wasn't sure what she would find since Galena had finished the job for her. René's gown went into the closet; having carried it the entire way herself. There she found a little safe for valuables, along with a note that read, "This safe is for the convenience of our passengers. The management wishes to advise you, however, that we cannot be responsible for any losses unless the property is checked with the ship's Purser."

The message did little to inspire confidence. Katherine stared at it, debating whether to put her Miriam Haskell jewelry in the safe. However, since she didn't know where to find the Purser and since the jewelry was costume, she decided to take a chance, though not without some trepidation.

She had been collecting Miriam Haskell pieces for the last five years, and it was one of her passions. It was not a particularly lawyer-like hobby, but then she wasn't a lawyer all the time, she reasoned.

Any concern over having enough to wear vanished immediately. Galena had packed enough clothes, bras, and thongs to last for three weeks rather than two. Katherine shook her head and stuffed the lingerie in the top drawer of her dresser.

This will probably give Jimmy and the guys something to talk about at the office, she thought.

After plopping down on the couch, she leaned back, and looked out the balcony doors. She was on vacation and the last thing she wanted to think about was the office.

Through the doors she could see a number of sailing craft and small vessels passing by the ship. Jet Skis crisscrossed each other's wake, bouncing across the water and leaving trails of foam. Some drivers waved at the passengers who were watching them from the rails.

Katherine and Beth had agreed to meet in half an hour and only fifteen minutes had passed.

Close enough.

She opened the door, stepped out into corridor, and

promptly collided with the man she had seen on line earlier, knocking his book and papers to the ground.

"Whoa there," he said, catching her by the shoulders.

"I'm so sorry," Katherine said, stooping down to help him collect his things.

The man stooped next to her. "No problem. Did I hurt you?"

"No, not at all. I ran into you. I think I stepped on your foot."

"You did, but I'm a tough guy," he said, smiling. He took her by the elbow and helped her up. "My name's John Delaney. Looks like we're neighbors,"

"Hi, neighbor," Katherine said, holding out her hand. "Katherine Adams."

Delaney shook hands with her.

"I'm three doors down."

"This is my cabin," Katherine said.

"So I gather."

She rolled her eyes. "That was dumb. Of course it's my cabin. Oh, here's your book," she said. Conscious of Delaney's fleeting glance at her missing finger, she quickly put her hand behind her back. "Are you a lawyer?"

"Yep."

"Me, too."

"Really? Let me guess: You specialize in hit-and-run cases."

Katherine opened her mouth, then closed it again, giving him a flat look. "That was bad."

"Sorry. I couldn't resist. Where are you from, Katherine Adams?"

"Atlanta."

"Great city. I've been there a lot of times."

"How about you, John Delaney?"

"New York."

Both of them moved aside to allow some people to pass.

"Are you with a firm or by yourself?" Katherine asked.

"Actually, I teach law at John Jay College in New York."

Before Katherine could ask another question, the door to Beth's cabin opened. A look of surprise appeared on her face when she saw them standing in the hallway.

"Am I interrupting anything?"

"No, John and I just ran into each other," Katherine said. Then, remembering her earlier conversation with Sherri Wallace, she added, "literally."

"I see. And now you're getting acquainted in the hall."

Katherine took a breath.

"John Delaney, this is Beth Doliver. Beth . . . John. He's from New York, too."

"Really? Where?" asked Beth.

"I live in Manhattan on the Upper West Side. How about you?"

"Scarsdale. We moved out ten years ago," said Beth. "The city got so crowded, we figured it was time."

"It's beautiful up there," said Delaney. "Well, I'd better get unpacked. It was nice running into you, Katherine— or is it Kathy?"

"Katherine . . . K. J. to my friends."

Delaney considered that for a second and nodded slowly.

"K. J.," he repeated. "I like it. See you both later. Good to meet you, Betty."

Katherine held back a giggle and slipped her arm through Beth's. "C'mon, *Betty*, let's go explore the ship."

"Betty," Beth grumbled.

FOR THE next thirty minutes they wandered around taking in the *Ocean Majestic*'s sights. It truly was a floating hotel. They consulted a map next to the elevators that showed the ship's layout and took the stairs up one flight, emerging onto a sunlit deck where a calypso band was playing. People were out strolling and lounging on chairs. They climbed another flight of stairs and looked down into an impossibly blue pool. At the end of the ship—Katherine later learned it was called the "stern"—they found a miniature-golf course and a rock-climbing wall. The jogging track Derek had mentioned was painted in green. Eventually, they worked their way back to the *Ocean Majestic*'s bow and found yet another pool. It was quieter and had less frantic activity than the first one. Nearby a bar was serving complimentary drinks. They each took one.

The gym was located at the stern of the *Majestic*. Katherine looked it over and decided that it was fine—more than fine, actually. The spa was next door. When they entered, a perky twenty-something attendant with a British accent gave them a guided tour of the place. She told them the Aphrodite (the spa's name) offered a range of services from facials and massages to seaweed wraps and hot-rock treatments. Katherine hadn't the vaguest idea what a hot-rock treatment was, but having once been covered in green slime when she visited a spa in the Bahamas with her ex, she decided to pass on it along with the "famous" seaweed treatment. The attendant was disappointed and assured her it would remove all of the toxins from her body. As an alternative, she and Beth scheduled massages and facials later in the week.

After leaving the spa they wandered into the Seafarer Lounge and saw what Derek was talking about. The variety of dishes and amount of food, all temptingly laid out buffet style, was staggering. Katherine took one look at the chocolate cakes and puddings and made a mental note to hit the gym the first thing each day.

By far the most impressive sight they encountered during their wanderings, other than an ice-skating rink, was a three-story shopping mall, complete with a cobblestone street. It looked like it was lifted straight out of the French Quarter in New Orleans. The mall ran down the center of the ship and contained four different cafés with tables and gas lamps in front of them. A candy shop had set up two free yogurt machines outside and a line of people had already formed. Those passengers who had interior cabins—and there were a few—could look out into the mall and watch the shoppers. At the moment all the stores were closed since they were still in port. The stores ran the gamut from Tiffany's to kiosks selling suntan lotion. A sign said they would open at six o'clock when the ship reached international waters.

At the far end of the mall was a casino with glittering bright lights and garish colors. Katherine had been in casinos before and wondered whether they were all decorated by the same person. Purples, yellows, and reds were everywhere, along with mirrors and the ubiquitous security cameras, or "eye in the sky," as they were called in the business. Of course there were no clocks or windows. Management knew the longer you stayed, the greater their chances were.

One of the few useful things she got from her marriage to the heart surgeon was an appreciation for the game of blackjack. On their first vacation to Las Vegas after his residency he explained that dealers and floor bosses were the most chauvinist people in the world. They believed women didn't have the brains or discipline to play blackjack correctly.

"Just give 'em a roll of quarters and send them over to the slots. It'll keep 'em occupied for hours," one of the managers had told him.

The heart surgeon made the mistake of passing that comment along to Katherine, whose mind was a highly organized and mathematical one. Once she determined to learn the game, she had no problem memorizing the basic strategy charts, or in keeping the count correctly, or in managing her money properly. Where he got frustrated, lost control, and began betting larger and larger sums to catch up his losses, she never did. He dropped eleven thousand dollars that week and refused to talk about it ever again. She won back just over nine thousand dollars and quietly returned the money to their savings account.

Katherine had visited Las Vegas a number of times, as well as casinos in Puerto Rico, Europe, and the Bahamas. During those visits she managed to amass enough winnings to pay for two cars, an antique armoire, a couch, and a number of paintings for their home. The rest she put into a trust for her children. Early on she concluded the trick was to walk away from the tables while you were ahead, and she did exactly that. Eventually the house would grind you down—it had to, given the difference in bankrolls.

It had been many years since she'd visited a casino and the game's allure was still there. It always would be, but there was no percentage in giving them another chance. Katherine decided if she played during the trip, it would be five-dollar bets.

After two hours of exploring, the women were exhausted and stopped at the ship's library to rest.

"I've never seen anything like this," said Katherine. "A couple of guys at the office went on cruises with their wives, but you just don't believe it until you're here."

"It's amazing," Beth agreed, flipping through the itinerary they'd received at check-in. "I put us down for a late dinner seating. Did you know they have four other restaurants on this ship besides the two main dining rooms?"

"No."

"We can switch to an earlier dinner if your friend wants to join us," Beth suggested.

"He's not a friend. I told you, we just ran into each other."

"Sure, K. J. You run into a fellow lawyer who just happens to be single and we haven't left port yet. The guy's a hunk."

"You're impossible. He teaches law at *John Jay*."

Beth stuck out her lower lip.

"*Another* professor? Do you think he's kinky, too?"

"If he is, I'll sign you up for the spankings. How are we supposed to dress tonight?"

Beth consulted the leaflet. "It says here 'casual.'"

Katherine was about to ask another question when the cruise director, a voice they were to become very familiar with over the next few days, came on the loudspeaker. He announced they were pulling out and invited everyone on deck to wave good-bye to Miami. It was a silly thing to do, waving good-bye to a city, but Katherine and Beth went on deck anyway.

People lined the rails and watched as the land slipped by. On the shore, parents put children on their shoulders and waved at the great white ship moving silently past them into the Atlantic. The ship's whistle blew a farewell blast, and soon the spit of land that marked Miami's lower boundary began to fall farther and farther away until at last it was just a hazy outline. The sky assumed a warm reddish quality marking the transition between night and day, something photographers call "magic time." It was simply beautiful. Katherine looked toward the horizon, took a long breath, and stared dreamily out across the water. They stayed there another twenty minutes and then headed back to their cabins, agreeing to meet at eight-thirty.

Katherine ran a bath, threw some oil beads into the water, and stepped in. *I'm taking a bath in a marble tub in*

*the middle of the Atlantic Ocean. If this isn't decadent, I
don't know what is.*

She made a mental note to send her kids an e-mail as
soon as she found out where the business center was
located, then leaned her head back and slipped lower into
the water, letting the tension drain out of her body. Her
thoughts turned inward after several minutes.

She loved being a lawyer; it was fun, and she was good
at it. Every case had something new to deal with. There
were similarities, of course. The same issues about who
got what and how much alimony would be paid or not
paid tended to come up frequently, but the facts remained
unique. Several years earlier, she decided that not having
to deal with criminal cases was a good thing. Every time
she went to court she was struck by a similar impression:
Ninety-nine percent of the people she saw looked like
they belonged there.

Thank God I'm out of that rat race.

Domestic relations wasn't every lawyer's cup of tea;
most attorneys hated divorce cases and steered clear of
them. Katherine, however, enjoyed the work. Not the
fighting, which could get downright nasty, but keeping
families together and seeing whatever hurt the parents'
breakup caused would not be visited on the children. It
wasn't the most exciting area of the law, but she was a
solid trial lawyer and her clients liked her.

A secondary benefit of not having to deal with criminal cases was that she was better able to keep her post-
traumatic stress attacks under control. They were
debilitating, painful, and reminiscent of having a coronary.
Thanks to the medications she took, and her removal
from the U.S. Attorney's office, the attacks remained under control. But as the doctors explained they could re-
emerge at any time. So far she had been lucky. When
Beth had asked about her love life, Katherine danced

around the topic despite the fact that Beth was her best friend. She slid the washcloth up her leg and stared at her hand, the one with the missing finger. "Damaged goods," she said softly. It was how she thought of herself. Richard Jenks had rocked her world and sent her into a dark place. It took years to pull herself up to the light and allow herself the luxury of trust once again. Then the heart surgeon pulled the rug out from under their marriage. His methods differed but the end result was the same. She built a wall for her self-protection and it had remained in place. It was so high it was often difficult to see over it.

Her will to live had saved her from a raving madman and kept her alive for four days and nights in an Ohio forest. And it was that same will she drew on to keep going after her divorce. Her children needed her. Her friends clung to the belief that Mr. Right was just around the corner—the perfect soulmate. She wasn't so certain anymore. Maybe this cruise was just what she needed.

Katherine settled lower in the water and allowed her mind to drift. In several minutes the rising heat made her eyelids heavy.

TEN

At the stern of the ship two men watched the foaming trail the *Ocean Majestic* left on the water. Moonlight gave it a slightly opalescent quality. The man on the left was tall and slender with a dark complexion and intense brown eyes. His companion, shorter and more powerfully built, leaned casually against the rail, watching. The shorter man's shoulders seemed to strain against his jacket. After a few seconds he turned away from the water and looked up at the rock-climbing wall, then down at the people strolling past him on the deck. A few nodded, but he didn't nod back, or even acknowledge those who said good evening. His partner continued to face the water and appeared to be talking to himself, except he wasn't. A wire from an earpiece ran behind his ear and down the back of his neck, disappearing into his sports jacket. Despite the warm night, they were the only two men on deck wearing jackets. The thin man had a tiny microphone clipped to the lapel of his coat. The rushing wind and slap of water against the ship's sides made it impossible to hear what he was saying, even if someone were standing close enough to do so. His partner adjusted his position slightly, placing himself between his companion and the passersby.

ON THE *Ocean Majestic*'s bridge, the navigator glanced at the ship's radar screen and mentioned to the officer on duty that another ship had been keeping pace with them since they left Miami. Presently, it was about two miles off their stern quarter. Second Officer Owen McCalister walked over and looked at the screen. McCalister was a man of about sixty years old who was completing his last tour of duty before he took early retirement.

"What ship is it?" he asked.

"The *Marie Star,* sir. It's a cargo transport—Liberian registry," answered the navigator.

"Do they have a plan on file?"

"Aye, sir. I took the liberty of calling it up. They're bound for Naples, Italy."

McCalister shrugged.

"It's a free ocean. We may have company for a while. Let me know if anything changes."

"Aye, sir."

* * *

THE THIN man on the Promenade Deck finished his conversation and nodded to his companion. Checking over his shoulder to make sure no one was watching, he pulled the earpiece out and detached the microphone from his lapel, stuffing them into his breast pocket. When he was through, he and his partner separated and went to their cabins at opposite ends of the ship. On the deck directly above them, a third man sat in a lounge chair pretending to read a book. He closed it as soon as they were gone and also went to his cabin. All three ordered dinner in their rooms.

KATHERINE LAY on her bed, reading the book she'd bought at the airport. While she and Beth were sitting in the library she noticed two copies of it on their shelves, but kept the observation to herself. The bath had been wonderful—exactly what she'd needed. She felt clean and fresh again. She glanced at the clock. It was time to get dressed, so she closed the book and began putting on her makeup. When she was through, she selected a pleasant sea foam green sundress Galena had packed, along with one of her Haskell necklaces. She debated over the shoes for a few seconds, rejected the closed toe pumps as too formal, and finally went with a pair of sling-backs. Sexy, but not overly so. A quick spritz of perfume on the neck and she was ready to go. After she collected Beth they went down to dinner together.

The grand staircase of the Palm Court looked out over the dining room. It was one of two formal restaurants onboard the *Majestic*. The room's décor reminded Katherine of the lobby at New York's Palace Hotel. After a brief wait, the maître d' appeared, kissed their hands, and led them down the staircase to their table. Despite the fact that it was pitch-black out, he assured them they would have a marvelous view in the daytime.

"I *love* making an entrance," Beth whispered.

To Katherine's surprise, John Delaney was seated there. Across from him were a man and woman and two elderly gentlemen dressed in golf shirts and blazers.

"I had nothing to do with this," Beth said under her breath.

Delaney got up when he saw them and drew their chairs out for them.

"Thank you," said Katherine.

"Thank you," Beth echoed.

"That's so nice," the woman across from him remarked. "More men should do that. I'm Libby Stephens and this is my husband, Ellis."

"Beth Doliver," said Beth, shaking her hand. "This is Katherine Adams."

"Hi," said Katherine. She smiled and shook their hands as well.

Delaney remained seated and introduced himself. The other men at the table turned out to be priests, Reverend William Kelley and Father George Reynolds. Both were from New York and had been close friends for fifty years.

"It's nice to see you again, John," said Katherine.

"Small world," he agreed. "Good to see you, too. How're you doing, Betty?"

"Beth," Beth said, drawing out the word.

Delaney stared at her for a second. "Damn," he said. Then he flinched when he realized there were priests present and apologized.

"It's okay, son. We're not on duty," Father Reynolds told him.

He looked to be in his late sixties. Hair that had once been red was now fading to white and a pair of bright blue eyes were his most prominent features

"Sorry," Delaney mouthed to Beth, who smiled and waved it away.

"Katherine tells me you're a law professor," said Beth. "What do you teach?"

"Evidence and forensic studies."

"That's an odd combination," observed Father Kelley.

"Yes, it is. I only got into the law about ten years ago. Before that I was a homicide detective at the 43rd Precinct in New York."

"Isn't that in the Bronx?" Libby asked. "I used to live there before we were married."

"Sure is," Delaney replied.

"What made you decide to switch?" asked Katherine.

"I always wanted to go to law school. I just got side-tracked along the way."

"Will your wife be joining us tonight?" Beth asked, jumping slightly when Katherine kicked her under the table.

"Not unless she can swim. We've been divorced for about seven years. She remarried and lives in Scottsdale, Arizona, now."

"Oh, how sad," said Beth. "I'm sorry."

Mrs. Stephens nodded in agreement.

Delaney shrugged. "I suppose it was for the best. We're probably better friends now than when we were married."

"Were there children involved?" asked Beth.

"I have a son who's starting at Penn State next year on a track scholarship."

The waiter and his assistant arrived carrying rolls and butter and took their dinner orders. The conversations resumed as soon as they were gone. Everyone went through the usual litany of questions and answers about their background and what they thought of the ship. There seemed to be general agreement the *Majestic* was a marvel of engineering, luxury, and technology. The only holdout was Father Kelley, an affable slender gentleman with a shock of pure white hair. He maintained the original *Queen*

Mary was at least as impressive as the *Majestic* in her own way.

Though Katherine generally avoided discussing her personal life, she did get around to mentioning that she was divorced. John Delaney's presence at the table might have had something to do with that, but it seemed like a reasonable opportunity to bring the subject up. She then went on to tell everyone about her children in some detail. He smiled and listened with interest.

Dinner progressed from appetizer to main course and the conversations eventually broke up into smaller groups as frequently happens in large gatherings. John and Katherine took to each other from the start. She thought he had a kind heart from the way he spoke, and he was impressed that she didn't put on airs. There was something about Delaney that intrigued her, though she couldn't quite put her finger on it at the time. He was easygoing, intelligent, and had a good sense of humor. She also liked the shape of his hands and his thick brown hair.

Delaney liked the way she threw back her head when she laughed and the twinkle in her eyes that seemed to appear when she teased him. He also found he was having a difficult time keeping his eyes on Katherine's face. While they were talking they kept drifting to the neckline of her dress, which was cut rather low.

Beth smiled to herself and tactfully let them talk. At some point during the meal, Libby Stephens mentioned that her husband and Delaney had something in common— both were professors. This brought up the subject of what field Ellis Stephens taught. He explained he was in the biogenetics department at Columbia University.

"Forgive my ignorance, but exactly what does a geneticist do, Dr. Stephens?" asked Father Reynolds. "Or would you prefer 'Professor'?"

"I'd prefer Ellis, Father. Geneticists study how genes

are formed. There are a lot of different subfields I won't bore you with. Basically, my group has been trying to learn how altering a cell's DNA affects its development."

"Does that have something to do with those designer genes we read about in the newspapers?" asked Beth.

Stephens chuckled. "I love that term—'designer genes.' It sounds like something you'd buy at Saks. I suppose the simple answer is 'yes.' Our experiments though have centered on developing a stem cell."

"What's a stem cell?" asked Beth.

"It's the basic cell in the body," Delaney answered. "We all start out that way and then the cells specialize. Some become brain cells, some become heart cells, that kind of thing."

"Bravo, Professor," said Stephens, clapping him on the back. "I see your time in undergraduate biology wasn't entirely wasted."

"Actually, I read it in *Newsweek*," Delaney said, with an embarrassed grin.

"Is this related to cloning people?" asked Father Kelley.

Stephens shook his head.

"There are scientists in my profession who would like to take their research in that direction, Father, but I think there are a number of ethical issues that need to be decided first. Personally, I'm not in favor of it. My leanings are more toward the therapeutic side of the equation."

"Well, I'm relieved to hear you say that," Father Kelley told him. "Human beings are much more than a collection of cells and fluids."

"I agree. Can you imagine cloning some of the guests from *The Jerry Springer Show*?" said Stephens.

The joke drew a laugh from everyone at the table.

"I don't get what you mean when you say the 'therapeutic side,'" said Beth.

"I'm referring to the possibility of developing new organs or regrowing cells that have been damaged due to disease or injury."

"You mean like giving someone a new liver or a new brain?" asked Father Reynolds.

"The liver perhaps, but growing an entire brain is something that's beyond us right now. Even though the cells would be an exact match, we'd have to assume they contained the specific information . . . the memories . . . the emotions and experiences that make a person unique. There are so many neurological interconnections, we'd be taking a tremendous chance to simply cut out a damaged portion of the brain and insert new cells."

"I completely agree," the priest said. "Bill and I are pretty much retired now, but I can tell you, this is a hot topic within the Church. They haven't adopted an official position yet."

Father Kelley nodded his head in agreement.

"They'll work things out in time after the Ecumenical Council debates it. Those guys just love to debate."

"Liberal," Father Reynolds remarked, motioning to his friend with his thumb.

Stephens smiled. "We have just as much debate in the scientific community. There's tremendous competition to be the first one out with the technology."

As he spoke, his wife slipped her arm through his and gave him an affectionate squeeze. Stephens stopped talking for a moment as the waiter returned to take their dessert orders.

"What do you mean, 'competition,' Ellis?" asked Katherine.

"Well, this sort of thing has the potential to become a billion-dollar industry, if not a multibillion one," he explained. "The population of the United States is aging, no question about that, and health concerns are on the rise. Insurance companies figured out a long time ago

that surgical cures are less costly than maintaining people in hospitals and nursing homes for years on end. In
fact, they're the ones who've supplied us with many of
the research grants."

"Does Jack's company do that kind of stuff?" Katherine asked Beth.

"I don't think so. We're mostly into over-the-counter
medications and bedpans. We do a few prescription products, but they're not the mainstay of our business."

"One of the drug companies actually sent a man on this
cruise to try and talk us into signing a contract with
them," said Libby. "Can you imagine that?"

"Do you mean you've done it already?" asked Delaney.

Ellis Stephens looked down at the table for a moment
before answering. When he looked up again there was a
broad smile on his face. That was when Katherine noticed the attaché case by the side of his chair.

AFTER DINNER was over everyone went their separate
ways. Beth said she wanted to turn in early and gave
Katherine a private wink as she departed. The Stephenses
decided to take a turn around the deck, and the two
priests announced they were going to a late show in the
main theater. Katherine and Delaney were left alone.

"Looks like we've been abandoned," he said.

"Looks like it," she agreed.

"I was going to try my luck in the casino. Want to
come along?"

"Sure. It sounds like fun."

"I generally play the dice," Delaney explained, as they
started walking. "But I'm pretty decent at cards, too. I
can show you how to play blackjack if you like."

"Oh, I'm not much of a gambler, John."

"Honestly, I can teach anybody. I taught one of the

guys I work with, and he won over three hundred dollars in Atlantic City."

"That's amazing," said Katherine.

"Yep."

The *Majestic*'s casino was already crowded by the time they arrived. Streams of silver coins poured out of different slot machines accompanied by flashing lights and sirens, tempting even a casual passerby to see what the excitement was about. All three craps tables were filled to overflowing with people and bystanders who watched every roll of the dice intently. In the center of the room were the blackjack tables, a roulette wheel, and two tables featuring something called Pai Gow.

Delaney and Katherine looked at each other and smiled.

"Which one are you going to play?" she asked.

"Well, I'd like to show you craps if we can get a spot. I'm not really a big gambler—mostly nickels and quarters."

"I didn't know you could make such small bets," said Katherine. "I've got a whole purse full of change."

Delaney laughed. "Nickels and quarters means *dollars*—fives and twenty-fives. The red chips represent five dollars and the green ones are twenty-five."

"Oh, I see. Maybe it would be best if I just watched you for a while."

"Sure. Hey look, there's a guy leaving over there."

Delaney quickly stepped across the room and secured a spot, then motioned for Katherine to join him. She took a deep breath and followed.

"Sorry," he apologized. "Didn't mean to abandon you in mid-sentence, but sometimes you have to move fast in these places."

"That's okay. A man's gotta do what a man's gotta do."

Delaney smiled at her.

"Now if you look close, you can see that both halves of the table are mirror images of each other."

"It looks very confusing."

For the next few minutes Delaney explained the finer points of craps to Katherine. He placed two hundred dollars in twenties on the table, and one of the dealers gave him back a mixture of green and red chips.

"Every one of those chips out there represents someone making a bet," he told her.

"I see."

In reality, Katherine had already picked up on the table's pattern and how the betting scheme worked. Delaney however, seemed to be enjoying the instruction, so she kept quiet and played the naïve female.

"The dice are coming around to us after this shooter," he explained. He then turned to the man next to him and said, "Hey pal, could you move down a little bit and make some room for the lady?"

The man moved, his eyes lingering on Katherine's cleavage. She adjusted the top of her dress and squeezed in between them.

The player next to Delaney was a dark-haired man wearing a diamond Rolex on his wrist and three gold chains around his neck. He made several passes before he threw a seven. Then it was Delaney's turn. He placed a five-dollar bet on the COME LINE and carefully picked out two of the six dice as though the selection were a scientific process. He shook them a few times, then suddenly stopped and looked at Katherine.

"Are you *sure* you've never played this game before?" he asked.

"Positive. I watched my ex-husband a few times, but I think he lost."

Delaney's face brightened and he handed the dice to Katherine.

"Oh God, John, I couldn't," she said. "I don't want to lose your money."

"Shoot 'em, lady. The dice are gettin' cold," a man at the end of the table called out.

"C'mon, K. J., you gotta do it," Delaney urged. "First-time lady shooters are lucky; everybody knows that."

Katherine was about to decline again, but he looked like such a little boy, she gave in and took the dice.

"All right, but don't say I didn't warn you."

"Hey, Mack, did you just say she's a first-time shooter?" the man on Katherine's left asked Delaney, completely ignoring the fact that she was standing there.

Delaney nodded and in less than five seconds all the bets on the table doubled.

"How come he didn't ask me?" asked Katherine.

"Just shoot the dice," Delaney said, out of the corner of his mouth.

"New lady shooter coming out," the stickman announced.

Hmph, Katherine said to herself.

She shook the dice a few times as she had seen John do, then tossed them the length of the table. They bounced off the rear cushion and came to rest with one showing a six and the other a five.

"Eleven," the stickman announced.

There was a general round of applause from the men and an "Atta girl" from a fellow in a cowboy hat three players to her right. The stickman raked in the dice and passed them back to her.

"You want me to throw again?"

"Absolutely," Delaney beamed.

Katherine let out a long breath, picked up two of the dice . . . and promptly rolled a seven. This time the applause at the table was supplemented by a few cheers, just as it was the next time she rolled a seven, and the time after that when she did it again. On her fifth try she rolled a six. The stickman moved a plastic puck behind a corresponding number on the table. "Six is the point," he said. "Good luck, lady."

"Easy point," someone called out.

After nine or ten rolls, during which every number *but* six seemed to come up, the dice finally produced a six and the table erupted in cheers once again. The man next to her patted her on the back and said, "Whatever you're doing, keep it up, sister."

Gradually, green chips started to outnumber the red ones. Katherine noticed a fair amount of black chips had also begun to appear on the table which meant some people were now betting hundreds. She glanced at Delaney's bet. He had fifty dollars out on the COME LINE and another seventy-five dollars in smaller bets on numbers five, six, and eight.

She managed to hold the dice for the next thirty minutes, making pass after pass, all to the shouts and applause of the men. The cheering grew so loud people at other tables came over to see what the commotion was about. Though she didn't have a single dollar on the line herself, Katherine got caught up in the excitement. Eventually she rolled a seven. There was a collective groan as the dealers raked in the players' money.

The heavyset man who had tried to look down her dress turned to her and said, "That was a hell of a roll, sister. *A hell of a roll.* You take care now."

A few men said similar things. As Delaney and Katherine turned to leave, they were stopped by the fellow in the cowboy hat who came over to shake her hand.

"Thank you, little lady," he said, handing her three black chips.

"What's this for?"

"Well, ma'am, you did all the work. All I did was plunk

my money down and ride your roll. Let me tell you, I've seen some hot hands before but you was flat on fire."

"That's sweet," said Katherine, "but I couldn't take your money."

"Fair's fair," he said, holding up his hands. "Listen to me, now . . . you done great. If you don't want it, you can buy your husband here a new set of pajamas."

Katherine opened her mouth to protest further, but the man wouldn't hear it. She finally gave up and thanked him, dropping the chips in her evening bag.

"I *could* use a set of pajamas," said Delaney, giving her shoulders an affectionate squeeze.

She didn't resist or pull away, which surprised her a little.

"You don't look like the pajama type."

Delaney gave her an odd look.

"I don't? How about I buy you a drink and we discuss it further? I found a really nice lounge on the Viking Deck, and I'm exhausted from watching you."

"Sure," said Katherine. "Did you do well? It looked like you did."

Delaney opened his palm displaying eight black chips and three green ones.

"You won *eight hundred and seventy-five dollars!*" she gasped.

"Guess I'll be able to afford those drinks."

ELEVEN

While half the ship's passengers were watching a magician pass a hoop over a lady who appeared to be floating in midair, two men at opposite ends of the ship changed clothes in their cabins. The thin man cracked open his door an inch and peered out into the corridor to make sure no one was watching before he left his room. He was now wearing the white uniform of a ship's officer. His cabin was located directly above the two massive stern thrusters that powered the *Ocean Majestic*. From studying schematics of the ship he was aware there were four more engines at the bow, but they were of no interest to him at the moment. He turned right around a corner, moving at an unhurried pace and continued until he came to a door marked CREW ONLY. His partner, dressed as an engineer, was waiting for him. They descended two flights of stairs to the *Majestic*'s main engine room.

At two o'clock in the morning, Captain Marius Barroni required that only a skeleton crew be on duty. The crew consisted of three men, one of whom was asleep on a cot. The two others were watching an old black-and-white movie on a portable television set they had set up to help them get through the boredom of a night watch. The crew's presence in the engine room was a holdover from the old days. Newer ships were now automated. The men were there more for security purposes and to prevent curious passengers from wandering around and getting hurt.

The vast computer center that controlled the *Ocean Majestic* was located on the bridge. Any adjustments in course or alterations in speed Captain Barroni wanted were made directly from there. Gone were the days when captains would call down to engineering through copper tubes and yell for more power. That only went on in the movies.

The shorter of the two men was carrying a toolbox with him. When the crew members heard them coming down the stairs they started to get up, but the thin man dressed as an officer motioned for them to remain seated.

"Anything good on?" he asked.

"No, sir. Just an old Cary Grant movie," Mike Cleland answered. Cleland was fifty years old and had been in the merchant marine since he was twenty-five. He was part of the original crew that had launched the *Ocean Majestic* eighteen months earlier.

"Which one?" the thin man asked, in a perfect American accent.

"*Arsenic and Old Lace*, sir."

"No kidding. I love that movie. The guy who thinks he's Teddy Roosevelt kills me."

"Yeah, they don't make 'em like that anymore," Cleland agreed.

"Carry on, men," the officer said. "Cabin 6405 isn't getting any water pressure, and maintenance says we can only get into the crawlway from down here."

"What you mean 'we,' white man?" joked the short man.

The officer shook his head.

"No respect at all. Let's get moving before they wake up the hotel manager."

As soon as they were out of sight on the opposite side of the giant turbines, the mechanic stooped, opened his toolbox, and took out what looked like a brick-shaped block of clay. He inserted two wires into it then attached them to a small timing device. Reaching under the turbine as far as he could, he wedged it between the deck and the steel casing. He repeated the procedure with the other engine. Earlier, in the cargo area near the middle of the ship, he had placed another concealed package containing plastic explosives. When the mechanic finished he closed the box and got up to leave.

"You won't find the access crawlway under there," Mike Cleland said from behind them.

Both men turned to face him. Neither replied.

"Now suppose you tell me what the hell you're doing," Cleland said.

He never got a chance to utter another word. A third eye suddenly appeared in the middle of his forehead. A trickle of blood started to drain from it. The mechanic caught him as he collapsed and quietly lowered Cleland to the ground. The other crew member, who was still watching TV, died from a single gunshot wound to the back of his head. He was in the middle of laughing as Cary Grant chased an elderly man around his aunts' house.

The officer paused to watch the rest of the scene. When it was over he dragged the crewman's body back to the turbines. His partner already had the outer maintenance door open. It was used for servicing the engine and propeller shaft. The thin man stared down at the black night waters of the Atlantic churning four stories beneath him and with an effort pushed the first body out. Mike Cleland's body followed a moment later. Then a maintenance coverall soaked with blood followed, tumbling out the doorway. It took both men three minutes to hose away the blood on the deck, sending it out the scuppers.

Satisfied, they closed the door and treaded past the sleeping crewman and back up the stairs. He woke up two hours later to find he was alone in the engine room.

The man dressed as an officer made his way back to his cabin, quickly stripped off the uniform and changed to regular clothes. He placed the uniform and the silencer from his gun in a plastic bag and went out onto his balcony. A quick check of the balconies to his right and left told him it was safe. The package hit the water a second later and disappeared beneath the ocean's surface.

Perhaps I'll get a quick bite to eat, he thought.

On the way to the buffet he passed the third member of his team. That man had just finished placing an explosive charge at the back of the bow computer that controlled the ship's fire-deterrent system. Neither acknowledged the other's presence.

TWELVE

The next morning Katherine awoke to a light tapping on the door connecting her room with Beth's. She'd been having a dream about John Delaney. They had stayed up until almost four o'clock in the morning talking and she went to bed thinking about him.

She watched his eyes while he spoke. They were gentle eyes, but she had a feeling they could turn hard at a moment's notice. He had an easy, confident way about him that appealed to her, and he was a gentleman. He hadn't tried to push things when they said goodnight; he shook hands. She wasn't sure how she felt about that. Good, mostly, she decided.

Slowly, Katherine told herself, as she went to unlock the door. Once she did, she turned around and crawled back into bed.

Beth Doliver came in and took one look at her. "God, what time did you get in last night?"

"Four o'clock," Katherine mumbled, hugging her pillow.

"So?" Beth said, sitting on the edge of the bed. "What happened?"

"I got a three-hundred-dollar tip."

"What?"

"John wanted to go gambling and he asked me to throw the dice for him. I made a bunch of passes—that's what they're called. Afterward, some guy in a cowboy hat came over and gave me three hundred dollars in chips. I guess I did good. John won almost nine hundred dollars."

"Are you serious? A total stranger just handed you three hundred dollars? You must be good."

"It was dumb luck. What did you do?"

"I spent the evening with Victor."

"Victor?" Katherine asked, turning slightly toward her.

"Victor Vibrator, my best friend . . . besides you, of course," said Beth.

"Oh, for God's sake," Katherine said pushing Beth off the bed with her feet.

"C'mon," Beth said, slapping her on the behind. "I thought you were the one who wanted to hit the gym every morning."

"That's when I was conscious."

"Well, get conscious and let's go. Do you want to have breakfast first or work out?"

"How about if I sleep for another half-hour?"

"Coffee, K. J.," Beth said, leaning forward and whispering in her ear. "Coffee and bagels . . . mmm."

"You're not going away, are you?"

"Uh-uh."

"All right," Katherine said, throwing off the covers and getting up. "What time is it?"

"Almost nine-thirty. You sleep in the nude?"

"Don't get any ideas."

Katherine rubbed her face with her hands and tromped into the bathroom.

"What do you want to wear?" Beth called after her.

"My black athletic bra and shorts. I think they're in the second drawer on the right."

Beth went to the dresser and rummaged through the drawer. She found what she was looking for, and tossed them into the bathroom.

"Thank you," said Katherine.

A moment later Beth heard the sound of water running and teeth being brushed. On the corner of Katherine's nightstand was a pill bottle. Beth picked it up and examined it for a moment, then put it back with a shake of her head.

"Feel better now?" she asked, when Katherine came out.

Katherine gave her a flat look and finished dressing. She put on a pair of sneakers and wrapped a sweatshirt around her waist.

"Coffee?" Beth asked.

"Coffee."

It took only a few minutes to find the SEAFARER'S BUFFET. Katherine got her coffee and a plate of fresh cantaloupe along with some pineapple and grapes. Beth went for the eggs and orange juice. Both women slowed down as they approached the pastry display, looked at each other, and said "no" at the same time, then quickly walked past it to a table by the window. Outside, the sky was a sharp blue with only a few high clouds. Sunlight created a million sparkling lights on the water that moved hypnotically with the ocean swells. The top portion of their window was open, letting a warm breeze drift through.

"This is so beautiful," Katherine said. "Thanks for making me come."

Beth smiled at her.

"For a while I didn't think you would, but I'm really glad you did, K. J. I was ready for a vacation."

"I almost didn't," Katherine said. "You only gave me a week's notice and I practically had to beg two judges to sign my leave of absence. On top of that, I had to promise to buy lunch for an opposing attorney in one of my cases."

"He sounds like a rat to hold you up."

"Actually, it's a *she* and we're friends. But I'll figure out a way to get even."

Beth started to say something then appeared to change her mind. Instead she looked down at her plate and was silent.

"What?" Katherine asked.

"When I was in your room I noticed the pill bottle. You're still taking them?"

Katherine shrugged.

"Have to. The doctor says they keep the playing field level."

"Do they?"

"Some. The flashbacks don't hit so often anymore, but when they do. . . ."

"Sure," Beth said quickly, as an image of a terror-stricken twenty-year-old Katherine huddled in the corner of their bedroom flashed into her mind. The panic attacks usually came at night and were frightening to watch. Beth felt helpless when they did. After several years she had begun to despair about her friend ever leading a normal life again. When Katherine met the heart surgeon and they got married, Beth thought everything would be all right. It wasn't. Far from it.

Katherine saw the concern on her face and seemed to read her mind.

"I used to say his screwing around caused our divorce, but the truth is if I were a better wife, if I was able to open up and let him get close, maybe. . . ."

"There's no excuse for what he did, K. J."

"I don't know."

"Well, *I* do."

Beth reached out and took Katherine's hand.

"You just have to give it time and fight your way through."

"Right," Katherine repeated, half to herself.

Beth was about to say something else when the sound of raised voices coming from one of the corner tables pulled her attention away. Katherine looked up at the same time.

Two men were involved in a heated discussion. She couldn't hear what was being said, but from the body language it was obvious they were having an argument.

"Hey, isn't that the guy from our table last night?" Beth asked.

Katherine frowned and looked closer. One of the men was indeed Ellis Stephens; the other had his back to her.

"Yeah," she said. "That's the professor from Columbia—Ellis Stephens. His wife's name is Libby."

"That's it," said Beth. "Boy, he doesn't look happy. I wonder what's going on?"

A few other people must have wondered the same thing, because heads were beginning to turn. Stephens finally pushed back his chair, got up, and walked briskly out of the buffet. The other man sat there. After a moment he also got up and started walking toward the door. He only took a few steps before he became aware of the attention being focused on him. Passengers turned away and went back to their conversations. The man started for the exit again, but stopped abruptly as he and Katherine made eye contact. A look of surprise appeared on his face. He quickly reached into his pocket, took out a pair of sunglasses, and put them on. He left the restaurant using the side door.

"What the hell was that about?" Beth asked.

Katherine shook her head and stared after the man. "I don't know," she said slowly. "He looked really familiar to me."

"You *know* him?"

"Maybe."

"Well, it sure looked like he knew you. Where do you think you know him from?"

"No idea. God, I hate when that happens."

"Me too," said Beth. "Let's finish up and go exercise. I want to lie out by the pool and get a tan."

"Sounds good," said Katherine.

She was still staring at the buffet's side door when they left.

THIRTEEN

The crewman standing in front of Owen McCalister was nervous and justifiably so. Not only had he been sleeping on duty, two members of the engine room's night watch were missing.

The man's name was Miko Hutras, and he was a new addition to the *Ocean Majestic*'s crew, having signed on just four months earlier. A little over an hour ago he'd woken up to find himself alone in the engine room. His first reaction was to look around in case the other men were playing a prank on him. Such things were not unknown on ships, particularly with new crew members. But after looking for them for fifteen minutes, he began to worry. The senior engineer, Cleland, didn't seem like the joking type, nor did the other man with them. Hutras only knew him by his first name of Fred. He remembered Fred saying that he was from California. A lot of

Americans he met were from California. It was possible they had both finished the watch and gone back to their cabins to sleep, but that made no sense. They had never failed to wake him before, nor he them when it was their turn to catch some shut-eye. On top of that, Cleland's television was still there. Hutras checked the blackboard and saw both names were still signed in. "Jablonski, F." he assumed was Fred. He knew it was his duty to report anything out of the ordinary to the officer of the watch, and the last thing he wanted was to get anyone in trouble, especially men he would be working with for the next two years.

He was still in the process of searching the engine room, when the new watch came on. The senior man was a big Irishman named Harry O'Rourke. Hutras pulled him aside and told him what had happened.

O'Rourke listened and cursed under his breath. "How long did you say you've been looking?"

"About thirty minutes."

"No notes? Nothing?"

Hutras shook his head and looked at the sign-in Board as did O'Rourke.

"Goddammit. What the hell's the matter with Mike Cleland? He knows better than to pull this kinda crap."

Hutras shrugged.

"I don't want to get them into trouble, but I don't know what else to do."

O'Rourke told Hutras to wait where he was while he made a personal sweep of the engine room. He returned three minutes later, grim-faced. "Let's go. We need to report this."

OWEN MCCALISTER looked up when the buzzer at the bridge door sounded. He glanced at the security monitor and saw two crewmen standing outside. He recognized one as Harry O'Rourke from engineering. The other was a new man.

"Permission to enter, sir," O'Rourke said into the intercom.

McCalister set his cup of coffee down and pushed the entry button. There was an audible *click* as the door released and both men came in. McCalister returned their salutes.

"Morning, Harry. What's up?"

"Sir, we've got two men missing off the engine room's evening watch."

McCalister frowned. "What'd you mean 'missing'?"

"Missing," O'Rourke repeated. "I came on duty a little while ago and, uh . . . sorry, what's your name?"

"Miko Hutras," said Miko.

"Right . . . Miko here reported that Mike Cleland and Fred Jablonski were gone. The board shows them as checked in, but they haven't checked out. I sent a man down to their cabins to look for them. So far no sign."

"What time did they leave?" McCalister asked Miko.

"Well . . . I was . . . ah . . . getting some—"

"You were asleep when they left, right?" McCalister said, finishing the sentence for him.

Miko nodded his head.

As second officer on the *Ocean Majestic,* McCalister was responsible for the disciplinary matters. He was aware many of the crew took turns sleeping during the night watches and had brought this to the attention of the first officer, who told him to not make a fuss. As long as two men were awake at all times it was fine. McCalister was ex-Navy, and sleeping on duty didn't sit well with him, but orders were orders. The *Ocean Majestic* wasn't the Navy and standards tended to be more relaxed; nevertheless they had a solid crew, so McCalister bit his lip and went with the program. He wasn't happy about having to go over the head of his superior, but now that the problem had been dumped in his lap he had to follow the book.

He turned to the communications officer. "Ring Mr. LaRocca's cabin and ask him to report to the bridge immediately. When you've done that, please call Ben Stemholtz in security and get him up here. It's . . . let's see, nine forty-five right now. We'll need to let the captain know what's happened. Please call him and say that he's requested on the bridge."

"Aye, aye, sir," the man replied.

"You checked the entire area?" McCalister asked O'Rourke.

"Pretty thoroughly. There's no sign of 'em."

The ship's navigator and radar operator were both listening to the conversation and each got a hard look from McCalister. They immediately turned back to their consoles.

"Do you think they went off with some girls?" McCalister asked O'Rourke.

"I doubt it, sir. Mike Cleland's a married man with three kids. He's not the type."

"What about Jablonski?"

"I dunno. He's been dating some little gal who works in the spa. You want me to go and ask her if she's seen him?"

McCalister muttered something under his breath and picked up his cup of coffee. He took a sip and thought about how to handle the situation.

A minute passed while the men waited.

"Nope," he finally said. "You two head back to duty. Hutras, you're on report. I want you both to go over the engine room one more time. Call me if you find anything."

The men saluted and left the cabin. McCalister watched the door close and leaned back in his seat to wait for his captain and the first officer.

FOURTEEN

John Delaney sat by the pool trying to read his book. He was having only limited success because his thoughts kept straying to Katherine Adams. Somewhere in the background Frank Sinatra was singing "Young at Heart" over the poolside speakers.

Delaney was wearing a plain white T-shirt and a pair of blue swim trunks. After getting to bed at nearly 4:15 a.m. he decided to sleep late, but fifteen years of being a cop and working the morning shift had given him an internal alarm clock and he woke up promply at 7:00 a.m. just as he usually did. He showered, shaved, and went to the gym. It wasn't that he wanted to start lifting weights again. His head felt like it wasn't screwed on quite right that morning, but Katherine had mentioned that she liked to work out early so he took a chance. When he didn't find her there he was disappointed.

"Probably stayed in bed," he grumbled to himself.

Delaney flipped another page in his book and looked at the text. He frowned and turned the page back over again. It was the second time he'd read it and he still had no idea what it said.

Wonderful, he thought.

He took a breath and closed the book. Images of the evening before drifted back to him bringing a smile to his face. He couldn't remember having had a better time in a long while. Katherine was fun to be with—a damn fine woman, he thought. Since his divorce he hadn't dated much. There were a few relationships, but none of them had really gotten off the ground, except for one with an assemblywoman from the Bronx. That lasted almost an entire year before they went their separate ways. Every so often one of his friends or a well-meaning relative would try to fix him up on a date. People couldn't avoid doing that. All of them were nice girls, but he hadn't clicked with any the way he had with Katherine. She was funny without trying to put herself center stage, and she knew when to talk and when to listen. A potent combination, he decided.

Last night they'd talked about their families and their lives as they grew more comfortable with each other. Their talk had lasted until the wee hours of the morning. He liked the way her eyes lit up when she told him about her children. They sounded like good kids. He also liked the easy way she slipped her arm though his while they strolled the deck. She was quite a girl—rational, intelligent, and a looker to boot.

Delaney had a tendency to call women "girls," to the annoyance of several female colleagues. He didn't mean anything by it. It was just a habit he had picked up on the streets when he worked homicide. One professor, a woman who taught contracts, once made a point of telling him that calling a woman a "girl" was chauvinist, or worse, possibly sexist. Over the years he had tried to catch himself, but finally gave up and said "Screw it."

He might be a dinosaur, but sexist he was not.

In fact, John Delaney was very much the opposite. In his opinion, if a woman could do a job as well as a man, what the hell . . . she ought to have it. That mindset did nothing to endear him to his male colleagues, all of whom were attorneys and who probably comprised the most sexist group he had ever met—with the exception of cops. As a result, he chose a line down the middle, did his job, and went home.

His divorce seven years earlier had hurt him. After the initial shock wore off, he thought he could deal with the situation. And he did . . . for a while. The real blow came when his ex told him she was getting married again and moving to Arizona. That news floored him. He came from a close Irish family where people stayed together. They didn't marry insurance salesmen and move to other states. The hardest part was not seeing his son every day. In the beginning, the pain was almost more than he could bear. The boy was barely eleven at the time. Now it was just a dull ache. It took him four years to put his anger aside and make peace with her.

The situation with Katherine felt different from the beginning. His practical side whispered he that had only known her for just over twenty-four hours and shipboard romances tended to be just that. As a result his expectations remained cautious.

John Delaney, former cop and now professor of law, shook his head, leaned his chair back, and closed his eyes.

Fifteen minutes later he awoke when a single drop of water plopped onto his stomach. He opened one eye just a slit and saw Katherine and Beth standing over him holding a glass directly above his midsection. Both were trying to keep from laughing.

Another drop hit him.

Slowly, carefully, his left hand inched forward until it was close enough for him to grab Katherine's ankle. He did it so quickly, adding a growl for good measure, that both women screamed and several people around the pool jumped.

"Sorry," he apologized.

He got up and pulled two lounge chairs over for them.

"You nearly gave me a heart attack," Katherine said, slapping him on the arm. "I'm sorry, that was mean of us. Beth put me up to it."

Beth's mouth dropped open.

"Liar. Don't believe anything she says, she's an attorney."

"So am I," observed Delaney.

"Then you're ideal for each other. You can get married, stay home, and raise lots of little liars."

Katherine was still laughing when she sat down. Beth took a pair of sunglasses out of her bag and stretched out on the lounge chair.

"So, what did you do last night?" Delaney asked Beth.

"Oh, nothing much . . . just played around."

A funny look passed between the two women. Delaney saw it and decided to leave it alone.

"We went to breakfast, then had a great workout," Katherine said, changing the subject. "What about you?"

"Just the opposite."

"Huh?"

"I worked out . . . then ate."

"Oh." Katherine smiled. "I didn't think you'd be up this early. We both went to bed so late."

"I keep trying to be a lawyer, but the cop in me won't let go."

"How come you decided to change professions, John?" asked Beth.

"Well . . . it wasn't completely my decision—someone retired me."

"Retired you?" said Katherine. "I don't get it."

"My partner and I were working a robbery-homicide when a suspect we were interviewing suddenly pulled a gun and started shooting. I was hit in the chest three times and once in the leg."

"Oh my God," Beth exclaimed.

"Someone shot you? You're kidding!" said Katherine.

"Wish I was," Delaney replied.

He glanced around the pool and pulled up his T-shirt. Just below his right shoulder were three circular brown scars. Beth and Katherine gasped.

"Sorry," he said, pulling the shirt down. "I notice them

in the mirror every now and then and it seems like it happened to some other guy. I was on disability for nine months. When I came back the job just didn't seem quite the same, you know? I mean, all in all the department was pretty good to me. They thought I needed more time to recover, so they extended my disability. In fact, they extended it all the way through law school, and now here I am.

"Initially, I thought it was because I was a naturally cute, personable type, but it was an election year, and the mayor's office figured it would be good for their image. Not a lot of detectives get shot."

"Jeez, John, I'm so sorry. I feel like a jerk for asking," said Beth.

"Not to worry. I get to hang out with much nicer people now."

"Naturally cute?" Katherine repeated. "Boy, I can sure pick 'em."

Delaney propped himself on one elbow and leaned closer to her.

"Is that true? You picked me?"

"Don't push your luck. The jury's still out."

Delaney smiled. "I've got faith. I'll grow on you."

"You're lucky you're alive; those scars are so big," said Beth.

"It's not the size that counts," he replied. "When you get shot, it's like they tell you in real estate: Location is everything."

Beth made a dismissive gesture with her hand. "Men are always saying size doesn't count."

Katherine suppressed a giggle at the look on Delaney's face, but chose not to comment. Instead, she asked how he got into teaching.

"My undergraduate degree was in forensics," he explained. "When I was on the force I used to do lectures at the school for the evidence professor. He recommended me to the dean when he retired and one thing sort of led to another."

"Unbelievable," said Katherine.

"Yep . . . that's what all the women tell me."

"You're both unbelievable," said Beth, rolling her eyes. "Who wants to go for a swim? I'm broiling out here."

"You girls go. I'll stay and guard your stuff."

"Are you sure?" Katherine asked. "The water looks good."

"Go ahead. I'll enjoy the view."

"Oh brother," Beth muttered. She pulled off her workout top, got up, and jumped in the pool.

Katherine was wearing a pale blue T-shirt over a white one-piece swimsuit. The neckline opened all the way to her navel and it was cut high on her hips. It had a three-quarter back that covered just enough not to get her in trouble. Her daughter loved it, but her son James always looked slightly scandalized whenever she put it on. From past experience, she had a pretty good idea what the overall effect would be when she took the shirt off. The last time she'd worn it was on Miami's South Beach a few years ago. She and Alley were taking a mother-daughter weekend together, along with one of Alley's roommates. During the afternoon a number of college boys actually tried to hit on her. She thought it was ridiculous given the disparity in their ages, but for some reason the girls thought it was cool.

Apparently so did John Delaney.

Behind her Katherine heard him say "Holy shit," though she was quite certain he didn't intend her to. Aware that several other men were also staring, she took her time walking to the pool.

"Eat your heart out, Jimmy D.," she whispered, then dove in.

When they climbed out, Beth toweled off and announced she was going to a napkin-folding class in the forward lounge. Katherine passed and elected to keep Delaney company.

They both read for a while longer and then went for a walk around the jogging track on the Sun Deck. There were so many things to see onboard the *Majestic,* they were always running into something new. At one point they stopped to watch several teenagers negotiate the rock-climbing wall. They tried a game of miniature golf. Delaney lost twice. Eventually, they came across a staircase that led to a secluded portion of the top deck. A sign read ADULTS ONLY and a number of women were sunbathing topless.

Katherine took one look and headed back down the stairs. Delaney followed, but not before he made a point of walking to the opposite rail to see if the ocean was any different on the starboard side of the ship.

"What?" he asked, looking at her with an innocent expression.

Pathetic, she thought. She kept that observation to herself, figuring men would be men.

"Would you like to have some lunch?" she asked

FIFTEEN

While Delaney and Katherine were spending the rest of the day together, unknown to the passengers of the *Ocean Majestic*, a great deal of activity was going on among the crew. Two of its members had disappeared without a trace, and a thorough search of the ship had turned up nothing.

Captain Marius Barroni, sixty-one years old and a veteran of over forty years at sea, sat back in his chair on the bridge and looked at his two senior officers. Barroni was a little under six feet tall, with a heavy chest and powerful-looking shoulders. He had a neatly trimmed beard and had worked his way up through the ranks to become captain of the largest cruise ship in the world.

Crewmen, he knew, jumped ship for a variety of reasons ranging from drugs to family problems, but he had never come across anything like this. He knew Mike Cleland personally and had even shared a few drinks with him. Cleland struck him as a decent, stable man, with no history of mental problems—or *any* problems for that matter. Fred Jablonski was only vaguely familiar. He had the impression of Jablonski as a blond, solid-looking fellow with a dark complexion.

Barroni punched a few buttons on his command console and brought up a picture of the missing man.

Thirty-two years old, unmarried, divorced, with one child, he read. *Born in Lansing, Michigan*. Jablonski had been with the company a little over three years and the *Majestic* was his second assignment. The semi-annual ratings his superiors gave him were all above average, and there was nothing on his record to indicate he'd ever been in trouble.

"So, where the hell are you?" the captain said to himself.

If they'd been anywhere near land, he would have assumed both men had gone AWOL. The problem was, they were four hundred and fifty nautical miles out to sea and jumping ship wasn't much of an option. The search had been going on now for almost twelve hours. A feeling of unease that had been forming in the pit of his stomach for most of the day intensified. He turned to Ben Stemholtz, his senior security officer.

"Any ideas?"

"No, sir," Stemholtz answered. "I wish I had something positive to tell you. We swept the ship twice and came up empty both times. None of the crew reported seeing them after they went on duty and nobody saw them after their shift was up."

"Any talk of bad blood between them?" First Officer Anthony LaRocca asked.

"Not that I've ever heard," Stemholtz replied.

"Why do you ask that, Tony?" asked the captain.

"I was just trying to come up with different possibilities, like if they had a fight and went over the side together."

Stemholtz shook his head.

"I don't think so. Everyone I spoke to said they got along just fine."

"What about this Miko Hutras?" the captain asked. "Do you think he could have done something to them and claimed to be asleep as a cover-up?"

"That's possible, too, Captain," Stemholtz replied. "He doesn't seem like the type, but that's no guarantee. He could be a closet wacko and a great actor. When I asked if he'd be willing to take a polygraph, he didn't hesitate for a second."

"So where does that leave us?" asked LaRocca.

"It leaves us having to notify the company and the authorities unless they happen to turn up in the next seven minutes," answered Barroni. "We're at open sea, gentlemen, and two of our men are missing. At 1900 hours I intend to make the appropriate log entry and place a call to the home office. They're just going to love this."

Marius Barroni looked at the clock on the wall and took a deep breath.

SIXTEEN

Neither Ellis nor Libby showed up for dinner that evening.

"Shouldn't we wait for them?" asked Father Reynolds.

"They probably went to the buffet," Beth suggested. "How was the show last night, Father?"

"Very impressive. I've seen my share of magic acts, but this fellow was really quite good. He actually made a woman from the audience float from the back of the theater to the front of it."

"They also had a two-man strength act," added Father Kelly. "I thought those fellows were every bit as good as the magician. It's amazing what they were able to do. And how did you young people entertain yourselves?"

"John showed me how to shoot craps," said Katherine.

"Really?" said Father Kelley. "We stopped by the casino last night for a little while. George lost twenty dollars at the roulette wheel."

Katherine's surprise showed on her face.

"I didn't know priests could gamble."

"It's not against the rules—provided you don't go overboard with it."

"That may not be the best expression here, Father," observed Delaney.

"Overboard? Oh . . . I see." Father Kelly chuckled.

The conversations continued like that right into dessert.

"Hey, are you okay?" Delaney asked, leaning closer to Katherine.

"What?"

"I asked if you were okay. You seem a little distracted."

"I was just thinking about Mr. and Mrs. Stephens. Last night they said they would see us at dinner."

"They probably went to the buffet like your friend said."

"Sure . . . maybe."

Delaney frowned at her, but Katherine shook her head.

"It's probably no big deal, but Beth and I saw Ellis having an argument with some man at breakfast earlier today."

"What about?"

"I don't know. We were too far away to hear. Ellis didn't look happy, though. Also, the man he was arguing with really looked familiar to me."

"How so?"

"I'm pretty sure I've seen him before. The problem is I can't say where, and it's been driving me nuts."

"Don't knock yourself out," said Delaney. "It'll come to you."

Katherine shrugged. "I guess."

AT FIVE minutes past nine, Captain Barroni pushed himself out of his chair and picked up the phone. He was in the process of dialing the home office's emergency number when a slight shudder shook the deck beneath his feet. Barroni's hand froze. A second later another shudder passed through the deck. Owen McCalister and Tony LaRocca both stopped talking and stood up. LaRocca, the ship's first officer, was in good shape for a man of fifty-four. His hair was black and combed straight back. He walked over to the ship's status console and scanned it for any signs of trouble.

"What the hell was that?" he asked.

The intercom buzzed before anyone could answer.

"Bridge, this is the aft engine room. We've had two explosions down here and we're taking in water. I need the captain."

Barroni was on his feet immediately.

"This is Barroni. Who's this?"

"Harry O'Rourke, Captain. We got a major problem here."

In the background, Barroni could hear men yelling and shouting.

"Get a damage-control party down there at once," he said to LaRocca.

"Damage control ain't gonna do any good, Captain. I'm ordering my men out. The turbines on numbers one and two are blown. They're completely off their mounts, plus there's a six-foot hole on the port side and another one to starboard. I've got one man dead and two more badly injured. We also have a fire burning by the port screw, and I can't get the emergency suppressant system to come on. I need to seal this area *now*."

Barroni was silent for a second.

"All right, Harry. Get your men out and lock it down. Make sure the watertight bulkheads are secure. Help's on the way."

Almost immediately a buzzer went off on the command console. It was accompanied by the intermittent blare of an alarm.

"Fire in aft engine room," the communications officer said.

"We already know that," snapped Barroni. "Mr. McCalister, I want you to take personal charge of damage-control. I'll need a complete report as soon as you can get it."

McCalister saluted, grabbed a walkie-talkie from the charging stand, and rushed off the bridge.

"Captain, we've lost the rudder," the navigator reported. He moved the joystick control lever in front of him back and forth to demonstrate.

"What about the forward engines?" asked Barroni.

"All on line, sir. I can use them to maneuver, but we're swinging to starboard."

"Cut power to one quarter, Mr. Carlson. All ahead slow, maneuvering thrusters only. What is our present position?"

"Five hundred thirty-six nautical miles from Miami, twenty-four degrees, fifteen minutes north latitude, sixty degrees, twenty-five minutes west longitude."

"Very good," said Captain Barroni. "Communications, we will commence emergency procedures immediately. Are there any ships in this area?"

"Aye, sir."

"Please begin sending emergency messages out on all available frequencies."

Twenty-one-year-old Charlie Kaufman, the ship's communications officer, wiped the sweat from his forehead and put his headphones on. He began broadcasting the *Majestic*'s call for help. His uncle had gotten him the job when he took a year off from school to see the world.

Kaufman continued broadcasting distress messages and turned back to his captain a moment later.

"Sir," he said, "the *Marie Star* is sixty-five miles from our present position. She's reversed course and is headed this way at full speed. The U.S.S. *Theodore Roosevelt* is a hundred and eighty nautical miles southwest of us and advises they are also on the way. Their captain asks if he should scramble rescue aircraft at this time."

"My compliments to the captain of the *Roosevelt*, Mr. Kaufman. Tell him the extent of the damage is unknown right now and to please stand by."

"Aye, aye, sir."

Barroni turned to his first officer. "Tony, let's get down to engineering and see how bad this is. Mr. Kaufman, please notify operations in Arlington, Virginia, that we have an emergency on our hands. Tell them that we will update them as soon as more information is available."

"Yes, sir. Shall I have the passengers report to their emergency lifeboat stations?"

"Not yet. I want to see what we're dealing with first. Carry on."

Barroni and LaRocca both took walkie-talkies and left the bridge. They descended the stairs to the Sun Deck walking at a rapid but not urgent pace toward the ship's stern. Several passengers recognized the captain and said good evening to him and he responded in kind, giving no hint that anything was amiss.

SEVENTEEN

John Delaney felt the shudder in the deck and looked up in mid-conversation. Not being a Navy man, he wasn't sure what to make of it. The only thing he *was* certain about was that, according to their daily positioning chart, they were somewhere in the middle of the Atlantic Ocean in about 14,000 feet of water. He was also fairly confident most cruise ships did their best to avoid bumping into things, particularly something large enough to send vibrations through the hull. Delaney looked out the dining room window onto the deck and noticed a number of crewmen walking toward the ship's stern. They were walking quickly, and the last two were carrying fire extinguishers.

He leaned over and whispered in Katherine's ear, "K. J., listen to me and don't react. I think something's up. There was a vibration a moment ago—you may have felt it, too. I don't know what it was, but I think we may have hit something."

To her credit, Katherine nodded, then casually glanced

outside as he had done. She also saw the crewmen hurrying past the window.

"Look, this may be absolutely nothing at all," Delaney continued. "I don't want to panic anybody, but I want you and Beth to get up and go back to your cabins. When you get there, change into something warm. I'm going for a walk to see what's going on. Hopefully, it's just my overactive imagination. I'll meet you at your room in a few minutes. Okay?"

Katherine was about to insist on coming with him, but the look on his face stopped her. She stared at him for a second, then turned to Beth and said, "Let's go back to the room."

Beth frowned and hesitated before she answered, "Sure."

She was clearly confused by Katherine's sudden change, but she knew her friend well enough to understand when something was wrong. She pushed her chair back from the table.

Delaney then quickly explained to the priests what he had seen and what he thought was happening. Both men listened carefully. Neither made any fuss.

"Son, if there's a problem, George and I should see what we can do to help," Father Kelley said.

"You're a great guy, Father," Delaney told him, glancing over his shoulder. Five more crewmen were passing by the window—only this time they weren't walking, they were running.

"Unless I'm wrong, I think they're going to call passengers to the emergency stations in a few minutes. The best thing we can do is to follow the program."

The two priests looked at each other and then Father Kelley said, "All right. We'll be in our rooms. Let us know as soon as you hear anything."

"You got it, Father."

Delaney gave Katherine a quick kiss on the head and said, "I'll be back as fast as I can."

BY THE time Katherine reached the front of the dining room, a number of passengers had become aware something was wrong outside. Several people asked the waiters if there was a problem. Unfortunately, the waiters knew no more than they did.

When they got to the elevators, Beth said, "Okay, you want to tell me what's happening now?"

"John thinks we may have hit something."

"Hit something? What's there to hit in the middle of the ocean? You mean like an iceberg or—"

Beth suddenly swayed on her feet and had to reach for the wall to support herself.

"Wow . . . did you feel that?" she said. "The whole ship just moved."

"John wants us to go to our cabins and wait for him. He went to see if he could find out what's happening. He thinks they're going to call an emergency."

"Wait a minute," Beth said, pushing the UP button again. "He was just sitting there with us. How the hell would he—"

Six loud blasts of the ship's whistle cut her words short. A second later the voice of the cruise director came on over the loudspeakers.

"Good evening, ladies and gentlemen. Those six whistle blasts you just heard are an indication for you to return to your cabins immediately. We're having a technical problem with two of our stern engines, but Captain Barroni wants you to know that everything is under control and there is nothing to worry about. This is just a precaution. When you get to your cabins, please don your flotation vests and proceed to the emergency assembly stations marked on them, just as you did during our drill. There will be crewmembers in the hallways to assist you. I repeat, everything is under control, and this is *just* a cautionary exercise."

"Forget the elevator," said Katherine, taking Beth by the arm. "The stairs will be faster."

"Remind me not to open my big mouth again."

Along the way, Katherine told her that Delaney wanted them to dress in warm clothes.

"Makes sense," her friend agreed.

KATHERINE WAS in the process of tucking her shirt into her pants when Beth knocked at their connecting door and let herself in. She was already wearing her life vest.

"I look like Jack's secretary in this," she said, glancing down.

Katherine smiled, retrieved her own life vest from the closet, and put it on. While she was doing it a second announcement came over the loudspeakers asking everyone to proceed to their assigned stations.

"Let's go," said Beth. "I know you said John would meet us here, but that was before the announcement. He's probably on the way back already and can catch up to us on the deck."

Katherine frowned and thought for a second, then snatched a piece of paper and a pen from the desk. "I'll leave a note on the door for him."

"Whatever," said Beth. "But I wish you'd hurry. This wasn't supposed to happen."

Katherine finished writing and stepped into the corridor. She stuck the note between the door and the jamb so that it could be easily seen and wrote "J. Delaney" across the front.

Then they closed the door and started down the hallway.

*   *   *

WHAT DELANEY was seeing wasn't good. He heard the announcement about passengers returning to their cabins, but decided to follow the four crewmen in front of him carrying fire extinguishers instead. In the mounting commotion no one paid any attention. They went down four flights of steps and through a door marked CREW ONLY. Two more flights of stairs brought them to the bottom of the ship. There, Delaney saw two officers giving orders to a group of crewmen who were standing in front of the engine room door. The ship lurched again, only harder this time.

An argument of some kind was taking place between the officers and the men. One of them was pointing at the door and the officer was shaking his head "no," trying to keep the others back. Finally the man pushed him aside and grabbed for the handle, yanking the door open.

An orange fireball exploded out of the engine room with a deafening bang, immolating those standing in front of it. The concussion was hard enough to knock Delaney down fifty feet away. The men at the entrance died horribly. He couldn't believe his eyes. Not only were flames coming out of the doorway, seawater was rushing from the bottom of it at tremendous force. It tossed the remaining crewmen aside like rag dolls. Pandemonium took over. Men were screaming and others were trying to get a handhold on anything they could. Delaney got up and rushed forward to help as water continued to fill the passageway.

Captain Barroni and his first officer arrived at the stairway seconds later and stood there stunned.

"Dear God," said LaRocca, looking at the damage, his olive complexion suddenly pale.

Another tongue of flame snaked out of the doorway followed by a second explosion. The deck beneath Delaney's feet lurched again and he would have fallen if Barroni hadn't grabbed him. As the ship settled, Delaney and Barroni found themselves fighting to keep on their feet. The engine room was now below water and the deck was tilting downward at a crazy angle.

"Everyone out *now!*" roared Barroni. "Mr. LaRocca, secure the watertight doors immediately. I'm giving the order to abandon ship."

"Captain, what if we—"

"We are sinking, sir. *Get these men out of here.*"

Barroni keyed his communicator. "Bridge, this is the captain. We need to engage the fire systems. They're not on."

There was a pause.

"Sir, the board shows the fire systems *are* engaged," a young voice said.

"Try them again," Barroni shouted. "We've got an inferno down here. The sprinklers are not on. I repeat, *not* on."

"Trying them again, Captain." Another pause. "The board shows all green."

"Goddammit," Barroni cursed under his breath.

A muffled noise came from the opposite end of the passageway, followed by the sound of tearing metal and a loud crash. A second later, LaRocca's communicator beeped.

"Mr. LaRocca, this is Shaun Neimans. We've got two fires amidships. One is in the Cavern Nightclub and the other is in the arts and crafts lounge. The fire system isn't functioning. My men are using extinguishers. Is the captain with you?"

"I'm here, Mr. Neimans. The system is apparently down. Can you get the fire under control?"

"Negative, Captain. We're losing it. You're not gonna believe this, but the fire hoses have been sabotaged. Someone's slashed them at the couplings. I've sent for more extinguishers, but I don't think it's gonna make any difference."

There was a long pause before Barroni answered.

"Thank you, Mr. Neimans. I want you to seal the doors and have your men fall back to assist with the lifeboats. We are abandoning ship."

"Aye, aye, sir," Neimans replied, and the line went dead.

"Mr. Kaufman, are you there?" Barroni said, hitting the communicator button twice more.

"Y-yes, sir. I heard."

"You will please broadcast our position and sound the evacuation alarm."

"Yes, sir. Broadcasting position and *Mayday* call to all ships in this area. Shall I tell the *Theodore Roosevelt* to dispatch the search-and-rescue planes?"

Barroni stared at the bodies of his men floating in the passageway. "Yes," he said quietly.

It took only a moment for him to recover, and he turned to Delaney. "You should be with the other passengers, sir."

"That's a great idea," Delaney replied, still holding the body of an unconscious man. "Let's get these guys out of here and we can talk about it more."

"This area will be underwater in less than three minutes," Barroni said, as he helped Delaney carry the man back up to the stairwell.

Below them, his first officer was yelling orders and doing his best to get the remaining crewmen out one at a time. It took slightly under two minutes before he joined Barroni and Delaney on the other side of the bulkhead.

"Stand back," said Barroni. He hit the button to seal the door.

Nothing happened.

"Shit. We'll have to lock it manually," said LaRocca.

Barroni and Delaney grabbed the door and slammed it

shut. The metal was already hot to the touch. LaRocca flipped open a gray box to the right of the door and pulled down a lever. There was a dull thud as the lock snapped into place.

"I can't understand why the fire systems haven't come on," said LaRocca.

"They've been sabotaged," the captain replied.

The public address system came on once again and the cruise director, whose voice had now lost much of its upbeat nature, instructed all passengers to proceed to their lifeboat stations immediately.

DESPITE ALL the urgings by the crew for everyone to remain calm and not rush, panic seized the passengers of the *Ocean Majestic* turning them into a rabble. People were yelling and falling down the steps in their attempts to reach the lifeboats, which still swung from their davits. What started out as an orderly evacuation quickly turned to panic as the first signs of smoke began to appear in the passageways. It was coming not only from the stern of the ship but from the midsections as well.

Katherine and Beth fought their way down the staircase to the next landing, holding the banister for support. All the while, Katherine kept looking for Delaney. Two men in tuxedos coming up the other way barreled past them, nearly knocking Beth over in the process. Katherine made a grab for her just in time and barely stopped her from falling.

"Do you remember where we have to go?" Beth shouted.

"Station six on the Calypso Deck. That's three floors down."

In the middle of the landing between decks a crewmember using a bullhorn pleaded with people to go slowly, but no one was listening.

When they finally reached the next landing, Katherine looked out through the double doors that led to the outer deck and heard a man shouting, "There's a fire at the end of the ship. You can see the flames."

A moment later he was knocked to the ground by a group of people running toward the bow.

"*Jesus,* K. J.," said Beth, "did you hear that?"

"I heard it. Let's get to our stations. I'm sure the crew—hey, isn't that Libby Stephens?" Katherine pointed at a woman in the passageway who was desperately trying to get a crewmember's attention.

"Yeah . . . yeah, that's her. Hey, Libby, over here," Beth yelled, waving her arms.

Libby Stephens saw them and waved back frantically.

Katherine and Beth pushed through the throng of people until they got to her.

"I can't find Ellis," Libby shouted, clutching Katherine's arm.

"All right, just calm down," Katherine said. "Where was the last place you saw him?"

"I went to the arcade to do some shopping and he went back to the room. Then all the alarms started and I ran back, but the door was locked. My key card won't open it."

"He's probably already at the lifeboat station," Beth said. "Which one are you supposed to be at?"

"I don't know . . . I don't know. I couldn't get in the room. The station's marked on the life vests, and I—"

A white-uniformed crew member came trotting down the corridor toward them. Libby broke off what she was saying and tried to grab his arm.

"Young man, can you help me, please?" she called out.

The man never slowed down.

"Where did you say you saw Ellis last?" Katherine asked.

"We were in the shopping mall, and Ellis hates shopping, so he went back—"

"I understand," Katherine said, cutting her off. "I want you to go with Beth. She'll take you to our lifeboat. I'll go and find your husband. Put a life jacket on as soon as you get there. Do you understand me?"

"K. J.—" Beth began.

"Everything will be fine," Katherine said. "Just get her down there. I'll meet you both in a few minutes."

"But—"

"Get going. I promise I'll be right there. Which cabin are you in, Libby?"

"Cabin 5102. It's all the way at the front."

"Great. I'll see you both in a few minutes."

Katherine gave them a push to get them started, then turned and started running down the corridor dodging past people coming the opposite way. A diagram on the wall showed Cabin 5102 was located at the ship's bow. Thus far she was reacting on instinct. At that point she didn't know, couldn't know, the fires on the *Majestic* had been deliberately set or the extent of damage to the ship. She arrived at Cabin 5102 in under a minute and began pounding on the door, but there was no answer. She knocked harder and yelled, "Ellis, it's Katherine Adams. If you're in there, open up."

Katherine waited, listening for any sound inside. After several seconds she was ready to give up, assuming Ellis had already gone to the lifeboats, when she noticed the red PRIVACY PLEASE sign hanging from the doorknob.

She pounded on the door again and still received no answer. She thought rapidly. Maybe Ellis had fallen and hit his head after the explosions rocked the ship. In desperation, she began to look for something to force the lock with. Her eyes stopped on a fire extinguisher hanging on the wall. Katherine jerked it free and slammed it against the doorknob, hitting it with all her strength. Once . . . twice . . . three times. On the fourth try she screamed in frustration and struck again. The last blow succeeded in knocking the handle askew. Nearly exhausted, she tried once more. Finally, the knob broke and fell to the deck. Using all her strength, she kicked hard at the door with her right leg. It flew open, banging against the wall.

The room was empty.

Katherine bent over, put her hands on her knees, and waited until her breath came back. In a few seconds her chest stopped heaving and she turned to leave. Then, out of the corner of her eye she noticed the red stain slowly spreading onto the carpet. It was coming from the bathroom door.

"Ellis?" Katherine called out.

There was no answer.

Her heart was pounding in her chest as she pushed the bathroom door open.

Ellis Stephens lay on his back in a pool of blood, his eyes staring at nothing. The left side of his head was partially blown away from what could only have been a gunshot wound. There were two more holes in his chest. Bone and gray matter mixed with the blood on the floor.

Katherine gasped and backed away, flattening herself against the wall, her hand flying to her mouth in shock. She was neither prepared for the gruesome sight nor for the horrendous smell that hit her at the same time. For the first time since she was a little girl, Katherine Adams's stomach revolted and she threw up, her mind reeling.

This can't be happening.

But it was.

An inner voice told her to run, but she couldn't do that. It took considerable effort to force herself to look at

Ellis's body, shutting out the loudspeaker that intoned, "All passengers should be proceeding to their lifeboat stations immediately."

The attorney part of her took over and, one by one, her brain began to register important details about the scene.

The balcony door is shut; the beds are made; no signs of a struggle. There are three gunshot wounds—large ones, by the look of them, she thought. Katherine could see the outline of Ellis's wallet in his back pants pocket and made a note of it. She shoved her own fears further back in her mind and began to examine the rest of the room. In the corner was the aluminum attaché case Ellis had been carrying around with him since the first day of the cruise. She bent down and flipped it open.

Empty.

Another violent shudder in the deck jolted her back to the present. This time it was accompanied by a sway that nearly caused her to fall. Katherine took the scene in one last time, fixing the details in her mind, and backed out of the cabin.

The heat hit her almost immediately.

The middle of the passageway was on fire. It was filled with dense black smoke and orange flames. Close by, two crewmen were valiantly trying to hold the fire back with extinguishers, but it was obviously a lost cause. Slowly but steadily, they were retreating in her direction as the fire cut off their escape route to the lifeboats.

Katherine trotted down the corridor and came up behind one of the men and tapped him on the shoulder.

"*Jesus,* lady, you nearly scared me to death. You're supposed to be at your station already. We're evacuating the ship."

"Are you an officer?"

"Yes, ma'am. Like I said, you need to be at your station. You'd better follow me."

The other man glanced over his shoulder, took one look at Katherine, and shook his head. "We'll have to use the forward access way and cross over to the port side," he said.

"A man's been murdered in 5102," Katherine told them. "I need you to come with me."

"All right, ma'am," the officer said, taking Katherine by the elbow, "if you'll just stay calm we'll get you to one of the lifeboats."

Katherine jerked her arm away. "I just told you a man has been murdered. What's your name?"

"Nelms, ma'am, Lieutenant Ed Nelms. We're all under a lot of stress here, but if you'll just allow me to—"

Nelms was a balding, middle-aged fellow whose job was to manage food and beverage on the *Majestic*. He looked to be about fifteen pounds overweight. His uniform was streaked black and he was sweating profusely. From the expression on his face, he clearly didn't believe a word Katherine was saying.

"Listen to me," said Katherine, keeping her voice level. "My name is Katherine Adams and I'm a former Assistant U.S. Attorney. I'm neither crazy nor am I hysterical at the moment. I just came from Cabin 5102 and I'm telling you there's a man named Ellis Stephens lying in there dead. Half his head has been blown off and there are two large bullet holes in his chest."

Nelms opened his mouth, but closed it again and looked at the crewman next to him, who shrugged.

"Maybe you better go and see," he said.

Nelms turned back to Katherine, then pulled the walkie-talkie from his back pocket and keyed the button a few times.

"Bridge, this is Ed Nelms on Emerald Deck. I'm in corridor four amidships with Doug Carnes from Supply. We've got a lady with us who says a man's been murdered in 5102. I'm going to investigate."

"Say again?" a voice on the other end of the communicator said.

Nelms motioned for Katherine and his companion to follow.

"I repeat," he said, as they started down the corridor. "There's a lady with me . . . what's your name again, ma'am?"

"Katherine Adams."

"Katherine Adams," Nelms continued. "Ms. Adams has identified herself as an attorney and advises that she's seen a man murdered in Cabin 5102. I'm on my way now."

"The man's name is Ellis Stephens," said Katherine.

Nelms nodded and added, "Passenger says the murdered man's name is Ellis Stephens."

"Uh . . . affirmative, Lieutenant. I'll relay that to the captain. You've got about four minutes until we blow the third whistle. Most of the boats are away already. There's an aircraft carrier and tanker en route to us, but the first ship won't arrive for another three hours yet."

"Acknowledged."

"What's the third whistle?" asked Katherine.

"That's the signal for crew to abandon the ship," Carnes replied.

"Wonderful. Who do I talk to about a refund?"

All three of them arrived at Cabin 5102 and Nelms entered the room. Doug Carnes followed him.

"Mother of God!" exclaimed Carnes, taking a step backward when he saw Ellis Stephens lying there. His mouth dropped open in shock. "Christ. You weren't kidding," he said, to Katherine. "You know this man?"

"He and his wife were seated at my table. I met him a couple of days ago."

"Shit," said Nelms, staring at the body. "This is a goddam first."

"Bridge . . . Nelms here. I'm in 5102 with Ms. Adams and Carnes. The lady wasn't joking. There *is* a man here and he appears to have been shot in the head and chest and he is definitely dead."

"*Jesus,*" the voice on the communicator replied. "Captain says to get to your evacuation area on the double. You can make a full report then. We're closing the bridge now. Good luck, Lieutenant. Kaufman, out."

The walkie-talkie went dead. A second later three long blasts of the ship's whistle followed.

EIGHTEEN

Delaney, LaRocca, and Captain Barroni came to a halt at the top of the second landing. Three floors beneath them the first flames were beginning to appear in the stairwell, consuming everything in their path. Barroni put his hands on the door to feel for heat.

"All right, stand back," he said, to the others.

Delaney moved aside and crouched down, with LaRocca following suit. The captain took one last look at them, nodded, then grasped the release bar, and pushed the door open a crack.

"All clear," he said.

The three men stepped out of the stairwell onto the cobblestone street of Fashion Avenue. They were at the far end of the shopping mall and began jogging. Delaney glanced up as they ran and could see smoke was now coming from the upper floors. When the whistle blasts sounded, he threw a questioning look at LaRocca.

"That's our signal to evacuate," LaRocca explained.

Two more explosions, seemingly right under their feet,

knocked them all to the ground. Delaney regained his feet first. He glanced around and saw the cobblestones lining Fashion Avenue were beginning to buckle. Seconds later, the ornate gas lampposts at the end of the promenade began toppling over like Pick Up Sticks. Without warning, a shop window near them blew out, sending bits of glass and metal flying everywhere. All three ducked out of reflex and watched as two mannequins, wreathed in flames, slowly fell through the shattered opening. They lay there as the fire destroyed them.

"Let's go, men," said Barroni.

Delaney started to ask another question, but stopped when he noticed the captain was staring at something over his shoulder. A two-story cloud of black smoke was rolling toward them, obscuring the end of the mall they had just come from.

FROM THE middle of the access way, three stories above the mall, Katherine Adams saw three men weaving their way down the street like broken field runners. Incredibly, the promenade appeared to be coming apart around them. Two of them were dressed in white uniforms. The third was John Delaney.

"John!" she yelled out, waving her arms. *"John!"*

Delaney stopped and looked around, trying to pinpoint where the voice was coming from.

"Up here."

"Katherine," he yelled up to her. "Why aren't you at the boat?"

"Why aren't you?"

Delaney opened his mouth to reply, but Barroni cut him off.

"Is that Mr. Nelms?" the captain called out, squinting at the balcony.

"Yes, sir," Nelms yelled back.

"I have no idea what you're doing up there, sir, but please get that young lady off the balcony and meet us at station six."

Barroni stepped back to avoid a coffee table that suddenly fell over in front of the café.

"We need to go up two more decks to reach the boats," he told Delaney. "The stairway is on the other side of those elevators. Mr. Nelms will meet us there with your friend."

Delaney nodded and they started forward once more.

When Katherine reached the deck she was astounded to see everything was in utter chaos. The entire rear half of the ship was on fire. Flames coming from the stern were slowly changing the superstructure of the luxury liner into something unrecognizable and grotesque. Despite the best efforts of the crew, the situation was hopeless. In that moment, she knew the *Majestic* was lost. People at the stern who were cut off from the lifeboats were jumping overboard into the swirling waters of the Atlantic. Those who didn't leap clear of the ship, or who didn't remember to grasp the lapels of their life vests, were killed on impact when they hit. Katherine looked out in horror to see a score of dead bodies rising up and down on the ocean swells. The sight made her throat constrict. The only encouraging thing she saw was about two hundred yards from the ship, where a small flotilla of vessels had gathered together in a group. They had to be the surviving passengers in their lifeboats. She prayed Beth and Libby were among them.

A tremendous groan came from the interior of the *Majestic* and she felt a sigh run through the deck. Without warning, the ship slipped sideways in the water and she nearly pitched over the rail. Miraculously, John Delaney was there, grabbing her before she fell.

"John, I was so worried about you," she said. "You won't believe what happened."

"Tell me later. We need to get into one of those lifeboats. The captain has ordered us to abandon ship."

"I know," she said. "This is horrible."

Delaney smiled and hugged her, which did a great deal to help. The strength in his arms made her feel safe despite the chaos around them. Along with thirty-five other passengers, they waited their turn to board the boat. Once Delaney saw her safely inside, he reached back to give Tony LaRocca a hand. Ed Nelms followed them.

Katherine looked up at the deck as the crew swung the lifeboat out and began lowering it into the water. Captain Barroni stayed behind, still giving orders on his communicator. Only after the last passenger was safely away did he and the remaining crew members board their lifeboat and descend into the Atlantic.

NINETEEN

No one talked as the boat rode up and down the swells. They watched the fire slowly creeping along the deck, destroying anything capable of burning. It was a sad and terrible thing to see. By what miracle Katherine would never know, but the *Ocean Majestic* did not sink immediately as she and everyone feared it would. The stern gradually settled lower and lower until the bow of the ship stuck out of the water at a sharp angle. An angry red glow lit the sky above the once proud smokestacks.

The officer in charge of the lifeboat told them not to worry. He said distress signals had been sent out and he explained that two ships were heading toward them at top speed to render assistance. He told them the boat's radio was operating with plenty of power and broadcasting their position continuously. He assured them that everything would be all right.

After a few minutes Katherine stopped looking at the *Ocean Majestic* because the bodies floating on the water were simply too much to bear. Not only were there men, but women and children. Images of other faces, long dead, seeped into her mind and a familiar knot began to form in the pit of her stomach. To fight it, she turned her thoughts to her own children and closed her eyes tightly, trying to shut out the gruesome images, but they wouldn't leave no matter how hard she tried. A hundred yards away, the body of the Texan who had given her a tip in the casino drifted on his back in the water, held up by his life jacket. His mouth was open and his eyes were staring up at the night sky.

THE FIRST helicopters from the U.S.S. *Theodore Roosevelt* arrived about thirty minutes later, and the aircraft carrier came on scene six hours after that. During their wait, Navy frogmen from the advance search-and-rescue teams entered the water time and again, helping injured passengers into safety baskets. Once the helicopters were filled to capacity, they sped back to the ship only to return once more, scouring the area in an effort to locate anyone left alive.

The *Marie Star,* pushing its engines to the maximum, got there in slightly under three hours and immediately put boats into the water aiding in the rescue effort. Slowly, people were plucked from the sea, wrapped in blankets, and taken to sickbay for medical treatment. One by one lifeboats tied alongside the ships, transferring those lucky enough to have escaped the flames. In all, 2,635 passengers and crewmen were rescued, and slightly more than 900 people went to their deaths, making the fire on the *Ocean Majestic* one of the worst disasters in

modern maritime history. Three hundred yards off the
port beam of the *Theodore Roosevelt,* the *Ocean Majestic*
drifted silently in the current, a lifeless, burned-out hulk.

UNNOTICED BY the majority of passengers on the *Marie
Star,* two men separated themselves from the ever-
expanding group of people on her deck and made their
way to the opposite side of the ship. After checking to
make sure no one was watching, both men walked aft and
disappeared down a companionway that led to cargo hold
twenty-three. One was thin and the other short and
stocky. They opened a door that had deliberately been left
unlocked for them and slipped inside. The hold was gray
and filled with boxes and crates that were lashed securely
to the deck. At the far corner sat a large metal container
approximately ten feet square, marked HOSPITAL RIYADH
in Arabic letters. The thin man walked over and pulled on
the container's door handle. As he expected, it wasn't
sealed. With a grunt, he tugged harder and the door
swung forward on a hinge. Both men stepped inside and
found the clothes that had been left for them, along with
food and drink. The thin man shut the door, sliding a bolt
home and locking it from the inside. He spoke a few
words to his companion in Arabic. The other shrugged,
picked up a sandwich, and took a bite.

After several minutes they both sat down to wait for
the third member of their team.

Adnan al-Jabbar knew that capture or even death were
possibilities. It didn't matter. They were in Allah's hands
now and Allah protected his people. If death came, it came.
Adnan had lived in the United States since he was eight
years old and spoke English with no trace of an accent. He
was twenty-six. A devout follower of the Islamic faith, he
had been recruited for this holy mission at the last moment
when an original team member had become injured.

Better to live in paradise as an honored martyr, rather than suffer degradation and humiliation at the hands of the Americans. Unlike his stocky partner, who spoke very little, Adnan was buoyed by their success and supremely confident. He knew the other man only as Umar. Adnan leaned back against the side of the crate, closed his eyes, and said a prayer of thanks.

The Americans in all their arrogance would know no peace. They would learn nothing of theirs was beyond Allah's reach and that his retribution was terrible indeed. Adnan thought of his wife and two small children as he sat there. It had been nearly two weeks since he had seen them, and it would be another two days before the ship docked in Italy. Once they arrived he would collect the rest of his money, pick up a new passport, and catch the first plane home. The sum their employer offered would be sufficient to put both of his children through college, with quite a bit left over. He saw no inconsistency in accepting money. Perhaps he would buy his wife a new washer and dryer. She would like that. They could afford it now and there was always the promise of more employment.

When he looked up he saw that Umar was watching him in the dim light. He was a strange man and made him uncomfortable. Adnan smiled, but the smile was not returned.

"My friend, how much longer do you think it will be before our companion joins us?" he asked.

Umar slowly shook his head and continued to stare.

TWENTY

While they waited for the rescue ships to arrive, too exhausted to think clearly, Katherine rested her head on Delaney's chest and slept. He was solid and real and it was reassuring to have someone she could lean on. Sometime later, he gently spoke her name and touched her on the shoulder. She had been having the dream again and her forehead was bathed in sweat. When she awoke with a start, she knew two things simultaneously: the *Ocean Majestic* had been deliberately sabotaged; and she knew the name of the man who had been arguing with Ellis Stephens.

It had been twenty years since she had seen his face and all at once it snapped back into her head with startling clarity. Bennett Martin Williams was the same man she had prosecuted for bombing an abortion clinic in Clayton, Georgia, in 1988. He was older and heavier now, but there was no question in her mind that it was him. At the time she had been acting as Ray Rosen's assistant on the case and the plea bargain Rosen accepted had caused a serious rift between them. She wanted to go for the maximum. She could still remember the smirk on Williams's face, and the arrogant way he stared at her during Rosen's cross-examination.

In the end, he received a three-year sentence in a youth correctional facility, largely because he was only sixteen years old and was thought by the judge to be under the influence of his father, the Reverend Walter Williams, an activist with the Southern Baptist Brotherhood. Katherine's heart began to pound in her chest and she sat straight up in her seat.

"John . . . Ellis Stephens is dead."

"What? How do you know?"

"Because I *saw* him. There were two bullets in his chest and half his head was blown away," Katherine whispered.

"Are you kidding me?"

"I'm not kidding. I saw it, and so did he," Katherine said, looking at Ed Nelms who was seated across from them.

Delaney studied her face closely for a few seconds then turned to Nelms for an explanation.

Nelms leaned forward, dropping his voice. "Ma'am, I'd appreciate it if you would keep that information to yourself until we get onboard. I need to report this to the captain, and then we'll let the authorities know. Please stay close to me when we get on deck."

Katherine introduced Nelms to Delaney.

"Someone want to let me know what's going on?" said Delaney.

Katherine slid to the end of the bench until she reached the window. Delaney and Nelms moved with her. Once they were away from the other passengers, she explained in hushed tones what she'd seen. Delaney didn't interrupt; he simply listened. At one point he glanced at Nelms who nodded in confirmation.

What neither of them were prepared for were her revelations about Bennett Martin Williams. When she was through, Delaney leaned back and blew a long breath out.

Nelms asked, "Are you certain about this, Ms. Adams? Accusing someone of murder is pretty serious."

"I'm not saying Williams did it," Katherine told him, "but I think it would be a damn good idea to have a talk with him, assuming he's still around."

"Still around?" Nelms asked.

"Not dead," Delaney told him.

"Got it. All right, as soon as we get on deck, I'll find the captain and let him know what happened . . . then we'll go and have a *talk* with Mr. Williams. We'll have to get permission from the captain of the *Marie Star*, but I don't think that will be a problem."

An announcement from the crewman piloting the lifeboat interrupted their discussion. They got up and began to file onto the gangplank with the rest of the passengers. Onboard, a ship's officer approached and asked if anyone needed medical attention. They told him they didn't. Nelms identified himself and then moved off to the side and began speaking into his communicator. At several points during the conversation, he looked directly at Katherine and nodded.

While Nelms was talking she searched the deck for Beth and Libby. There were already several hundred passengers milling about. She looked for nearly a half-hour without success. Captain Barroni was still out on the ocean in his lifeboat going from body to body to check for survivors. Sailors from the *Theodore Roosevelt* joined him and the other crewmembers in their grisly task.

Several of the *Marie Star*'s crew came on deck with coffee and blankets for those who needed them. Katherine declined the offer of a blanket from a young man who looked about the same age as her eldest son, James.

The *Marie Star* was as different from the *Ocean Majestic* as a ship could be. There were no swimming pools or water slides—only container after container, running from the bow to the stern. The ship was painted almost entirely in a primer red, except for its sides, which were flat black. Katherine walked from one end to the other, trying to find her friends, and finally gave up. They had to be on the *Roosevelt*. Leaning against the rail, she squinted across the water, but the aircraft carrier was too far away to see anything clearly.

"You all right?" Delaney asked. It was the first time he had spoken in the last fifteen minutes.

"No . . . I'm pretty damn far from being all right."

He put his hands on her shoulders and turned her to face him.

"K. J., are you sure about this Williams guy?"

Katherine nodded and told him the details of Bennett Williams's case. The more she talked, however, the more it became obvious there was something wrong with her theory. All she had seen was an argument in the buffet with Ellis, and an empty attaché case.

What does that prove?

As a trial lawyer she could see a hole large enough to drive a truck through. If Williams *had* killed Ellis and then set fire to the ship, he risked killing himself in the process, which made no sense at all. But he had committed arson before, and the *Ocean Majestic* had clearly been sabotaged. That much was obvious. The fire systems, which should have come on, didn't . . . and, most astonishing of all, Nelms told them the hoses had all been cut. She voiced these concerns to Delaney, who was already thinking along the same lines.

"It doesn't add up, John."

"Agreed, but sometimes these nuts do lots of things that don't make sense. I worked a case once where a guy put a bullet in his own stomach just to deflect suspicion. The best thing is to get Williams alone and shake him down. You said he recognized you in the buffet, right?"

"I'm pretty sure."

"How did he react?"

"He was clearly surprised to see me and he promptly pulled a one-eighty and left through the side door."

"Sounds like he was trying to make himself scarce. Maybe . . . oh, here comes Nelms."

Delaney broke off what he was saying as Ed Nelms approached them.

"Captain Barroni is onboard the *Theodore Roosevelt*,"

Nelms told them. "He's going to talk with their captain and send a boat for us. Can you give me a description of what this Bennett Williams looks like?"

Katherine thought for a second. "He's got to be about thirty or thirty-one by now. He gained some weight since the last time I saw him, but my guess is he's somewhere around one hundred ninety pounds, and maybe six feet tall."

"About the same height as me?" Nelms asked.

"Yeah . . . I'd say so. He has close-cropped blond hair. I can't remember what color his eyes were—hazel, I think."

Nelms nodded and pressed the TALK button a few times on his walkie-talkie. Marius Barroni answered at once.

"Captain . . . Nelms here. The lady's given me a description of Williams. Six feet, short blond hair, and around thirty-five or thirty-six years old."

"Thank you, Mr. Nelms," the speaker cracked. "A boat's putting out for you now. Report to me at Captain Blaylock's cabin as soon as you get onboard."

Katherine, Delaney, and Nelms all looked across at the *Roosevelt* and saw a launch coming across the water toward them at high speed. Ten minutes later they found themselves standing on the deck of the U.S.S. *Theodore Roosevelt*. A brief disagreement ensued between Nelms and Delaney about whether the invitation also included him. In the end it was decided that Delaney should come as well. They were greeted by an officer in his late forties, wearing a golf jacket and a baseball-style cap. The cap had the name of the ship stitched across it in gold letters. His name was Scott Wardlaw, and he was accompanied by two men wearing security armbands. Wardlaw introduced himself, shook hands, but made no effort to introduce the others. He asked everyone to follow him. As soon as they started walking, the security guards took up positions on either side of the group.

They proceeded down a narrow corridor painted the same gray color as the rest of the ship. At the end was a staircase that led up to the next deck. Two sailors with side arms were standing guard in front of a large wooden door. To Katherine it looked more like something you'd find on a private home as opposed to a Navy ship. The guards came to attention as soon as they saw Wardlaw coming up the steps.

"As you were," he said, returning their salutes.

He knocked twice and a voice from within called out, "Come."

TWENTY-ONE

Captain James "Tiger" Blaylock's cabin wasn't what Katherine expected. She found herself in a living room with a thick blue pile carpet. On the far side of the room was a couch with two comfortable-looking side chairs facing it. A large liquid-crystal television set hung on the wall. On the opposite wall were a set of bookshelves. A French desk with a black leather top and brass scrollwork down the legs stood in front them.

Tiger Blaylock got up as soon as they entered. So did Marius Barroni and Tony LaRocca. Blaylock took the cigar he was smoking out of his mouth and came around his desk. He was a man in his early fifties with a clean-shaven head and an athletic physique. A pair of dark brown eyes and a strong jaw line conveyed the impression of intelligence.

"Ms. Adams, I'm James Blaylock," he said, extending his hand.

"Good to meet you, Captain," Katherine replied. "This

is John Delaney and Officer Ed Nelms. I'm afraid I don't know your rank, Mr. Nelms," she added.

"It's lieutenant, ma'am."

Delaney shook hands and Nelms saluted both the captains, who returned the courtesy.

"Welcome onboard the *Theodore Roosevelt*," said Blaylock. "I'm very sorry it has to be under these circumstances. Why don't you come over here and have a seat. Captain Barroni and I were just discussing you. Can I get you something to drink?"

"I'd love a Diet Coke, if you have one," said Katherine.

Delaney asked for a beer and Nelms said water would be fine.

Blaylock reached across his desk and pushed a button on his intercom. An orderly entered the room, took their orders and left. He returned a few minutes later carrying their drinks on a tray.

Tiger Blaylock sat on the edge of his desk and gestured to Barroni using the butt of his cigar as a pointer.

"Captain Barroni was just filling me in on what happened to your ship. Oh, excuse me," he said, reaching for the ashtray.

"You don't have to put it out," Katherine told him. "I love the smell of a good cigar. *Fuentes*, right?"

Blaylock's eyebrows went up and he exchanged a look with Barroni.

"Right," he said, amused by Katherine's observation. "I have a friend on a British guided missile carrier who manages to get a box over to me every now and then. Have to hide 'em from the wife, though. She's been on me to quit for the last five years. The crew gives me advance warning whenever she comes onboard to make an unannounced inspection."

This time it was Katherine's turn to smile. She really

did like the way cigars smelled and made it a point to not cramp a man's style if he wanted to smoke one in her presence. Given the times, it wasn't a particularly fashionable attitude.

"Thank you for coming to our rescue, Captain."

"My pleasure, ma'am. You have my deepest condolences if you lost anyone in this tragedy."

"I didn't lose anybody," Katherine replied, "but I may have misplaced my best friend, Elizabeth Doliver. She was with a lady named Libby Stephens the last time I saw them. Libby is the wife of Ellis Stephens, the man who was murdered. They weren't on the other ship and I'd really like to know that they're safe."

"I'm sure they are. Scott, do you think you could look into that for Ms. Adams?"

"Sure thing," said Wardlaw. "If they're with us, we'll find them. Can you give me their descriptions?"

"Beth is my age and about an inch taller than me. She's a brunette, pretty, and she was wearing blue jeans, a white sweater, and a gray windbreaker. Libby was dressed in a pantsuit . . . dark blue, if I remember correctly. She's in her mid-fifties . . . black hair with maybe a little gray."

"That shouldn't be a problem," said Wardlaw. He got up, saluted both captains, and left the cabin.

"I really appreciate it," said Katherine. "Thanks."

"The least I could do. You folks have been through a pretty rough time of it. Captain Barroni has informed me of what you and Mr. Nelms saw, but I'd like you to fill us in on the details. I'd also like to have what you say taken down, if you don't mind."

"That will be fine."

Blaylock punched a button on his desk intercom. "Chief, would you have Martinez step in here?"

There was a short pause while everyone made small

talk. It was followed by a knock on the door. A slightly built, Hispanic-looking young man entered carrying a tape recorder and a yellow notepad.

Blaylock introduced Raul Martinez to everyone. The introduction, Katherine realized, was not for social purposes, but to identify who was present. He explained Martinez was his secretary and knew shorthand. He would be taking down what was said in the room. No one voiced any objections.

It took Katherine several minutes to recount her story. During this time she provided them with the details of her background as an attorney and her involvement in Bennett Williams's case twenty years earlier.

"So you had no idea who this man was when you saw him?" Blaylock asked.

"I only knew his face was familiar. It didn't come to me until later . . . when we were in the lifeboat."

"And what led you to make that connection?"

Katherine shrugged.

"I don't know. It's just one of those things that pop into your head."

"I see. So, after you went to check on this . . . Stephens fellow," Blaylock said, looking down at his notes, "you found the door locked, broke in, and saw that he'd been murdered."

"Right."

"What made you decide to get Lieutenant Nelms?" Captain Barroni asked, speaking for the first time.

"He was the first ship's officer I saw. He and another man were fighting a fire in the corridor and I thought it would be a good idea to have a witness in case we sank or anything."

Tiger Blaylock shook his head and turned to Captain Barroni.

"Do you think your vessel is still seaworthy, Captain?"

"It's questionable," Barroni replied. "My guess is she'll stay afloat for a while, but *how* long, I can't say. At least two of those explosions put good-sized holes in her bottom, and she was listing pretty badly. Rudder control was gone, so any maneuvering ability that's left will be quite limited—only what we can manage with the bow thrusters. If the seas start picking up . . . ."

Tiger Blaylock understood the implications and nodded slowly.

"Did your automatic pump system come on?" he asked.

"They were operating, but there's no way they can handle the volume of water coming in."

"You're pretty sure about the ship being sabotaged?"

"There's no question in my mind, sir," Barroni replied.

"Agreed," said LaRocca.

"That goes double for me," Ed Nelms added.

Blaylock opened his mouth to say something else, but the intercom on his desk buzzed before he could.

"Captain, this is radio," a voice said. "I have a message for Captain Barroni."

"Do you want to take it in private?" Blaylock asked.

Barroni shook his head.

"Go ahead, radio. Captain Barroni is sitting across from me."

"Your company advises a salvage tug has put out from Bethesda, Maryland, and is proceeding to this location with all haste. They're expected to arrive at 0300 hours tomorrow. Two ships are also being sent out in relief. You are to take all steps necessary to ensure the safety of the passengers. They would like a casualty toll and the names of all deceased at the earliest possible time, sir."

"Thank you, radio," Captain Barroni called out. "With the captain's permission, please let my company know the message was received and I'll keep them informed."

"That'll be fine," Blaylock replied.

Although both men were captains and technically held the same rank, Barroni was following the accepted protocol of the sea by asking permission, since the *Theodore Roosevelt* was Tiger Blaylock's ship.

"I don't know about you, Captain," said Barroni, "but I'd like to have a firsthand look at Ellis Stephens's body. I'd also like to check and see if your men have been able to locate this Bennett Williams."

"I was about to suggest the same thing."

"If you have a photographer, or someone with a camera, it might be a good idea to take a few pictures. The authorities will want to see them eventually," said Delaney.

It was the first time he had spoken since they got into the room. Everyone turned and looked at him.

"Makes sense," Blaylock agreed. "You would be Mr. Adams?"

"Not yet," Delaney replied. "The name's John Delaney."

Blaylock frowned and consulted his notes again.

"Sorry. For some reason I thought you two were married. I put 'law professor' next to Ms. Adams's name."

"John's the professor," said Katherine. "I'm just a lowly divorce lawyer."

"Got it," Blaylock replied, scratching through his notes. "I apologize for the mistake."

"No problem. K. J. and I were discussing what to name the children when all the commotion broke out."

Blaylock smiled at the joke.

"I take it that makes *you* K. J."

"It does," said Katherine. "John takes some getting used to, but I think he's right about the photographs. By the way, he neglected to mention he was a homicide detective before he became a lawyer."

Blaylock considered Delaney for a moment.

"Right," he said nodding. "Do you want to come over with us, Ms. Adams, or remain here onboard?"

"I'll come," Katherine said, though it was the last thing she wanted to do. The fear of resurrecting the flashbacks again surged in her mind.

"What about you, Mr. Delaney? You're a civilian, so I can't order it, but I suspect your expertise would be valuable. It would have to be on a volunteer basis, of course."

"I seem to remember my father warning me about volunteering for anything in the Navy, but yeah, I'll be happy to come. I'd love to nail the guys responsible."

"Guys?" Blaylock asked, his face suddenly losing its pleasant aspect.

"Just a guess, Captain. But if what I'm hearing about hoses being cut and the fire system being out is true, there's a good chance Williams wasn't acting alone, assuming he did it, of course."

The two captains exchanged glances, then got up at the same time and headed for the door.

TWENTY-TWO

By the time they reached the deck Katherine was surprised to see streaks of red and purple on the eastern horizon. The sea was placid and glassy calm. She looked toward the *Marie Star*, at the people there. They were watching the few boats still in the water as they recovered bodies. In the predawn light the aircraft carrier's central tower rose up stark and forbidding. Four F-18C Tomcat fighters were anchored to the deck a hundred feet away. A short distance from her was a Viking 2C with its pancake-shaped radar above the plane's fuselage. There were other planes, but Katherine didn't know them. The only reason she could identify any at all was because her youngest son, Zach, was into model building and could quote at will most of the specifications of the Navy's fighter arsenal. He was so fond of bringing his models to the breakfast table in the morning and telling her about them, she decided some of the information must have rubbed off.

Though she had never set foot on a Navy vessel before, she found that she could recognize the Sea Sparrow missile launchers (also based on her conversations with Zach). She drew a sharp glance from Tiger Blaylock when he started to point out the Close-In Weapons System and she completed the sentence for him.

Surprised, the captain asked her how she knew.

"Oh, I pick up little bits of information every now and then," she replied, hoping he wouldn't press the matter. He didn't.

In truth, Katherine's mind was in turmoil about going back to the *Ocean Majestic*. The intense heat from the fire had turned the once beautiful liner into a blackened, mis-shapen thing that now reminded her more of a floating tomb than a ship. Without thinking, she slipped her arm through Delaney's. His presence seemed to steady her. He smiled and gave her a look that was both calming and reassuring, luxuries she hadn't allowed herself in a long time.

Before Captain Blaylock would allow anyone to leave he dispatched a team of damage-control specialists and firefighters across to make sure it was safe. Katherine stood on the deck next to the catapult launcher and watched the boats tie alongside the cruise ship. Sailors wearing orange coats and helmets with flame-resistant neck coverings used the davit lines to climb onboard, then disappeared belowdecks. They reappeared a half-hour later and lowered a gangplank at the stern, which was nearly all in the water, for the damage-control team, who began scouring the ship to assess its condition. It was another hour before they radioed that it was all right to come across.

The sun was already well above the horizon by the time Katherine and the others reached the *Majestic*. They entered through a maintenance access door on the first deck and were met by a grizzled-looking chief warrant officer named DeCharles, who was in charge of the damage-control party. He told them the aft engine room was completely flooded but that the watertight doors seemed to be holding.

"There was more than one explosion," Barroni said. "Have your men been able to locate the other damage?"

"Yes, sir," DeCharles replied. "Near as we can tell, there's a hull breach near the starboard bow and another amidships on the port side. Both sections are sealed, but she's continuing to settle. We've got the portable generators up, so you'll have electricity—at least for a while."

There was a pause.

"How long do we have?" asked Barroni.

"At the rate she's going, sir, an hour . . . maybe a little longer. I wouldn't want to cut it closer than that."

"Other than the two holes in the engine room, you're saying there's another hull breach?" Blaylock asked.

"Has to be, Captain. My guess is, it's somewhere near the stern section. I've got my men looking for it, but this is a big boat."

Blaylock nodded and thought for a moment.

"Thirty minutes, Chief. No more. Then clear all the men off and get them back to our ship. Advise the captain of the *Marie Star* to make a final sweep for survivors. When he finishes, I'd like him to put some distance between us. In fact, it might be a good idea to pull all his people out of the water. Do you agree, Captain?" he asked, turning to Barroni.

Barroni took a deep breath and answered, "Yes."

"All right, it's settled then," said Blaylock. "Thirty minutes. I'd like one of your officers to go with Chief DeCharles and our photographer so we can take pictures of the damage. The other photographer can come with us."

"Mr. LaRocca?" Captain Barroni said.

"Aye, aye, sir. I'll see to it."

"Good," said Barroni. "Let's stay in touch with the handsets. I want to know the moment there is any change in the ship's status."

"Right," said LaRocca.

The first officer, the photographer, and DeCharles all headed down the corridor toward the stern.

"Mr. Nelms, which cabin was it?" asked Barroni.

"5102, sir."

"Lead the way, if you please."

Katherine heard the exchange and understood what they were talking about: The *Ocean Majestic* was sinking, which did little to increase her comfort level. While they were making their way toward the bow, she fought a sudden desire to run down the gangplank and get back to the safety of the *Theodore Roosevelt*'s launch. An image of Ellis Stephens's face and his dead eyes drifted into her mind. This was something she *had* to do. Delaney put an arm around her shoulders and gave her a tight-lipped smile.

"It's always tough going back to a murder scene," he said. "The first time is a shock, but the second time, you know what to expect and your mind starts working on you. Are you okay?"

"Um-hm."

"Good girl. When we get there, why don't you wait outside and let me have a look around first? Barroni says it's fine with him."

"I'm not scared, John. I'm just not looking forward to it, that's all. He was such a nice man. Libby's going to be devastated."

"I didn't say you were scared. But the point is, I've got some background in working crime scenes and it's easy to taint valuable evidence if you're not careful. That's why police freeze off an area until forensics can go over it."

"I understand," said Katherine. She registered the change in Delaney's voice as he shifted back into cop mode.

The long hallway leading to Cabin 5102 was now lit only by the emergency light, giving it an eerie aspect. Many of the cabin doors had been left open and reflected light from the ocean played against the walls, moving and changing with the swells. The absence of noise only added to the situation.

Christ, this looks like one of those cheap horror movies, thought Katherine. *Sure . . . "take a cruise," Beth says. "We'll have an incredible time."*

Katherine shook her head and kept walking. Her friend was partially right: She *was* having an incredible time—though not in the way they'd planned.

When they reached the cabin, the photographer, Nelms, Katherine, and both captains stepped aside allowing Delaney to enter. He stood there studying the room for several minutes before he spoke. There was enough sunlight spilling in through the balcony doors to see without a problem. Near the bathroom, the bloodstain now looked more black than red. Katherine turned her head away, knowing who it belonged to. Ellis's attaché case still lay in the corner against the wall. Except for the blood, there was no indication anything was wrong.

Delaney squatted down for a closer look at something.

"Anybody think to bring a flashlight?" he asked.

"Got one," said Nelms. He began fishing around in his

pocket and produced a small key ring with a tiny cylindrical ornament on one end. He handed it to Delaney, who stooped again and shined the light at a spot on the floor. He examined it for a few seconds then took a dollar bill out of his wallet and placed it next to the spot. Everyone craned their heads into the room to see what he was doing.

"What's your name?" he asked the photographer.

"Brian, sir. Brian Moss."

"All right, Brian. I want you to step in here with me. Stay close to the dresser and take a couple of pictures of this."

"Sir?"

"There's an imprint," Blaylock said, pointing. "It looks like the heel of a man's shoe."

Katherine squinted and looked closer. In the blood was the partial outline of a man's shoe.

"It might belong to Mr. Stephens," said Nelms.

Delaney nodded and stood up as the photographer adjusted the lens on his camera.

"It might. I won't know until we can compare it. Ellis was a big guy . . . maybe six foot one or six two. This doesn't look nearly that large."

"The dollar bill is to give it scale, right?" asked Barroni.

"Right, Captain. You'll make detective yet. If you'll note the direction it's facing, whoever made this was heading *out* the front door. From where I'm standing, you can see the body, and it's facing the other way."

When Delaney said that, Brian Moss stopped what he was doing to look.

"*Fuck!* he exclaimed, taking a step backward and bumping into the dresser. The color drained out of his face and his mouth dropped open in surprise.

"My sentiments exactly," said Delaney. "Get a photo of that attaché case too, if you would."

The young sailor nodded and started taking pictures, his mouth still open.

"Brian, when you're through, step over to the bed and take one of the pillowcases off the pillows. I want you to put the briefcase into it then see if you can scare up a shoe from that closet. Okay?"

"And be careful to not get your own prints on anything," warned Tiger Blaylock. "This is all going to be evidence."

"Yes, sir," Moss replied.

"You guys are good," said Delaney.

"Too many Sherlock Holmes books when I was a kid," Blaylock answered.

"Old Sherlock had the right idea. Did you know police got the idea about using fingerprints from Conan Doyle's writings?"

"I knew that," said Nelms.

When everyone looked at him, he added, "I *did*," in a defensive tone. "It was a question on one of those quiz shows."

"I don't know about anyone else," said Katherine, "but my prints are probably here. I touched the case earlier."

"Got it," Delaney replied.

He spent a full ten minutes examining Ellis's body, while Brian Moss, still pale, reluctantly inched closer and took several more photos. At one point Delaney stepped over the pool of blood, picked up one of Stephens's hands, and looked under the fingernails. He frowned at what he saw.

"What is it?" asked Katherine.

"I need a penknife," he replied, patting around his own pockets.

Once again Nelms came to the rescue. He produced a small folding knife and handed it to Delaney, who got a piece of paper from the desk and put it under Ellis's hand. Then he carefully scraped some material out from under the fingernails letting it drop onto the paper. When he was through, he folded it and handed the paper to Tiger Blaylock.

"As soon as we get back on the ship, I'd like to put this in a plastic bag and seal it. We'll label it 'evidence,' then sign and date it. We can send it to the authorities as soon as possible. It's very important that no one else touches it until then."

"Why go to all the trouble?" asked Barroni.

"It's to preserve the chain of custody," Katherine explained.

"I'm pretty much done here," Delaney told them. "Does anyone know what cabin Williams was in?"

"Let's see if we can find out," said Barroni. He keyed his hand communicator twice. "Tony, are you there?"

"I'm here, Captain. Chief DeCharles and I are trying to find that other breach."

"Is there a ship's computer anywhere near you?"

"The communications center is up on deck two. We just passed it."

"Do me a favor. If our computer's operating, see if you can punch up the passenger list. I want to know what cabin Bennett Williams was in."

"Righto. I'll be back with you in a minute or two."

The walkie-talkie went silent. A short while later, LaRocca came on with the information they needed.

"Cabin 7130, Captain."

"That's two decks up," Barroni told Delaney. "Do you want someone to come with you?"

"Sure. A keycard would be helpful if you guys have one; otherwise I can use K.J.'s method to get in."

Ed Nelms reached into his pocket and produced his access keycard.

Delaney stuck out his lower lip, impressed. "Regular Boy Scouts, you guys."

"We try to be," said Barroni. "Ed, go with him in case he needs anything else."

Nelms and Delaney left the cabin and disappeared around the end of the access way. They found a staircase on the opposite side of the ship and came out on the Calypso Deck. Nelms led the way to Cabin 7103 and slid the plastic card into the lock. After opening the room he stood aside to let Delaney enter first. It took less than a minute to find the gun hidden in the third drawer of the dresser. It was under Williams's clothes. While Nelms was searching the closet, Delaney crossed the room, grabbed a pencil from the desk, and returned to the dresser. He reached down, slid it through the trigger guard, and held it up for Nelms to see. "Bingo," he said.

Nelms turned around and blinked. "I'll be a son of a bitch."

"Exactly. Strip one of those pillowcases off the bed, would you?"

Nelms did as he was asked and held it open for Delaney to drop the gun in.

They spent another few minutes checking for anything that looked like it might have come from Ellis's briefcase—papers, videotapes, photographs, or computer disks—but they came up empty. The last thing left was the closet safe.

"I don't suppose there's any chance you brought a blowtorch with you?"

" 'Fraid not," said Nelms. "When passengers forget the combination or lock themselves out, we have to call maintenance. They're the only ones who can get in. Can't you detective guys do some trick with a credit card?"

"Only in the movies," Delaney told him. "Let's head

back. Maybe we can get your buddy in engineering to help."

Katherine, Blaylock, Barroni, and Brian Moss were waiting for them in the hallway. Her eyebrows went up in a silent question when she saw them. Delaney winked at her and patted a bulge under his shirt.

"Do you have any way of getting into a safe?" he asked Barroni.

"Sure. I can have someone from maintenance come across and—"

A beep from his walkie-talkie interrupted the rest of his sentence.

"Captain . . . LaRocca here. I think we'd better get our people out as soon as possible. The stern quarter is settling *much* faster than we thought. Chief DeCharles and I haven't been able to find the other hull breach, so we're assuming it's below the waterline. I don't like what I'm seeing right now."

"How much longer do you need?" Barroni asked Delaney.

"Ten minutes," Delaney answered.

"Did you get that, Tony?" Barroni said into the communicator.

"We don't have ten minutes, sir. And that's no exaggeration. I'm ordering the men out now. The chief said to tell Captain Blaylock he's doing the same."

"Got it," said Barroni. "We're out of here. We'll meet you at the boat. If you get there first and it looks like she's going down, you're to put as much distance as you can between the *Majestic* and yourself. Is that understood?"

"Aye, aye, sir, but—"

"That's an order, Tony. Get moving. Sorry, Mr. Delaney, but we'll have to make do with—"

The rest of Captain Barroni's words froze in his mouth as a deep, protracted groan came from the very heart of the ship. It was followed by a sudden and very noticeable shift in the deck.

"Move it, people," snapped Blaylock.

Within seconds they were all running down the corridor toward the staircase. It came as a shock when Katherine realized they were actually going downhill. As the stern of the ship moved lower in the water, the bow continued to lift upward. Once again the terrible groaning started and from somewhere deep within the heart of the ship itself came a loud crash. Visions of being pulled under by the massive ocean liner tugged at the corners of her consiousness as she sped down the steps.

By the time they reached the gangway it was at such a steep angle the bottom quarter was already underwater. For a second Katherine nearly panicked because the *Roosevelt*'s launch was gone. She looked around wildly and saw that LaRocca had brought it behind them. Delaney and Blaylock helped her climb over the safety rail. She had to jump the last few feet into the waiting arms of a crewman. Nelms, Delaney, and the photographer were next, followed by Blaylock. For the second time in twenty-four hours, Marius Barroni was the last to leave his ship. His feet had barely reached the deck of the launch when a series of explosions came from the interior of the *Majestic*'s hull.

"Gun it, sailor," said Blaylock.

"Hang on," the helmsman responded, ramming both throttles forward. The launch leaped ahead and began to gain distance from the ship looming above them.

"*Mother of God*," one of the damage-control sailors exclaimed. "She's going."

Katherine and everyone else in the launch turned to look. Water boiled around the *Majestic's* stern. A second later the launch began to pitch violently as the ocean became unsettled. Suddenly, they found themselves looking at a wall of water that seemed to rise out of nowhere and began rushing directly at them.

"*Displacement wave to stern, Captain,*" a sailor yelled.

"Steer away from the *Roosevelt*," ordered Blaylock. "Point her directly out to sea."

"Aye aye, sir, directly out to sea," the helmsman repeated, throwing the wheel hard over.

Katherine would remember what happened in those next few seconds for the rest of her life. Despite the launch's speed, the wave overtook them and broke directly over the top of the boat, swamping it. She grabbed for the nearest railing and hung on with all her strength. Even though it was May, the temperature of the Atlantic was still frighteningly cold. Water poured in, knocking everyone to the deck. The bow of the launch pitched downward, then up again, lifting them higher and higher. In another second they were plunging into a trough at a frightening speed. A second wave, forced from the water by the *Majestic*'s mass, began rolling toward the launch. Somehow they managed to stay afloat. The engines strained to gain distance from the nightmare behind them. Eventually, the waves subsided, replaced by large swells that lifted and dropped them sickeningly.

"Look," someone yelled.

"Jesus," Nelms whispered.

Cold, wet, and shivering, Katherine turned back to see an invisible giant lift the bow of the *Ocean Majestic* out of the water and stand it on its end. Her eyes opened wide at the sight. Then without a sound, the great cruise ship, larger than most buildings, began to disappear foot by foot. It was gone in under a minute.

TWENTY-THREE

A sailor placed a blanket around Katherine's shoulders as soon as she got onboard the aircraft carrier. She was taken belowdeck and given a change of clothes. The ship normally had a complement of five thousand men and women, and with the addition of a thousand more people, things were becoming pretty crowded. Another thousand were aboard the *Marie Star,* which maintained its position a few hundred yards away. A female crewmember named Roberta Sanchez escorted Katherine to the main mess hall and got her something to eat. Roberta told her she was from Miami and had joined the Navy after her first year of college.

"My grades weren't that great, so I figured a couple of years working my butt off wouldn't do me any harm," said Roberta. "It turned out to be a good idea because they're training me to be an aircraft maintenance specialist. When I get out I'll be able to land a job with one of the airlines."

Roberta was about the same age as her daughter and meeting her reminded Katherine she had to get a message home to let everyone know she was all right. Roberta told her where the Communications Center was located.

Until Katherine took the first bite of her sandwich she didn't realize how hungry she was. She devoured the whole plate of food in no time. Roberta sat back and watched in frank admiration. Katherine wrapped her hands around a steaming mug of coffee and let the warmth seep into her fingers. There were other passengers in the mess hall. A few she recognized—most she didn't.

She sipped the coffee and looked around, hoping to see

Beth or Libby, but neither of them were there. The more she thought about it the more worried she became and eventually asked Roberta if she would check with the first officer about her friends.

"No problem, ma'am. I'll be right back. I'm sure they're fine."

After Roberta was gone, Katherine scanned the hall for Delaney. There was no sign of him either, which annoyed her because she wanted him there.

Typical man, she thought morosely. *Never around when you need them.*

She was getting used to the easy confidence he projected. He made her feel safe. And then there was that tingle she felt when he put his arm around her the night before the *Majestic* sank. It had been so long since she allowed herself the luxury of those feelings she wasn't sure what to do about them now. She thought of telling him about her past and the night terrors, but she was afraid. Afraid of killing the relationship before it had a chance to get off the ground. She wanted to trust John, to finally open up and trust someone, still . . .

"This sucks," she said to herself.

All sorts of things competed for attention in her mind. Much of what happened simply made no sense. It was true Bennett Williams had been violent in his youth. She detested his type with all her heart. Arrogant and controlling, he hadn't shown the slightest hesitation about trying to burn six people to death at the Arlington Abortion Clinic, fifteen years earlier. But why kill Ellis Stephens? Theft was a possibility, though even that didn't ring true.

If you steal something you do it because you want whatever it is you're taking. Committing suicide in the process doesn't fit.

Fifteen minutes later, Roberta returned with Beth Doliver in tow.

The moment Beth saw Katherine she shouted her name out and ran across the dining hall to hug her.

"Thank God you're okay," Katherine said. "I was sitting here imagining the most horrible things. Where's Libby? Is she—"

"They told her about Ellis," Beth said quietly.

Katherine grimaced.

"How is she taking it?"

"How do you think? She got hysterical and they had to sedate her."

"Oh, Christ."

"The good news is, they've got that prick Williams in custody."

"They do?"

"Four of the ship's security people jumped him and put him in handcuffs. He's down in their jail screaming up a storm. He says he's going to sue everybody."

"Fine," said Katherine. "Tell him to take his best shot."

"I'm sorry to interrupt, ma'am," said Roberta. "But Captain Blaylock asked if you could join him in his cabin."

"What? Oh . . . sure," Katherine replied. "Is it all right if Beth comes, too? By the way, Elizabeth Doliver . . . Roberta Sanchez."

"We've already met. And yes, the captain would like you both."

"I'll come under one condition . . . you stop calling me 'ma'am.' 'Katherine' will be just fine."

"Yes, ma' . . . I mean Katherine. Sorry—Navy training," Roberta said with a smile.

"Super. Lead the way, sailor."

"What's your rank?" Beth asked, as they walked to the elevators.

"Rank's not the right term, ma'am. In the Navy we use 'rate.' I'm rated as an E-3—that's a seaman. I'm also an aviation technician, or A.T. It's a specialist's rating."

"Cool. By the way, my name is *Beth*. And I'm the same age she is, so you can knock off that 'ma'am' stuff with me, too. It makes me feel like someone's grandmother."

"Will do," said Roberta, "except when the captain or another officer is around. 'Rules is Rules,' as they say."

Delaney was waiting for them when they arrived at the captain's cabin. Marius Barroni was also there, as was his first officer, Tony LaRocca, and Scott Wardlaw, the man Katherine had met earlier. On the way up, Roberta filled them in on who was who among the crew. Wardlaw, it turned out, was the *Theodore Roosevelt*'s executive officer, which technically meant he was second in command of the ship. Katherine also recognized Raul Martinez, the young sailor who had taken down their statements earlier. This time another man was present whom she didn't know. Unlike the others, he was dressed in a formal black uniform with gold leaves on his cap. It took only a second for her to decide he was a Navy lawyer.

After dismissing Roberta Sanchez, Captain Blaylock asked everyone to take a seat. He waited until the door closed before introducing Joel Kincaid, a slender man in his late thirties. Kincaid had gray eyes, a prominent nose, and brown hair. Blaylock explained that he was with the Judge Advocate General's office.

"Maybe you'd better take over, Mr. Kincaid," said Blaylock.

"Yes, sir. As I see it, we have a variety of problems to deal with here. The first has to do with who has the authority to exercise jurisdiction."

"I'm sure that'll make Ellis Stephens very happy," said Delaney.

Kincaid turned to Delaney.

"I wasn't trying to be humorous, Mr. Delaney. This is not a joking matter. Captain Blaylock asked me to attend this meeting because multiple sovereign countries are involved, and we're dealing with an apparent civilian murder."

"Apparent? Damn, I completely overlooked the suicide angle. Let's see . . . how many gunshots were there?" Delaney began ticking them off on his fingers.

"All right, point taken," said Kincaid. "We're dealing with a murder. Nevertheless, what I said about different countries having jurisdiction is literally true. Being a lawyer, I'm sure you can appreciate the problem. To begin with, the *Ocean Majestic* was registered in Italy. The decedent was an American citizen; so is Williams—assuming he's going to be charged. At the moment, we're only holding him for questioning. This a United States Naval vessel, so we're bound to abide by the laws of military justice."

"Which means?" asked Katherine.

"Which means we have a choice," Kincaid replied. "We can do one of three things. We can turn Mr. Williams over to the authorities in the States; we can hold him for the Italian police or Interpol, whichever one gets here first; or we can release him. The last option would be up to Captain Blaylock should he determine there's no probable cause. We've already been contacted by the Italian government and you can imagine what their position is—they want him. The Navy's Judge Advocate General, the president, and the attorney general are all meeting in Washington right now to determine the proper response to the Italians' demand."

"Doesn't Captain Barroni have a say in this?" asked Beth.

Marius Barroni shook his head.

"If my ship were still afloat, then I'd be in charge of the matter. Captain Blaylock is the master of this vessel, and it was his crew that plucked the majority of the passengers from the sea while they were attempting salvage operations."

"Salvage operations?" Delaney repeated.

"My official log entry will be to declare the *Majestic* was lost at sea while the United States Navy was trying to salvage her at my request."

"I don't get it," said Beth.

"The reason Captain Barroni is making such a declaration is to strengthen our right to hold Mr. Williams," explained Kincaid.

"If the Italian authorities get their hands on him, it'll be five years before he comes to trial," said Barroni. "By the same token, if he's handed over to Interpol, they'll take him to Geneva to stand trial at the International Court and—"

"The Swiss don't have the death penalty," said Katherine.

"Exactly, Ms. Adams," said Kincaid.

Katherine looked from Kincaid to Barroni, who raised his eyebrows, and returned a tight-lipped smile to her. Barroni leaned forward in his seat. "Nine hundred people are dead, Ms. Adams. I intend to see that the person responsible for this pays, and I don't mean by spending the rest of his life making license plates."

For the first time since she met him, Marius Barroni's face had none of the pleasantness she had come to associate with it. Instead, he looked distinctly feral.

Delaney leaned back in his seat. "You have my apologies," he said to Kincaid.

"Good man," said Blaylock. "If everything works out, that son of a bitch won't simply . . ."

The captain's voice trailed away. And at almost the same time everyone in the room turned toward Raul Martinez, who had been taking down what they were saying.

There was a pause.

Startled, Martinez glanced up from his notes at the sudden silence and blinked.

"Uh . . . sorry, Captain. My pencil broke. I don't think I got that last part at all."

"Pity," said Blaylock. "See you're better prepared the next time, sailor."

"Aye, sir."

"I intend to convene a . . . what the hell is it called?" Blaylock asked Kincaid.

"A Board of Inquiry to determine probable cause."

"Right, right, a probable-cause board. There's a conference room on B Deck that we can use. Captain Cardwell of the *Marie Star* is coming over. He'll sit on the board along with Captain Barroni and myself, so we have three senior officers as regulations require. Joel will give you a rundown of what to expect."

"I know Ms. Adams and Mr. Delaney are both attorneys," Kincaid began, "but military inquiry boards are a little different from what you may be used to. To begin with, you're here in the capacity of witnesses, not to represent anyone. Obviously, you can't make any objections and you shouldn't volunteer information, no matter how much you might want to. Do I make myself clear?"

"Clear," said Katherine.

Delaney nodded.

"Now, Ms. Doliver, as I understand it you were a witness to some interaction between the deceased and the accused—is that correct?"

"If you mean did I see an argument between Ellis Stephens and a man—yes."

"I thought that's what I said."

"You did . . . kind of."

"Understood," Kincaid replied. "Sometimes you have to explain things slowly to a lawyer."

"The problem is," said Beth, "I don't know this Bennett Williams from a hole in the wall. I saw him in the buffet and a little while ago when he was arrested, but even then I didn't get a very good look. He was facedown most of the time."

"I was just getting to that. Do you think you would recognize him again?"

Beth's brows came together and she thought for a second.

"Sure . . . I think so."

"That's fine. You'll also be called as a witness. Once the hearing starts, I'll ask you to make an identification."

"You plan on holding a lineup?" Delaney asked.

"That's one of the differences between our naval code and the procedures most states follow. At a probable-cause board all I need is an identification. A lineup isn't required. Of course, we'll have to sequester the identifying witnesses until they're actually called."

"What are you going to do to me?" Beth asked.

"Sequestered means you won't be allowed in the hearing room while testimony is being given. Considering our other evidence, I don't think this will take very long. We've got a pretty solid case—at least at this level."

"Is Williams going to have an attorney?" asked Katherine.

"One of my colleagues, Jason Snelling, will represent Mr. Williams. Jason's very bright and very aggressive, but in view of Mr. Williams's background, and the fact that we found a gun in his cabin, we shouldn't have any problem holding him for trial. There'll also be a law officer present to handle any technical questions that might come up."

"You understand we're pretty much screwed without the slugs from the body to make a comparison," Delaney pointed out.

"True," Kincaid agreed. "Unfortunately, we'll just have to sail with the wind we've got."

"Cute expression," Delaney observed.

Kincaid ignored the remark and looked back at Beth. "Is there anything else you can recall that might be of help?"

"Only that Ellis told us one of the drug companies had sent a man on the trip who was bothering him about selling his invention to them."

"Invention?"

"Maybe I'm not using the term right . . . K. J., help me out . . . it was something about the brain and genes."

"Stem cells," said Katherine. "At dinner the first night out Dr. Stephens told us that he and his group at Columbia University recently made a breakthrough in growing stem cells in a dish. From what I understood, once they have the basic cell, they can grow it into anything . . . a heart . . . a kidney . . . anything."

"That was it," said Beth.

Blaylock and Kincaid exchanged glances and made notes on their legal pads.

"Did Dr. Stephens ever say Williams was the man bothering him?" asked Kincaid.

"No," said Beth, "not that I recall."

"Would it be possible to find out who Bennett Williams is employed by?" asked Katherine.

Barroni answered, "If I could talk with my home office they might have that information on file."

"Scott, why don't you take Captain Barroni to the Communications Center and see if we can get a call through? Where are they headquartered, Captain?" asked Blaylock.

"The company is based in Rome, but the main corporate office is located in New York."

"Well, it's eleven o'clock in the morning there," Blaylock said, glancing at his watch. "I expect they're up by now."

"When you speak with them, ask if they could fax a hard copy of whatever they have to us," Kincaid told him.

"Can you get that in evidence without a hearsay objection?" asked Katherine.

"Good point, Ms. Adams. Captain, if I could go with Captain Barroni and Mr. Wardlaw, I'll dictate the proper language for his people to use so we don't get snagged on a technicality."

Blaylock nodded, returned Joel Kincaid's salute, then got to his feet.

"Very good. We'll convene in one hour. Mr. Martinez will show our guests how to get down to the conference room."

TWENTY-FOUR

The conference room was a plain affair. At the front was a long table, with three chairs for the board members. Eight more rows of chairs had been set up on either side of an aisle that ran down the center of the room. Katherine walked past the two security guards who flanked the entrance. Delaney was behind her. She took in most of the room's features with a single glance. Since there was no place for a jury, she assumed the naval code of justice didn't require one at that stage of the proceedings. Two smaller tables had been hurriedly brought in and were placed on either side of the aisle. Out of habit, she began walking to the one on the right, before she remembered she was there as a witness, and took a seat in the audience. Bennett Martin Williams and his attorney, Jason Snelling, were already seated at the table on the left. Kincaid was opposite them arranging his papers. The trial lawyer part of Katherine registered that the witness chair would be directly in front of him. It was the same thing she usually did during a trial. Another armed security guard was stationed at the front of the room.

Williams was dressed in a one-piece orange jumpsuit with the word PRISONER on the back. He glowered at Katherine as soon as he saw her and touched Snelling on the elbow to get his attention. Jason Snelling was wearing the same formal black uniform as Joel Kincaid. He was a sharp-featured man, perhaps thirty-five, with intense green eyes and close-cropped brown hair.

Katherine and Snelling briefly made eye contact. Williams leaned over and said something in his lawyer's ear and Snelling nodded slightly, but his expression remained unchanged and unreadable.

"That our boy?" Delaney asked, taking a seat next to Katherine.

"Yes."

Williams observed their interchange, and turned his attention on Delaney for a moment, then shook his head in disgust and turned back around.

"I have that effect on a lot of people," Delaney remarked. "Can't say I'm mad about his tailor."

Katherine started to answer him, but stopped when she noticed an odd expression had appeared on Delaney's face.

"What are you staring at?"

"Check his right forearm," Delaney whispered.

"What about it?"

"See those scratch marks?"

Katherine stared harder and turned back to Delaney for an explanation.

"Those scrapings I took from under Ellis's fingernails," he prompted.

"Skin?"

"The lab will have to confirm it, but that would be my guess."

"Wow," Katherine whispered.

Before she could say anything further, the door at the front of the room opened and all three captains walked in and took their seats. The third man was tall and rail-thin, with iron-gray hair. He wore a formal black coat with two gold epaulets. Captain Blaylock waited for the stenographer and the video technician to finish setting up their equipment before introducing himself and the other board members. The last man to enter was dressed in a Judge Advocate's uniform and seated himself at a small desk on the left side of the room.

"Must be our law officer," Delaney said under his breath.

When everyone was settled, Tiger Blaylock addressed himself directly to Bennett Williams.

"Mr. Williams, my name is James Blaylock; I'm the captain of this ship. This is Captain Marius Barroni, and this is Captain Seldon Cardwell, of the *Marie Star*. According to naval regulations we are here today to conduct a probable-cause hearing. Do you understand what that is, sir?"

"I understand this whole thing is bullshit," Williams replied. "I was a passenger on that ship the same as everyone else and I'm also an American citizen. I'm not in the Navy, so you have no right to hold me. This is false arrest."

"On the contrary, Mr. Williams, as captain of this ship, I *do* have the right to hold you *and* charge you with a crime. This is not a court-martial, only a board of inquiry. *If* we determine there is probable cause to continue holding you, we will do so. You will be then turned over to the appropriate civilian authorities for prosecution. Do you understand that?"

"This is a bunch of crap. I'm telling you it's a setup."

Williams stopped speaking when his attorney put a hand on his forearm and got to his feet.

"If it please the board, my name is Jason Snelling, and I have been appointed to represent Mr. Williams. I ask that you excuse my client, who is understandably upset by recent events. He finds himself in the middle of a maelstrom, accused as the perpetrator of a heinous crime. We are going to enter a plea of not guilty to all charges. In addition, and with all due respect to this board, I must also tell you that we object to the manner in which it has been constituted."

"What is your objection, Lieutenant?" Blaylock asked.

"Captain Barroni, is . . . was, forgive me, Captain, the master of the *Ocean Majestic*, the commercial liner that sank off our starboard quarter only hours ago, yet he is now sitting on a board of inquiry to determine whether the only suspect should be charged with that crime. Under such extraordinary circumstances I can't see how any man, let alone the captain of the very vessel that's been lost, could render an impartial decision."

"If the board please," Joel Kincaid said, rising to his feet, "there is ample precedent. Lieutenant Snelling is quite correct, these are extraordinary circumstances. And if this were a court-martial I would agree with him, but it's not. This is only a board of inquiry. There are no other senior officers present, nor is there a civilian authority to turn Mr. Williams over to. I suggest the board *can* make a decision to keep Mr. Williams in administrative detention, not only for his own good, but for the *safety* of the passengers and this crew. Anticipating the lieutenant's concern, I have taken the liberty of bringing along several cases that support this point. I have extra copies for the lieutenant and the board."

"Let me see what you've got," said Blaylock.

Kincaid handed Snelling a sheaf of papers, then approached the table and gave each of the captains a set. He also handed a copy to the law officer. Katherine later learned the man's name was Alan Cohen. Everyone waited while the board and Cohen read through them. The minutes ticked as Blaylock and Cardwell made notes on their pads. Barroni barely glanced at his. When he finished reading, he stacked them together in a single pile and turned them face down.

"I'm satisfied," he said.

Blaylock looked at him then turned to Seldon Cardwell.

"Captain?"

Cardwell nodded once. "Agreed."

"Does the law officer have anything to add?" he asked Cohen.

"Captain, I've read over the cases," said Cohen, pushing his glasses back onto the bridge of his nose. "None of them are exactly on point, but what it comes down to is a discretionary call on your part."

"Very well," said Blaylock. "Your objection is noted, Lieutenant. We will proceed with the inquiry. Call your first witness, Mr. Kincaid."

Williams gave a derisive snort, loud enough for everyone in the room to hear.

"I call Katherine Adams," said Kincaid.

Katherine got up and went to the witness chair. Even before her oath was administered, Snelling was on his feet again.

"If the board please, I would like to invoke the Rule of Sequestration."

"All right," said Blaylock. "Everyone who is going to give testimony today will have to step outside. There's another conference room directly across the hall where you can wait."

Delaney, Beth, Libby, LaRocca, Nelms, and a sailor Katherine recognized as the damage-control chief she had met earlier on the *Ocean Majestic* all got up and left the room. Kincaid waited until the door was closed before turning back to her.

"You are Katherine Adams?"

"Correct."

"And you were most recently a passenger on the *Ocean Majestic,* were you not, ma'am?"

"I was."

"Ms. Adams, would you tell the board where you reside?"

"Atlanta, Georgia."

"And what is your profession?"

"I'm an attorney."

"Are you in private practice, or do you work with a firm?"

"I'm a partner with the firm of Boyd, Simons, Levitt, and Adams."

"May I ask how long you've been with them?"

"It will be eight years this Christmas. Before that, I was with the United States Attorney's office in their criminal division."

"How long did you work there?" Captain Cardwell asked.

"Twelve years."

"Really? Why did you leave?"

"I got tired of the clientele and I was ready for a change," said Katherine. "I specialize in domestic relations now."

"Domestic relations?" asked Cardwell.

"Divorces, adoptions . . . things like that."

"Sounds like a pretty big change to me," he said, smiling at her.

"Not as big as you'd think."

For the next five minutes, at Kincaid's prompting, Katherine went through the details of her educational background and other boilerplate information, knowing they were just preliminaries to the real stuff. She didn't have long to wait.

"Now Ms. Adams, you and I have spoken about this case before, haven't we?"

"Yes, we have."

"Would it be correct to say that you and Mr. Williams have met each other prior to today?"

"Yes, it would."

"Please tell the board under what circumstances you met."

"I was one of the attorneys who prosecuted Bennett Williams and another man for arson and the bombing of an abortion clinic in Clayton, Georgia, approximately twenty years ago."

Seldon Cardwell, who was in the process of jotting down something on his pad, looked up sharply when Katherine made her statement. He turned and stared at Williams, who stared back at him. Cardwell pursed his lips and made another entry as Kincaid continued with his questions.

"Did that matter come to trial, Ms. Adams?"

"Yes, it did."

"Would you be good enough to tell the board the result?"

Before Katherine could answer, Snelling rose to his feet and made an objection.

"I recognize this is not a trial and the rules of evidence are relaxed. However, they have not ceased to exist. If Lieutenant Kincaid wants to introduce evidence of a prior conviction, there is a proper way to do it. What the lieutenant is asking Ms. Adams to testify to is pure hearsay, and it cannot be considered by this board at all."

Blaylock frowned and glanced at Barroni, who raised his eyebrows in response.

"What's the correct thing to do?" he asked Alan Cohen.

"The captain should ask Mr. Kincaid if he has any response to Mr. Snelling's objection."

Blaylock shook his head. "All right, Mr. Kincaid?"

"I do. The lieutenant is correct. This isn't a trial, and Ms. Adams *would* be testifying to hearsay. The proper way to introduce a prior conviction is to get a certified copy of it from the court, and then offer it into evidence. But as I pointed out earlier, we are not on land, and I can't just run down to the courthouse and pick up a copy of the papers. These are highly unusual circumstances. The board has the discretion to overrule a hearsay objection and consider the testimony for what it is worth. I suggest there is little danger of prejudice because you are men of long experience and no jury is present. As an alternative, we could suspend the hearing and communicate with the courts in Atlanta and ask them to fax a copy of the conviction to us."

"Do you want to suspend the hearing as Lieutenant Kincaid suggests, Mr. Snelling?" asked Blaylock.

"May I have a moment to speak with my client, Captain?"

"Certainly."

Snelling bent down and whispered something in Williams's ear. Williams shook his head and whispered back to him. They continued talking with each other for nearly a minute until Blaylock prompted, "Mr. Snelling?"

"Captain, neither my client nor I want to delay this inquiry. Therefore, subject to my objection we can proceed."

Blaylock looked at the law officer, who nodded.

"Very well. Ask your question again," said Blaylock.

Kincaid restated his question for Katherine.

"Mr. Williams entered a negotiated plea of guilty to a charge of aggravated arson. He was sentenced to a term of three to ten years in federal prison," Katherine told them.

"I see," said Kincaid. "Did you have further contact with Mr. Williams after the trial, Ms. Adams?"

"No. The next time I saw him was on the *Ocean Majestic*. That was two days ago, in the buffet. I forget the name of the deck, but it was the one on the top floor with the pool and the solarium."

Barroni smiled at Katherine's description of the ship having a top floor.

"Would you describe what you saw there for the board please?"

"Yes. My friend Elizabeth Doliver and I were having breakfast when we heard raised voices coming from a corner of the room. I looked up to see Ellis Stephens. He was having an argument with a man. I didn't recognize Mr. Williams right away. Eventually Mr. Stephens left, and Mr. Williams started to follow him."

"What happened then?"

"When Mr. Williams saw me, he seemed surprised. He took out a pair of sunglasses, put them on, and went out through the side door."

"Is that when you recognized him, ma'am?"

"No. I knew his face was familiar, but it didn't come to me until I was in the lifeboat."

For the next few minutes Katherine proceeded to recount what she did after the fire alarms went off. She told them about meeting Libby Stephens on the stairway and the reason she went back to check on Ellis. Then she told them what she saw in his cabin. All three captains leaned forward, listening intently.

"You actually saw gunshot wounds on this man?" asked Barroni.

"I did."

"Pardon me, Ms. Adams, but have you ever seen gunshot

wounds before? I mean, are you familiar with what they actually look like?" Seldon Cardwell asked.

"I've seen them. I worked several murder cases in the organized crime division while I was with the U.S. Attorney's office."

"You mentioned something about an empty attaché case," said Tiger Blaylock, looking down at his notes.

"Right."

"I'm confused. Why is that important?"

"I met Ellis Stephens during dinner on our first night out. And he was carrying that case. I saw him a number of times after that, and he always had it with him. He never let it out of his sight."

"Do you have any idea what was inside it?" asked Blaylock.

Katherine shook her head. "No. My guess is—"

"Objection," said Snelling. "Captain, I don't mind Ms. Adams testifying about things she actually saw or heard, but having her speculate as to what was inside a briefcase is improper."

Cohen swiveled around in his seat and nodded his agreement to Blaylock.

"It appears your objection is good, Lieutenant," said Blaylock. "Anything else, Mr. Kincaid?"

"That's all I have. Your witness," Kincaid said to Snelling.

Jason Snelling came around the defendant's table to bring himself closer to Katherine.

"Ms. Adams, being an attorney you understand what this proceeding is all about, so I'm going to skip the preliminaries. If there's anything I say that you're not clear on, stop me, and I'll rephrase the question, okay?"

"No problem."

"Now, as I understand it, two days ago you and your friend heard raised voices in one of the restaurants on the

Majestic, and those voices attracted your attention. You looked up, recognized the deceased and my client, though you didn't know who he was at the time. Is that correct?"

"Yes, it is."

"It would be fair to say that you have no idea what they were talking about, do you, Ms. Adams?"

"No, I didn't hear them."

"And it would also be true that you don't know what started the argument?"

"No, I don't."

"Now, the last time you and Mr. Williams had any contact was some twenty years ago, right?"

"Right," said Katherine.

"And he was sixteen years old then, wasn't he?"

"As best I can recall, yes."

"Ms. Adams, you testified earlier that you went to Ellis Stephens's cabin, found it locked, broke in, and saw that he was dead."

"Right."

"And you observed what you believed to be gunshot wounds to the deceased's chest and head?"

"Right," Katherine replied again.

"Following that, you noticed an empty attaché case lying on the floor."

"Correct."

"Now you certainly didn't see Bennett Williams shoot Ellis Stephens, did you?"

"No, I didn't."

"And you didn't see him remove anything from the attaché case?"

"No, I didn't."

"Because you have no idea what was in that case, do you, Ms. Adams?"

"No idea," Katherine agreed.

"In point of fact, it could have been completely empty, couldn't it?"

"I suppose that's possible," said Katherine. "I have no way of knowing what Ellis Stephens was carrying."

"It's also possible, assuming the contents of that case were valuable, Mr. Stephens might very well have delivered them to the ship's purser for safekeeping, isn't it?"

Katherine took a deep breath and rubbed the bridge of her nose with her fingers. Apart from her divorce, this was the first time she had ever been a witness in a legal proceeding. The experience was giving her a new perspective.

"He might have," she said. "He might also have sent them back to the States by carrier pigeon. I'll make it easy on you, counselor. I didn't see Bennett Williams shoot Ellis Stephens. I don't know what Ellis was carrying in his briefcase, and I don't know what their argument was about the other day. All I know is what I observed."

"Yet you're here accusing him of the destruction of a seven-hundred-million-dollar vessel and the murder of hundreds of innocent people."

"I'm not accusing your client of anything. I reported what I saw and what I know about Mr. Williams to the proper authorities. They're the ones who've decided to hold him, and quite frankly I think it's a great decision. I don't trust him any more now than I did twenty years ago. Got it?"

A slight smile appeared on Jason Snellings's face. There was a long pause before he answered.

"Got it. The witness is excused."

Seldon Cardwell looked at Captain Blaylock, who shook his head slightly and stretched in his seat.

THE NEXT witness was Libby Stephens. Her eyes were still red-rimmed when she took the stand. It appeared she was keeping herself under control only with some effort.

In response to Joel Kincaid's questions, she told them her husband had been carrying his research notes in his attaché case. She described in a general way what they were about and why Ellis was fearful of letting them out of his possession. She then went on to identify Bennett Williams as the man who had approached them at breakfast two days earlier with a business proposal from his company.

"Were you present when Mr. Williams and your husband discussed this proposal?" asked Blaylock.

"No, I excused myself and left the table. I always let Ellis handle those sort of things."

"I see. So you don't specifically know what Mr. Williams wanted?"

"We discussed it afterward, and Ellis told me."

Snelling of course objected on the grounds that any testimony Libby Stephens might give regarding what her husband said would be inadmissible. Blaylock listened carefully and took a moment to consult with Alan Cohen before he sustained the objection.

The only other thing Kincaid was able to get in during his examination was that Libby believed her husband was upset because news of his research had gotten out so quickly.

Beth Doliver told the board essentially the same story Katherine had. She confirmed everything up to the time Katherine left her to find Ellis.

She was followed by Ed Nelms, who testified about seeing Stephens's body and the gunshot wounds. He also told them about the fire hoses being slashed.

As the morning progressed, the board heard testimony from DeCharles, the *Roosevelt*'s damage-control chief, and Tony LaRocca. Both were in agreement the ship had been deliberately sabotaged.

When Joel Kincaid rested his case without calling

Delaney, Katherine was shocked. At first she thought he'd made a mistake and had simply forgotten him. She felt the color in her cheeks rise and leaned forward to mention it, when Kincaid turned and winked at her. That was when she realized he was holding Delaney back as a rebuttal witness.

Smart. He's leaving himself a last shot.

GIVEN BENNETT Williams's temperament and his earlier outburst, it was something of a surprise when Jason Snelling called him as a witness.

"Mr. Williams, let's just cut to the chase and let me ask you straight away, did you kill Ellis Stephens?"

"Absolutely not."

"Did you at any time enter Ellis Stephens's cabin and remove *anything* from his attaché case, sir?"

"No, I did not."

"Mr. Williams, did you have anything to do with sabotaging the *Ocean Majestic*?"

"Do you think I'm insane? Kill a man in the middle of the Atlantic Ocean, then set fire to the ship and kill myself, too? *No* . . . I had *nothing* to do with that at all. I was a passenger on that boat the same as everyone else."

"Ship," Snelling corrected.

"Ship . . . sorry."

"But in fact, you weren't a passenger on the *Majestic* like everyone else, were you?"

"Excuse me?"

"What I'm saying, Mr. Williams, is that you weren't on the *Ocean Majestic* for pleasure, were you?"

"Well . . . no," Williams replied, his eyebrows coming together.

"And you didn't just happen to run into Ellis Stephens. You were there on business. Wouldn't that be a true statement?"

Williams waited a few seconds before he answered. "Yes, I was there on business."

"And that business specifically involved Ellis Stephens, didn't it, sir?"

When Snelling asked his question, all three of the captains exchanged glances. Whatever he was trying to accomplish, it sounded more like a cross-examination than a direct.

"Yes," Williams answered.

"Would you mind telling the board whom you work for, Mr. Williams?"

"Gotchal Biomedical Technologies."

"How long have you worked for them?"

"A little over six years."

"What is your position with the company?"

"I'm the regional manager of their sales and marketing division. My group is in charge of new product development. When we heard about Dr. Stephens's breakthrough, the company sent me on the ship to see if we could make a deal with him."

"Why?"

"Well . . . over the last few years we've developed several genetic stem-cell products that we thought would do the trick for us, but for one reason or another, none of them panned out. Our most recent patent, R-380, has a great deal of promise, but even that's incomplete. This was an ideal opportunity to get a jump on the field. Dr. Stephens's work was the missing piece of the puzzle. It was all we needed to put us over the top."

"And did you make a deal with Ellis Stephens?"

"Unfortunately, no. We offered him a cash advance of fifty thousand dollars plus royalties, but he refused to consider it. That was on the first day of the cruise. In fact, Dr. Stephens got upset that we knew anything about his research at all. Under the circumstances, I decided not to push things further and waited until the next day, hoping that he would calm down. I tried speaking with him again at breakfast, but he flew off the handle. That's the argument she and her friend were talking about," Williams said, indicating Katherine and Beth.

"When you say fifty thousand dollars, do you mean you were willing to write Dr. Stephens a check in that amount in return for signing with your company?"

"I mean we were going to pay him fifty thousand dollars in cash. I was carrying it with me."

"I see," said Snelling. "Do you still have that money with you?"

Williams laughed to himself and shook his head.

"I wish. It's sitting at the bottom of the ocean. It was locked in my safe when the fire alarms went off. My company won't be happy, I can tell you that. They'll probably think I blew it gambling."

"But you didn't blow it gambling, did you, Mr. Williams?"

"No. I didn't blow it gambling."

"Mr. Williams, I want you to turn around and face the members of the board." Snelling waited for Williams to turn. "Look them straight in the face. I'm going to ask you again, did you kill Ellis Stephens?"

"No, I did not," Williams said, emphatically.

"Do you know anything about his murder?"

"No, I don't."

"Anything at all?"

"Nothing."

Snelling waited a few seconds for effect before turning to Captain Blaylock.

"That's all I have," he said.

Blaylock nodded and asked Joel Kincaid, "Do you have any more witnesses to call?"

"I have just one witness for rebuttal, if it please the board."

"None of this pleases the board," said Blaylock. "We'll take a ten-minute break and reconvene here at 1300 hours."

When the captains got up, Blaylock nodded to the guards at the back of the room. They came forward, waited for Bennett Williams to rise, and then escorted him out. Both attorneys, Ed Nelms, and DeCharles followed them. As soon as they were alone, Beth turned to Katherine.

"Where's John? How come that Kincaid guy didn't call him as a witness?"

Katherine held up a hand and looked over her shoulder before answering.

"He's going to call him when they return. That's what he meant when he said 'a rebuttal witness.'"

"Oh, I get it," said Beth. She slid closer to Katherine and lowered her voice. "Listen, K.J., do you really think Williams killed Ellis and then set fire to the ship? He comes off like an arrogant asshole, but—"

"John and Nelms searched his cabin and found a gun," Katherine whispered. "Williams also has scratch marks on his right arm."

"So?"

"John took some scrapings from under Ellis's fingernails when he examined his body. They've sent them to the lab for identification. We think it will come back as human skin."

"Do you mean Ellis scratched him?"

"If they had a struggle, there's a good chance of it," Katherine said. "The board's going to have a hard time letting him walk. Our problem is, we don't have a body to compare it to, or the bullets from the gun."

"Jeez," said Beth, "poor Ellis. I can't believe this has

happened." Tears began to fill her eyes. "He was such a nice guy, and Libby's so sweet. I was talking to her out in the hallway. Did you know this was their first vacation in years and they've got two kids in college? This whole thing stinks."

Katherine put an arm around Beth's shoulders and pulled her closer. Neither woman said anything for a while. They just sat there. Finally, Katherine took a deep breath and said, "It really does stink. The next time we go on vacation, I'm flying."

Beth looked at her and smiled, wiping the tears from her eyes with her sleeve. "I'm so sorry, K. J. I wanted this to be special for us. Something we'd always remember."

"We'll remember it, all right. It's not your fault."

"Do you want to go back?" asked Beth. "Nelms told me the company is sending two ships out to meet us."

"I can't think about that right now. We'll talk later. What do you know about Gotchal Biomedical? I've heard the name before, but I can't place it."

"They're a medium-size company with a dozen or so different products on the market. Natural immunization stuff, mostly. They try to design cells that will help the body's immune system fight liver disease and stuff like that. I met their president at a party last year. If I remember right, they're owned by a German conglomerate."

"Does Jack's company do business with them?"

Beth shook her head. "Nah, we're pill pushers and bedpan makers—they're into high-tech stuff."

Katherine thought for a second. "Do you believe Williams's testimony about wanting to pay Ellis fifty thousand dollars?"

"I don't know . . . probably. The first company to hold the patent on stem-cell technology won't be able to count the money they make."

Katherine shook her head.

"But to murder someone and then sink a ship, killing . . . God, I don't know how many people. It's just sick,"

"There are all kinds of sickos in the world, K.J. You ought to know that—you've dealt with enough of them."

Katherine did know.

"I guess," she said. She leaned back and looked up at the ceiling. "I miss my kids."

"I miss Jack," Beth said, resting her head on Katherine's shoulder.

They were still alone with their private thoughts when people began filing back into the room. After the captains took their seats, the guards escorted Williams in. Joel Kincaid was the last person to enter.

"All right, Mr. Kincaid," said Blaylock. "Before the break you indicated you wanted to call a rebuttal witness."

"Yes, sir," said Kincaid, getting to his feet. "I call Professor John Delaney."

Blaylock glanced at one of the guards at the back of the room and the man opened the door. Delaney entered and took the witness chair. Kincaid got through the preliminaries on his background and qualifications quickly and came right to the point.

"Now, Professor Delaney, would you tell us what the results of your examination were?"

"Certainly. I observed that Ellis Stephens, a white male in his mid-fifties, had been shot in the chest twice at close range and once in the head. You could tell the proximity of the wounds because there were powder burns present around two of them. Mr. Stephens was dead when we arrived."

Libby Stephens, who had come back into the hearing room with the others, was sitting in Katherine's row. When she heard what Delaney said she began crying again. Beth slid closer to her and put an arm around her shoulders. Bennett Williams twisted around in his seat and stared at them for a moment, his expression unreadable. He turned back around a second later. All three of the captains also paused at the interruption. Blaylock gestured for Kincaid to proceed.

"Professor, were there any other observations you made in the room?"

"There were. I saw an empty aluminum attaché case lying on the floor near the cabin window. Ms. Adams actually pointed it out to me. I also took the opportunity to examine Dr. Stephens's body closely. Based on the size of the entrance wounds, they appeared to have been made by a large-caliber handgun, probably a 9mm or a .38, but it would be impossible to say definitively without the bullets."

"I see. What else did you do while you were there?"

"I looked for anything of forensic significance. From the trail of blood I saw, it appeared that Dr. Stephens was shot shortly after he opened the door. The stains were just inside the room, near the entrance. My guess is there was a scuffle of some sort and whoever shot him dragged the body into the bathroom. This was obvious from the marks on the carpet.

"I also took scrapings from under the decedent's fingernails and recovered a white substance, which I placed in an envelope. I initialed it and turned it over to the lab here on the ship for identification."

"Do you have an opinion as to what that substance was, Professor?"

"My preliminary thought is that it was human skin, but the lab will have the final say."

"Is that the only way we can know, Mr. Delaney?"

"That's about it. Unless Mr. Williams wants to tell us where those scratch marks on his right arm came from."

"*Bullshit!*" Williams shouted, jumping to his feet. "I got these trying to stop a woman from climbing over the railing. You fuckin' people have already made up your minds. Why don't we just cut this whole farce short and you can make your decision now."

The guards at the back of the room came off the wall and started for him, but stopped when Tiger Blaylock held up his hand.

"Have a seat, Mr. Williams. No one has made up their mind about anything yet. That's why we're here. Quite frankly, these outbursts aren't doing your cause any good. A lot of people are dead, and a ship costing the better part of a billion dollars is at the bottom of the ocean. This is not a pleasant experience for anyone here today, so why don't you just sit down, be quiet, and let us finish what we've started."

Bennett Williams looked as if he was about to reply, but Blaylock cut him off before he could do so.

"The fact is, you're not in the Navy," the captain continued. "You're a civilian, as you pointed out earlier. And believe it or not, we're doing our best to protect your rights and follow the procedures available to us. You also happen to be a guest on this ship. So, if you're incapable of returning the same courtesies we're extending to you, I'll have you gagged and bound to your chair. Do I make myself clear, sir?"

Williams stood there, his chest rising and falling in time with his breathing. He locked eyes with Blaylock, who stared back at him, unblinking. After several seconds, Williams sat down again. Blaylock turned to Kincaid and nodded.

"Assuming you're correct and the substance you found *was* human skin, is there a way to identify who it came from?"

"There is," said Delaney. "A DNA test would have to be conducted. I spoke with the chief medical officer earlier. Unfortunately, you don't have the facilities here to do it."

"I see. Was that the extent of your investigation, Professor?"

"Actually, no. I decided to have a look around Mr. Williams's cabin and I found this little goody there."

Delaney reached under his chair and pulled the handgun, now sealed in a plastic bag, out of the pillowcase. He placed it on the table in front of Seldon Cardwell. The captain blinked in surprise and leaned back in his seat. At the head of the room, the security guard's mouth opened at the sight of the weapon. Katherine quickly glanced at Jason Snelling, whose face suddenly had gone pale. For a space of time no one spoke as Kincaid allowed the full impact of what had just happened to sink in.

"Professor, are you familiar with this weapon?"

"I am," Delaney answered. "It's a Taurus Millennium 9mm semi-automatic. The barrel is three and a quarter inches and it's built on a black polymer frame."

"You told us a little earlier that you believed Dr. Stephens was killed with a large-caliber handgun. Would this qualify?"

"Oh, yeah," Delaney said, looking straight at Bennett Williams.

BLAYLOCK GRANTED Snelling another recess to confer with his client, but the board's decision to hold Williams for prosecution was a foregone conclusion when they returned. Snelling made a last attempt to save his case by re-calling Williams as a witness and showing the reason he had brought a gun onboard the ship was for his protection due to the large amount of money he was carrying.

"Did you ever advise any of the officers you were carrying a gun in your luggage?" asked Barroni.

"No."

It all fell on deaf ears, and the board's vote to hold Williams was unanimous.

TWENTY-FIVE

Warren Wilkerson stood on the sidewalk outside NBC's studios watching the news on their television screens with about twenty other people. A streaming video was rerunning the story about Bennett Williams being held in connection with the *Ocean Majestic*'s sinking. For the last two days little else had dominated the news. People looked on with morbid fascination. The death toll was just shy of a thousand people.

In Washington, D.C., the president appeared on television and announced there would be a prayer service for the deceased in National Cathedral that Friday. He assured the country everything possible was being done to bring those responsible to justice. Within two days of the tragedy, senators and congressmen were calling for an investigation into how secure the shipping industry really was, as public outrage over the incident mounted.

People shook their heads at the unfolding events as more and more details came to light. Warren Wilkerson shook his head too, particularly when Ellis's name appeared on the screen as one of the deceased. It was a shame about Ellis, he thought. After a few minutes he continued along the street. When he got to Rockefeller Center he walked down the steps to the Sea Grill restaurant and asked for a seat in the corner. Though it was a pleasant summer day and there were plenty of tables outside, he wanted seclusion. A waiter appeared and took his drink order. Wilkerson waited.

At the table next to him were two men. They also had drinks, though their glasses were still full. Their salads had also not been touched. Neither spoke, but their eyes were alert, carefully watching patrons going in and out of the restaurant. Eventually, the man closest to Wilkerson called for their check. He paid in cash and left a fifteen percent tip on the table. Then he and his companion got up and left. Neither looked around as they walked out.

Wilkerson noticed the briefcase right away. But instead of calling to the men, he reached out, hooked his leg around it, and slid it under his own table. The case was quite heavy.

He was in no rush and ordered an appetizer consisting of black caviar and chopped egg on little pieces of toast. Caviar wasn't something he ate every day and he wasn't sure if he would like the taste, but he had always been curious about it. A television set over the restaurant's bar had a newscast showing the same videotape a passenger on the *Ocean Majestic* had taken. Wilkerson watched for a few seconds and glanced down. One of the sleeves on his suit had become a little frayed. He let out a long sigh and made a mental note to stop by Saks on the way home and order a new one. Then he picked up the briefcase and left the restaurant.

TWENTY-SIX

The *Ocean Explorer* arrived on station in the middle of the Atlantic in just over twenty-four hours to relieve the *Marie Star* and the *Theodore Roosevelt* of their passengers. Her sister ship, the *Meridian Princess*, was expected the following day. Delaney, Beth, and Katherine were in the last group to be transferred because the Italian authorities had asked them to come to Genoa to give testimony regarding the tragedy. They were told the entire process would take less than a week. The Italians supplemented their request with three international subpoenas. Once their testimony was concluded the cruise company promised to fly them home. The U.S. ambassador who conveyed the message made it clear that both the Italian and United States governments wanted their cooperation, so they had little choice but to agree.

Roughly sixty percent of the people who started the cruise took the *Explorer* back to Miami. Many of them had either lost loved ones or no longer had the heart to complete the vacation they had begun so hopefully three days earlier. The balance of the passengers elected to continue on with the *Meridian Princess* when she arrived. The *Theodore Roosevelt*'s crew did their best to be good hosts, but the recent disaster hung over the ship like a pall. When the *Marie Star* had transferred the last of her passengers to the aircraft carrier, she gave three long blasts of her whistle and got under way for Genoa.

The sudden influx of people made things so crowded on the *Roosevelt*, it caused the chief engineer to rearrange several planes in order to redistribute the surface weight more evenly. Everyone was managing as well as they could under the circumstances.

For her part, Katherine wanted to leave as soon as possible, but a ship-to-shore phone call with her children that Scott Wardlaw was kind enough to arrange eased her mind. It was the sheerest good luck when she phoned Alley's apartment, she also found her son James there. They were having dinner. Despite the harrowing experience, her daughter insisted she at least *try* to enjoy as much of the vacation as she could over the next few days. James agreed.

"If you're going to be stuck in Italy, Mom, you should make the most of it," Alley said. "You haven't had a real vacation in years."

"I'm not really in a party mood anymore."

"Besides," Alley continued, "Beth said you met a really cute guy."

"Beth?"

"She called us earlier and told us you'd probably want to come home the first chance you got."

"Beth Doliver called you?" said Katherine.

"It's supposed to be a secret," James told her over the extension. "Alley's right, though. You need to chill. We're all fine here, plus we're in the middle of exams now, so we couldn't hang out with you even if we wanted to."

"What about Zach?" asked Katherine. "I'm supposed to be home next week."

"Zach's fine," said James. "He got your e-mail and he's been following what happened on the news. He told Dad he'd be staying with him a few days longer."

"I can just imagine what your father and Kimberly said to that."

"Her name is *Kendra*," James chided.

"Whatever."

It was now the heart surgeon's fourth marriage and the various wives passing through his home were confusing. Being honest with herself, Katherine admitted the mistake might have been a trifle petty since she had never really tried to get them straight.

"Zach's turning into a tough little guy," James said, switching subjects. "I spoke to him on the phone last night and I asked if your staying longer would cause a problem. He told me everything was already worked out."

"Really?"

"Yep," Alley added. "I spoke with Dad, too, and he sounded . . . well, surprised. He told me Zach just marched into the kitchen and announced he was staying until you got back. Then he asked him if he could drive him to school a half-hour early on Monday."

"Wow," Katherine said, impressed at her sixteen-year-old. "What did Kim . . . uh, Kendra say?"

"Nothing," Alley told her. "I think they were both so taken aback by Zach's approach, they gave in without an argument. I mean it wasn't like they had a lot of choice considering you're still floating around on the ocean."

"I could be home in a couple of days. The hearing is only—"

"Stop worrying—we're fine," said Alley. "Zach's fine, too. If he wasn't, I'd leave school and get him. You know that."

"I know. Good for Zach . . . and good for you, too—the both of you."

"Right," said James, "Go ahead and have the time of your life. I know it's tough, but give it a try, okay?"

"I'll think about it. You said this was on the news?"

"Yeah, it's all over the place. They're saying you were instrumental in helping to get the guy responsible," James said.

"He's only a suspect right now."

Katherine sketched in the rest of the details for them. When the conversation was over she felt better for having talked with her children, although she wished she could have spoken with Zach, too. Afterward, she went to find Beth.

"Sneak," Katherine said, sitting down next to her friend.

Beth held up her hands defensively. "I only told them you'd probably want to turn around and go home. They're good kids."

"Did you speak with Zach as well?"

"Just for a few minutes," Beth said, taking a sip of her coffee. "I called Jack to let him know I was all right. He conferenced me down to the university and then to Atlanta. Listen, we don't really have a lot of choice in the matter anyway, so we might as well try and relax."

"That seems to be the consensus," Katherine said. "Just out of curiosity, what are we supposed to do once we get to Italy? All our clothes went down with the ship. Not to mention my Haskell jewelry . . . the son of a bitch. I really liked those pieces."

Beth nodded sympathetically.

Katherine continued, "And I hesitate to point out all your stuff is gone, too, unless you want to run around in these naval uniforms."

Beth glanced down at the T-shirt and jeans she was wearing and shrugged.

"I think I look pretty sexy," she said. "A pilot and an assistant crew chief both propositioned me yesterday."

"You're beautiful, but I'm serious, we—"

"Not to worry, I spoke with Ed Nelms this morning. Everybody's in the same position. The *Meridian* is the *Majestic*'s sister ship and the company's giving each passenger thirty-five hundred dollars to replace what we've lost. Anything we can't get onboard we can pick up in Portofino or Cannes."

"*Cannes?* Cannes costs a fortune . . . so does Portofino. We'll be lucky if we can buy a decent pair of stockings between us."

"Then we can go to Nice or Genoa. They've got great shopping there."

"You're unbelievable," said Katherine, shaking her head.

"I'm not going to let you run home, K. J. We started this goddam vacation together and we're going to finish it together, subpeonas or no subpeonas. Besides, rumor has it a certain law professor is staying, too."

Katherine blinked.

"John's staying?"

"Um-hmm."

"I've only seen him about five minutes since the hearing."

"Maybe he's playing hard to get," said Beth. "Where's he been? This coffee's good, by the way."

Katherine leaned forward and lowered her voice. "They've got him doing research on their computer. He's positive Williams wasn't acting alone."

"How come?"

"Because they brought back a few pieces of metal from the *Majestic*'s hull and examined them under a microscope. There were traces of nitrate and something called RDX, the same stuff they use to make plastic explosives. It would be nice to find out who sank the ship and why."

"Maybe you should let the authorities handle this, K. J."

"Why? We need to find out what really happened. We can't just let—"

"K. J. . . ."

"What?"

"This is me you're talking to, remember?"

"What do you mean?"

"You know exactly what I mean. You can't bring back those girls who Jenks killed, and you can't change what happened to the *Ocean Majestic*. Just let the authorities—"

"That has nothing to do with it," Katherine told her. "What happened was more than twenty years ago."

"And it's been inside you ever since. You were the one who lived."

"You're wrong."

"Am I?" Beth asked quietly.

"Absolutely . . . I don't know, maybe a little. I'm sure the psychiatrists would say there's a connection. They see connections in everything. The fact is I want to put Williams away for good this time, and make sure he never has the chance to hurt anyone again."

Beth took a deep breath and let it out.

"If Williams was working with other people, don't you see they could come after you next—or John, or even me, for that matter."

"We need to get to the bottom of this."

Beth remained unconvinced and shook her head in resignation.

"Exactly what *is* John looking for?"

"He wouldn't say. But it has something to do with the cruise company's records. He's being very mysterious about it."

"Which probably means he doesn't have the first clue and is just trying to impress you."

"I don't think John cares about impressing anybody. He's kind of a bulldog once he gets his teeth into something."

"Sounds kinky," said Beth, lifting her eyebrows theatrically.

Katherine pushed her away.

"What about Jack? Doesn't he want you to come home?"

"He's probably busy chasing Irene around her desk,"

"Who's Irene?"

"You know . . . his secretary." Beth illustrated by holding her hands in front of her chest.

Katherine frowned and thought for a second.

"Oh, you mean the one who's built like your life vest," she laughed. "You're not serious, are you?"

Beth smiled.

"No, Jack's a sweetheart. But he does want me to take some time and rest up. According to the ambassador we're not going anywhere for at least a week. When I told that to Jack, he arranged a corner suite for us at the Splendido."

"Really? said Katherine. "The one that looks over the harbor?"

"That's the one."

Katherine sighed. "I love Portofino. It's so beautiful, so serene. I haven't been there since my honeymoon."

"Then say yes."

"Yes."

Beth screamed and threw her arms around her.

BETH DOLIVER'S description of the *Meridian Princess* was accurate. Except for a few minor differences in color scheme and some lobby furniture, the ship was a virtual twin of the *Ocean Majestic*. The speed and efficiency at which the crew transferred the remaining passengers amazed Katherine. At the company's insistence, all of the *Majestic*'s original employees returned home on the *Explorer*. Whether this was for humanitarian reasons or due to the investigation wasn't clear. Judging from the heightened security and debriefing they all went through, Katherine assumed the latter. Two teams of six people sent by the cruise line had quietly interviewed all of the passengers by the time they arrived in Genoa. Officials from the United States consulate as well as from the Italian government met them in the main lobby and handed out new passports, replacing the old ones that had been lost when the ship went down. The *Majestic*'s original itinerary called for them to spend two days in Genoa, then head up the coast to Nice.

Gradually, the horror of what had happened began to fade and people returned to more normal routines. Father Kelley and Father Reynolds both elected to stay on. They held memorial services in the ship's theater for those who had been killed and counseled anyone who felt like talking. Katherine, Delaney, and Beth all attended the first service.

Bureaucracy, they soon learned, was much the same the world over. The ship had no sooner docked in Genoa than they were met by a government official who informed them that Italy's prime minister was trying to sort out which party representatives would sit on the investigative committee. He assured them a decision would be reached by the end of the week and recommended a number of restaurants and sights they might wish to take in during their stay.

While everyone waited for the Italians to get on with their hearings, conversations eventually returned to more mundane topics. However, the empty chairs in the dining room provided a stark reminder of the recent tragedy.

SANDWICHED BETWEEN France and Tuscany, the city of Genoa is more a commercial and industrial center than a tourist stop. Despite a large, impressive harbor and rolling hills, the city tends to be somewhat colorless compared with her more spectacular neighbors, Florence and Rome.

On their second day there, Katherine and Beth went for a stroll along the Via Cairoli, browsing the fashionable shops. John Delaney was with them. For the first hour they just wandered around and he managed to put up a

brave front; however, sometime during the second hour a
glaze settled over his eyes and he announced he was going to visit the aquarium. They promised to meet for dinner back at the ship.

Beth watched him depart in a taxi and said, "Men are
amazing. They can spend four hours traipsing around a
golf course or go on a ten-mile hike, but take 'em shopping
with you and they're as good as dead in no time."

Katherine giggled, slipped her arm through her
friend's, and they continued down the street toward the
Old City. Along the way she noticed three-quarters of the
population seemed to be driving or walking around with
cell phones attached to their heads. Even bicycle riders
were using them.

High up on a hill at the end of a narrow street sat one of
the city's more prominent buildings, the Castello d'Al-
bertis. Katherine remembered it from her her last trip. The
castle was now a museum surrounded by a park with rare
flowers and artificial caves. The original owner, a sea captain, had built it as a residence in the late 1800s complete
with something he labeled a Turkish room, that resembled
the cabin of his last ship. During her visit she and the heart
surgeon had taken a sightseeing tour. The guide told their
group that Genoa was the original home of Christopher
Columbus, who was born there in 1451. What he didn't say
was that Columbus left as soon as he got cab fare out of
town. She remembered the two maps on display in a glass
case and wondered how Columbus had ever managed to
find anything. One showed his anticipated route to Japan,
2,700 miles away to the west. Unfortunately, Japan was
12,200 miles away, with North and South America in between.

The women turned right at the end of the street and
entered the Piazza de Ferrari where they took a break at
a little café on the square. Katherine ordered a Campari

and sipped it slowly as she and Beth people-watched. It felt good to unwind. The center of the square was dominated by one of those large, bubbling bronze fountains Italians love so much. It was a mild day and a breeze blew through the water creating a mist in the air. Across the square was the old opera house that had been damaged by bombs during World War II. She and her husband had seen a production of *Don Giovanni* there. The acoustics were so poor, neither could understand the singers.

Once she and Beth had rested, they made their way to Via Garibaldi, a narrow cobblestone street often referred to as "the street of palaces." At one point many of Genoa's prominent families resided there, the most notable being Columbus, but Marco Polo had also lived on Via Garibaldi, as did Charles Dickens, Rubens, Flaubert, and Wagner.

They came upon an art gallery that had a painting by Canaletto on display. Its presence was a surprise for Katherine, because she'd seen posters and reproductions of it before. The artist's use of light and perspective never failed to amaze her. Oddly, it brought back memories of when she and the heart surgeon were first married. He had just begun his residency and money was tight—not poverty, but not far from it. As a young wife she had to watch every cent and occasionally skipped meals to make sure he had enough for himself. During her lunch hour she would go to the museum and sit and look at the Canalettos. Afterward, when the heart surgeon came home and asked her how her day had been, she would make up a story about meeting a friend for lunch and tell him how wonderful the meal was. Life was different then. She was different then. Katherine reflected on this as she stood in front of the shop window. Much of the trust she gave so freely was gone now along with her naïveté.

Her mind shifted back to the present and the painting in front of her. She studied it, wondering if Canaletto might have also been hungry when he painted it. There was no answer to that, and she and Beth continued to meander along the block. She thought about that painting several times during the day, with its cobblestone courtyard and muted colors. Though elegant, there was a loneliness about the scene. On the way back to the ship it came to her that Canaletto was probably hungry too, but in a different way.

KATHERINE STEPPED out of the bath, wrapped a towel around her, and padded over to the bed where the packages were stacked. One of the last places she and Beth had stopped was a fashionable lingerie shop, the Italian equivalent of Victoria's Secret. She dropped the towel, slipped on a matching pair of panties and bra, and stood there in shock. The bottom wasn't a thong, but it was so small it left almost nothing to the imagination.

She twisted around and looked over her shoulder in the mirror, checking to see if she might have put it on the wrong way.

No luck.

Damn. These look like a twelve-year-old could wear them. She checked the other panties and saw they all had the same cut.

No wonder there are so many Italians, she muttered.

She thought about calling Beth, but remembered her friend said she wanted to go to the business center and send some e-mails. Katherine finished getting dressed and went to knock on Delaney's door. To her surprise, he was still in his bathrobe.

"Hey, lazy bones. I thought you'd be dressed already."

"I'm in the midst of a crisis," he replied. "Come in."

Katherine stepped into the room, kissed him on the cheek, and sat on the edge of his bed.

"What's up?"

"After I left you, I stopped to pick up a few things I needed. I don't know what the deal is with these Italians, but I went to about five or six men's shops near the Piazza Corvetto, and I couldn't find a decent pair of boxers."

"Really?"

"Yeah."

"And?" Katherine asked, lifting her eyebrows.

Delaney hesitated, then walked over to the dresser, opened a drawer, and pulled out two pairs of the tiniest Speedo-type underwear she'd ever seen. One was black and the other was dark blue.

"Whoa," Katherine said, impressed.

"Exactly. How the hell am I supposed to go out in these? They look like something a teenage lifeguard would wear to Jones Beach."

"Hmm," Katherine said, "I don't know . . . they're pretty sexy and you've got a nice body. . . ."

"Aw, for chrissake, K. J., I'm forty-six. I've been wearing boxers since I was ten."

Katherine shrugged. "Not much choice. You could always go au naturel. It would be our little secret. Well . . . maybe 'little' isn't exactly the right word."

Delaney gave her a flat look.

"I won't tell a soul, John, I swear. C'mon, we need to head down to dinner."

Delaney stared at her for a few seconds, then marched into the bathroom with as much dignity as he could muster. He grabbed a pair of cream-colored trousers from the back of a chair and emerged a minute later wearing the pants and a loose-knit white shirt.

"*Very* nice," Katherine said, looking him up and down.

He mumbled something under his breath as he slipped his feet into a pair of brown loafers.

Katherine got up from the bed and put her arms around

his neck, bringing her lips close to his ear. "If you do a dance for me later, I'll put a dollar in your—"

"Let's go," he said.

His expression was so funny she had to bite her lower lip to keep from laughing, which wouldn't have helped the situation. It also didn't help when she pinched him on the butt as they were getting into the elevator and whispered, "Nice ass."

Delaney was so surprised he spun around nearly knocking down one of the other passengers. He mumbled an apology and glared at Katherine, who smiled back at him innocently.

"John, you really should be careful."

As THEY walked through the dining room toward their table, Katherine did her best to keep a straight face, but was not really succeeding. The corners of her mouth seemed to be twitching uncontrollably.

They said hi to Beth and sat down.

"One word about the Speedos and I'll personally throw you overboard," he said out of the corner of his mouth.

That was the straw that broke the camel's back. Katherine hurriedly got up and headed for the ladies' room, quivering with laughter.

"Everything okay?" Beth asked, when she returned.

"Oh, yeah," she said, wiping a tear from the corner of her eye. "My liner was just running. Everything all right with you?"

"Yep. I decided to call Jack instead of e-mailing him. He's been a little under the weather, but he said he was doing fine. Of course he always says that. He sends his regards, by the way. Are you going to Portofino with us tomorrow?" Beth asked Delaney. "K. J. and I are renting a car."

"If you've got the room. We're stuck here until Friday

and I'd like to see it. I was going to take a bus, but I'd rather hitch a ride with you guys."

"No problem," said Beth. "The agency told me we have an Alfa something. I only saw a photo, but it looked decent and it's got a big trunk . . . or maybe it was a hatchback. I don't know."

"I'm sure it'll be fine," Delaney said. "The ride is pretty short, from what I understand."

"Seventeen miles," Beth told him. "K. J. and I figured we'd spend a day there, then drive up the coast to Nice. How about you?"

"I hadn't given it much thought. I was pretty much going along with the program—until I met you, that is," Delaney said, nudging Katherine with his elbow. "I don't have a hotel. Do you think that will be a problem?"

"Not at this time of the year," said Beth. "We're staying at the Splendido."

They continued to make small talk throughout the meal. Delaney took part in it, though he seemed to be shifting about in his seat a little more than usual. Katherine had a good idea why, but wisely elected to keep any more comments to herself. Thankfully, Beth took the lead and kept the conversation going.

"So, have you found any more bad guys, John?" she asked.

"Not really. They hooked me into the cruise company's mainframe and I tried chasing down a few leads, like people having the same employers and similar addresses, but I came up with zilch. We even checked with C-4 manufacturers to see if any passengers' names showed up as customers. Nothing there either. It's frustrating, because I know that little creep couldn't have pulled off sinking the *Majestic* by himself. He definitely had help."

Katherine rubbed Delaney's arm affectionately and asked, "Did you get to see any financial records?"

"What do you mean?"

"I assume the people Williams worked for paid for his ticket. I'd be interested to see if they paid for any other passengers or even if they used the same travel agency."

Delaney stared at her for a second.

"That's good, K. J.," he said with frank admiration. "I don't know why I didn't think of it myself."

"Behind every great man . . ." Katherine said.

"There's an even greater woman," Beth added, finishing the sentence for her. The women gave each other a high-five for emphasis.

"Do you think whoever did it could be on this ship, too?" Beth asked, glancing around the dining room.

"It's possible," said Delaney. "But in all likelihood they took the other ship back home."

"I don't see why you can't let the police handle this," said Beth. "I don't want anyone else getting hurt."

Delaney shrugged.

"You might have a point. How about if I take you ladies dancing?"

"Uh-uh, three's company. You two kids head on. I'm going to curl up in bed with a good book."

"No," Katherine protested. "Come with us."

"Thanks, but I'm worn out. Be sure and play nicely."

She got up and gave Katherine a kiss on the forehead. Delaney got a kiss, too. He also got the message loud and clear when she leaned over and whispered in his ear, "If you hurt her, I'll kill you."

"Yes, ma'am," he whispered back.

Katherine watched her friend walk away.

"She's so awesome."

Delaney nodded in agreement.

"Yeah, I like her." He started to say something else and then stopped and looked at Katherine, his expression suddenly serious.

"Listen, K. J., I don't want to get between you two. You girls came on this vacation together. I'm pretty much a recent addition. Beth probably feels like she's a fifth wheel right now. Do you know what I'm saying?"

Katherine smiled. "That's pretty sensitive for a dinosaur."

"I have my moments."

"Don't have to worry about Beth Doliver. She's got no problem telling you what she thinks if something's bothering her. We talked it over this afternoon and she's fine with our seeing each other."

"You talked about me?" Delaney said, surprised.

"Well, of course we talked about you," Katherine said, pushing her chair back. "C'mon, take me dancing."

"Yeah, but still. . . ."

Delaney got up as well and took Katherine's hand as they walked through the dining room. He was pleasantly surprised when she stopped and kissed him.

"What's that for?"

"For being a dinosaur."

ON THE *Majestic* the adult nightclub had been called The Cavern. On the *Meridian Princess* its name was The Grotto. Katherine looked the décor over as they walked down a flight of rough-hewn stone stairs and decided there wasn't much difference between the two. Unlike most ships, which catered to teenage and twenty-something crowds, the *Meridian Princess* had set aside The Grotto for their "mature clientele," as a sign on the door suggested. There were two other nightclubs on the ship that played New Age music, rap, and something called techno-rave. Although The Grotto didn't offer any waltzes, their music was lively and up to speed. Just to keep everyone happy they threw in an occasional slow dance now and then. Katherine preferred the faster music, but it was a nice change of pace and she enjoyed holding Delaney and feeling his hard chest against hers. She also didn't object when his hand occasionally strayed from her waist to the top of her hips and made contact with her buttocks. He had a flat stomach and it felt good to run her hands up his solid back.

The management had spared no expense where atmosphere was concerned. The dance floor consisted of large, translucent squares that were constantly changing colors. Green laser beams crisscrossed the room, moving in time to the music, and every thirty minutes or so someone threw a switch on a dry-ice machine producing knee-deep fog. The effect was surreal when the lasers passed through it.

By his own admission, Delaney was not the most graceful of dance partners, but he made a reasonable effort for Katherine's sake. Katherine was a natural and followed his lead without difficulty, making the experience an easy one. The dance floor gradually grew more and more crowded and after two hours they found themselves perspiring and flushed. She couldn't remember when she had had such a good time. During a break she sat down at their table to wait while Delaney went for drinks. She watched him cross the dance floor, noticing a little hitch in his stride which made her giggle.

When their drinks were gone they decided to call it quits for the evening and walked back to his cabin together. She wasn't surprised when he invited her in nor when he kissed her, nor even when his hands started to roam.

"Hmm . . . I'm not the only one with a cute tush," he whispered in her ear.

Katherine started to reply, but the words were lost when he bent down and kissed the nape of her neck and then her throat. She put her arms around him, closed her eyes, and tilted her head back, suddenly conscious her heart was beating rapidly. After a few seconds their lips found each other's and her breathing quickened even further. It felt like the room was spinning, a wonderful, heady sensation that she hadn't experienced for a very long time.

Outside, the waters of the Mediterranean gently lapped against the sides of the ship, and the stars were diamonds in a black velvet sky. Katherine put her natural caution aside and went with the flow.

TWENTY-SEVEN

A long blast from the *Marie Star*'s whistle caused Adnan al-Jabbar to look up. It was followed by a low rumbling vibration he and his companion felt through the ship's decking.

"The anchor," said Jabbar. "We must be in Genoa."

Umar nodded once and stretched. He held his watch close to a battery-powered lantern and checked the time. It was 3:30 a.m. He had been cooped up in the ship's cargo hold with Jabbar for longer than he wished and was ready to leave. Umar disliked people who talked too much, and Jabbar was a talker. For the last two days the fool had kept up a constant stream of conversation. He complained about the Americans and their mortal insults. He complained that they showed no respect to Allah. He complained that Americans were an arrogant, immoral people who had too much money. Umar pretended to listen. He cared nothing about Allah nor did he care about the Americans. They were simply the means to an end. Political affiliations, like religious causes, only complicated things. His loyalty was to

money and what it could buy. In a few years the radical
Muslims would direct their vitriol toward the Russians, or
perhaps the Japanese. It really didn't matter, there would
always be groups to target.

Umar looked at his watch again. They would be coming soon. The third member of their team had failed to
rendezvous with them, but that didn't matter either. A
fifty percent split was preferable to a third. Perhaps the
man was dead. Theirs was a hard business. He glanced at
Adnan, who was still prattling on and on about what a
glorious victory they had achieved.

Overconfident fool, he thought. *If the Americans ever
become angry enough to act, they could wipe out Adnan's
native country in a single day and still have time to
purchase their big-screen televisions for their Sunday
football games. Adnan's fellow terrorists were pathetic,
no more than fleas who believed they could somehow control the dog.*

Two minutes later there was a tap at the container door.
A pause followed, then three more taps. Umar lifted the
bolt and cracked the door open. Seldon Cardwell helped
him slide it aside.

The *Marie Star*'s captain stepped into the room and kept
his voice down. "Most of the crew are asleep now. We only
have three men standing watch, and they're at the other end
of the ship. I've checked the pier and it's deserted too. If
you move quickly and quietly you'll be out of here in under
two minutes. These are for you."

Cardwell reached into the pocket of his coat, removed
two thick envelopes, and handed one to each man. Adnan
placed a hand over his heart, made a half-bow, and stuck
the envelope in his duffel bag. Umar opened his and began
flipping through the contents. Besides an airline ticket and
a passport, the envelope contained twenty thousand dollars
in cash. He also examined the passport for a moment. His

face showed no reaction as he read the handwritten note there.

"Very good," he said.

"And what of our companion?" asked Adnan. "Have you heard anything?"

"Unfortunately not," Cardwell replied. "He knew the risk when he took this assignment. You both need to get moving now. The gangplank is located at the third corridor. Good luck."

But Umar didn't leave. He reached into his jacket, fished out a package of cigarettes and stuck one in his mouth. He muttered a curse in Arabic when he patted his pockets for matches and couldn't find any.

Cardwell watched him with mounting impatience.

"Take this," he said, tossing his own lighter to Umar. "But wait until you're clear of the dock to light up."

Umar nodded and stuck the lighter in his pocket.

No one offered to shake hands.

With Adnan leading the way, Umar followed. They located the gangplank, checked to make sure everything was clear, and started down it. Once they reached the pier they headed straight for the parking lot. A late model Mercedes sat by itself against the rear fence. Umar went to the driver's side, reached under the rear wheel and found the keys. He then pushed the remote control button that released the trunk while Adnan went to the passenger door. It was still locked. He tapped on the roof of the car to get Umar's attention.

Umar pointed the remote control at the lock and pressed the button again. Nothing happened. The door remained locked. Muttering under his breath, he came around to Adnan's side.

"Move."

Adnan stepped aside and watched while Umar tried the key.

Still nothing.

"Let me," said Adnan.

Umar pursed his lips and handed the key to his companion.

Before Adnan could insert it into the lock a hand clamped over his mouth and yanked his head backward sharply. He felt a searing pain in the middle of his back. Adnan tried to scream as the knife slid upward into his body, puncturing his right lung. He felt it go in again a second time. Blood flooded into his lung, choking him, and his arms began to flail. Suddenly all the strength seemed to be draining from his legs. In desperation, he threw himself away from the car and spun around, reaching for Umar's throat. A thousand colored lights exploded before his eyes as Umar plunged the knife into Adnan's stomach and thrust upward, piercing his heart.

Umar released his hold of Adnan's shoulder and withdrew the knife as his companion collapsed to his knees. Their gazes locked. Umar took a step backward and watched impassively as Adnan fell over onto his side.

A flicker of understanding finally appeared in Adnan's eyes before they glazed over. Umar moved his foot away from the pool of blood seeping from his companion's body and stooped to open Adnan's duffel bag. He removed Adnan's passport along with the airline ticket. Placing both on the ground he used the cigarette lighter Cardwell had given him to burn them. In less than a minute, only ashes remained. Satisfied, he kicked them away, and slowly thumbed through the rest of the money in Adnan's envelope. When he was through he tucked it securely at the bottom of his own bag.

Better still.

It took some effort to drag Adnan's body to the edge of the pier. He pushed it in, then waited for several minutes until it slipped beneath the surface of the water. In the car

Umar found a Michelin roadmap in the glove compartment and studied it.

Once he located where Portofino was he started the engine.

TWENTY-EIGHT

At 10:30 a.m., Delaney, Beth, and Katherine packed the Alfa Romeo and set off for Portofino, taking the back roads instead of A12. The trip was scenic and mercifully short. Their car did have a good-sized trunk, as Beth had said, but its back seat was better suited to small children than a fully grown man—at least in Delaney's opinion. At six foot two he felt like a pretzel. The journey should have taken less than a half-hour. Unfortunately, Beth made a wrong turn and somehow managed to wind up in the town of La Spezia.

In deference to Delaney, they decided to take a break and explore the town's twisting old streets. It was a charming place set amid Italy's rocky western coastline. They wandered for an hour and eventually stopped at the Trattoria Lanterna for lunch and directions. The waiter, whose English was nearly as bad as their Italian, listened to their request politely and shrugged elaborately. He returned a minute later with the restaurant's owner.

"Is no problem, signora," said the owner. "Unfortunately, you can no get there from here."

"What do you mean you can't get there from here?" asked Katherine.

"No, no . . . is no possible from this road."

"Well, what road do we take?" asked Delaney.

The owner thought for a moment and translated the

question for the waiter. Another man, seated at a nearby table, joined in the discussion uninvited. But instead of providing an answer, they began arguing among themselves while Beth, Katherine, and Delaney waited. They exchanged glances, waiting for the argument to subside, which it did not. It grew more heated. Delaney finally had enough, tossed a few euros on the table, and motioned for the women to follow him. They slipped past the men, who were still arguing loudly when they left.

"Can't get there from here," Katherine grumbled to herself as they approached the car. Beth spread a map out on the hood and studied it. After two minutes of turning it one way and then the other, she let out an exasperated breath and handed it to Delaney.

"You drive," she said. "This doesn't make any sense. It's an approximation of where things *used* to be. The bridge we're supposed to take should be over there, but it's not, plus there's another one a half mile down the road that's not even listed."

THE RESTAURANT owner was partially correct. It wasn't impossible to get to Portofino, only difficult. En route they managed to visit the towns of Lerici and Rapallo before finally arriving at their destination. Like most resorts along Italy's northwest coast, Portofino reminds one of a picture postcard, sitting at the base of three steep tree-covered hills, with a magnificent harbor in front. Once an ancient fishing village, the town spreads out in an S-curve along the water. The remarkable Hotel Splendido where they were staying overlooked the scene from high atop a hill. Delaney had the good sense to call ahead when they were in La Spezia and make a reservation for himself. Apart from the price, which nearly took his breath away, he decided the place was all right. It was mid-afternoon by the time they checked in.

Definitely not worth six hundred bucks a night, but it'll do, he thought. *Thank God we're only staying one day.*

The bellman put his suitcase on a metal rack and opened a set of double doors onto a small balcony. A swimming pool, complete with a blonde and a redhead sunbathing topless, was two floors below. Delaney stood there admiring the view for a few seconds before he realized the bellman was waiting for his tip.

"Oh, sorry, pal," he said, reaching into his pocket. "Lost my train of thought there for a second."

"No problem, signore. *Grazie*. Enjoy your stay. If you need anything, please feel free to call me. My name is Benito."

"Will do."

Wind gently moved the purple bougainvillea hanging over the balcony. Far below in the town, Delaney could see the homes and buildings along the harbor, their shades of yellow, white, red, and orange faded from years of exposure to the elements. On the water a number of pleasure craft, ranging from sailboats to yachts, drifted lazily by. Tourist season was already in full swing judging from the crowds who strolled along the quay. He breathed in the salt air and folded his arms across his chest.

"Beautiful," he said to himself.

He tried to picture what the town would be like without all the people, just walking along and holding Katherine's hand. The image brought a smile to his face. Last night they had almost gone to bed together. But for some reason she had demurred, though only just. He was certain about that. He wanted to make love to her. In fact, he wanted to make love to her more than anything, but he knew better than to try to push, particularly with a girl like K. J. Her sudden change of mind was a little disturbing and the cold shower he took later had helped.

A tap on the door brought him out of his reverie.

"Just a minute."

When he opened the door, Katherine was standing there. She had changed into a yellow sundress that made her look like a college girl. Her hair was tied back in a ponytail that nearly reached her shoulders.

"Hi," he said. "You got ready in a hurry. Where's Beth?"

"She's waiting down in the lobby. I thought you might like to join us for some exploring. I promise no shopping and I'll even buy you a gelato."

"What's that?"

"It's Italian ice cream. It comes in about a hundred flavors and it's better than the American kind—no calories."

"No calories, huh?" said Delaney. "Two good-looking gals and no calories. A guy can't lose."

Katherine gave him a hug and they went downstairs to collect Beth, who was talking to the concierge.

Beth said, "Armand was just telling me most of the antique stores are in Genoa, but they have a few good ones here, too. He gave me a map of the town with everything marked. Isn't this exciting?"

"I'm beside myself," Delaney said dully.

Beth gave him a funny look.

"I promised to buy John a gelato," Katherine said, giving him a quick glance.

"Ooh, that sounds good," said Beth. "Let's head down to the harbor. I'm sure we can find a place there."

The tourists were increasing in number and the harbor wasn't much better. It was crowded with small fishing boats and yachts, some more than a hundred feet long. Earlier that day, two cruise ships had dropped anchor, depositing more than two thousand people on Portofino.

So much for a relaxing stroll in a quiet fishing village, Delaney thought. But, rather than dampening the women's enthusiasm, he kept it to himself and went along with the program.

Beth's prediction about a gelato shop was correct. They located one on the first street they came to. At her urging, Delaney tried the tiramisu flavor. He took a tentative lick and raised his eyebrows.

"Pretty good," he said.

She gave him a wink.

Portofino's streets were narrow and uneven. Delaney listened to Beth and Katherine's conversation as they walked. Beth covered a great many topics: people, places, the economy, and northern Italy in general. She knew a lot about a lot of things. He didn't participate because it was much more interesting to listen. They spent the next hour seeing what the town had to offer, which turned out to be the usual collection of tourist merchandise. The two antique shops weren't much better, and even Beth was willing to concede defeat after a while.

"I remember it being nicer that this," she said.

"I guess things changed," said Katherine. "It is picturesque though."

Beth sighed. "I'm ready to head back to the hotel. The concierge told me they serve tea and hors d'oeuvres at four o'clock."

"Sounds good to me," said Delaney.

"Me too," Katherine agreed.

At the end of the harbor they turned onto Viale Baratta and started back up a tree-lined hill. It was fairly steep and the temperature was in the mid-eighties. When they came to an opening that afforded a good view of the town, Beth insisted they stop so she could take a video.

"Move to your left a little," she said, gesturing with her hand. "I want to get the ships in."

Katherine and Delaney obliged.

"What should we do?" Delaney asked.

"I dunno, wave or something. Look like you're on vacation."

Katherine and Delaney waved.

"That'll come out really good," Beth told them. "Now why don't you take some of K. J. and—"

Delaney heard the car's engine before he saw it. His head came around sharply in the direction of the noise. A split second later, a black Mercedes came tearing over the crest of the hill directly at Beth, who appeared to be frozen in place.

Katherine screamed.

Only a last-second lunge by Delaney saved her life. There was a loud crack as the car made impact with something. Beth was knocked to the pavement. The car's front tire hit the curb before it swerved back onto the road. It continued to the bottom of the hill and came to a screeching halt. No one got out.

Delaney started after it, but he got only a few steps before the driver gunned the engine again and sped off up a side street.

Katherine had her arm around Beth's shoulders. She was shaken, but except for a bruise on her left cheek she appeared all right. There was another bruise on her knee and her blouse was torn at the neck. The camcorder lay on the ground in pieces along with parts of the car's side mirror.

"Are you okay?" asked Delaney, stooping down next to them.

"I think so," Beth said, rubbing her arm. "The sonofabitch hit my wrist."

When she started to get up Delaney put a hand on her shoulder.

"Slow, slow," he said. "Let's have a look at you first."

A man and a woman coming down the street ran over to help them.

"We saw the whole thing," the man said. "Are you hurt?"

"I'm fine," Beth said. "Let me up."

Delaney and the man helped her to her feet.

"We saw the whole thing," the woman said. "That moron could have killed you. I can't believe he drove off like that. Do you want us to call a doctor?"

Beth shook her head as Delaney checked her wrist with his fingers.

"Did anyone catch the license plate?" he asked.

"No, he was moving too fast," the man said.

"There's nothing broken," Delaney told Beth. "How are you doing?"

Beth started to answer, but changed her mind and looked down the block where the car had disappeared. *"Asshole!"* she shouted.

"Can I call someone for you?" the man asked, taking out his cell phone.

"No, I'll be all right, thank you. I'm more mad than hurt right now. That bastard broke my camera and I just got it the other day."

"Forget the camera," said Katherine. "You're lucky you're alive."

Beth walked over to where the pieces lay. She picked them up and stared at them for a second, then tossed them over the side of the hill.

"Brother, this is some vacation," she said. "Let's get back. I need to clean up."

She thanked the man and woman again and assured everyone that she could walk back to the hotel under her own power.

TWENTY-NINE

Katherine went to the room with Beth in case she need anything while Delaney reported what had happened to the hotel manager, who was shocked. He then went to the bar to wait for them. A half-hour later, the women came down again and joined him. Beth's bruise had begun to darken and she was walking with a slight limp. As a result of some carefully applied makeup, the mark on her face was less obvious, though it still looked painful.

"Don't say anything," Beth said, noticing Delaney's glance. She and Katherine sat down. "Right now all I want is a good stiff drink."

"How are you feeling?"

"I'm okay. It'll take more than a couple of bumps to finish me. I'm tough."

Delaney smiled.

"Beth was on the field hockey team in college," said Katherine.

"Impressive. I took the liberty of ordering some of those little sandwiches for us; they should be here in a minute. You want to go to the police and report what happened?"

"I guess. Do you think it will do any good?"

"Probably not . . . unless they get lucky and stumble across the car. I doubt whoever was driving will hang around. He's probably in Genoa by now."

"Figures," said Beth. "I suppose I can make an insurance claim for the camera, but I'd love to get that bastard."

"Here come the sandwiches," said Katherine, seeing the waiter approaching them. He was balancing three plates on one arm and carrying a bottle of wine under the other.

"And the assistant manager," Delaney added.

"*Perdono, signora,*" the assistant manager said to Beth, handing her a piece of paper. "There was a phone call for you earlier."

"Oh, thanks."

"*Prego.*"

Beth opened the paper and her eyebrows came together as she read the message. "It's from Jack's secretary. 'Please call right away,' she says. Great. This was two hours ago."

"My apologies," said the manager. "The young lady who took it left for the day. I just noticed it in your box and thought you might wish to see it. The lobby phone is available in the corner."

"No problem," Beth told him. "Thanks, again."

"My pleasure." The assistant manager made a small bow and returned to the front desk.

Beth winced as she got up. "I guess I'd better call. The place might be on fire."

Katherine watched her friend walk away. "Beth's a rock. Nothing bothers her."

"Yeah, she seems like a neat lady. I take it you guys have been friends for a long time."

"Since our freshman year in college."

"That would qualify as a long time."

"It's not *that* long," Katherine said, poking him in the ribs.

This was the perfect opportunity to tell him about her past and the attack on her and how it had affected her life. She found that she was caring more and more for John as each day went by. He had an irresistible smile and it felt good to be around him in a way she couldn't quite articulate. But she didn't want anything to spoil what was growing between them. Twice she found herself approaching the topic and twice she pulled back, afraid it might push him away. She ended up angry at herself for being a coward.

"Did you ever find out if any of the *Majestic*'s passengers purchased C-4?" she asked instead.

"I left my cell phone number with the ship's computer guy. He promised to call if they turned up anything. They're also cross-checking the credit cards and payment records like you suggested, along with any C-4 purchases that might have been made in the last year."

Katherine opened her mouth to reply, but stopped when she saw Beth's expression from across the room.

"What's up?" asked Delaney.

"I don't know. She doesn't look right. I'd better go see if something's wrong."

"Want me to come?"

"No. I'll be right back."

Beth hung up the phone. Even from where he was sitting, Delaney could see that she was upset. The women exchanged a few words, then hugged each other.

"Aw, Jesus, *what now?*"

Beth didn't return to their table. She headed directly for the stairs. Delaney pushed back his chair and went to Katherine.

"We just got some bad news. Jack had a heart attack earlier this morning. He's in the hospital."

"Is he okay?"

"I don't know," said Katherine. "She spoke to Jack's office, but they don't have any news yet. She went upstairs to call Columbia Presbyterian."

Delaney shook his head. "Is there anything I can do? How's Beth taking it?"

"Not good. Whichever way it turns out, I'm sure she'll want to head home immediately."

"Absolutely," Delaney agreed. "Just let me know when we need to leave."

"You're sweet, John. Let's meet in your room in a few minutes. I want to give her some privacy."

BETH KNOCKED on Delaney's door ten minutes later. When she came in, it was obvious she'd been crying. Her mascara was smeared and her eyes were red.

"Jack's okay," she told them. "He did have a heart attack, but it was a mild one. I spoke to him for a few minutes and he sounded fine, but . . ."

"But?" said Katherine.

"K.J., I've gotta leave. Jack doesn't want me to, but there's no way I can stay here while he's in the hospital."

"Of course," said Katherine. "John and I were just discussing it. Do you want me to call the airport and see about reservations?"

"I already called them. Genoa's last flight leaves in forty-five minutes, so that's out. Air France has a flight from Nice at 8:20 p.m. That's a little less than four hours from now. According to the desk clerk, there's a train from Rapallo that leaves at 5:05 p.m. If I move, I can just make it. I'll have to call the U.S. consulate and square it with the Italian authorities."

"Don't worry, I'll take care of everything," said Katherine.

"How far is it to Nice?" Delaney asked.

"About a hundred and thirty miles," Beth told him.

He thought for a second, then reached for the phone.

"Hey . . . this is John Delaney in Room 312. Would you have the valet bring our car around right away, please?"

"John—"

"K.J. and I will drive you."

"But—"

"You're not taking a train and that's that."

"Did you check if the plane has two seats available?" asked Katherine.

"You don't have to come with me, K. J. I'll be fine."

"It's not a matter of your being fine. You wouldn't leave me, and I'm not leaving you."

Their car was waiting outside the lobby. Delaney tossed Beth's suitcase in the trunk and got behind the wheel. He guided the Alfa down the steep hill and onto Via San Michele. Like most cars in Europe it was equipped with a stick shift and he found himself continuously changing gears along the narrow streets. When they reached the A12, he slid the car into fifth and accelerated smoothly into the traffic pattern. Katherine had had the good sense to get directions from the concierge and was acting as navigator. She routed them through Genoa onto the E80 and then onto Autoroute 8. Eventually, Italian road signs gave way to French. Everything was clearly marked so they had no difficulty finding the airport in Nice. Delaney kept the car moving at a solid 100 k.p.h. and managed the trip in just under two hours.

The discussion about whether Katherine would accompany her friend back continued during the ride. Katherine wanted to go and Beth was against it. Delaney listened, but expressed no opinion. He knew her leaving was probably the right thing to do and was relieved when he found out it wouldn't be possible. The plane only had one seat left. The news made him feel both good and bad at the same time, and he ended up irritated with himself for being selfish.

They walked Beth to the terminal, made sure that she got her ticket, and helped check her bag. They kissed good-bye at the gate and Beth promised to call as soon as she knew more about Jack's condition. Katherine refused to leave until the plane took off.

"WOULD YOU like to get a bite to eat?" Delaney asked, as they headed back to the car.

"Sure. You must be starving."

"I could do with a little something."

She slipped her arm around his waist and hugged him.

"Thanks for everything, John," she said softly resting her face against his chest.

He kissed her on the top of her head.

The airport was only four miles from the center of town and Katherine suggested they leave their car with the valet at the Hotel Negresco.

"How, if we're not staying there?" Doug asked.

"They won't mind."

"Are you sure?"

"The people at the Negresco are such snobs they figure no one who isn't a guest would have the gall to leave a car there. Just tell whoever takes it to keep it out front. A five-euro tip usually helps."

Delaney chuckled.

"You're an amazing woman, Katherine Adams, but when they come to take you away, don't ask me to bail you out. I'm just a simple hometown boy."

"You're the one driving," she pointed out.

"Great—I'm an accessory."

As Katherine predicted, the valet at the Negresco opened the door and listened politely to Delaney's request, then smoothly accepted five euros without the slightest hesitation. They walked around the corner to Rue de France, a lovely old street with dozens of restaurants stretching from one end to the other. Like most European streets, it had a tendency to change names every few blocks, becoming Rue Massena and then Rue Giofreddo—all in the space of about two hundred yards. The cop part of Delaney picked up on this. The third time they passed a lamppost with yet another name on it, he came to a halt and looked up and down the street. It was all the same as far as he could see. He shook his head. If the French wanted to give each street a new name, who was he to argue?

They found a little restaurant with the prices clearly marked on a menu in the window and ate dinner outside. Katherine ordered a glass of white wine and he ordered a beer with his meal. While they were waiting for their food to arrive, Delaney picked up an English newspaper someone had left on the next table and glanced at it.

"The French always have the best crime stories," he said.

"How come?"

"I'm not sure, but they read like novels. I worked a case with the Parisian police once and got hooked on them. The bad part is that you have to read the first installment to know what's going on. They don't provide summaries like we do in the States."

When they were through with dinner they walked some more and looked in closed shop windows before strolling back along the Promenade Anglais to the hotel. Despite the fact that it was 10:00 p.m., plenty of people were out.

The wind off the bay began to freshen, bringing a watery fog with it. People moved in and out of the street-lamps' yellow light, turning the promenade into an old painting. Delaney took off his jacket and slipped it around Katherine's shoulders.

"You've been pretty quiet for the last hour," he said. "Everything all right?"

"I'm just worried about Beth, that's all."

"She'll be fine," he said, trying to reassure her. "It sounds like her husband will be, too. I've got a neurologist buddy who works at Presbyterian. If you like, I can call and check on how he's doing."

"That would be really nice. Jack's a good man and he's

good to Beth. You'd have to be discreet about it—I wouldn't want them to think we're prying."

"We are."

"I know. But I don't want them to think it."

Delaney was positive there was some type of distinction there, but he decided not to press the issue and simply said, "Right."

Their car was waiting for them. So was the valet who drove it all of fifteen feet from a parking space near the entrance to the front door. He opened Delaney's door (Katherine let herself in) and discreetly looked the other way while Delaney fished around in his wallet for a tip. This time he handed the man one euro. The valet glanced at it, raised a disdainful eyebrow, and wished them a good night.

"If I'm ever reincarnated, I'm coming back as a valet at this place," Delaney said, as he put the car in gear.

The return trip was more leisurely due to the wet road conditions and fog. A brief moment of awkwardness came and went when they kissed good night outside Katherine's door. They were both exhausted and promised to see each other at breakfast.

KATHERINE AWOKE at 6:00 a.m. the next morning. Throughout the night the fog continued moving up the coast, enveloping the tiny fishing village. Instead of seeing a crystal blue ocean and green tree-covered hills, she opened her balcony doors to find a world of white and gray.

Yuck, she thought, closing the doors again. She considered waking Delaney and inviting him to go for a run with her, but wasn't sure if he would appreciate it, given the early hour. She decided to let him sleep, pulled on pair of shorts, a T-shirt, and the running shoes she'd bought in Genoa, and went downstairs for breakfast.

Coffee first.

A waiter was busy putting out place settings when Katherine poked her head in the restaurant and asked if it was open. He motioned for her to come in and take a seat.

"*Buongiorno, signora.* Would you care for some coffee? Juice, perhaps?"

"Good morning. Coffee would be fine—black with a little sugar, please."

"And to eat?"

"If you have any fresh fruit, that would be wonderful."

"We just got some melon—very delicious. I had some a while ago."

"That sounds great."

The waiter went into the kitchen and came back a few minutes later with a bowl of cut up melon chunks and a cup of espresso. Katherine examined the espresso with a frown.

"Excuse me. I asked for coffee."

"*Sì*, this is coffee."

"I believe it's espresso."

"Ah . . . you wanted the American coffee, yes?"

"Exactly, do you have that?"

"No. I'm so sorry."

"Oh."

"When in Rome you must do as the Romans do, *si*?"

"This is Portofino."

"Is the same. Please . . . try it. I promise you love it."

Katherine took a deep breath. "All right."

"*Prego.*"

The waiter bowed and left. After a few seconds, Katherine screwed up her courage, and took a sip. The coffee wasn't bad—it was awful. Worse, it had the consistency of mud. She put the cup back down and pushed it away. From the kitchen's doorway the waiter glanced back and smiled at her, obviously pleased she was making an attempt. Katherine responded with a weak smile.

But the moment he turned his back, she snatched up the cup and dumped the contents into a potted ficus plant near her table.

"Sorry, fella," she whispered to the plant. "It's you or me."

The ficus didn't reply, which was just as well.

Seated in a corner of the room, Umar Maharan, late of the luxury liner *Ocean Majestic* and more recently the cargo vessel *Marie Star*, watched her impassively. Despite an open newspaper in front of him, all of his attention was concentrated on Katherine Adams, his black eyes devoid of emotion. It was much the same way a leopard might regard its prey.

Patience, he said to himself.

Maharan glanced out the window at the fog-shrouded town as the ghost of a smile touched the corners of his mouth.

Patience. This will be interesting.

Nearly fifteen minutes passed before the American woman finished eating and got up. Without waiting for his check, Umar placed a few euros on the table and followed her outside, his fingers closing around the knife concealed in his jacket pocket.

Maharan was dressed in a black Windbreaker, tan pants, and a conservative blue shirt and could have easily passed for any of the tourists visiting Portofino that summer. Waiting until Katherine was a reasonable distance in front of him, he began to follow. He was not perturbed when she broke into a light run and disappeared in the fog. From the map he had studied he was aware the town had only one main street. There were few places for her to go.

She will return this way eventually, he thought, pleased at his good fortune.

Despite the holiday season, Portofino's streets were quiet at that hour of the morning.

Better and better, he thought, quickening his pace. *Run all you wish, lady.*

His knife had a five-inch blade and was made of Solingen steel, the same one he had used to kill Adnan. By rights he should have been in Syria by now, but there were loose ends to tie up, or so his employer had told him. It was regrettable the man wasn't with her. He would deal with him later, when the time was right.

Katherine was partway down the hill when she heard the scrape of a boot on the pavement behind her. Out of reflex she turned and glanced over her shoulder. It was not quite 7:00 a.m. yet and all the really sensible people were still in bed. She came to a halt, paused for a second or two squinting into the fog.

Nothing.

For a moment she thought about waiting for the weather to clear, but rejected the idea. It had been three days since she'd last exercised and middle age wasn't going to win the battle without a fight. *Besides*, she thought, *there's something romantic about running in the fog.* It reminded her of one of those old black-and-white movies. *Casablanca* maybe. Pulling a deep breath of air into her lungs she resumed her run. At the bottom of the hill she increased her pace, falling into an easy rhythm. Her body began to warm as blood flowed more quickly to her arms and limbs. It felt good to exercise. Faded yellow and orange buildings appeared and disappeared in the fog. Most were about four stories high. To her left she could hear the rumble of boat engines in the harbor, and occasionally she spotted a few tall black masts moving back and forth on the water. The air tasted of salt. Several merchants were out lowering their shop awnings, as they got ready for the day.

When she reached the main plaza she slowed to a walk, wiping the perspiration from her forehead. An old woman was busy sweeping the street. Katherine smiled at her and she waved back. One or two other people were also out. The fog closed in behind them after a few yards. Except for the slosh of water against the boats and an occasional creak of the rigging, everything seemed quiet and still in the early morning air—until she heard the footfall again. When Katherine turned around, the footsteps halted. She waited for a few seconds, but no one appeared.

You're jumping at ghosts, she said to herself, as she started walking once more.

Portofino had grown up at the base of the Ligurian foothills in Italy's extreme northwestern section. "The top of the boot" as locals called it. It has a number of streets, but only one main road which winds along the harbor. She shook off a feeling of disquiet and quickened her pace. The sounds she heard were definitely footsteps and it was odd that they stopped when she did.

Occasionally the dense fog parted long enough to give her a glimpse of the harbor and the boats.

Conscious she wasn't alone, Katherine began listening more carefully. Someone was definitely behind her. She couldn't tell how far back they were, but there was no question in her mind now. After another twenty yards she stopped abruptly and spun around, thinking it might be Delaney.

He's the only one who knows I'm here and if this is his idea of a joke, I'll . . .

To her surprise, the footsteps didn't stop this time; they quickened and began coming toward her. Suddenly the fog lost a great deal of its charm. Instinct took over. Katherine ran. Her heart was pounding heavily in her chest by the time she reached the end of the street. The footsteps were still coming—only faster. To the right was a path and she made for it without hesitation. Asphalt soon gave way to hard-packed dirt. In less than fifty yards, bushes and trees began to appear. She was on a narrow trail in a forest with no idea where she was going.

In the back of her mind she vaguely recalled something about an old abandoned castle a German baron had once built on the cliffs above the town. She squinted into the mist, trying to get a sense of direction, but in the low light the trees only appeared as shadowy shapes flashing past her. The sound of a snapping branch told her whoever was back there was much closer now. Katherine clenched her teeth and accelerated to full speed. Branches whipped at her arms and legs and tree roots reached out threatening to grab her ankles.

Another glance over her shoulder. Visibility was less than fifteen yards and, in the stillness, the sound of her own feet striking the ground seemed unnaturally loud.

All at once the forest floor changed again. The path split off to the right and vanished into a copse of trees. To her left was a gravel walkway that ended at a series of stone steps. Katherine took the steps two at a time. She came out atop a broad cobblestone terrace at the base of the castle. Thick reddish walls loomed above her. Another set of stairs led up to the main entrance. She thought quickly. If she could circle around the house she might be able to lose whoever was following her.

After they had transferred to the *Meridian Princess*, the cruise director gave an "Italy orientation talk" where he warned everyone about Gypsies, itinerant nomads who moved from town to town throughout Europe. They were said to be skilled pickpockets, but weren't above making a direct assault on the unwary under the right circumstances. At the same time another memory seeped back into her mind, one that drained the strength from her arms and legs. She couldn't live through this again. She prayed whoever was behind her would give up.

The "castle" turned out to be a large manor house, though compared to the average home in Portofino, it was easy to see why locals referred to it that way. Katherine forced herself into motion and climbed the second flight of stairs onto the main terrace. It was a good bit larger than the one below. Through breaks in the fog, she caught glimpses of the bay in the distance. Katherine turned and studied the house. Most of its windows were long gone and it appeared to be little more than a colossal wreck.

Checking behind her again, she padded silently to the end of the terrace in the hope of finding a way to the back. Someone was coming up the steps now, no longer bothering to conceal the sound of their footsteps. All of her instincts yelled "run," but she forced herself to stay calm and think.

Panic and you're dead.

If it was a Gypsy wanting to mug her they would be disappointed, because she had no money. All she had was the key to her hotel room. Visions of being raped and worse began to tug at the corners of her consciousness.

There was a path, but it was badly pitted and broken. To its right was a steep drop that would take a person all the way down to the harbor if they lost their footing. To make matters worse, the stones were covered in moss and lichen. The only good thing about it was that it appeared to go in the right direction. All she had to do was circle around her pursuer and head back to the town for help. A second before Katherine turned the corner she caught a glimpse of a powerfully built man in black emerging at the top of the steps. She couldn't tell whether the man saw her, but if he did there was nothing she could do about it now.

Moving quietly, she picked her way over the broken stones, listening to see if he was coming.

So far so good.

But the moment she turned the corner she knew she was

in trouble. The path ended at a patio with a sheer drop on three sides. There was no way out except though the house. Any attempt to climb down the rocks would be suicide. She was trapped. Katherine ran to the doors at the rear of the home and tried them. The first was locked. Her luck was better with the second. Its wood was bleached and badly weathered and the iron reinforcing bands had long since gone to rust, but it moved when she pushed on it. Katherine peered into the darkness for a moment, then suddenly drew back. A spiderweb was stretched across the entrance and in the center was a white spider about the size of a half-dollar.

Cursing under her breath, she carefully began to dislodge a corner of the web. Ever since she was a child she had hated spiders. Fortunately, the spider felt the vibration and scrambled off, vanishing into a crack.

Good, Katherine said to herself, stepping into the room.

A dank smell, musty and heavy with age, filled her nostrils as her eyes adjusted to the darkness. She was in a cellar. It was quite empty, of course. Whatever furniture had been there had long since been removed. Now, only a thick layer of dust and leaves remained, covering the floor. Katherine moved to a set of stairs in the corner and tested the first step. It seemed solid enough. Fearing the slightest sound would alert her pursuer, she crept quietly upward, coming out in a hallway. It was as barren as the cellar, but at least the air was fresher. She took a deep breath. Cellars everywhere seemed to have the same smell. The hallway was narrow and gloomy, illuminated only by the light of a solitary window at one end. She took a second, allowing her heart rate to slow as she gained her bearings. Her mouth felt like cotton and she swallowed several times to restore some moisture to it.

There were a number of doors running off either side

of the hallway so she picked the first and went in. Perhaps it would lead to a way out. No luck. The room turned out to be a kitchen. An old-fashioned icebox still remained, its door hanging open, apparently too heavy to have been carried away by scavengers. A series of wooden cabinets had pulled away from the wall and now lay broken on the floor. Katherine stood still listening for nearly a minute. Other than wind passing through the trees outside there was nothing out of the ordinary.

Maybe he gave up.

Just to be safe she waited a little longer. Out of curiosity she decided to see what lay beyond the kitchen. The castle's great room, like everything else in the house, was empty save for a large fireplace. Four windows, which might have offered spectacular views of the surrounding landscape had it not been for the fog, were open or hanging lopsided in their casements. A carved limestone mantel above the fireplace reminded her of the one in her own home.

Cautiously, she moved along the wall to the nearest window and peered out. The fog had shredded itself into ribbons and was thinning. Two hundred feet below, the sound of waves striking the rocks reached her. There was no sign of anyone on the lower terrace, still it might be prudent to wait a little while longer. Katherine turned away and examined the room more closely. It would have been large by any standards—probably fifty feet across. The original wainscoting and paneling were still intact, as were the crown moldings. Like the basement, they were all covered in dust. Leaves and debris were scattered across the stone floor. Katherine leaned against the window frame, wondering about the people who had built the house as the minutes passed.

Through the archway she could see the house's main door in the center of a great hall. She had only caught a glimpse of the man following her as he came up the steps, but he didn't look anything like a Gypsy. She supposed Portofino had its share of crime, but picking on a jogger who was obviously not carrying anything of value didn't make sense. A number of other possibilities occurred to her, each more unpleasant than the last.

When she was satisfied enough time had elapsed, Katherine walked across the room into the hall. The front door was paneled and rounded at the upper corners, coming to a point in the middle, reminiscent of the type churches used during the Renaissance. Even before she reached it she saw the deadbolt. It was locked. Frustrated, she gave the knob a twist anyway.

"It will be better if you stay where you are, lady," said a voice behind her.

Katherine spun around and saw the man in black standing in the kitchen doorway. He was short, olive-skinned, and had a deep chest. His eyes were so dark they were nearly black.

"I don't have any money," she said, backing away.

The man nodded.

"Just stay where you are, Mrs."

But Katherine didn't stay where she was—she bolted to her right for the staircase that led to the upper level. Umar muttered something in Arabic under his breath and started after her.

From the second-floor balcony, Katherine looked back in horror as he removed a shiny object from of his pocket. The switchblade sprang open with a click, locking into place.

"Why are you doing this?" she asked. "I told you I don't have any money. What do you want?"

"*You*, lady, only you," Umar replied, never taking his eyes off her.

He continued to advance slowly, holding the knife just behind his right hip. Katherine was trapped. She tried to scream, but her voice seemed to have left her. And then a strange thing happened.

A dark shape burst from the room behind him and crashed into the assailant. With a grunt Umar went down, his shoulders arching backward. John Delaney hit the floor and came up in a crouch. His right fist lashed out as Umar was getting up and connected with the side of the Arab's head. Umar slashed backward with his knife. He slashed again, but Delaney stepped in, blocking the blow and trapping Umar's arm against his side. He landed three more punches to Umar's jaw.

With a snarl, Umar yanked his arm backward freeing it from Delaney's grasp. A thin red line of blood appeared along Delaney's left side. Umar lunged and Delaney sidestepped, bringing his forearm down across the Arab's wrist. The blow dislodged the knife, sending it clattering to the floor. Umar struck at Delaney's kidney, buckling his knees. Both men came together, each grappling for control, and they went down in a tangle of arms and legs. Umar was on his feet first. His right leg caught Delaney under the chin and sent him crashing backward into the wall. Before Delaney could recover he was hit again. The blow was so heavy it nearly lifted him off the ground. It was followed by another and then another.

KATHERINE COULD see Delaney was in trouble. She also saw the assailant's knife lying on the ground a few feet away and started to reach for it.

"Stay where you are," Umar warned.

The distraction was enough to give Delaney the time he needed to drag a breath into his lungs. With a roar he launched himself off the wall slamming his shoulders into Umar's stomach. They both went down again.

"I'm gonna fuckin' kill you," Delaney shouted, hitting Umar in the face twice more.

The Arab succeeded in knocking Delaney off him. Slowly, both men got to their feet and faced each other. Umar's face was bruised and bleeding and the blood on Delaney's side was more obvious now. Umar glanced down at his switchblade and began to shuffle around toward it. Delaney responded by placing himself between the assailant and the knife.

"You'd like that knife, wouldn't you, you little fuck? Well, you're going to have to come through me to get it."

"So be it."

Without warning, Umar lowered his head and charged Delaney like a bull, catching him by surprise. Both men careened backward through a closed door, destroying it in the process. Katherine immediately dove for the knife, picked it up, and ran to the room where they were struggling.

A wide punch to Delaney's head missed and he replied with a jab to Umar's face. It was followed by a solid right cross that staggered the Arab.

A minute passed and then another as the fight between the two men continued. It was becoming obvious, given his greater height and reach, that Delaney was the more effective boxer. Umar spat out a mouthful of blood and began pressing his attack, alternating his punches with kicks to Delaney's side. Each time the Arab landed one, it brought a grimace of pain to Delaney's face.

But the next time Umar prepared to charge, Delaney was ready. A second before he made his move, he noticed the Arab pivot onto the ball of his back foot and shift his weight forward. Delaney sidestepped the rush and Umar made contact with nothing. Unable to check his momentum, he careened into the balcony railing, which disintegrated on impact.

Katherine would remember his scream for the rest of her life and the sickening thud that followed when he hit the stone floor below. The scream stopped abruptly.

Delaney walked over to the landing and looked down, then bent over and put his hands on his knees as he waited for his breath to return. Katherine dropped the knife and ran to him.

"John, are you okay?"

"I'm getting too old for this crap," he replied, between gasps. "Who the hell was that?"

Katherine took him under the elbow and helped him straighten up.

"I don't know. I was out for a jog and . . . *oh my God!*"

She broke off what she was saying when she saw Delaney's left side. His shirt was now completely soaked with blood. With a grimace, Delaney gingerly lifted it up to reveal a four-inch gash just below his rib cage. Blood slowly oozed from the wound and ran down his side.

"Hmm," he said, probing the area with his fingers.

"Hmm?" Katherine sputtered, "What do mean 'hmm'? You're *bleeding*."

"Yeah, I guess."

He held up his hand before Katherine could say anything else.

"I'm fine, K.J. It's looks worse than it is . . . honest. Help me get this shirt off."

Delaney undid the buttons and shrugged out of it. He folded the shirt into a square and pressed it against his side.

"We need to get you to a doctor, John. You stay here and I'll go for help."

"I'm well enough to walk back," he assured her. "I want to know a little bit more about your playmate. You have *no* idea who he is?"

Katherine shook her head as they walked down the stairs.

"I swear to God. I got up early and went downstairs for breakfast. I think he was in the dining room. In fact, I'm positive about it. We never said a single word to each other. When I finished eating, I went for a run. I guess he must have followed me. And speaking of following me, where did you come from?"

Delaney didn't answer right away. Instead, he dropped down on one knee and used his free hand to check Umar's body. The expression Katherine had come to identify as his "cop face" returned.

"I was at the restaurant a couple of minutes after you left. The waiter told me you went out to run. I thought I'd surprise you, only you got away from me in the fog. I asked some old lady who was sweeping the street if she saw you, and she said she thought you were headed up toward the castle."

Delaney paused and looked at the surroundings.

"Doesn't look anything like a castle, if you ask me. Anyway, I followed and didn't see any sign of you. What I did see was handsome here creeping around the house. He didn't look like he was up to any good, so I . . . ah, here we go."

Delaney tapped something solid in Umar's pocket and pulled out his passport, flipping it open. He frowned when he saw the name.

"Otto Magnuson . . . from Switzerland."

"If he's Swiss, I'm Minnie Mouse," said Katherine. "I don't know what his accent was, but it definitely was not Swiss."

"Any idea what he wanted?"

"Robbery, I thought. But after he pulled that knife, I don't know. He probably wanted to rape me."

Delaney nodded and continued his search. He found the thick yellow envelope in Umar's breast pocket and let out a low whistle when he saw what it contained.

"Pretty much lets out robbery as a motive, doesn't it?" he said. "This guy's loaded. There's got to be thirty or forty thousand dollars here."

"Jesus," said Katherine. "We need to let the police know about this."

"You ever deal with the Italian police?"

"Not really."

"Well, I have, and I trust myself. It makes no sense for this guy to just show up here in town and single you out. He might be some kind of wacko, except he didn't act like one. He acted more like a professional."

"What do you mean?"

"I only got here at the tail end, K. J., but from what I saw he was coming at you with the knife behind his hip— that's something a professional would do. Street punks try to be flashy and use the knife to intimidate. They like to flip it back and forth from hand to hand. It's the same with rapists—they work through intimidation. This guy was planning on using that knife."

"Oh, Christ. *Why me?* I don't get it."

Delaney pushed himself up and shook his head.

"I don't know. I'm just happy I was here, that's all."

Katherine put her head on his chest. "You saved my life, John."

"Glad to be of service," he said. "Let me finish examining Mr. Magnuson, then we'll head back and notify the authorities."

Katherine dutifully stepped away. Oddly, Delaney didn't do anything for the next minute except stare at Umar's body. It was as if he were trying to solve some complex equation. Eventually, he walked around the corpse and stopped at his feet, then bent down for a closer look at the soles of Umar's shoes. When he finished, he pulled the back of Umar's Windbreaker away from his neck and did the same with his shirt.

"There are no labels," said Katherine.

"Good girl. Take a look at his shoes and tell me what you see."

Katherine cocked her head to one side, but did as instructed.

"They're new."

"Right. Unless this guy was suffering from some kind of phobia, it appears he went to a lot of trouble to conceal his identity. Do you see anything else?"

Katherine looked up and down the body for a few moments and eventually shrugged.

"Fingertips," Delaney prompted.

One of Umar's hands lay palm up on the ground. Delaney reached out and uncurled the fingers, holding them open for Katherine to see. The ends were all badly scarred. It took a moment before the significance of this dawned on her—*the man had no fingerprints*.

"What does it mean?" she asked.

Delaney shook his head slowly.

"I don't know, but I don't think he was here on vacation. If Otto, or whoever the hell this is, was staying at the hotel, I'd like to know when he checked in. This passport's a new issue," he said, flipping through the pages. "It doesn't have any stamps yet—not even an Italian one. This whole thing stinks, K.J. Is there anybody back home who's mad at you?"

"Plenty of people," she answered, "but most of them are ex-husbands from my divorce cases. I can't think of anyone who would go to this length."

"Wonderful. Let's go. We'll talk as we walk."

Katherine pointed at the body. "What about him?"

"I don't think he's going anywhere, except maybe in a body bag."

THIRTY

It took them a half-hour to find the local constable, whose house was located at the end of a steep street. Delaney managed the climb with some difficulty and was breathing heavily by the time they got there. A slightly built man in his early sixties came to the door in response to their knock. He had a full head of white hair and intelligent blue eyes that immediately darted to the blood-soaked shirt Delaney had pressed against his side. He introduced himself as Carlo Cansini and led them into his living room. Cansini listened without interruption as Katherine and Delaney recounted what had happened at the castle. They identified themselves as attorneys and told him about the disaster on the *Majestic*. Delaney also mentioned his background as a detective. Cansini's only reaction was to raise his eyebrows and incline his head in acknowledgment.

At one point Cansini's wife poked her head out of the kitchen and asked him something in Italian. They exchanged a few words before she disappeared again, giving Katherine and Delaney a brief glance. It was followed by the sound of a receiver being lifted in the next room and a rapid conversation.

"I have asked my wife to call for the doctor," Cansini explained. "She is also calling both my assistant and a photographer. I assume neither of you will object if we retrieve your passports from the hotel? You understand I must confirm your identities?"

Delaney and Katherine nodded and said they understood.

"Excellent," said Cansini. "Now, signora, you said you rose early this foggy morning to go for a run. And during your exercise you encountered a man who followed you to the castle and attempted to assault you."

"I said he attempted to kill me with a knife, and he would have done so if John hadn't stopped him."

"Forgive me, but I must ask these tiresome questions. Is part of my job, no?"

"Go ahead," said Katherine.

"You never saw this man before today?"

"Never, except at breakfast before I went out."

Cansini shook his head in puzzlement.

"Strange. Would you not agree?"

"Very."

"It gets even stranger," said Delaney. "The guy had no labels on his clothes and the prints were burned off his fingers, probably with acid. He was also carrying an envelope with about forty thousand U.S. dollars in it. And he had this."

Delaney reached into his pants pocket, pulled out Umar's passport and placed it on the side table next to the couch.

Cansini used a pen to open it.

"Otto Magnuson," the constable read.

"The passport's probably a phony," Delaney told him. "If you notice, there's no entry stamp—or any stamp, for that matter. It looks as new as everything else Mr. Magnuson was wearing. I'm no expert on Switzerland, but he doesn't look like any Swiss I've ever seen. To me his accent sounded distinctly Arabic."

"Ah, you spoke with him then?" asked Cansini, without looking up from the passport.

"Yeah. You might say we had a brief conversation."

"How so?"

"He was trying to stick a knife in me at the time."

Cansini closed the passport and turned to Katherine.

"Do you have any idea why this man would wish you harm, signora?"

"No, I don't. I thought he wanted to rape me, but that doesn't seem—"

The rest of Katherine's sentence was interrupted by a knock at the door. Cansini excused himself and went to open it.

The doctor turned out to be an attractive hazel-eyed woman in her early thirties named Valentina Sanzelli. She was slender and casually dressed in a skirt and blouse.

"Ah, Valentina, thank you for coming," said Cansini. "I'm sorry to disturb you so early. This is Signore John Delaney, a professor of law from the United States. And this is Signora Katherine Adams, also a lawyer. They were both on the cruise ship that sank several days ago."

Valentina Sanzelli's eyebrows arched in surprise. She shook hands with both of them, then set her medical bag down on the couch.

"We heard of it on the news. It must have been horrible."

"It was," Katherine told her.

The doctor cast a critical eye at Delaney's blood-soaked shirt.

"So . . . I will assume you are my patient. Let's have a look at you."

Delaney pulled the shirt away, revealing the gash in his left side. The blood had already turned black and the area immediately around the wound was slightly red. The doctor frowned when she saw it and frowned again when she noticed the bullet scars on his chest.

"I was a police officer before I became an attorney," Delaney explained.

"I'm relieved to hear it wasn't an angry client."

Delaney smiled. "Or an angry ex-lover. That's the story my buddies want me to tell. They say it sounds more exciting."

"I suspect the original is exciting enough. Carlo, may I use your couch, please? I need to clean this wound and it would be better if Signor Delaney is lying down."

"Of course," said Cansini, gesturing toward the couch.

"Can I do anything to help?" asked Katherine.

"Some peroxide perhaps, and a sheet."

"I'll get them," said Cansini.

Delaney lay down on the couch and exchanged a look with Katherine. She smiled at him. Fifteen minutes and sixteen stitches later, the doctor declared he was well enough to get up. She gave him a tetanus shot as a precaution and told him not to do anything strenuous for the next few days. He started to ask her a question, then stopped when he realized it was actually to Katherine that she was giving her instructions. Katherine listened carefully. Delaney looked back and forth between the two women and then glanced at Cansini, who seemed mildly amused, but chose to stay out of it. Before Valentina left, she inquired as to how long they would be staying in Portofino. She told Katherine she wanted to check on Delaney's condition before they departed.

"Oh, Carlo, I nearly forgot. I met Federico on the way here. He said he and Gilberto would meet you at the castle."

"Very good. Thank you, Valentina."

"I appreciate it, Doc," said Delaney, looking down at the stitches. "How much do I owe you?"

"I'll send the bill to your hotel later today. The important thing now is for you to get some rest, eh? We have an apothecary here in town. I can prescribe something for the pain if you wish."

"Nah . . . I'll be fine."

Before they could say good-bye, Cansini's wife answered another knock at the door. She returned carrying a fresh shirt for Delaney. He recognized it as one of his own.

"I took the liberty," said Cansini. "I hope you do not mind."

"Good thinking."

As KATHERINE walked back to the castle a variety of feelings came at her. She felt a growing affection for the man who had saved her life, and anger bordering on hatred for the one who had tried to take it. Emotions held in check for the last few days came rushing to the surface. Her first instinct was to call her children and tell them that she was getting on the next plane home. More than that, she wanted to do something and was frustrated because she didn't know where to begin. Once during the doctor's ministrations she and Delaney made eye contact and he seemed to read her mind. He gave her a wink accompanied by one of his smiles.

There was little question that John was right; whoever the man was, he hadn't singled her out by chance.

But why? It simply made no sense.

She began a mental review of her cases, past and present, trying to pinpoint someone, anyone, who hated her enough to do such a thing. Each possibility ended at a stone wall. There were plenty of upset people on the opposite side of her suits—but *murder?*

The fog was nearly gone by the time they arrived at the courtyard. It left glistening drops of moisture on the cobblestones' surface and in between their crevices. At some point—Katherine couldn't say when—her fear was slowly replaced by something else. She found that she was clenching her fists so hard her knuckles hurt, so she drew a deep breath of air into her lungs and let her fingers relax. The methodical portion of her mind, the lawyer who could look at a case and see possibilities and solutions few of her contemporaries were capable of, began to take over.

The assailant was where they left him, only he now had

company. Two men hovered nearby and waved when they saw Cansini. The photographer was an elderly fellow with coarse gray hair and stooped shoulders. He was using an old box camera with an upright flash to take pictures, the kind you used to see newspapermen with. He went about his business quietly and without fuss. Katherine watched as he placed a tape measure alongside Umar's body and snapped four shots in succession, tossing the spent bulbs on the ground. He then took a series of close-ups of Umar's hands and shoes before excusing himself to go into the house. A short while later a series of flashes could be seen coming from the second-floor balcony.

Cansini introduced the other man to them as his assistant. His name was Federico, a slender teenager with a Roman nose and dark good looks. Federico carried a small yellow pad that was already filled with notes. He showed them to Cansini. The constable looked them over and gave him a satisfied nod.

"Federico is leaving us in September to study criminal justice at the University in Torino," he explained. "He already knows more than many criminologists."

"That is because my uncle is an excellent teacher," said Federico.

"Ah . . . you give away family secrets," said Cansini, wagging a finger at him. "What have you found?"

"Very little, Uncle Carlo. This man had almost nothing on him except these," Federico held up a plastic bag with several items in it. "Other than a hotel key, a car key, his watch, and a cigarette lighter, he was carrying nothing else. Gilberto took photos, of course."

Cansini said, "While the pictures are being developed, I would like you to take the car and drive into Rapallo. We should see if there are any fingerprints on these items. This is a most unusual situation."

"Did you notice his fingertips, Uncle?" asked Federico.

"I did. Signor Delaney told me about them. He is a former homicide detective who now practices the law."

Federico's eyes grew a little wider.

"Really? I would love to speak with you about this, signore . . . if it is no imposition. One day I hope to be an inspector, as my uncle was. He was Genoa's chief of police for twenty-five years."

This time it was Delaney's turn to be impressed. "No kidding?"

Cansini inclined his head in acknowledgment as he dropped down on one knee for a closer look at Umar's fingers.

"Very strange," he said, getting back up. "Those scars are obviously not accidental. You say neither of you ever saw our Swiss gentleman before today?"

"Nope," said Delaney. "It's just lucky I caught up with K. J. when I did."

"Excuse me . . . *K. J.*?"

"That's me," said Katherine. "And no, other than in the hotel's restaurant earlier, I never saw this man before. When I asked him what he wanted all he said was, 'You, lady.' "

Cansini shook his head slowly. "Strange indeed. Obviously his neck is broken, but we will do an autopsy anyway. Procedure, you understand? I must ask you both to remain in Portofino until the investigation is concluded. I trust this will not be inconvenient."

"No problem," said Delaney. "Can I do anything to help?"

"*Grazie.* But I think we can manage. Will it be all right if I also retain your passports for a day or two?"

"That's fine," said Katherine.

Cansini smiled.

"I was certain you would cooperate. It should only be a couple of days at most. Perhaps we can meet later and discuss this matter further."

"Name the time," said Delaney. "Our only constraint is that we have to testify in front of the Board of Inquiry in Genoa this Friday about what happened on the cruise ship."

Cansini spent ten more minutes more going over the body. He turned Umar's pockets inside out and examined his clothes in much the same way Delaney had. When the photographer returned, he asked him to take a few more shots of the cut-out labels, and then he asked Katherine to show him where she had entered the house. She led them to the back patio.

The door was still open and the spiderweb was still there. The white spider had returned and was slowly making its way toward a struggling insect near the bottom of the web. Katherine stared transfixed at the spider for several seconds, then suddenly bent down and picked up a branch lying on the ground. She destroyed the web while Cansisi watched her with interest.

"I don't care for predators," she said.

The corners of Cansini's mouth turned down. "Nor do I, signora."

When the constable finished his investigation he walked with them back to town. He shook hands with Delaney, kissed Katherine on the hand, and said he would call on them at their hotel at 6:00 p.m.

Delaney stood there watching the old man climb the street to his house until he disappeared around a corner.

"Chief of police in Genoa, huh?" he said. "That's one smart guy, K.J. I like the way he handles himself."

Katherine was inclined to agree. Carlo Cansini's demeanor might have been low key, but he didn't miss much. She could tell he was disturbed by the attack . . . not because a woman was involved, or because she was an American tourist, it was because it made no sense. She went over the details again in her mind, hoping to find something that might have escaped her notice, but eventually gave up. It wasn't until Delaney cleared his throat that she noticed they were back at the hotel.

Instead of going in, however, Delaney went up to one of the valets and spoke with him. When he was through, he took out a couple of euros and slipped them into the man's palm.

"Our buddy's car is around back," he said. "Let's go."

"Don't you think we should wait for Cansini?"

"I'm not going to touch anything. I just want to have a look-see at the vehicle. The bell guy said he was driving a black Mercedes and that he was a crummy tipper. According to him, Magnuson parked his car here yesterday, even though he wasn't staying at the hotel."

"Where was he staying?"

"No idea. The bellman put the car in the lot himself last night and noticed it was still here this morning. He thought it was odd because he couldn't find Magnuson's name on the guest roster to bill the charges to, so he asked the manager about it when he came on duty."

THE HOTEL Splendido's parking lot was located at the bottom of the hill behind the main building. It held about twenty cars and there was no attendant present. Except for a low hedge aound the lot's perimeter, the only security was a chain hanging between two posts across the entrance. Beth's red Alfa Romeo was parked in the far corner and Umar's Mercedes was in the second row. Delaney and Katherine exchanged glances when they saw the trunk was open. They found out why as soon as they got closer.

Federico was already there dusting for fingerprints. He

lay on his back on the front seat and was in the process of lifting a set of them from the driver-side window when they walked up. Black smudges on the other windows indicated he'd already gone over the vehicle thoroughly. He looked up when he heard Delaney's footsteps.

"Ah, Signore Delaney and Signora Adams, my uncle said you would be here, but I didn't think you would arrive so soon."

"He did, huh?" said Delaney. "Clever guy, your uncle."

"Yes, very."

"You find anything?"

"Nothing of promise, I'm afraid. The trunk was empty and the registration papers say only that the car was rented in Firenze. It doesn't look like Signore Magnuson planned to stay very long. Oh, forgive me—this is for you."

Federico fished around in his shirt pocket, pulled out a piece of paper, and handed it to Delaney.

"What's this?"

"It's the license number of this car and the phone number and address of the rental agency in Firenze—Florence, to you. My uncle said—"

"Yeah, yeah, I know what your uncle said. He said I'd be wanting the information. Thanks. Did you get any decent prints?"

"A few. It always pays to check, of course, but I don't think they will be helpful. Signore Magnuson was a very careful man, I think."

"I think you're right. Tell your uncle I appreciate it. We'll be at the hotel or wandering around town."

"The Splendido has an excellent lunch," said Federico.

"Great. It's okay if you want to check out our car while you're here. It's the red Alfa over there," Delaney told him. "And don't tell me Uncle Carlo already asked you to do that."

Federico shrugged.

"The guy's unbelievable," Delaney muttered. "All right, see you later, kid. Keep up the good work."

"Grazie, buongiorno."

"Whatever."

"Arrivederci," Katherine said, trying to keep a straight face.

They walked back to the hotel together and went to their rooms to change clothes. Delaney knocked on Katherine's door fifteen minutes later. She had changed to a tan skirt and a green pullover. He wore a pair of jeans and a conservative white Ralph Lauren shirt with the sleeves rolled up. They both went to the restaurant together.

"You look like a college professor," she said, after they sat down. "How's your side?"

"It pinches a little, but I'll live. More important, how are you doing?"

Katherine shook her head and stared out the window at the sea. She didn't answer right away. Absently she reached up and brushed a strand of hair out of her eyes before turning back to Delaney.

"I'm all right."

"Are you?" he asked quietly.

Katherine nodded. "John, I know these things happen, but knowing doesn't help you deal with them any better. I've been giving this some thought and I want you to know I love being here with you, but—"

"But you've decided to cut the trip short and head back home. I pretty much figured you would."

"Are you angry?"

Delaney shook his head.

"Nah . . . I guess it's not a bad idea. I love being with you too, but this vacation's got a black cloud over it. It's not enough a guy at our table gets murdered, we nearly burn to death on a cruise ship, and miss drowning by the skin of our teeth, now a phantom shows up and tries to kill you. Sure, 'take a cruise . . . have a few laughs,' my friends said.

"I'll ask Cansini if he can fix it so we give our testimony to the Genoa board via telephone. If he gives us the green light, I'll change my reservations and we can go back together."

"John, you don't have to do that."

"*Yes,* I do. First, there's no way I'm letting you go home alone. Second, I kind of like hanging around you."

"Honestly?"

Delaney's eyes met hers and his expression grew serious.

"Yeah, K. J."

Katherine reached across the table and took his hand.

"Thank you for saving my life."

When he smiled it changed his face a great deal. The amused look that usually played at the corners of his mouth dropped away, leaving only a gentle caring man in its place. Katherine felt her eyes growing moist and she turned her head away.

"Besides, your kids probably miss their mom," Delaney said, changing the subject.

Katherine thought about that for a moment and shook her head.

"I don't know. Both of the older ones are in college now. They've got their own lives to live. Zach recently started wearing cologne to school; he's my baby. I think he's discovered there's another sex out there."

"How old did you say he was?"

"Sixteen."

"Good guess. He's staying with his father, right?"

"Right."

"Do you guys get along?"

Katherine shrugged. "Better than we used to. It took

thirteen years, but I suppose that's progress. Frankly, the less I see of him the better."

"Sorry, I didn't mean to open up a can of worms. It took me a while to get over my breakup, too. I was pretty much worthless for about four months.

"I teach with a guy named Nick Berkley. He's a part-time professor and does domestic relations on the side, like you do. Nick's always saying that divorce is like hitting yourself on the head with a hammer. The only good thing is you eventually stop."

Katherine smiled in spite of herself.

"I don't think I ever heard that before. We had a pretty good marriage . . . at least I thought it was good, until I came home and found him in our bed with another woman—a pharmaceutical sales rep."

"Jeez . . . what'd you say in a situation like that?"

"Not much. I had the bed burned and filed papers two days later. He called a bunch of times wanting to reconcile, but hell . . . I'd already bought a new bed and all."

This time it was Delaney's turn to chuckle.

"Things just didn't work out, huh?"

"Well . . . we couldn't come to terms with what we wanted out of life."

"Such as?"

"Such as, he wanted an open marriage . . . and I wanted him dead."

The last comment caused Delaney's Campari to go down the wrong way and he started coughing. Katherine reached over and patted him on his back until he stopped.

"Remind me not to piss you off," he said. "By the way, you'll be pleased to know that I'm not into that stuff. When it comes right down to it, I'm a pretty dull guy. You know . . . one woman, one man. That sort of thing."

"*You* are anything but dull, John Delaney," Katherine told him.

Throughout the main course they spoke of what their lives were like back in the real world. Despite all they had been through in the last few days, it was the first time they had talked on that level. They covered everything from children and morals to abortion and their own religious beliefs. No cross-examination was ever conducted so skillfully. Katherine was pleased to learn that Delaney's mother was still alive, and more pleased still when he told her he saw her at least once a week.

In return, Delaney learned that Katherine had two sisters and a brother. She was a dyed-in-the-wool Democrat; he was a solid Republican. There were other differences of course, but in the end, their growing feelings for each other made them seem minor. Several times she started to tell him about her panic attacks and how they had affected her life and her past relationships, but each time she drew away from the subject.

Two hours passed before they looked around and noticed the terrace was empty. One level below them was the hotel pool where guests were sunbathing and swimming. A part of her wanted to do the same. At that moment she would have loved nothing better than to freeze time.

She realized Delaney had stopped talking and was looking at her.

Katherine leaned across the table and kissed him.

"What's that for?"

"For being my knight in shining armor."

"Oh, yeah, that's me . . . Sir John the Confused."

Katherine didn't respond. She simply looked at him with serious eyes. It only took a second before he got the message.

"Sorry," he said quietly. "It's just my way sometimes. I can't think of any woman I'd rather slay a dragon for, K. J. You can make book on that."

Katherine started to reply, but never got the chance. Some time ago, she'd decided that public displays of affection were best left to teenagers. So when Delaney got up and came around the table and kissed her full on the mouth, she wasn't fully prepared for it.

A discreet throat-clearing behind them caused her to go red in the face.

"Forgive me," Cansini said from the doorway.

"We were just exchanging notes on the case," said Delaney, resuming his seat. He gestured for the constable to join them. Katherine straightened her hair and let her heart rate return to normal.

Cansini said, "Ah . . . I was certain there was Italian blood in your family. I compliment you on your innovative technique, signore. Federico and I generally use the phone."

Katherine chose not to reply. She smoothed her skirt and smiled at the old man.

"I thought we were going to meet later," said Delaney. "You come up with anything?"

"Perhaps. I'm in agreement with you, the unfortunate gentleman you met is probably not Swiss. I checked with their embassy and they have no record of a passport number matching the one he was carrying. And as you correctly pointed out, there are no entry or exit stamps, so it seems our Mr. Magnuson must have dropped from the sky.

"I suspect Federico's examination of the automobile will also yield little information. I have checked its registration number with the Genoa police and it appears the car was stolen in France, then driven here. The license matches a rented vehicle in Florence, but it's for a different car entirely."

"So where does that leave us?" asked Katherine.

"Very much in the dark, I am afraid, signora. I think we

will all agree that it was not coincidence that brought Signore Magnuson to Portofino."

"That's just peachy," said Delaney.

"We may know more when Federico returns from Rapallo. Their laboratory is more complete than ours."

"You've got a lab?"

"A small one. Like you, the science of forensics is a passion with me. The dean of your school sends his regards, by the way."

Delaney stared at the constable who smiled back at him.

"Sounds like you've been doing your homework. I'd have done the same thing in your place."

Cansini inclined his head. "I shall take that as a compliment. I am grateful you are not offended. There has been one piece of good luck, though it may come to nothing."

"Like what?" asked Katherine.

"I was able to get a fingerprint on the cigarette lighter Magnuson was carrying. It belongs to a man called Seldon Cardwell. Is the name familiar to either of you?"

The crease between Delaney's eyebrows deepened. "I've heard that name before."

Cansini looked at Katherine, who shook her head.

"I've heard it, too, and recently," she said. "I hate when this happens, because it's going to drive me . . ." Katherine's voice trailed away and her mouth opened.

"What's wrong?" asked Delaney

"Seldon Cardwell was the name of the *Marie Star*'s captain. You remember. He was one of the men on the hearing panel."

Delaney snapped his fingers.

"Jesus, K.J., you're right. I remember him now. Barroni was on the right and he was on Blaylock's left—a tall thin guy."

"Perhaps you could explain," Cansini prompted.

"The *Marie Star* was one of the two ships that rescued us after the *Majestic* caught fire," Katherine told him.

"I see. Could Signore Magnuson have been one of the passengers, perhaps?"

"Maybe," said Delaney. "It's easy enough to find out. Why don't we get ahold of the company's manifest? If Magnuson was a passenger then his name should be there."

"He might have been a crew member," Katherine suggested.

Delaney shook his head in the negative.

"I don't know how many crew the *Marie Star* had, but I'm willing to bet I saw every one of them during our trip here. It's worth checking on, though."

"Most interesting," said Cansini. "This was the ship that brought you to Genoa?"

"No," Katherine said. "We were on the *Meridian Princess*. The *Marie Star* is a tanker. They left once all the passengers were transferred."

Cansini thought for a second.

"Would you care to accompany me to my office? We can place a few phone calls from there and perhaps unravel this mystery a little further."

"Let's do it," said Delaney, pushing himself back from the table.

CANSINI'S OFFICE looked like something out of a movie to Katherine. His wife, who also doubled as his secretary, nodded to them when they came in and asked if they wanted anything to drink. No one did. In the corner was an old rolltop desk with a wooden chair behind it. The only photo on the wall was one of Cansini being presented an award of some kind at a ceremony. Three smaller pictures in silver frames sat on a credenza. One was obviously Mrs. Cansini; the other two were attractive dark-haired young ladies.

"My daughters," Cansini said, noting Katherine's interest.

"They're very beautiful."

"Thank you. I'm most fortunate they take after their mother. Luciana was my assistant when I worked with the Genoa Police Department."

"Your nephew said you were the chief."

"It was a long time ago," Cansini replied. "Let us go into the next office."

Cansini walked to a plain brown door at the rear of the room and held it open for them. In direct contrast to the outer room it contained an array of modern equipment. Two computers with twenty-inch flat-panel screens sat on a long table along with a fax machine, a copier, and a VCR. The room was lit by fluorescent lighting.

Cansini went to the nearest computer screen and sat down, motioning for Katherine and Delaney to join him. He picked up the phone and dialed a number. When someone answered he began speaking rapidly in Italian. Four more calls followed. Katherine was able to catch only bits and pieces of his conversation, but from the notes he was making she could tell it wasn't going well. Cansini would write down a few words or a phone number only to cross them out again seconds later. After thirty minutes he hung up and rubbed the bridge of his nose.

"Bureaucrats are the same all over the world, no? I have spoken with the Genoa authorities, and they agreed to request a passenger list from the cruise company . . . but it will take time. The harbormaster in Genoa told me the *Marie Star* unloaded its cargo and set sail early this morning. Doubtless they are now outside our territorial waters, so I contacted the minister of commerce in Rome and spoke to his assistant. He suggested I call the Liberian consulate. You can imagine the wealth of cooperation I received there. Last, I was referred to our own department of justice, who informed me that I must make a request in triplicate."

"How long will that take?" asked Katherine.

Cansisi tossed his pencil on the desk and leaned back in his chair.

"Have you ever dealt with the Italian government, signora? The *Marie Star* could be halfway to Jupiter by the time we get a response."

"Maybe I can help," said Delaney. "Would it be all right if I make a phone call or two?"

"Please," said Cansini, gesturing toward the phone.

"What do I have to do to call the States?"

"Dial zero one one, the area code, and then the number," Katherine told him.

Delaney winked at her and started to dial.

THIRTY-ONE

The 43rd Precinct in the Bronx was built in the neo-Renaissance style popular in the early 1900s. An elaborate, but nonfunctioning wrought-iron balcony sits above the main entrance and two ornate lamps flank either side of a cast bronze door. In contrast to the building's light tan color, a brownstone stoop was installed in 1955 after the old one became unusable. A pair of planters, empty of flowers for as long as anyone can remember, adorn the stoop. The station was constructed before central air-conditioning. Each office now has portable units that work sporadically. In an effort to make conditions more tolerable during the summer months, when temperatures in New York can climb well into the nineties, the city recently installed fans in the hallways. The fans push air around in a desultory fashion while a steady stream of uniformed and plainclothes officers come and go. The 43rd was where John Delaney worked for thirteen years.

Detective Betty Berkowitz, a plump, matronly woman, answered her phone on the second ring. She was a fourth-generation cop with a set of lungs that could be heard two blocks away, the result of growing up around a brother and two longshoreman uncles.

"Robbery, Berkowitz."

"Betty, this is John Delaney calling from Italy. How're you doing?"

"Delaney?"

"Yeah. Can you hear me okay?"

"I hear you fine. Did you say you're in Italy?"

"Right. How's everyone there?"

"Never mind me, how the hell are you? We heard you were on that cruise ship that went down in the Atlantic. Everybody's been going nuts trying to find out what happened. We even called the college to see if they had any word on you, but no one could tell us a goddamn thing. Were you hurt?"

"No, I'm fine, Betty. Listen, I need a favor. I need to get ahold of the passenger list from the ship."

"What's going on?"

"I'm on someone else's dime right now, so I'll make this quick. I'm in Portofino at the moment and I'm calling from the office of their Chief of Police, Carlo Cansini. He's standing here next to me."

"Right. Got it."

"I met a gal on the ship named Katherine Adams. She's here, too—"

"Hang on for a second," Betty interrupted. "Hey, Mike, pick up. It's John Delaney on the phone. He's calling from Italy. You sound like you're around the corner, John."

"I know. It's a great connection."

"*Mike*, pick up the goddamn phone, would you?" she yelled again. "He's calling from Portofino."

There was a pause and a click as Detective Mike Franklin came on the line.

"Hey, big-shot lawyer. What's a matter with you? You too good for your friends anymore? We heard you were on that fuckin' cruise ship that sank . . . the *Ocean* something."

"He was," Betty said. "Shut up and listen for a second."

Delaney spent the next five minutes bringing them up to speed on what had happened aboard the *Ocean Majestic*. Then he told them about the assault on Katherine.

"So you think the two are related?" Franklin asked.

"I don't have a clue, Mike. Right now I just want to get ahold of the passenger list. I also want to know who the crewmembers on the *Marie Star* were."

"The what?"

"The *Marie Star*—it was one of the ships that picked us up. I'm thinking if the passenger list turns out to be a dead end, there's a good chance the assailant might have been a member of the crew."

"Why's that?"

"The local police here just came up with a clean print on a dead man's cigarette lighter. Turns out it belongs to the ship's captain, a man named Seldon Cardwell."

"So let me get this straight," said Franklin. "We've got a dead perp who attempted to make a hit on this lady you're with and a possible connection to one of the two ships that picked you up. What has this got to do with the NYPD?"

"Nothing . . . I don't know, or maybe something. I only know that one man was murdered and nine hundred people are dead and a billion-dollar ship was deliberately sunk. Now, out of the blue there's an attempted hit on the lady who first saw the murdered man's body."

"What's the deal with this woman?" Betty asked over the extension.

"She's an attorney from Atlanta and a former prosecutor with Justice."

"That's not what I meant, John. You just run into her in Portofino or what?"

There was a pause and Delaney glanced at Katherine before he answered.

"I met her on the cruise. I'd rather not go into the details, but she's pretty special to me. So I'd have to say my interest isn't strictly professional."

Betty Berkowitz and Mike Franklin looked at each other across the room. Franklin gave his partner a thumbs-up.

"Sorry, John," said Betty. "I wasn't trying to pry . . . well, not too much. It'll be a minor misuse of police power, but I think Uncle Phil has a friend at the Port Authority. How 'bout I give him a call and see what I can shake loose for you? What number are you at?"

Delaney repeated the number. He also gave her Cansini's fax number and e-mail address.

Franklin said, "Listen, pal, at the moment I don't have the first idea how to get a list of who's who on the crew of a Liberian tanker. Let me put my thinking cap on and I'll see what I can come up with. Is the number you just gave Betty the best way to reach you?"

"For the next twenty-four to forty-eight hours," Delaney told him. "Assuming Chief Cansini doesn't object, Katherine and I are heading back to the States as soon as we can change our reservations."

Cansini nodded his agreement and Delaney continued.

"Yeah, the number is a good one. If things work out we should be back home in a couple of days."

He said good-bye to both of them and hung up.

"Your conversation sounded encouraging," said Cansini.

"They're good people. I worked with them for thirteen years. If the information is out there, they'll get it."

"I'd like to know what the fax says," said Katherine.

"Of course," Cansini replied. "With respect to your leaving, I do not see a problem. I'll have to check with Genoa, of course. In the meantime, I would like to take recorded statements from each of you, if you don't object."

Katherine and Delaney both said it was fine. They were not, however, prepared for the second part of Cansini's request; he wanted their statements in the form of a polygraph examination.

At first Katherine didn't know whether to be angry or offended, but the more she thought about it, the more she was inclined to agree. She knew polygraphs weren't admissible in United States courts because they were not as reliable as their supporters made them out to be, but since she had nothing to hide she said it was fine with her.

Delaney had frequently used polygraphs in his investigations when he was a cop. Like Katherine, he also agreed.

THE FOLLOWING morning, the hotel manager rang Katherine's room and told her that Cansini had dropped by earlier with a note asking if she and Delaney would meet him at his office at 11:00 a.m. She thanked him, placed the receiver back on its hook, then rolled over and kissed Delaney on the cheek.

"The constable wants to see us in two hours. Did you sleep well?"

Delaney propped himself up on one elbow and kissed the nape of her neck, sending a shiver down her spine.

"Oh, yeah. That was the most fun I've had without laughing."

Katherine responded by slapping him on the leg.

"You shouldn't make a joke about everything."

"Sorry. I can be very annoying. I tend to do that when I'm at a loss for words. Yeah, I slept great. You fit very nicely in my arms."

"Good," said Katherine, putting her head on his chest and snuggling closer.

Delaney ran his fingers slowly up and down her back producing a contented sigh. She responded by rubbing her face against his shoulder.

"You found my weakness," she murmured.

"Really? I thought it was all that Miriam Haskell stuff you collect."

"This is cheaper and it has fringe benefits," she whispered.

"Such as?"

The law professor's eyes went wide as Katherine showed him.

AT FIVE minutes to eleven, Katherine Adams and John Delaney knocked on Cansini's door. They were met by his wife, Luciana, who ushered Katherine into the back office and asked Delaney to have a seat in the living room.

"Can I get you something to drink, signore? Some coffee, perhaps?"

Delaney was about to say yes when he suddenly remembered what Italian coffee tasted like and politely declined. He opted for a Pellegrino instead. Luciana went into the kitchen and returned a moment later with a glass of sparkling water. She handed it to him and sat down on the couch, folding her hands in her lap.

It was hard for Delaney to guess her age because she was one of those women who were able to manage an elegant appearance without trying. Her eyes were a warm brown that bespoke intelligence, and she moved with an easy grace. Dressed in an understated manner, her figure was still trim and fit. He thought for a moment and decided Luciana had to be somewhere in her early sixties. A few strands of gray were mixed in with her black hair which she wore in a bun at the back of her neck.

"Is this your first visit to Portofino?"

"Yes, it is."

"A poor introduction for you and the signora, I'm afraid. We don't generally have such incidents here."

"I'm sure."

"This is for you, by the way," Luciana said, handing him several sheets of paper. "They came in a little while ago."

The cover sheet of the fax read NEW YORK CITY POLICE DEPARTMENT at the top and contained a handwritten note from Mike Franklin in the message box asking that Delaney call him when he got back.

Delaney started going down the list of names, positive they were another dead end. He was conscious Luciana was watching him and equally certain that she already knew there was no Otto Magnuson on the passenger list, but he went through the pages anyway.

"Zero," he said, offering the papers back to her. "I had a feeling we weren't going anywhere with this. If your husband wants a copy it's fine with me."

"I've already made him copies, but thank you for offering."

"You're a good secretary."

She smiled. "I know."

"Mr. Cansini is a lucky man," Delaney said, raising his glass to her.

"I know that, too. More important, *he* knows. It's a

shame you have no idea who this man was. It makes matters more complicated, yes?"

"Definitely, yes."

"Carlo told me you and the signora are not married."

"That's true."

"And you have been separated from your spouse for many years. This is also true?"

"Many years," Delaney agreed. "I think the same is also true for Ms. Adams."

Luciana made a little clicking sound with her tongue.

"So . . . this would eliminate the unhappy wife or husband—very confusing," she said, with a shake of her head. "Have you known each other long?"

Delaney shifted in his seat. He was beginning to feel like a witness under cross-examination.

"Not very," he said. "We only met on the cruise."

"Ah . . . romantic. And now you are lovers. How wonderful."

"Excuse me?"

"I say . . . now you are lovers."

"Who said anything about our being lovers?"

"Signore, Portofino is a small town. It is very difficult to keep secrets here, no?"

"Apparently. Does it show that much?"

Luciana reached out and squeezed his hand.

"Only a little, but is more obvious to a woman. Yesterday, my sister and I were having lunch two tables from you and the signora. Neither of you looked up during the whole meal, so I tell Carlo, I think you are lovers."

Delaney laughed to himself.

"Yeah . . . well, I guess we were a little wrapped up in ourselves. You know how it is."

"Of course. I knew I would marry Carlo the first time I saw him. He was only an inspector then."

"How long have you been married?"

"Forty-one years next month."

Delaney let out a low whistle. Before he could reply further, the door to the inner office opened and Katherine stepped out. She was followed by Cansini and a small, owlish-looking man who Delaney guessed was the polygraph examiner.

"Everything was wonderful," Cansini told him. "I apologize for this inconvenience, but you understand why it is necessary."

"No problem," said Delaney. "I've just been visiting with your lovely wife. Are you ready for me now?"

"I'm pleased to see you survived Luciana's interrogation," joked the constable. It earned him a light slap on the arm from his wife.

"She didn't exactly use a rubber hose on me, but she's definitely sharp," Delaney told him. "It's a good thing you came out when you did because I was ready to crack."

Cansini chuckled.

"As I know only too well. This shouldn't take long. Professore, may I introduce Arturo Pezza? Arturo is with the Rapallo Police Department and will administer your exam."

"Great," said Delaney, shaking hands with Pezza. "I'm ready when you are."

"If you wish, Signora Adams may remain in the room."

Delaney shrugged and said it was fine with him.

Once inside, he took a seat next to the table where the polygraph was located. It was a small, unpretentious-looking machine in a beige box. A four-inch-wide sheet of graph paper was folded next to it. From experience, Delaney knew the three colored lines appearing on the readout as ragged peaks and valleys were the results of Katherine's exam. The machine was an older model;

most polygraphers now used computers. During his years as a detective he had witnessed numerous exams and even took one himself at the insistence of internal affairs after a shooting incident in Washington Heights.

He sat calmly as Pezza attached a piece of rubber tubing around his chest, and a pulse clip to his forefinger. Another tube was placed around his left ankle to measure his systolic blood pressure. All body signs would be recorded by three needles on a rolling sheet of graph paper, just as Katherine's had been. When the exam was finished, Pezza would check his answers and match them up against how his body's involuntary systems had responded to the questions.

In the hands of a competent examiner the polygraph had a high level of accuracy and was a useful tool to determine if a subject was lying. Personally, Delaney liked using them, even though he knew they had a poor record where sociopaths were concerned. That type had no emotional attachment to telling the truth or telling a lie. For them it was all a matter of manipulation. This was why polygraphs weren't allowed in courtrooms.

Pezza's questions began slowly covering the more innocuous aspects of Delaney's life. How old was he? Where did he live? Was he a lawyer? From there, they moved on to when he and Katherine had met and what had happened at the castle. Typically, all of the questions were asked so as to require a simple yes or no. Pezza sat behind Delaney, monitoring the machine's readout and occasionally stopping it to place a mark on the moving graph. Such marks coincided with the questions. Katherine, Luciana, and Cansini also took seats behind Delaney so as not to distract him.

His exam lasted a good deal longer than Katherine's had. Delaney expected this, since he was the one who had killed Magnuson. At one point near the end of the exam, the fax machine in the outer office rang and Cansini excused himself.

While her husband was out of the room, Luciana leaned over and whispered something in Katherine's ear. Katherine stared at her for a second before her face broke into a smile and she nodded in response. Neither Delaney nor the examiner saw the exchange.

"All right, just a few more questions, signore," Pezza told him.

"Fine."

The little man stopped the machine to add more ink to one of the reservoirs.

"Very good. We are ready now," he said. "You stated that you fought with the man who was trying to kill you and Signora Adams at the castle. Is this true?"

"Yes."

"And during the fight, this man broke through the balcony railing and fell to the first floor?"

"Yes."

"Is it true he was dead when you got the bottom of the steps?"

"Yes."

"And afterward, you and Signora Adams examined the body for the purpose of identifying him?"

"Yes."

"Did you remove a passport and an envelope containing money from the body?"

"Yes."

"Did you remove anything else?"

"No."

"After your examination, both of you came directly to the constable without stopping?"

"Yes."

Pezza was about to tell Delaney that was his last question, when Luciana handed him a note. The examiner stared at it for a second, blinked, and turned around to look at her. She and Katherine both nodded their heads vigorously and gestured for him to continue. He rolled his eyes and swiveled back around.

"Excuse the interruption," he said to Delaney. "The wound in your side—it was inflicted by the deceased man?"

"Yes."

"And you were following Signora Adams by chance that morning?"

"Uh . . . yes," said Delaney.

"Because she is beautiful and you are in love with her?"

Huh? thought Delaney. He heard Cansini re-enter the room at the same time. Not wanting to mess up the exam he ignored the odd question and simply answered "yes."

Pezza looked at the next question and shook his head.

"And having made love to Signora Adams, you will never again look at another woman?"

"What the fuck?" said Delaney, twisting around in his chair.

Pezza blinked again as blood pressure and pulse readings on the graph shot across the paper. Cansini, who also heard the question, folded his arms across his chest and gave his wife a reproachful look.

"Answer the question," said the women.

There was a pause as the needles returned to normal.

"Yes," said Delaney, looking at Katherine, "No other women."

"Well, I would say we are concluded," Pezza announced.

The little man got up and came around the table to free Delaney from the machine, which he did quickly, and then placed some distance between himself and his examinee. For a moment it appeared that Delaney was going to say something, but he changed his mind and settled for leveling a baleful look at Pezza, who held his hands up in defense.

After the good-byes, Katherine hung back for a second and exchanged a "low-five" with Luciana before following Delaney out the door.

THIRTY-TWO

The trip back to Atlanta connected through New York's Kennedy Airport and would have been interminably boring if not for the fact that Katherine and Delaney managed to get seats together. Cansini fixed matters with the Board of Inquiry, who took their statements over the phone. Thanks to a 400 m.p.h tailwind, they made it home in just over eight hours and twenty minutes. Katherine had a two-hour layover between flights and Delaney insisted on staying with her until she was ready to board. While they waited, she used her cell phone to call Beth Doliver.

"Hey Beth, it's me. How's Jack doing?"

"Katherine, where are you?"

"I'm at Kennedy Airport at the moment waiting for my connecting flight. John's with me."

"I thought you weren't coming back for another week," Beth said. "Jack's fine. It was only a mild heart attack, but he's driving both me and the doctors crazy. They ordered him to stay home for a couple of weeks and begin a walking program. And they also put him on a low-fat diet, which he absolutely hates. Everything the cook brings him he sends back."

"Just bear with it," said Katherine. "He's had a rough time."

"Yeah, well, if you decide to rent a husband for a few days, let me know and I'll ship him down to you."

"Tell Jack to be a good boy or I'll have John send some of his cop buddies by to arrest him."

"So how did it go with you two?" Beth asked, lowering her voice.

"You're right. I missed the kids a lot, so I decided to head home a little early," Katherine answered.

There was a pause. Beth frowned and looked at the receiver before she got the message.

"Oh, I get it. You can't talk, right?"

"Exactly. Tell Jack I miss him, too. I'll give you a call once I get back to Atlanta."

Beth gasped. "K. J., did you get laid?"

"Hello? Hello? God, I hate these cell phones. I think we're losing our connection, Beth. I'll call you later. Bye."

"Liar," Beth whispered into the phone.

As soon as Katherine hung up, her friend started giggling, then ran upstairs to tell her husband the latest news.

DELANEY AND Katherine checked the nearest video screen for her departure time and the flight's status. They still had thirty minutes to go. They promised to call each other in a couple of days once things settled down. For the first time since she had known him, John didn't have much to say. She wasn't sure what to make of his change of mood until he blurted out that he was "a little down about their parting."

Until that moment she placed him in the strong, silent category, but his unexpected disclosure caused a lump to form in her throat. They hugged in the middle of the terminal, oblivious to the sea of people drifting by, then sat down on one of the benches and held hands.

While they were waiting, Delaney listened to his

messages. One of them was from Mike Franklin. When it ended, he flipped his cell phone closed and told Katherine they were still drawing a blank on the *Marie Star*'s crew.

The gate agent called Katherine's flight as they were in the midst of discussing whether it would be easier for Delaney to fly down to Atlanta for a weekend or for her to fly up to New York. Another hug and three more kisses and Katherine was on the plane home. It was Sunday afternoon.

SHE HANDED the parking lot attendant her ticket and waited for the bad news: a seventy-two-dollar bill. The young man passed her change back through a sliding drawer, along with a "Frequent Parker Card" that contained a number of duck-shaped punches, one for each day she had been gone. Katherine shook her head at the ducks and pulled her Mercedes out onto Camp Creek Parkway.

IN ATLANTA, the police refer to I-285, a ninety-nine-mile loop that circles the city, as "the speedway." It consists of eight separate lanes and passes through three different counties that comprise the metro area. Motorists routinely ignore the 65 m.p.h speed limit in favor of more reasonable speeds (in their collective opinion) that hover somewhere around 80. All this is done on the assumption that the police have an unwritten rule that says they'll "give" a driver 10 m.p.h. over the speed limit. The police, of course, know nothing about such a rule and hand out tickets by the handful on a daily basis.

Katherine managed the drive home in one piece despite two near misses. She stopped at the mailbox and found it empty, then remembered her mail was being held until the end of the week.

Just as well.

After pulling her car into the garage she rolled her suit-case to the bedroom and considered unpacking, but decided to wait. The message light on her phone was flashing. She ignored that too and flopped down on the bed. It was good to be home.

She lay there thinking about John Delaney and how their relationship had changed. A little voice inside her head cautioned her that shipboard romances tend to fade quickly in the light of day. But this one seemed different. Delaney was different. He was intelligent, witty, consid-erate, and a wonderful lover. For the next half-hour she debated whether to call him. She knew that if there was any chance of their going forward she had to tell him about her past.

Tomorrow, she decided.

It wasn't that she didn't want to call. She did—very much. It was just hard shaking the trepidation. Common sense told her to take things slowly, assuming that was still possible now. Instead, she phoned the heart surgeon's house. A slightly breathless voice answered the phone. Kendra, the latest Mrs. Adams, had always re-minded her of someone trying to do a Marilyn Monroe impression.

"Hello?"

"Hi, Kendra. It's Katherine. Is Zach around?"

"Oh, Katherine. It's so nice to hear from you. How was your vacation?"

Apart from nearly drowning and getting murdered, it was marvelous, Katherine wanted to say. Instead, she said, "It was fine."

"I just adore cruising, don't you?" Kendra breathed. "Spain is such a lovely country."

"I was in Italy." *Maybe she doesn't read the papers*, Katherine thought, then corrected herself, wondering if Kendra read at all.

"Of course, it *was* Italy, wasn't it? Did you get to see a bullfight?"

Katherine held the receiver away from her ear and looked at it for a second.

"Uh . . . no. I think they were closed for the season."

"Oh, what a shame. Zach isn't here. He went cosmic bowling with a few friends. Would you like him to call when he gets back?"

Katherine searched her memory trying to recall exactly what "cosmic bowling" was. It came to her a moment later. Cosmic bowling had been a fad several years ago. Her two oldest children tried it for a while before they lost interest and moved on to other things. She remembered droves of high school kids descending on local bowling alleys and bowling to rock music, flashing lights, and fog machines. It was basically a disco with bowling balls.

"Sure. Just tell him I called and that he should come home tomorrow after school."

Katherine hung up and pressed the message button on her answering machine.

There was the usual array of calls from merchants offering estimates on new gutters to deals on siding (despite the fact that her home was made of brick). The air-conditioning people left a message reminding her that it was time for her annual checkup. One message she was particularly gratified to hear was from Sherri Wallace, who thanked her for sticking by her during the divorce, and said that she would be leaving a cake at the office later that week. Katherine smiled. She was about to save the rest of her thirty-one messages for the following morning, when her partner Barry Levitt's voice came on.

"Hi, K. J., this is Barry. I don't know if you're checking your messages from overseas, but give me a call as soon as you get this."

There were two more just like it later on the tape, and another from a person named Charles Watson, with the *Fulton County Chronicle*, a local newspaper that reported on legal cases.

Katherine dialed Barry's number.

"Barry . . . K. J., I just got your messages. What's up?"

"Katherine, where are you?"

"I'm back in Atlanta. What's up?"

"Oh . . . not much. What time are you coming in to-morrow?"

"Early. It'll probably take me three days just to clear off my desk. Why?"

"We're, uh . . . Bert wants to have a firm meeting first thing in the morning. Can you make it at eight-thirty?"

"Sure. Is something the matter?" Katherine asked, noting the odd tone in his voice.

"I guess," said Barry, "but I don't want to talk about it right now. I'll see you tomorrow, okay?"

"*No*, it's not okay, Barry. You leave three messages asking me to call you as soon as possible, then keep me hanging. I'm not a stranger, I'm your partner. Now what's the matter?"

"K. J., I really can't talk about it right now. I'll see you tomorrow morning."

"Barry—"

Katherine didn't know whether to be angry or offended when the line went dead.

Angry, she decided, slamming down the receiver.

She'd known Barry Levitt for more than ten years and this was the first time she could recall him acting this way. It was almost as if he was embarrassed to speak with her, something totally out of character for him.

Though Barry Levitt was a trial lawyer, he rarely set foot in court anymore. For the last eight years most of his time had been devoted to running the law firm as its managing partner, a job no one else wanted, and one at which he seemed to excel. He was a low-key and competent individual with an easygoing manner that everyone in the office appreciated. He and Burt Boyd were the firm's senior partners.

For a moment Katherine considered calling him back or phoning one of her other partners, but she was too tired for office politics just then. Instead, she fixed herself a cup of peach tea, turned on the stereo, and lay down on her bed to listen to Stan Getz play light jazz. She was asleep in ten minutes.

THE LAW firm of Boyd, Simons, Levitt, and Adams was located on the twenty-seventh floor of a modern building on Atlanta's perimeter. From a large picture window in the lobby, clients could see Atlanta's downtown skyline sixteen miles away. The lobby was paneled in dark cherry wood and decorated with a number of antiques, thanks in large part to Katherine's influence. The last chrome-and-leather sling-back chair had made its trip to the Salvation Army eight years earlier along with a Picasso-style area rug their original decorator sold them. It was replaced by a Bokhara carpet that went well with the wooden floors. Just as Barry Levitt had become managing partner by default, Katherine had stepped into the role of unofficial decorator, a title the male members were only too happy to confer on her.

She arrived at 8:20 a.m. and the first person she saw after coming though the double doors was her secretary, Galena, who was filling in at the reception desk. Katherine's smile faded when she caught Galena's expression. Her secretary motioned with her eyes to a man sitting on the couch.

Katherine immediately understood. The man saw her at the same time and got up. His features reminded her of a ferret.

"Ms. Adams, I'm Chuck Watson with the *Fulton County Chronicle*. I've left you several messages, but never got a reply, so I thought I'd drop by and take my chances. If you have a moment, I'd like to talk with you about the Bennett Williams suit."

"I'm sorry," said Katherine, "I'm really not familiar—"

"Katherine!" Burt Boyd called, coming out of the conference room to hug her. He was all smiles and good cheer. "I'm glad you could make it."

She got the message and kept quiet as Boyd turned to Chuck Watson.

"Why Mr. Watson, I'm surprised you're still here. I told you earlier this is not a good day for us. We have a firm meeting scheduled this morning. It would be best if you make an appointment."

Watson's nose twitched as he looked from Boyd to Katherine, then he took a camera out of a canvas shoulderbag.

"No problem," he said. "I'll call you later today, Ms. Adams. How about if I get a photo of you in the meantime?"

Boyd immediately stepped in front of Katherine and held his hand up.

"I don't think so."

"It's her decision, isn't it?" insisted Watson. "Our readers have a right to know what's going on, Mr. Boyd."

"If Ms. Adams wants to have her picture taken, you and she can discuss it later, but what happens in this office is *my* business and the answer is *no*. Do I make myself clear?"

"Generally, most attorneys are happy to—"

"Good day, Mr. Watson," said Boyd.

Watson stared at him for a second, shook his head, and walked out the front door. As soon as he was gone,

Katherine turned to her partner and asked, "What the hell's going on, Burt?"

Edward "Burt" Boyd had been a fixture on the Atlanta legal scene for forty years. He was the quintessential Southern gentleman with a head of white hair and an endless supply of bow ties. He wore one to work every day. The only concession he had made to the firm's "casual Friday" rule, adopted several years earlier, had been to take his jacket off in the office. Boyd was known throughout Atlanta as a tenacious litigator.

"Let's talk in the small conference room," he said.

"Fine."

Katherine was already aware that something was seriously wrong when she entered the room. Unlike the larger conference room behind the reception area, the small one doubled as a working library for the partners and associates. Row after row of books comprising the *Georgia Code*, the *Southeast Reporter* (first and second series) and the *United States Code* lined its walls. There were other volumes as well, all with different-colored bindings, from the maroon *Shepards Reports* to the turquoise *Southeastern Transaction and Litigation Guides*. In the corner was an end table with a coffee machine. Katherine said hello to her other partners and poured herself a cup.

"All right, does someone want to tell me what this is all about now?"

Barry Levitt began. "We have a problem, K.J. I apologize for not speaking with you last night, but this is an awkward situation. First of all, welcome back and, second; we're all delighted you weren't hurt in the tragedy. It must have been terrible."

"Thank you, Barry."

"Have you had a chance to catch up on the news since you've returned?" asked Burt Boyd.

"No, I just got home last night."

Boyd and Jerry Simons exchanged glances and turned back to her.

"I'm sure you're aware how much media attention has been focused on the *Ocean Majestic*'s sinking," said Levitt. "Accusations of negligence are flying everywhere. At the moment, there's a feeding frenzy looking for someone to blame. You helped that by handing the authorities Bennett Williams, K. J."

"Right," Katherine said, as visions of bodies drifting on the ocean swells flashed into her mind.

"Wrong," said Boyd.

"Excuse me?"

"Bennett Williams was released several days ago. His DNA turned out to be negative. The FBI obtained samples of the murdered man's hair from his wife and compared them to the scrapings they took from Williams's fingernails. They didn't match, K. J. On top of that, they tested the gun and determined that it hadn't been fired recently.

"A federal magistrate held a preliminary hearing in New York and ruled there was insufficient evidence to hold Williams. He ordered him released from custody."

"It was all over the papers," Levitt added.

Katherine felt like she had just been punched in the stomach.

"Unfortunately, that isn't the worst of it," Levitt continued. "While your friend Williams was in jail, he retained Tyler, King, and Elkins to defend him. They served us with this."

Levitt took a thick sheaf of papers out of his attaché case and slid them across the table to Katherine.

"It's a suit for one hundred million dollars against the firm for false arrest, defamation, negligence, and intentional infliction of emotional distress, among other things. The marshal was here on Thursday trying to serve papers on you. Since you were still out, I took the liberty of accepting them on your behalf."

Barry Levitt retrieved another set of papers from his attaché case and passed them to Katherine.

"Naturally, we contacted our malpractice carrier the moment they arrived. The bad news is they're refusing coverage because the incident didn't occur in the ordinary course of our legal representation."

Katherine stared at the papers in disbelief, her mind reeling. After a few seconds she forced herself to slow down and think deliberately.

"This is great," she said, pushing the papers away.

Levitt went on. "That's not all, K. J. We've also been in contact with the State Bar of Georgia. They're filing a complaint against you."

"What the hell for? All I did was to report what I saw."

"Which is exactly the problem," Levitt explained. "Apparently Bennett Williams was sixteen years old at the time he was convicted and his record was sealed by court order."

The meaning behind Barry Levitt's words slowly began to register. Katherine wasn't worried about defending the lawsuit, but there was a larger problem now. She had revealed information from a sealed record regarding a minor. Even though twenty years had elapsed, judges took a dim view of attorneys who violated their orders. As a result, she could be facing a charge of criminal contempt, and if Barry was right, the bar was going to file a complaint against her for that disclosure. She was aware the State Bar tended to choose their battles carefully. Rarely did they go after large firms. They concentrated mostly on sole practitioners, or lawyers who were involved in high-profile cases. This one was about as high profile as a case could get.

"So what are we going to do?" Katherine asked.

"Obviously, we'll retain independent counsel to represent us in the civil matter," Boyd told her. "The costs will have to come out of our own pockets, assuming I can't get the insurance carrier to reconsider their position. I'm meeting them tomorrow. But the bottom line is, it ain't gonna be cheap.

"We've given this considerable thought, K. J., and if they do bring criminal charges against you, you'll have to hire your own attorney to defend you. Obviously, we're all personally acquainted and it wouldn't be proper for anyone in the firm to get involved—besides, none of us practices criminal law. The same goes for the bar complaint.

"The fact is, your history with this Williams occurred before you joined this firm, and the rest has nothing to do with any legal work you've performed here," said Boyd.

Katherine nodded and remained silent, certain more was coming.

"The other thing is, I . . . *we* . . . think it would be a good idea for you to take a leave of absence from the office for a while . . . until this blows over."

"I see."

"Now don't go looking at me like that," said Boyd. "This is for the good of the firm. A civil suit is one matter, but now we've got that horse's ass of a reporter snooping around. The last thing we need is more adverse publicity."

"You know how they like to blow things up, K. J.," added Levitt. "No matter what you say, they'll report it in the most blatant fashion they can to sell more papers. The only thing that rag is good for is to wrap fish."

"Um-hm."

"Yeah, you know what they're like," Boyd echoed.

In fact, Katherine did know what the *Fulton County Chronicle* was like, far more than her partners did. It was a third-rate newspaper always on the lookout for scandal

rather than news. They had a habit of publishing un-
founded and uncorroborated stories, then quoting themselves as *authoritative sources* in subsequent editions for
the facts they made up in the earlier ones. Their reporters
tended to be people who couldn't make it with legitimate
newspapers. During her time in the U.S. Attorney's office,
Katherine had been involved in a number of cases that
drew national attention, and it took just one or two contacts
to convince her that any connection between the *Fulton
County Chronicle* and the truth was coincidental at best.

"What would you like me to do?" she asked quietly.

"Take a couple of weeks off until things settle down,"
said Boyd. "Jerry and I will handle your cases. I'm pretty
sure none of the judges will give us any trouble in light of
the circumstances."

"A couple of weeks?" Katherine repeated. "When was
the last time you heard of a civil case being resolved in a
couple of weeks—or a bar complaint, for that matter?"

"We're not saying you should stay out of the office,
K.J.," said Levitt, "but we've got a lot of clients who'll
get nervous when they hear their law firm is being sued
for a hundred million dollars. That reporter Watson will
make sure of it. The less heat we have to take, the better it
will be."

"And my being gone is supposed to help matters?"

"None of us like this, but it's something we've all
agreed on. I hope you understand," said Barry.

Katherine pushed herself back from the table and got
to her feet.

"I understand that I have three partners who are looking
out for themselves and have the backbones of jellyfish."

Before anyone could answer she turned and walked out
of the door.

Galena was waiting for her in the lobby. "K.J., I'm so
sorry."

"You knew?"

"I'm filling in for Vonda; she's out sick. Boyd called me at home last night and had me type this letter for you," she said, handing Katherine a white envelope. "They all signed it," she added, lowering her voice. "I didn't want to give it to you with that reporter here."

Katherine looked at the envelope and could guess what was in it. She slipped it into her purse without reading it.

"What are you going to do?"

"I don't know. Right now I need time to think and to clear my head. If you can pull a list of my clients together along with their phone numbers, that would help. I need to talk with them and see if they'll agree to substituting counsel. Fax it to my house when you get the chance, okay?"

"This whole thing sucks," said Galena. "How could Bennett Williams not be involved? The newspapers said they found a gun in his cabin and that he had scratches on his arms. I don't get it."

"Neither do I. I'll talk to you later."

Katherine's head was still spinning when she got on the elevator. As soon as the doors shut she leaned against the wall and closed her eyes. There was a knot in her stomach growing larger by the minute and she was having difficulty thinking straight. Her partners wanted her to leave.

For the good of the firm, Boyd had said. She was so angry she wanted to scream or cry. She didn't know which.

How could Bennett Williams not be involved?

Katherine walked across the parking deck to her car. All the evidence was there: the gun, the scratches—even his background. . . .

"Oh, Ms. Adams," a voice behind her said.

Katherine was in the process of putting her key in the door lock and turned around instinctively. The camera's flash caught her off guard. She blinked and held a hand up above her eyes. The photographer was Chuck Watson.

"Didn't mean to startle you," he said. "I just wanted to get a picture for the paper in case something came up later and we couldn't meet."

"You put my picture in your paper without permission and I'll sue you," Katherine said. "This is a restricted area, Mr. Watson. What are you doing here?"

"I guess I must have taken a wrong turn," he lied. "It's a big place. When I saw you get off the elevator, I thought, hey why not? Maybe she's free now."

I'll just bet you took a wrong turn, you little weasel. "Actually it's not a good time for me at the moment—"

"Is Boyd, Simons going to hire outside counsel to defend them in the suit?"

"I'm really not at liberty to say, Mr. Watson. You'll have to direct that question to Burt Boyd or Barry Levitt."

"How do you feel about being asked to leave the firm?" Katherine stared at him for a second.

Well . . . news certainly travels quickly, particularly when people are trying to cover their asses.

"First of all, I wasn't asked to leave, and second, I really don't have the time or inclination to do this right now."

"Do you think you're in danger of being disbarred?" Watson asked, ignoring her.

"I have no comment. Now, if you'll excuse me—"

"Just one more question, ma'am. A hundred million dollars is a lot of money—are you worried about the outcome of the suit?"

Watson had to take a step back to avoid being hit by her car door.

"I have no comment," she repeated.

"Look . . . I really would like to get your side, Ms. Adams. We're running the story tomorrow and I thought you might have something to say."

Katherine tossed her briefcase on the front seat and got behind the wheel.

"I do have something to say. If I were you, I'd move my foot unless you want it run over. And if I see my picture in your paper, I'll hire a lawyer."

"Check the constitution, counselor," Watson replied with a smile that never touched his eyes. "You've been all over the news for the last week. That makes you a celebrity *and* it gives me the right to take your photo. Hundred-million-dollar lawsuits don't happen every day in Fulton County. Our readers would like to know what's going on. You know what I mean?

"Let me ask you this: Would you say that you have a personal vendetta against Bennett Williams?"

Chuck Watson never got an answer to his question. The Mercedes's engine roared into life. Katherine threw the car into reverse and stepped on the gas.

If he gets his foot out of the way in time, fine—if not, that's fine, too.

She knew exactly what he meant when he referred to her as a celebrity. Whether she liked it or not, the incident on the *Ocean Majestic* and Bennett Williams's arrest had thrown her into the limelight. The correct term, according to the Supreme Court, was a "limited celebrity." It meant that as long as what was being reported wasn't malicious or intended to deliberately harm her, Watson could pretty much do as he pleased under the guise of freedom of the press. There were other legal niceties, but it all came down to the same thing: Her civil rights, *particularly* her right to privacy, had just taken a giant step backward.

THIRTY-THREE

Katherine didn't remember the ride home. But somehow she found herself sitting in her driveway. She parked the car at the rear of the house and closed the gates behind her. The last thing she wanted was uninvited guests.

She walked around the big English Tudor home to her patio and sat down by the fountain she loved so much. It was an indulgence she had built several years earlier. The fountain was made of black wrought iron and was nearly nine feet high with four separate tiers. Three elegant, long-necked swans adorned its base and water bubbled out of a spigot at the top into a series of shell-shaped bowls that spilled into one another, cascading down to a brick retaining pond. It was a sight that never failed to relax her.

She couldn't say how long she sat there watching and listening to the water, but when she finally got up there were long shadows on the ground and the sun was just above the treetops. She walked to the front of the house and saw a yellow manila envelope had been left at the front door. She picked it up and let herself in. The sender's address read, "State Bar of Georgia." She tossed it on the end table without opening it, went to her bedroom, and lay down on the bed.

The phone rang several times during the night, but she made no effort to answer it, nor did she try to hear who was calling when the machine picked up. The following morning she awoke with a headache and trudged into the kitchen to get two Advil.

A quick glance in the refrigerator told her most of the food was no longer fit for human consumption.

Wonderful, she thought.

Zach was coming home after school and he usually showed up starved. Going food shopping wasn't something she wanted to do, but there was little choice in the matter.

Now what? she asked herself. *Behave normally* was the obvious answer. *But this isn't exactly a normal situation, is it, Katherine?*

For the first time since she'd graduated law school she began to get an inkling of how some of her clients must have felt.

God, this bites, she thought.

That window of insight closed as quickly as it opened. Every day for the last eight years, rain or shine, cold or hot, she had gotten dressed and gone to her office. Now that wasn't possible.

For the good of the firm. Boyd's words replayed themselves in her mind. *For the good of the firm.*

Katherine closed the refrigerator and got a white porcelain carafe out of one of the cabinets and then filled the coffeemaker with water. Unfortunately, the tin where she kept her coffee was empty. She stared at the remaining grounds on the bottom for several seconds. Without warning she suddenly spun around and threw the carafe across the kitchen. It smashed into pieces against one of the cabinets.

"For the good of the firm."

Katherine stepped over them and went to take a shower. It was eleven o'clock in the morning when she finally left the house.

The Kroger Supermarket where she normally shopped had recently been remodeled and was now styled as a "super-supermarket," according to a banner in one of the windows. It was already crowded with young mothers, retirees, and housewives in tennis outfits. Katherine pulled a shopping cart from a line of about fifty others and began walking up and down the aisles. Every so often she picked up an item and tossed it in. She continued on automatic pilot for the next twenty minutes. On two different occasions she walked down the same aisle without realizing it. After a resigned breath she decided the shopping cart was full enough.

The checkout line had three people in front of her. While waiting her turn Katherine glanced at the national tabloids and saw that Elvis had been sighted again, former president Clinton was dating a fifteen-year-old porn star, and a two-headed dog had been born in Iowa that bore a striking resemblance to its owner. The paper didn't say which head it was.

Her eye continued to roam over the magazines until it came to rest on the stack of regular newspapers. For a second she couldn't believe what she was seeing. There on the front page of the *Fulton County Chronicle* and the *Atlanta Journal* was a full-page photograph of her getting off the elevator the day before. The picture, which was less than complimentary, had a headline above it that read "Prominent Atlanta Lawyer Sued for 100 Million Dollars."

Katherine nearly went into shock and immediately snatched a copy off the rack. The article said that a lawsuit filed by Bennett Williams had named her as one of the defendants along with her law firm. It went on to detail her background as a former prosecutor with the Justice Department and described the case she and Williams had been involved in.

"Do you have any coupons today?" a pleasant-looking woman behind the register asked.

"What?"

"Do you have any coupons?"

"Oh . . . uh, no."

"Are you a member of the Kroger Club?"

"The what? I'm sorry," Katherine said, trying to concentrate.

"It's a club that gives you discounts. It will only take a minute to sign you up. I have a—"

"Look, I'm sorry. I can't do this right now."

She tossed a dollar on the conveyer belt for the newspaper and left her shopping cart where it was.

"But, ma'am," the lady called after her. *"Ma'am. . . ."*

Katherine never heard the rest of the sentence because the automatic doors closed behind her. When she got to her car she slid behind the steering wheel and read the rest of the story. Not only did it talk about the recent tragedy on the *Ocean Majestic*, it was slanted in such a way so as to make it look like she had been harboring a grudge against Bennett Williams for years.

This reporter attempted to interview Adams, but she refused to speak with him, falling back on that time-honored phrase "no comment." Williams's attorney, Gary Pagel, of the prestigious New York law firm Tyler, King, and Elkins, said his client ". . . has been terribly damaged by the irresponsible and reprehensible statements made by Katherine Adams." Pagel said they were looking forward to their day in court.

Katherine tossed the paper aside and started the engine. She began driving with no destination in mind. She just drove.

Eventually she found herself in the parking lot at Perimeter Mall and went into one of the bistros to have lunch. An attorney she knew by sight, but not personally, was seated in the second booth from the door and glanced up when she entered. He nodded by way of acknowledgment and gave her a weak smile. His companion, another lawyer, twisted around in the booth, looked at her, and then said something under his breath to his friend.

When the hostess finally led her to a table, she sat there feeling self-conscious, exposed, and certain half the people in the restaurant were staring at her. Katherine finished her lunch quickly and left.

THIRTY-FOUR

For the next two days Katherine stayed home, wandering around the house arranging and rearranging furniture. Too self-conscious to go out, she felt she was adrift on the sea alone. The one saving grace was Zach. When he got off the school bus she was waiting for him and he all but launched himself at her, a huge smile on his face.

Like any teenage boy he wanted to hear every detail about how the *Majestic* had sunk. What was it like to see a dead person? Did it gross her out? Had she ever seen one before? Though she had no desire to relive the episode, Katherine related the events as faithfully as she could, leaving out the part about the attack on her life in Portofino. Whether it impressed her sixteen-year-old she didn't know, but she was grateful when the flood of questions finally subsided.

John Delaney called a number of times and left messages for her, but she didn't return them. In fact, she didn't return any messages people were leaving, including those from her partners. On the second day, Burt Boyd surprised her by coming to her home. Katherine didn't invite him in; they stood in the doorway and talked. Boyd said he felt bad about what had happened and assured her they were still a team. He said he was concerned about how she was holding up and he asked about her children. Then he started asking questions about the cases she had been handling. She told him to go to hell and shut the door in his face.

Three more days passed. It was two o'clock in the afternoon when the front doorbell rang.

Katherine looked up, trying to decide whether to answer it or not. She was in the process of sketching the fountain in her backyard, something she hadn't done in years. Drawing had always been a passion, and she didn't know what caused her to take it up again. Probably having too much time on her hands, she decided. To her, sketching was more than just a way of relaxing or passing time. When she drew it was as if she and her subject were alone in the world. Katherine had been drawing since the fourth grade.

On nice days during art class, her teacher sometimes took the students outside. She would lie on her back, looking up into the branches of an ancient oak tree that grew on the school's lawn, her fingers moving over the sketchpad. Shadow and light in the spiderweb of branches emerged in astonishing detail.

Her drawings were more than mechanical reproductions. The sketches bristled with life and feeling. Her teacher recognized her ability right away and encouraged her to keep at it. Art soon became Katherine's favorite subject.

Her parents, however, were practical hardworking people who viewed drawing as a hobby, not something a person should spend their life doing. Ambivalent at first, they soon actively discouraged her from taking time away from "legitimate" school subjects and wasting her time daydreaming. Her teacher even made a special trip to Katherine's home and tried to explain Katherine's talent to them. The speech fell on deaf ears and the sketchpad was put away.

Over the years the pad reappeared from time to time, especially after her children were born and again after her divorce, though it never stayed out very long. The talent was still there, but so were the day-to-day demands of a legal practice, so the pad waited. She'd come across it several days ago in a hall closet while she was cleaning.

When the doorbell rang a second time, her charcoal paused above the paper. Katherine muttered something under her breath and got up.

Galena Olivares was standing at the front door.

"Galena, how did you get down here? I thought I locked the gate."

"Glad to see you, too, K. J. I ruined a pair of pantyhose climbing over your fucking gate. Jesus, you look like shit."

"Thank you for noticing. Why are you here?"

"I'm your secretary, remember? It's like you dropped off the earth. What's with you?"

"I'm just taking it easy for a while."

"That's what you people call it, huh?" said Galena, looking up at the house.

Katherine didn't respond.

"Anyway," she continued after a silence, "you gonna invite me in or keep me standing on your doorstep?"

Katherine took a breath. "I'm sorry," she said hugging Galena. "I don't mean to be a bitch."

"You're a lawyer—you can't help it."

Katherine pushed the door open and led Galena into the living room.

"Can I get you something to drink?"

"I'll take iced tea, if you have any."

"Have a seat. I'll be right back."

* * *

GALENA OLIVARES sat down and looked at her surroundings. The living room of Katherine's home was almost forty feet in length and nearly the same in width. An antique Marie Teresa chandelier suspended from a high vaulted ceiling dominated the room's center. The entire room was paneled in maple. A large lead-glass window looked out onto the patio and Katherine's fountain. To the right was a fireplace with a carved limestone mantel.

Katherine returned with two drinks and sat down across from her.

"So, how're you doing?" asked Galena.

"If I were having any more fun I couldn't stand it."

There was a pause before Galena continued.

"All of your clients have been screaming for you."

"There's not much I can do for them right now. Burt signed the pleadings as co-counsel and he's the firm's senior partner. He's got the right to take over the cases if he wants to."

"I understand what you're going through K. J. I spoke to everyone—with the exception of that idiot, Wilson. I swear they'll all follow you if you decide to leave."

To emphasize her point Galena fished around in her purse and produced a small legal pad containing a list of about thirty names, all of them Katherine's clients.

Katherine looked at the list for a few seconds and handed it back.

"It wouldn't be ethical. Technically, they belong to the firm. It would also be a violation of our partnership agreement for me to solicit them."

"Who said anything about soliciting? They did this on their own. I'm telling you, every one of them told Burt they didn't want him to represent them. Sherri Wallace told him to drop dead when he refused to give her your cell phone number. Your partners are just covering their asses. The whole thing's a bunch of crap. And you want to know what else?"

"What?"

"Jimmy said he'd go with you if you decide to leave. He can't stand Boyd either. It's the same with Phyllis."

Katherine stared at her secretary, not quite knowing what to say.

"I'll give it some thought," she said after a minute. "The last thing I had in mind was going out on my own and starting a firm."

"Well, don't think about it too long. The clients are willing to stay with you if you leave, but the longer you wait. . . ."

"I know, I know. I just can't make a decision like this on the spur of the—"

Katherine stopped speaking when Galena's cell phone went off.

"Hello? Oh, hey. Yeah, I'm here with her right now. Just a minute. It's for you," Galena said, handing the phone to Katherine.

Katherine frowned at her and mouthed, "Who is it?"

Galena shrugged and continued to hold the phone out.

Exasperated, Katherine gave in and took it. "This is Katherine Adams."

"Yeah . . . well, this is John Delaney and I've got a bone to pick with you. Where the hell have you been? I've been calling all week. I must have left a hundred messages."

"Oh, John," she said. "I know you've been calling. It's just that I—"

"I think I'll go have a look at that fountain," said Galena. "I'll be back in a bit."

A Cheshire cat smile appeared on her face and she started for the back door, just managing to avoid the swipe Katherine took at her backside.

"Look, I know what's going on and how you must be feeling right now," Delaney told her. "Bennett named me as a defendant, too, along with all three of the captains who sat on the board, the United States Navy, Regal Cruise Lines, and anyone else he's ever met. I thought we had something together, K. J."

Katherine paused before she answered. She didn't have to be a mind reader to know Delaney was angry or that he was holding off really letting her have it. He was right—she should have returned his calls. She knew it. But how could he understand what she'd been going through? How could anybody? Being a lawyer was almost as much a part of her as being a mother. She knew she could never go back to Boyd, Simons, Levitt, and Adams again. Their relationship would end the way all her relationships ended.

Her apology came out in a rush, along with emotions she had been holding in check for the last week. The outpouring was unexpected, not only by Delaney, but by Katherine herself, and when it was over, the comfort of hearing each other's voice began to have its effect.

THIRTY-FIVE

Through the window Katherine could see Galena sitting on one of her lounge chairs, watching water bubble out of the fountain. She waved to her, but Galena didn't see it.

Katherine sighed and leaned back on the couch, closing her eyes. She'd been on the phone for nearly a half-hour.

She said, "This may sound silly, but I'm really happy

to hear your voice. I've been going through a rough time the last few days. I just needed to be by myself and think things through."

"It's not silly and I understand," Delaney said. "Galena's been filling me in on the local news. If you'd like, I've got a friend named Guido who'll be happy to pay that reporter a visit and break his knees."

Katherine smiled in spite of herself.

"Everything hit me at the same time. I know the lawsuit is worthless, but there were those photos in the papers, then my partners asking me to leave, and now the State Bar's involved. They filed a disciplinary complaint against me for disclosing confidential information about a minor."

"Oh, bullshit," said Delaney. "First of all, Williams isn't a minor anymore. Second, let's start thinking like lawyers. We were dealing with an extraordinary situation involving a massive loss of life in the middle of an ocean. Considering the circumstances, my guess is that your *first* duty was to prevent any more deaths and see that justice was done. The Bar loves to get involved in cases like this because the public will think they're doing a good job.

"I spoke to Rudy Abrams—a buddy of mine. Rudy and I went to school together and he practices down there. He's willing to represent you—gratis. Do you know him?"

"The name's familiar," Katherine said. "But I don't think we've met."

"He says he ran into you at a seminar a few years ago. He does a lot of this stuff."

Katherine thought for a second and tried to match the name with a face but couldn't.

"Anyway, Rudy's a good guy," Delaney went on, sensing her reluctance. For some reason there was a wall rising up between them again. Katherine was pulling away and he didn't know why.

"I gave him your number," he went on. "He probably called already and left a message."

"It's possible. I haven't been answering the phone."

"I know. So start answering it and rejoin the world."

"I'll try," she said, only half-believing that she would. "What's going on with you?"

"Well, apart from missing you and trying to ease back into a normal schedule, not much. I came up with a dead end on the *Marie Star*'s crew list, by the way."

"I don't get it," said Katherine. "How could Seldon Cardwell's fingerprint get on that cigarette lighter?"

"No idea. Both the FBI and Interpol interviewed him in Gibraltar, and he said he had no clue. He told them he'd lost it a couple of weeks earlier and never saw it again. Oh, and you might be interested to know the Feds came up with a match on Otto Magnuson. His real name was Umar Maharan and he had connections to Hamas."

Katherine frowned.

"Hamas?"

"The Middle Eastern terrorist organization. They're the ones Yasir Arafat used to claim he had no control of while he was slipping them weapons and money on the side."

"I *know* who they are," said Katherine. "What do they have to do with me? We both know Maharan wasn't on vacation in Portofino, and he sure as hell didn't swim there. He *had* to be on one of those ships, John."

"Maybe he was just looking for an American to kill."

"Maybe, but that doesn't add up either. Didn't Cansini tell us the car he was driving was stolen in France before it was driven to Portofino?"

"Yeah. He changed plates with a rental car out of Florence."

"I can't imagine Portofino being at the top of any terrorist hit list. He was there for a specific reason, and I think it involved me. I've been racking my brain for the last week trying to figure out why, and the only thing I can come up with has to do with Ellis Stephens. Maybe it was something I saw in his room, or maybe something Ellis said to me. I think all that money Maharan was carrying is also related."

"You're saying it was a professional hit?"

"I don't know. I need to speak with Libby Stephens. She gave me her number. I've got it here somewhere and I've been meaning to call her, but I haven't had the energy over the last few days."

"This whole thing is bull," said Delaney. "Look, why don't you come up to New York and spend a few days with me? We'll go see her together."

"You wouldn't want me in this condition."

"K.J., I'd want you in any condition," he said seriously. "C'mon. I'll even spring for dinner and tickets to a play."

"No . . . there's a lot you don't know about me, John. I should have talked to you when we were in Italy—before we got involved."

"We're talking now."

"It's just that . . . John, I can't. I'm damaged goods. You don't want to get involved with someone like me. It will end badly. It always ends badly," she added in a whisper.

"Let me tell you something I learned a long time ago. Having a partner—someone you can rely on, someone who's there to watch your back, makes life a whole lot easier. People are stronger when they're a team, K.J., and they can face down any problem. I believe that—I really do."

"But—"

"But nothing. Making love to you in Portofino was wonderful. In fact, it was just about the most wonderful thing that's ever happened to me. I know how guys are supposed to be, but I couldn't have gotten out of the starting blocks if I didn't want you. I hope you hear what I'm saying. I want *you* as a person—problems and all, good and bad, not just your body, which is kind of spectacular by the way. With me, it's a package deal."

"Oh, John. . . ."

All at once the floodgates opened and things Katherine had been holding inside began to pour out. She told him about Richard Jenks and what he had done to her so many years ago. She told him about the flashbacks and the medicine she had to take. Post-traumatic stress syndrome the doctors called it. She told him how the heart surgeon had shattered her trust and how it affected her relationship with men. Intimacies she had shared only with her psychiatrist in the past came out in a rush. He was silent when she finished.

"Katherine, what you went through was rotten. I'm not making light of it, but it doesn't affect the way I feel about you, not one little bit. I didn't run when you started screaming in your sleep the first night we were together. I won't run now and I won't run later. I held you until you quieted down. I'm good at holding people. That's what partners do."

"You *knew*?"

"Some of it. Not all the details, of course, but I'm telling you they don't matter. The woman I want is on the phone with me, traumatic stress and all, problems and all. A college girl was attacked by a sicko. Everyone our age has a past, and it doesn't mean squat to me. Trust comes with time. You have to earn it. We'll earn it together, if you'll give me a chance—give us a chance."

"John," Katherine whispered.

There was a long pause as Delaney held his breath. This was the make-or-break moment.

"What play?" Katherine finally asked.

"*What play?* Any play—any play you want, or a concert, or the ballet. Just name it."

"I suppose I could call Zach's father and ask for a favor," she said. "Only, I just got him back and they might have plans. I don't want him to feel like he's being shuttled back and forth."

"Of course. But if you're right about this, we need to get moving on it before someone else does."

Katherine had already thought about that—a great deal. Now with Galena's sudden appearance and her suggestion that she start her own firm, there was one more thing to complicate matters.

In the end, it was Zach who decided the issue. If someone *had* made an attempt on her life, it stood to reason his associates might do so again—and the last thing she would tolerate was her child being at risk.

"I'll call you back tonight," she said.

When the call was over, Galena poked her head in the room and asked, "Is it safe?"

Katherine laughed.

"Sure. I'm going to New York for a few days, but I'll definitely think about what you said. Why don't you, me, Jimmy, and Phyllis all sit down together and a talk when I get back?"

Galena's face lit up and she gave Katherine a hug.

"I knew you would do it. I have a friend in the leasing department of the 2600 building, right across from us. A tenant recently moved out on them and they're dying to rent the space."

"Whoa," said Katherine. "I haven't agreed to anything yet."

"Sure, sure. I'll call Jimmy and Phyllis and let them know the good news."

"There *isn't* any good news," Katherine insisted. "All I said was that we would talk when I get back."

"Right. No problem. So you're going up to see the professor, huh? He's looks really cute from his photographs and he's always so nice on the phone. Not like some of those other losers you've dated. He's funny, too."

"When did you see photographs of John?"

"He was in the papers. He looks like a hunk. Is he tall?"

"About six-two," Katherine answered.

She took Galena by the elbow and walked her to the door. "I've got a lot of phone calls to make. I also have to pack to get ready in time."

"There's a flight at six thirty-five tonight and another one at eight fifty-eight," said Galena. "Tomorrow morning the first flight out is at ten twenty. Oh, and Montez Miller called. She said she could fit you in for a nail appointment this afternoon if you need to see her."

Katherine stopped in mid-stride and folded her arms across her chest. "She just happened to call?"

"Uh . . . yeah."

"Mm-hmm. And which flight do I have reservations on?"

"The one in the morning."

THIRTY-SIX

That evening at dinner Katherine broached the subject of going up to New York for a few days to her son. She also called James and Alley and explained the situation to them without getting into specifics. No one had a problem with it, including the heart surgeon, who surprised her by agreeing to take Zach again without an argument. He even asked if there was anything he could do to help.

Zach said the same thing. As they rode to school the next morning, he listened soberly while Katherine explained why she was going and what the lawsuit was about. He assured her he would be fine and then asked if she needed any money, because he had a few hundred dollars saved up. It nearly caused her to start crying. She held it in for his sake. When they arrived at the front door, she kissed him good-bye and promised to call every day. She sat behind the steering wheel watching her youngest son walk toward the school's entrance for several seconds before she put her car in gear.

So big. So much like a man, she thought. The tears came then.

She thought about her conversation with Delaney while she drove to the airport and it made her feel good in a way she hadn't felt for a long time. A seed of hope that it would be different this time began to grow in the corner of her heart.

"People live in hope," her father had once said to her.

It was one of those trite expressions that didn't mean much at the time. But then maybe her father was smarter than she thought.

THIRTY-SEVEN

Katherine walked down the concourse at LaGuardia Airport to where Delaney was waiting. He was dressed in a blue oxford shirt, maroon tie, dark brown pants, and a tweed coat.

"You look like a law professor today," she said, kissing him.

"And you look wonderful."

She rested her face on his shoulder breathing in the scent she had come to associate with him. They hugged for a long time.

"It's good to see you," she whispered, though it was mostly to herself.

At baggage claim they waited for her luggage along with the other passengers on her flight. Her suitcase came out fifteen minutes later.

"We'll have to catch a cab," Delaney explained. "A friend of mine is using my car today."

"That's fine."

He handed her suitcase to the driver who put it in the trunk, and waited for Katherine to get in before he followed. A brief discussion ensued with the driver about the best route into the city. Delaney told him to take the Queensboro Bridge, but the cabbie insisted the Triborough was faster. They argued for another minute before the driver saw he wasn't going to win and gave up.

"The Triborough's more scenic," Delaney said as they pulled onto Grand Central Parkway. "Unfortunately, the fare comes out about eight dollars more, not counting the toll. It's an old game."

There was a pause before he continued.

"I'm really glad you're here, K. J."

"I am, too," she said, snuggling closer.

"After we drop your stuff off at my place, we can run over and talk to Libby. I called her last night and she's cool with it."

"How's she doing?"

Delaney made a see-saw motion with his hand.

"Yeah." Katherine said.

"I want to ask her some more about that stuff Ellis was working on. I agree with you about the whole business being connected. The problem is I don't have the first clue why or how. Maybe between the two of us we can figure it out."

"Have you checked into who owns the *Marie Star*?" asked Katherine.

"Not yet. They're a Liberian registry; that much we do know. We sent a couple of inquiries, but as of this morning they haven't responded. It's the same runaround Cansini got."

"How did you find out about the crew?"

"Cardwell faxed us a copy of the ship's roll himself— 'us' being my friends on the force."

"I see."

During the cab ride they explored various theories as to why the *Ocean Majestic* might have been sunk, as well as the attempt on Katherine's life. None of them held much promise. They were both as much in the dark as they had been nearly two weeks earlier. As they were crossing the Queensboro Bridge into Manhattan, Katherine looked down at the swirling gray waters of the East River. To her left, the distinctive shape of the United Nations rose up and on her immediate right were four huge smokestacks of a building Con Edison had affectionately dubbed "Big Alice." It was one of the city's main power plants.

Ever since the famous New York blackout of 1965 that turned vast areas of the five boroughs dark for several hours, Big Alice had become something of a landmark. A second, lesser-known event, or series of events, depending upon your point of view, occurred nine months later when New York's birthrate unexpectedly soared.

Delaney's home was a pleasant surprise. One of New York City's first grand apartment buildings, the Dakota is a Beaux-Arts style building with enormous windows that look out over Central Park. It was constructed in

1884 and was largely responsible for upgrading the area surrounding it, which consisted mostly of shanties and open land at the time. People thought it was so far uptown, they told any friends who wanted to move there they might as well be living in the Dakotas. The name stuck. Over the years, legends grew up around it and it even earned a place in the National Ghost Register due to several sightings of a young boy wandering through its halls. In reality the Dakota has only seven floors, but it appears much taller due to its Renaissance style and a peaked slate roof. The dormers and turrets all contain windows, but they are there more for architectural balance than function. An ornate arch, flanked by a pair of urns and wrought-iron lanterns, opens into a large courtyard. It's been one of the most photographed buildings in New York for decades.

"You live *here?*" Katherine asked as the cab came to a stop.

"I inherited my aunt's apartment from her about twelve years ago."

"I'm impressed."

"Uh . . . yeah," he replied, slightly embarrassed. "Aunt May was loaded. For reasons no one in the family can explain, she took a liking to me and left me her place."

Katherine looked into the courtyard and up at the roof, slowly nodding her approval.

"We used to drive past this on the way to the Museum of Natural History when I was little," she said. "I always wondered about it. It's beautiful."

"C'mon in and I'll give you the cook's tour."

An elevator carried them to the fourth floor of the building. The door to Delaney's apartment opened into a living room at odds with the image he projected, at least in Katherine's opinion. She was prepared for a typical man's apartment with minimal decorating and everything

lined up along the walls. Instead, she was pleasantly surprised to find a beautiful Oriental rug and a pleasant
arrangement of overstuffed traditional furniture set at an-
gles around the room. Austrian drapes adorned the windows and there was even an antique mahogany secretary
in the corner. Delaney's bedroom was decidedly
masculine, accented by a tiger-skin chair and a king-size
sled bed that reminded her of something Ernest Heming-
way might have used. All the furniture was of good quality without appearing ostentatious.

Katherine herself wasn't sure what her reaction would
be to spending the night at his place. It was a good sign
that she felt comfortable right away. It also helped that he
wasn't taking the situation for granted despite the fact
that they had already slept together. He showed her the
guest bedroom and asked where she wanted her suitcase.

"How about in your room?" she replied.

A big smile creased his face. She loved that smile, and
his having the best butt in Manhattan, maybe the whole
city, didn't hurt either.

Katherine spent a few minutes unpacking. She appro-
priated a portion of the master closet for her clothes and
the same amount of space on the bathroom vanity for her
makeup and hair dryer. When she finished she found that
Delaney had prepared lunch—salad for her and a sandwich for himself. Another surprise.

"I really like your furniture. Your aunt had excellent
taste," she said, as they sat down to eat.

"Oh, this is all my stuff. Aunt May left me the condo,
but she gave her furniture to my sister."

"*You* did all this?" Katherine said, putting her fork
down. She twisted around in her seat and studied the
apartment again.

"Yeah."

"You're amazing."

"That's what I keep telling you."

Katherine shook her head. "What time are we meeting Libby?"

"In about an hour. She lives in Kew Gardens. I said we'd drop by around three o'clock. If Pinky doesn't have my car back by the time we're ready to leave, we'll have to catch another cab."

"Pinky?"

"A buddy of mine. We grew up together. He's an inspector with U.S. Customs now. I thought he might get some information for us about who the owners of the *Marie Star* are, so I asked him to help. They keep tabs on all the ships that go in and out of New York Harbor."

"Sounds good."

"Pinky used to be with the NYPD but he transferred to Customs a couple of years after I left the force."

"How come he needed your car?"

"Before 9/11 his office was located at the World Trade Center, but they had to get other space after the buildings went down. They're scattered all over the place now until they get their act together. It's a real mess. The administrative offices are in lower Manhattan and ownership records are in Brooklyn, in Canarsie."

"Where in Canarsie?" asked Katherine. "I grew up there."

"I dunno. We can ask Pinky when we meet him later."

"That can't be his real name."

Delaney smiled. "It's not—it's Paul Marchefski."

"So how do you turn that into Pinky?"

"A few years back he went to Rockaway Beach with a girl and I guess the date wasn't going so well. He fell asleep on the blanket and when he woke up she was gone, except she'd left her pink beach bag behind. He tried reaching her for a couple of days and even went to her house but he couldn't find her."

"Was she kidnapped?"

"No. It turns out she'd met an old college boyfriend and they took off for Atlantic City together. That stupid beach bag sat on his desk for nearly a month before he found out. By then he had already filed a missing person's report. When word got around, the rest of the guys in the station started ribbing him. You know how cops are."

"That's terrible," said Katherine. "I hope you didn't participate in it."

"Uh . . . yeah. I'll give him a try on his cell and see what the story is."

While Delaney was calling, Katherine went into the den and placed her own call to Beth Doliver.

"Guess where I am?" she asked.

"Where?"

"I'm calling from John's apartment. It's the nicest place. Did you know he lives in the *Dakota*?"

"You're in town?" Beth asked, surprised. "When did you get in?"

"A couple of hours ago. John invited me up for a few days. How are you feeling and how's Jack?"

"I'm fine. Jack's doing great, too. You just came up for a social visit, you slut?"

Katherine laughed. "Actually, it's part social, part business. We're heading out to see Libby Stephens in a little while."

There was a pause before Beth spoke again. "K. J., we talked about this. I thought you were going to let the police handle it. I'm serious."

"You worry too much," said Katherine. "I have a lot to tell you when we see each other. In the meantime, I want you to be careful. John and I both think the car that almost hit you wasn't an accident."

"You're crazy, and I don't worry too much," Beth insisted. "I can't see how some nut in Italy relates to a ship sinking in the middle of the Atlantic Ocean. I understand Bennett Williams had help and I don't want his friends coming after you, K. J."

"You haven't been following the papers, have you?"

"Not really. I've been home most of the week with Jack. He started his walking program yesterday."

Katherine's revelation about the judge letting Williams go came as a shock to her friend. Nevertheless, it didn't dissuade Beth from insisting that she drop the matter.

"I'll be fine," Katherine told her. "Besides, I've got John to protect me. If you and Jack are free, maybe we can all get together for dinner tonight or tomorrow—that is, if Jack's up to it."

"Tomorrow would be better. Where will you be later?"

"After we see Libby, we're meeting a customs inspector friend of John's. His name is Pinky, if you can believe it."

"What does the Customs Department have to do with this?"

"We're trying to find out who owns the *Marie Star*. It's a long shot, but the information might be helpful."

Beth took a resigned breath. "I'll give you a buzz later."

"Okay. Love you."

"Love you, too. Say hi to John for me."

By two-thirty Pinky Marchefski hadn't reappeared nor did he answer his cell phone, so Delaney left him a message and they went downstairs and asked the doorman to hail them a cab. He gave the driver the address, then held his breath as the man made a U-turn in the middle of Seventy-second Street, cutting across four lanes of traffic, totally oblivious to the curses being shouted at him.

Libby Stephens's home was in a pleasant residential neighborhood. A sign above the mailbox read STEPHENS. There was another sign on the front lawn that said FOR SALE. Katherine and Delaney saw it at the same time and exchanged glances as they walked to the entrance. The door opened before he had a chance to knock.

"Oh . . . it's so good to see you both," Libby said, giving each of them a hug. "Come in. Come in."

She ushered them into the living room and poured glasses of tea from a crystal pitcher for everyone. For the next fifteen minutes they caught up on recent events. Libby told them about Ellis's memorial service, and they expressed their regret at not being able to attend. While they were talking, Katherine glanced around the room. Both the kitchen and the hallway were stacked with cardboard boxes.

"After the funeral, I decided to put the house on the market," Libby explained. "I'm moving to Florida. My mother and two sisters live in Orlando and both of my boys are going to school in Gainesville. That's only about an hour away."

"Isn't this all kind of sudden?" asked Katherine.

"Extremely. The house was only on the market for three days before we got an offer. They generally sell fast in this neighborhood, but I couldn't believe how quickly it happened. To be honest, I really wasn't prepared for anyone to buy it so soon. But with Ellis being gone, there's no reason for me to stay. We were going to celebrate our anniversary next month. . . ."

Libby's voice trailed off and her eyes became moist. She turned her head away and looked out the window at the lawn. Katherine got up and put an arm around her.

"I'm sorry," Libby said. "Every time I think I'm over it, it happens again."

Delaney shook his head.

"You'll never be over it," he told her softly, "and you shouldn't. Ellis was a good man. I didn't know him very well, but I liked him right from the start."

"Thank you, John. Tell me how I can help."

"It's like I mentioned on the phone. K. J. and I are convinced Ellis's death and the sinking of the *Ocean Majestic* are related. What I didn't tell you was the day we arrived in Portofino, a man named Umar Maharan tried to kill Katherine."

Libby gasped.

"That's why we came to see you. I know this is tough, but I'd like to ask you a few questions about Ellis's work if you feel up to it."

Libby was clearly shocked about the attack on Katherine. She took a deep breath and dabbed her eyes with the corner of a handkerchief.

"That's the third time today I've ruined my eyeliner," she said. "Go ahead and ask your questions, John. I'll do my best. You do know I've been over all this with the FBI and the police?"

"Right," said Delaney. "I've read the reports. We just want to see if maybe they missed something. It's a long shot, but you never can tell."

"Okay."

"For example," said Katherine, "who else knew you and Ellis were going on a vacation? Bennett Williams obviously wasn't on the ship by accident. He said as much himself at the hearing."

"Let's see . . . our children knew, of course, and so did my mother. Esther and Maury Blum also knew . . . they're our next-door neighbors. They were watching the house while we were away. Then there's Jamie and Keith and, oh yes . . . Warren Wilkerson and the travel agent. She had an odd, foreign-sounding name. Diviana, I think. She works for Roberts Travel."

"Great," said Delaney.

He took a small yellow pad out of his pocket and scratched some notes on it. "Esther and Maury, your neighbors, I got that. Who are the others?"

"Jamie is Jamie Yamaguchi. She's one of Ellis's assistants, a graduate student. I'm not sure what her major is. Molecular biology, if I remember correctly. Keith Haynes is also an assistant, but he has a PhD in genetics. He's been with . . . was with, Ellis on the project for the last five years. I was very hurt when neither of them came to the memorial service."

"Did you expect them to?" asked Katherine.

"Of course. Keith and Maureen are good friends. They've been here for dinner at least a dozen times. I didn't know Jamie that well. She was only with us for the last year, but she seems like such a nice, sweet girl—very bright."

Katherine nodded.

"And who was the other person you mentioned?" asked Delaney. "Warren Wilkerson?"

"Warren is the department dean. The poor man is just devastated by what happened. He was the one who suggested Diviana."

"Diviana?" repeated Delaney.

"The travel agent they used," said Katherine.

"Oh, right." Delaney said, adding a few more notes to his pad. "Can you think of anyone else who knew you were leaving?"

Libby looked up at the ceiling and began ticking off the people she had mentioned on her fingers.

"No. That's about it. The others might have mentioned it to different people, but I'd have no way of knowing if they did."

"Are your neighbors home now?"

"I'm afraid not. They both teach at Hunter College and usually get back around six o'clock."

"How about the dean, this Wilkerson fellow? Would he be at the school now?" asked Katherine.

"I imagine so," Libby told them. "Warren is usually the last one in our department to leave."

"What about Yamaguchi and Haynes?" asked Delaney.

"Possibly. But I haven't seen or spoken to either of them since I got back. It's a little disappointing, considering how long they worked with Ellis. Neither of them even sent a card or called."

"Did they all get along well?" asked Delaney.

"I always thought so. Ellis would have told me if he was having any problems with them. We've known the Hayneses for fifteen years."

Delaney and Katherine looked at each other.

"I hope you don't mind my asking this," said Delaney, "but if Williams didn't kill your husband that leaves the question of who did. Was Ellis in any kind of trouble, or was anyone mad at him?"

"The police asked me the same thing, John, and honestly, I can't think of a single person who had anything against Ellis. Everyone liked him."

Katherine asked, "Do you have any idea how Williams knew you were on the ship?"

Libby shook her head. "Ellis and I talked about it several times, and neither of us had a clue. I asked Warren the same thing when I got back, and he didn't know either. He's been so upset by what happened, he ordered a whole new security system for the department."

"Is there *anything* you can think of that might be helpful?" asked Delaney.

"Not really. I'm sorry, John."

"Don't be. We're just trying to get to the bottom of this. If we come up with a connection, we'll let you know."

Before they left they got Libby's phone number in Florida and promised to stay in touch. They kissed Libby good-bye and headed back toward Queens Boulevard where Delaney thought they stood the best chance of catching a cab. It was two blocks away.

He tried Pinky's number again while they were walking and still couldn't get an answer.

"That's odd," he told Katherine. "Pinky's normally as reliable as hell."

"Do you think anything's wrong?"

"Nah. Pinky can take care of himself. He's probably tied up or can't get any reception wherever he is."

THIRTY-EIGHT

By the time they reached Queens Boulevard the sky had darkened and it was starting to drizzle. Typical of New York, all the cabs did a disappearing act as soon as the rain began. Delaney tried hailing one for fifteen minutes while Katherine set aside her traditional notion of equality between the sexes and waited in the doorway of a shoe repair shop. When the last group of taxis passed, he glanced over his shoulder at her and shook his head.

"How about if we take the subway?" she called. "There's one over there."

"You sure?"

"It's better than drowning."

He gave her a flat look and signaled for her to join him. He put his arm around her shoulders and they crossed the street together to the Union Turnpike Station. In Manhattan they changed to the A train and got off near Columbia University's campus. A security guard told them the Physical Sciences building was located on the opposite side. They found it with no problem. It was a large modern structure that seemed out of place among the stately old buildings. The Bio-Genetics Department occupied the third floor and had a good view of the Low Memorial Library.

At Katherine's suggestion, Libby phoned ahead to secure an appointment for them with the dean. After a short wait, the departmental secretary appeared and escorted them to Wilkerson's waiting room at the rear of the building. She told them to make themselves comfortable.

Wilkerson showed up a few minutes later. He was in his early sixties and might once have been an athlete, but had let his body go, judging from the way his stomach now hung over his belt. He was perhaps an inch or two shorter than Delaney and had gray-brown hair and a deep tan. After the introductions, Wilkerson told his secretary she was free to leave for the weekend. Though his manner was friendly and open, Katherine got the impression that it was clearly his place and he knew it.

Wilkerson's private office was well appointed. To the left of his desk hung several framed degrees showing his accomplishments. One of them indicated his undergraduate work had been completed at Stanford University in chemical engineering; another showed he had received a doctorate some years later. A picture window at the side of the room gave an expansive view of the quadrangle and the school's walking paths. It had stopped raining by then, and outside students studied their textbooks while others, less academically inclined, played Frisbee. Some socialized in small groups.

"What can I do for you, Professor?" asked Wilkerson. "Libby tells me you and Ms. Adams are friends of hers."

Delaney opened his mouth to reply, but it was Katherine who answered. She knew taking the lead might come off as aggressive, but Wilkerson spoke as if she wasn't there and it annoyed her.

"Do you have any idea how Gotschal Biomedical knew Ellis Stephens was taking the cruise?" she asked, coming directly to the point.

"Honestly, I do not, Ms. . . . ah, Adams, isn't it? The

FBI investigators posed the same question and I've thought about it quite a bit. The truth is I don't know. Sometimes this happens in situations like this."

"What situations are you referring to?" asked Katherine.

"Corporate spying. It's sad to say but money can turn people's heads—particularly a lot of money, which is often the case with high-tech research. Ellis and his group made an incredible breakthrough in the area of genetics. What they accomplished will make it possible to grow new organs from scratch. No more waiting for the right donor to appear or the problem of rejection. It's quite incredible. But in the highly competitive world of genetic research, some companies can be quite unscrupulous."

"I see," said Katherine. "Besides yourself, who else knew the Stephenses were taking a vacation?"

"Very few people, I suspect. I communicated the news of Ellis's discovery to the president of the school, of course, and told him Ellis would be taking a couple of weeks off . . . with my blessing, I might add. He'd been working so hard. I probably mentioned it to my wife, too. Then there was Ms. Yamaguchi and Dr. Haynes. And I suspect the travel agent I sent them to had to know since she made their reservations."

"Right," said Delaney. "Libby told us you were the one who recommended her, a Diviana something. . . ."

"Diviana Patel. She's a delightful young lady who works for Roberts Travel. They have an office on Lexington and Eighty-sixth. I can give you the number if you wish."

"That would be great," said Delaney. "Thanks."

Wilkerson leaned back in his chair and shook his head.

"I've been sick to my heart over this. I don't know if you know it, but I was the one who suggested that Ellis take the cruise. I wish I'd never opened my mouth."

Delaney gave him a sympathetic look. "You shouldn't beat yourself up. There's no way anyone could have foreseen what happened."

"I know, but still—"

"Dean Wilkerson," Katherine interrupted. "Libby mentioned neither of Ellis's assistants showed up at the memorial service. Did that strike you as unusual?"

Wilkerson frowned.

"Actually, yes. Ellis, Keith, and Jamie were a tight-knit group, so I was more than a little surprised when neither made an appearance. I'm not saying anything against them, mind you, but I'd be less than honest if I said it didn't bother me, because it did.

"In Dr. Haynes's case we found out why quickly enough. It turns out Keith took a job overseas with Metadine Research. His departure was abrupt, but in all fairness, I'd have to say it's a wonderful opportunity for him. Still, the lack of even two weeks' notice was very troublesome."

"Metadine?" Delaney repeated.

"They're a French company. Keith took over as head of their research department. He's in Paris right now, training, from what I understand."

"In the same area of work he was doing here?" asked Katherine.

"No, no, no . . . he signed a non-disclosure agreement with us. The university has a policy that all the research conducted here belongs to the institution. That applied to everyone, except Ellis and a few others who were with the school before it was instituted. From what I understand, Dr. Haynes's work will be in a related field of genetics. Something to do with developing a new medication for rheumatism."

"Didn't Libby say Keith Haynes was married?" Katherine asked Delaney.

"She did. Do you know if his wife accompanied him?"

Wilkerson lifted his shoulders.

"I imagine she did. I mean, we never discussed it, but she must have. The only communication I've had from him was a letter recently telling me he was getting settled in, but I can't see why she wouldn't. Would you like me to call her?"

"That would be very helpful," said Delaney.

Wilkerson reached forward, picked up a Rolodex from the corner of his desk, and began thumbing through it. It took him a moment to find the number. A small crease appeared between his eyebrows after the phone rang several times and a message came on. Wilkerson listened to it, then hung up.

"It appears we have the answer to your question, Professor. There's a recording on the line saying the number has been disconnected."

"Are you sure you dialed it correctly?"

"I think so."

Wilkerson punched in the number again and put the phone on the loudspeaker so they could hear.

"That's moving pretty quickly," said Katherine. "How long ago did he leave? It can't be more than two weeks."

"Almost three to be exact," Wilkerson told her. "I must say this is a little odd."

"I suppose we can talk to him by phone," said Katherine. "What about Jamie Yamaguchi . . . is she at school today?"

"I'm afraid I don't have good news regarding her either," said Wilkerson. "Ms. Yamaguchi has taken a leave of absence to get married and won't be back until the end of the month."

"Really?" said Katherine. "Were you aware she was getting married? Libby didn't mention anything about it to us."

Wilkerson smiled.

"To be honest I'm really not up on the comings and go-ings of Ellis's assistants. Matters of that type are gener-ally handled by the faculty adviser, which in this case would have been Ellis. As a graduate student Ms. Yam-aguchi was pretty much a free agent. If I recall correctly, she completed her class work last May and has been working on her doctoral thesis since that time."

"Here?" asked Katherine.

"Ellis procured her an assistantship, which is a job of sorts. The university pays her . . . not a lot, but a reason-able stipend. Our assistants don't have any specific hours in terms of punching a clock. What generally happens is they put in about twenty hours a week while pursuing their degree. Sometimes they'll teach undergraduate classes or conduct research, as Jamie was doing."

"And you had *no* idea she was leaving?" asked De-laney. "Aren't you the head of the department?"

"Certainly, but this is something that's handled by a supervising faculty member and our secretary. I'm sure it's the same at your school. From what they tell me it was a case of young love and all that."

Their conversation with Warren Wilkerson lasted an-other ten minutes and ended pretty much the way it had be-gun. He answered their questions, but provided very little in the way of useful information. Each avenue Katherine and Delaney explored led to a stone wall and increasing frustration on their part. The only topic Wilkerson flatly re-fused to discuss was what the university's plans were with regard to Ellis's research. He told them the matter was un-der consideration by the board of trustees and that every-thing would be done to ensure that Libby received adequate compensation.

"But I thought it was Ellis's idea," said Katherine.

"That's what the whole argument with Bennett on the ship was about. His company wanted to buy the research."

"I'm afraid this is something our lawyers will have to work out, Ms. Adams," Wilkerson said. "Unfortunately, Ellis never had an opportunity to patent his work, and as such, the university's position is that the research should be the property of the school since it was developed here."

"Does Libby know about this?"

"Not yet. We're still in the talking stage—at least until the board makes up its mind. I'm confident it will work out to everyone's satisfaction."

Wilkerson stood up, indicating the meeting was at an end.

"Is there anything else I can do for you? I really must be running along."

Katherine asked, "Dean, would it be possible to use your library? We need to do a little research of our own."

"Of course," he said, walking them to the door. "Technically, our facilities are open to teachers in other universities as a courtesy, but I think we can bend the rules a bit to include you."

"Is that the law library over there?" Katherine asked, looking out the window at a large columned building on the other side of the quadrangle.

"No, it's housed separately. You can see it to the left of that sculpture," Wilkerson said, pointing.

"Very kind of you," Katherine replied. "Do you know if they maintain a corporate database record for the various states?"

Wilkerson chuckled.

"I don't believe anyone has ever asked me that question before. But I'm sure if it's out there, Columbia has it. The librarians will be glad to help. We've got a great staff—very knowledgeable."

"Wonderful," said Katherine, shaking his hand. "Thanks again."

FROM HIS window Warren Wilkerson watched Katherine and Delaney walk across the campus. They paused for a moment at the library steps, but appeared to change their minds and kept going in the direction of 116th Street. Without taking his eyes off them he reached back, picked up the phone, and dialed a number.

"Yes?" a voice answered after the second ring.

"They were just here."

"What did they want?"

"They were digging around about Haynes and Yamaguchi, and wanting to know who else knew Stephens was going on a vacation—the same questions the FBI asked."

"Not surprising. He was a cop before he became a law professor. They all think alike. Frankly, the woman worries me more than he does."

"It was the same with her," Wilkerson said, "except she wanted to know if our library had court records and corporate databases."

"Why do you suppose she wanted them?"

"I'm not sure. I suspect she plans to dig into the ownership of the *Marie Star.*"

There was a pause.

"That wouldn't be in her best interests."

"Hasn't there been enough killing already?"

"Enough so that two more won't be noticed. I'd rather avoid it, but we can't afford for them to complicate matters right now."

Warren Wilkerson's heart began to thud in his chest and he found that his mouth had gone dry. Beads of perspiration broke out on his forehead. How could anyone talk about cold-blooded murder this way? Nine hundred people were just numbers to this person.

"Surely there has to be something we can do . . . something else."

"Let's hope so . . . for their sake," the voice said, and the line went dead.

THIRTY-NINE

Katherine and Delaney walked across Amsterdam Avenue to wait for a bus. The sun was trying to poke its way through the clouds. Oil slicks left by passing motorists mingled with puddles on the ground, producing false rainbows that disappeared as quickly as they were formed.

"What would you like to tackle next?" asked Delaney.

"Dinner. It's almost seven o'clock and my stomach is making some very unladylike noises."

"Jeez, I'm sorry, K. J. I got so wrapped up, I totally forgot about the time. What are you in the mood for?"

"How do you feel about sushi?"

"I don't eat anything I can use for bait."

Katherine laughed. "Okay, surprise me. Here comes the bus."

Delaney's cell phone rang as the doors were opening and Katherine stepped aside to allow the passengers to exit. Her foot had barely touched the first step when she felt him grab her forearm. One glance at his face was enough to let her know something was wrong—very wrong. She shook her head to the driver and indicated for him to go on.

"How?" she heard him say.

Katherine opened her mouth to speak, but he held up his hand.

"What time did it happen?"

The person on the other end of the line said something she couldn't hear and a look of anguish clouded Delaney's features.

He took a deep breath. "Yeah," he said. "We're at the corner of 114th Street and Amsterdam. How long will it take you?"

Another pause.

"All right, see you in ten minutes."

Delaney pressed the disconnect button on his cell phone and rested his forehead against a lamppost, squeezing his eyes shut.

"What is it, John?" Katherine asked, putting a hand on his shoulder.

He opened his eyes and rubbed his face with his hands. After a second he took a deep breath.

"That was Mike Franklin. Pinky Marchefski's dead. He was killed in a hit-and-run on Centre Street earlier today."

"Oh, my God," Katherine said, pulling him to her. "I'm so sorry."

They stood there holding each other for several minutes. Delaney's eyes were red when they separated. He looked away and wiped them. Katherine searched for the right words to say, but nothing came to her. She didn't know his friend, but she was devastated by his loss. All she could do was repeat how sorry she was. Neither of them spoke until an unmarked police car pulled up to the curb. A dark-haired man was behind the wheel.

"Here's our ride."

Detective Mike Franklin got out and he and Delaney hugged.

"How did it happen, Mike?" asked Delaney.

"All I know is that it was a hit-and-run," Franklin told him. "I was at Manhattan South when the call came in. Apparently Pinky was crossing a street near his office and some prick came flying by, nailed him, and then took off. The uniform working it found your vehicle registration in Pinky's wallet. What the hell was he doing downtown so late?"

"He was doing me a favor," Delaney answered. "Mike, this is Katherine Adams. K. J., meet Mike Franklin."

"Pleased to meet you," Franklin said, shaking her hand. "I see Delaney's taste in women is improving. You're the ship lady, right?"

Katherine smiled. "Right."

"Let's get in," said Delaney.

They took the West Side Highway and reached Centre Street in just under twenty minutes. The police were already there and had the area roped off to traffic. A photographer was busy taking pictures. An ambulance was also on site along with two paramedics and a half dozen uniformed cops. When a plainclothes detective saw them, he detached himself from the crowd, and came over. His partner stayed behind and continued interviewing the witnesses.

Franklin introduced Detective Ricky Benetiz to them. Benetiz was a ten-year man on the force recently assigned to the traffic fatality division, a position it was apparent he had little enthusiasm for. He was in his mid-thirties and looked to be just shy of five feet eight. His appearance came off older due to a receding hairline and a thin mustache. He was wearing a wrinkled tan suit and a white button-down shirt. Both looked like they could have used a good ironing.

"So what was Marchefski doing with your vehicle registration?" asked Benetiz. "I understand he was a cop before he transferred to Customs."

"Yeah . . . he was a cop," said Delaney, staring at his friend's body on the stretcher. "We used to work together. He was doing me a favor and I let him borrow my car."

"What kind of favor?"

"I asked him to see if he could check into the owners of a ship—the *Marie Star*."

"How come?"

"About ten days after the *Ocean Majestic* went down, Ms. Adams and I were in Portofino, and someone made an attempt on her life. The guy had no fingerprints and he was using phony ID. Our theory is the two incidents are related. Ms. Adams was the one—"

"Right, right. Who discovered the scientist's body," Benetiz finished. "I read about that in the papers. I forget his name."

"Ellis Stephens," said Katherine.

"Yeah, Stephens. Then you fingered the wrong guy, or something. No offense."

"None taken," said Katherine, meeting his eyes.

"The news reports said you prosecuted Williams a few years back for arson when you were with Justice. The story's been all over the news for the last week."

"That's right, too," said Katherine.

Delaney said, "Mike was checking on the crew for me and Pinky was trying to try find out about the owners. The guy who tried to kill Katherine had a cigarette lighter on him."

"So?" said Benetiz.

"The Italian police tied the lighter to a man named Seldon Cardwell, the captain of the *Marie Star*. Cardwell told them he didn't have any idea how the perp got it. And to make matters more interesting, the hit man was a fellow named Umar Maharan, who worked for Hamas."

"Any reason you're referring to him in the past tense?" asked Benetiz.

Delaney filled Benetiz and Franklin in on what had happened to Umar. When he was finished, Franklin shook his head and clapped Delaney on the back.

"When you left the force you said all you wanted was a nice quiet job."

Delaney nodded absently, but didn't respond. After a second or two his brows came together.

"What's up?" Franklin asked, picking up on his expression.

"Who was the first cop on the scene?"

"Nick Brown, over there," Benetiz answered, pointing to a cop who was in the process of writing out a report.

"Did he take an inventory of Pinky's personal property?"

"Sure . . . it's S.O.P. You know that."

Without another word, Delaney started walking toward Officer Brown.

"Detective Benetiz says you were the first one on the scene. Is that right?"

"Yes, sir," the patrolman replied.

"Where's Marchefski's personal stuff?"

"I bagged everything and put it in my patrol car, except for the vehicle registration. I gave that to Sergeant Benetiz."

"Was there a briefcase?"

The officer frowned. "Not that I saw. He just had a wallet, keys, a cell phone, and some loose change. That's about it."

"What's up, pal?" Franklin asked as he joined them. Benetiz and Katherine were close behind.

"Mike, do you remember that ratty old briefcase Pinky used to carry around? It belonged to his dad or something."

Franklin nodded. "Yeah. It was an old-fashioned thing with a flap and buckles. Did you see anything like that?" he asked, turning to the officer.

"No, sir. Like I said, it was only the usual stuff. You want me to get the bag from my unit?"

"What's the big deal with his briefcase?" asked Benetiz.

"Every time Marchefski worked a case, he kept all his notes in a briefcase," Franklin explained. "We used to call it his traveling office."

"So maybe he didn't use it this time. Or maybe he left it home."

"Maybe," Delaney replied, scanning the surrounding area. "Do you know where the Customs parking lot is located?"

"Not really," said Benetiz. "It's gotta be around here somewhere. But everyone's probably gone by now. I'm not even sure where the Customs building is now. I can check in the morning if you want."

"Tomorrow's Saturday," Katherine said. "Hang on for a second."

She took her cell phone out of her purse and called directory assistance. A second later she had the phone number for the U.S. Customs Service, along with their address.

"Which way is Hudson Street?" she asked.

"It's about two blocks up," Officer Brown answered, motioning over his shoulder with his thumb.

"They're located at number sixty-five Hudson Street, on the eleventh floor. Maybe there's a security guard who can tell us where the lot is."

Benetiz nodded and signaled for Officer Brown to join them and they started up the street together.

Katherine's prediction was correct. The Customs Department did have a security guard stationed in the lobby. They introduced themselves and explained the situation to him. The guard told them where the employees' parking lot was located. Delaney gave Officer Brown a description of his car. Brown then used his walkie-talkie to relay that information to his partner and asked him to check it out. At Delaney's request the guard had one of his co-workers escort them up to Pinky's office.

The second guard, a fellow named Sanderson, confirmed what Benetiz had said earlier: The building was pretty much deserted at that hour of the night. He took them to Marchefski's office. There was no briefcase. Even the legal pad on Pinky's desk was devoid of any notes mentioning the *Marie Star*. Another dead end.

On the way back to the elevator, Katherine noticed a light at the end of the hall and asked Sanderson about it.

"That's probably Curtis. He's one of our computer programmers. If he has to make up next week's schedule he stays late every now and then."

Katherine threw a silent question at Delaney.

"It's worth a try," he said.

As the group approached Curtis's office they exchanged puzzled glances. The sounds of a man and woman having sex could clearly be heard coming from within. Delaney and Benetiz poked their heads around the corner.

Curtis turned out to be an overgrown teenager in his late twenties with a bad complexion, scraggly goatee, and long, unwashed hair. He was wearing a T-shirt and jeans and had a lollipop stick in his mouth. He was so preoccupied with the action on his computer screen he never heard anyone enter the room. When Benetiz touched him on the shoulder he let out a yelp and would have fallen over the back of his chair had Delaney not stopped him in time.

"Shit. You nearly scared me to death," he said to Delaney. Then he noticed the others standing there, turned red in the face, and quickly flicked the monitor off.

"I didn't think anyone else was in the building," he

stammered. "I'm on my own time now. I was just . . . uh. . . ."

"Relax, sonny," Benetiz told him. "We were just checking someone's office. You can go back to what you were doing as soon as we leave."

Curtis cast a nervous glance at Officer Brown, who returned his look without blinking.

"It's not illegal to look at this stuff, you know."

"No, it isn't," said Benetiz. "Like I said, we were just checking someone's office."

"So I'm not in any trouble?"

"No, you're not in any trouble."

"What's going on?"

"One of your co-workers was killed by a hit-and-run earlier," Benetiz explained.

"No shit. Who was it?"

"Paul Marchefski," said Delaney.

Curtis's mouth dropped open, and his lollipop nearly fell out.

"No way. He was just up here a couple of hours ago. I don't fuckin' believe it."

"What was he doing?" asked Katherine.

"Some research. I was helping him with the database. Mr. M wasn't too good with computers. Christ, I'm sorry to hear about this. He was a real decent guy."

"Do you remember what you were looking for?" asked Katherine.

"Sure. He was trying to track down the owners of some ship."

"Can you recall the ship's name?" asked Benetiz.

Curtis shook his head. "He never mentioned it. I just got him into the records and he took over from there."

"Do you know if he found the information he was after?" asked Katherine.

"I think so, because he asked me if I could loan him a

floppy disk. I can't believe this shit; people are fuckin' sick."

"Yeah, people are sick," Delaney agreed. "Did you see what he did with the floppy?"

"I'm pretty sure he stuck it in his briefcase along with his legal pad."

Delaney, Benetiz, and Franklin all exchanged glances but didn't say anything.

"What'd I say?" asked Curtis.

"Nothing," Delaney answered. "We're just interested in what Paul was working on. Can you get us into this database?"

"Uh . . . maybe it would be better if you guys wait until morning and my supervisor says it's okay. I mean, I'm not trying to be uncooperative, but I don't know you and I don't want to get into any trouble."

Benetiz and Franklin both took out their badges identifying themselves as detectives and showed them to him. Officer Brown, on the other hand, remained silent, fixing Curtis with a dour look. He got the message quickly. Everyone watched as his fingers moved over the keyboard. After a moment, page after page began to appear on the computer screen.

"This is LISA," Curtis explained, referring to the database he was looking at. "We keep a list of every commercial and private ship that makes port in the United States. It shows whether cargo was off-loaded or on-loaded, and whether taxes and duties were paid, etcetera etcetera. Do you know what you're looking for?"

"A ship called the *Marie Star*," Katherine told him.

"The *Marie Star*," Curtis repeated, typing the name into the search field. There was a brief pause before an image of a port inspector's certificate came up.

"Here we go. The *Marie Star* is a Liberian registry. She sailed out of New York Harbor on June eighth, bound for

Genoa, Italy, and then Saudi Arabia, with what looks like hospital supplies . . . two hundred thirty beds; mattresses; tongue depressors; cases and cases of cotton swabs; meds; and a bunch of other stuff. You want me to print out the whole manifest?"

"Sure," said Delaney.

"Are you positive they sailed on June eighth?" asked Katherine.

"Absolutely. The Port Authority cleared them at 6:20 p.m. on a rush request. Now this is a little odd. . . ." Curtis broke off what he was saying and read further.

"It looks like there was a last-minute change of plans here, because the original route they filed called for them to go to Argentina on June twelfth."

A second document appeared on the computer screen. Curtis leaned back to let the others see.

"What does that mean?" asked Franklin.

Curtis shrugged.

"Maybe nothing. Ships'll change a route plan if their company needs them to make an extra stop, but it usually doesn't involve switching hemispheres. These guys pulled a complete one-eighty."

"So?" said Benetiz.

"So you're the detective. You tell me," Curtis said.

Benetiz gave him a sour look and turned to Katherine.

"Why'd you ask him about June eighth?"

"A couple of reasons," she explained. "First, the *Ocean Majestic* set sail from Miami on June *ninth*. This ship left the day before and traveled south toward Miami instead of east toward Italy. Maybe it's something and maybe it's nothing, but they were one of the two ships that rescued us.

"Detective Franklin secured a list of the passengers along with the names of the *Majestic*'s crew. And the man who tried to kill me wasn't among them. That leaves the crew of the *Marie Star*. It's the *only* place he could have come from."

"How come?"

"Do you remember that fingerprint John told you about on the cigarette lighter?"

"Yeah," Franklin said. "The one belonging to the *Star*'s captain. He told Interpol he hadn't seen the lighter for a couple of weeks."

The crease between Benetiz's eyes deepened as the implications dawned on him. He looked from Katherine to Franklin and back again.

"How could that be if he sailed the day before you?" he asked.

Katherine turned her palms up and gave him a tight smile. "Great question."

Benetiz considered what he'd just heard and turned to Delaney.

"Okay . . . you're the law professor. Do we have jurisdiction over this?"

Delaney nodded.

"The murdered scientist on the *Ocean Majestic* was a Columbia University professor named Ellis Stephens. He lived in Queens. There were also a lot of New Yorkers who bought it when the ship went down. Half of them were burned to death."

"Go on."

"Unless Paul Marchefski's briefcase turns up in the next few minutes, I'm guessing the hit-and-run wasn't an accident. He was deliberately killed for what he found."

As if in answer to the question, Officer Brown's walkie-talkie chose that moment to go off.

"This is Baxley," a voice on the other end cracked. "We've got the car. There's no briefcase here that I can see."

"Ask if he checked the trunk," said Delaney.

Brown nodded.

"Mickey, you check the trunk, too?"

"Of course I checked the trunk. It's clean, except for a spare tire, a jack, and what looks like a bunch of law school exam finals."

Brown and Benetiz looked at Delaney.

"I haven't had a chance to grade them yet," he said. "Tell him thanks and ask if he can drive the car around to the front entrance."

"The prof says thanks and wants you to bring his car around to the front," Brown repeated into the mike.

"Will do."

"What does that document say about the ship's owners?" Katherine asked, pointing at the screen.

"Let's see," said Curtis, bringing up another page. "Here we go. It's the Farrington-Medlin Group, a New York limited partnership."

FORTY

Delaney's car turned out to be a white 1960 Jaguar XK-150 convertible, complete with wire wheels and knockoff rims. The dashboard was burled walnut and still had the original airplane flip switches Jaguar used before they went to push buttons. Katherine studied it after they got in and decided it was a lot like the man who owned it: conservative and solid, with a lot of strength under the hood. She felt good being with him, but there was a feeling of disquiet in her stomach that was growing worse by the minute. When they arrived uptown, Delaney parked the Jag in a lot on Columbus Avenue and they walked back to his apartment holding hands. Neither of them spoke much, nor did they make love that night.

A theory was forming in Katherine's mind that she couldn't shake. It upset her and made sleep impossible. From the one-word answers she was getting from Delaney, she was pretty sure he was thinking along the same lines. Neither would put their thoughts into words just then and she lay awake into the early hours of the morning watching as the space between the bedroom drapes grew lighter. At 5:00 a.m. she finally gave up, slipped out of bed, and wandered into the kitchen to make a cup of coffee.

Delaney came in a half-hour later, wearing the bottom half of his pajamas. He sat down across from her and frowned at her shirt.

"Nice shirt."

"I forgot to pack a nightgown."

"Careless of me to leave it lying around in my drawer like that."

She stuck out her tongue, went to the cupboard, and took out a heavy-looking mug and filled it with hot coffee for him.

Despite the banter, Delaney's mood was as somber as it had been the night before, and for the first time since she had known him he seemed to be struggling to make conversation.

"I was thinking it would be a good idea to take a ride across to New Jersey. I'd like to see if we can get ahold of Jamie Yamaguchi's roommate. If she has a phone number for her we won't have to wait until Yamaguchi gets back from her honeymoon. I'd also like to see if we can reach Keith Haynes in Paris and talk with him."

Katherine considered that for a moment. "It'll be more efficient if we split up. You interview the roommate and I'll go to Columbia and use their library. I'd like to see what I can come up with on the Farrington-Medlin Group."

"Are you sure?"

The cup was halfway to Katherine's lips. She paused and put it back down on the kitchen table, then stared out the window. The sun was already over the tops of the buildings on the other side of Central Park, bathing the trees in soft yellow light. Shadows were sharply angled and black. In the street below, taxis and passenger cars were beginning to appear in increasing numbers as New York's morning traffic swelled. Yesterday's rain had blown out to sea, leaving a sharp blue sky and a few scudding white clouds that held the promise of a fine summer day.

To the south Katherine could see the old Plaza Hotel at the corner of 59th Street and Fifth Avenue with its green dormers. It had closed recently and was being turned into condos and a shopping mall. A few blocks beyond that was another building, new and modern, a combination of glass, steel, and rust-colored granite. It rose seventy-five stories above the pavement. Katherine looked at it for a long time before she responded to Delaney's question.

"I have to know, John."

"We could let the cops and the FBI take it from here. It's only a matter of time until they put two and two together."

"I know," she said quietly. "Can I use your computer? It shouldn't be too hard to find a phone number for Metadine."

"Sure. It's in the den. I'll jump in the shower in the meantime."

It took Katherine only five minutes to locate a telephone number for the Metadine Corporation. It was located in Paris as Warren Wilkerson had told them. She picked up the phone and dialed, only to curse to herself when she got a recording saying the call couldn't be completed. She tried again, this time adding the country code, and got through on the second ring.

"Metadine, bonjour."

"Bonjour," Katherine said. "Do you speak English?"

"Oui . . . yes, a little," a young woman's voice answered. "How can I help you?"

"This is Katherine Adams in New York. I'm trying to locate Dr. Keith Haynes. I believe he is a new employee there."

There was a pause.

"Ah . . . just a moment and I will connect you, madame."

The wait was longer than Katherine expected. After two minutes she began to worry that she'd been forgotten and was about to hang up when a heavily accented man came on the line.

"This is Dr. Jacques Moussard. Can I help you?"

"Dr. Moussard, this is Katherine Adams calling from the United States. I'm trying to reach Keith Haynes. I believe he's just come to work for your company."

"As are we, madame. We've had no word from Dr. Haynes for three weeks now. I notified the police of this only yesterday."

Katherine was incredulous. "He never showed up?"

"Never. We sent a car to Charles de Gaulle Airport to meet him, but he was not on the flight. Everyone here has been very concerned. I even called his university, but they could tell me nothing. You are a relative, perhaps?"

"No. I'm an attorney. I was on the cruise liner that sank in the Atlantic a few weeks ago. Dr. Haynes was working with a man I met, and I wanted to ask him a few questions."

"Ah, the *Majestic*. Yes, we heard about it here in France, too. A terrible, terrible tragedy. Dr. Haynes was a colleague of Ellis Stephens, yes?"

"Yes. That's the man I met."

"My condolences, madame. It must have been a horrible experience. I said as much to Dr. Wilkerson."

"I see. When did you speak to Warren Wilkerson?"

"Last week . . . no . . . it would have been nearly two weeks ago. As I say, we have been most worried about Dr. Haynes, so I placed the call. Unfortunately, he had no more information than we did. This is when I thought it best to notify our police. The man seems to have totally vanished."

I'll just bet he did, thought Katherine. *Along with his wife.*

"Were you and Dr. Haynes personally acquainted?"

"No, no. I knew of his work and read several papers he and Dr. Stephens had published together, but we never met."

"I'm curious, Dr. Moussard . . . how was it he came to apply for a job with your company? Paris is not exactly across the street."

"Genetic research is not large field, madame. Sooner or later everybody in it tends to meet everybody else at the conferences and symposiums. Metadine has had excellent relations with Columbia University for many years. In fact, several of our own scientists have held positions there as, ah . . . how do you say, 'fellows.' When Dr. Wilkerson suggested Keith Haynes for our position we leaped at the opportunity."

"Do you remember the first time you contacted him?"

"I would have to consult my calendar, but it was quite recent, I think. Not more than a few weeks. We concluded the arrangements quickly. I don't mind telling you this whole affair is extremely troubling. We have been praying there is a reasonable explanation for his disappearance."

So have I, thought Katherine.

"Let me see if I understand correctly. You sought out Keith Haynes based solely on Warren Wilkerson's recommendation?"

"That and his published work, as I told you. Every major company in our field has been pursuing stem-cell research. We thought it would be a coup to obtain a man of his qualifications. Dr. Stephens would have been our first choice, but, ah. . . ."

"I understand."

When Katherine placed the receiver back on the hook she found that her hands were shaking. She exhaled and inhaled twice to calm herself. Wilkerson had lied to them. That was now clear. But *why?* A number of explanations occurred to her, though none made any sense except one—money. Wilkerson said as much himself. Katherine closed her eyes and leaned back in the chair.

Money. This is about money.

A footfall caused her to turn and she saw Delaney standing in the doorway with a towel around his waist. His hair and shoulders were still wet. The smile on his face faded the moment he saw her.

"What?"

"Wilkerson lied to us."

Delaney folded his arms across his chest and leaned against the doorjamb.

"I'm appalled . . . a man of his stature."

"I just got off the phone with Keith Haynes's boss in Paris, a gentleman named Jacques Moussard. He told me that Haynes never showed up. He just turned in a missing persons report to the Paris police yesterday."

"Right," said Delaney, "and. . . ."

"And he spoke to that bastard Wilkerson nearly *two weeks ago,* trying to find out where Haynes was. And do you know what else?"

"I can hardly wait."

"Guess who suggested Haynes for the job in the first place?"

"Wilkerson."

"Bingo."

"Son of a bitch," Delaney said under his breath. He took a deep breath and looked at Katherine. "Suddenly, I'm not getting a good feeling about Jamie Yamaguchi's hasty marriage, K. J."

Katherine held his gaze for several seconds before she pushed herself away from the computer and stood up.

"It'll take me thirty minutes to get dressed. If I can't find what I want at Columbia, I'll go down to the courts and look through their records. Why don't you call the roommate and set up an appointment while I shower?"

"Right."

She reached out and touched Delaney's shoulder as she walked by. She almost got to the bedroom before he spoke again.

"Katherine, we'll to have tell our people about this. You know that, don't you?"

She stopped walking but didn't turn around.

"I know," she said over her shoulder, then continued into the bathroom.

Katherine turned on the water, stepped into the tub, and closed the frosted-glass door behind her, blocking the rest of the world out. The water was hot and the shower soon began to fill with steam. She let it beat against her back and neck. The same thoughts that had kept her awake during the night returned with increasing clarity. Everything was so neat . . . so precise: Haynes had vanished, Yamaguchi was conveniently out of town, and Ellis Stephens was dead. Wilkerson was smooth, all right. They might even find him at the bottom of it all, but she didn't think so. What she did think made her want to scream. Piece by piece a picture was beginning to form. The problem was that she didn't want to see it.

"This shouldn't have happened," she said to herself.

Katherine finally shut the water and stepped out of the tub. After clearing away a portion of the mirror she stared at her reflection for several seconds. Then she went to get dressed.

Delaney was waiting when she came out of the bedroom. She had chosen a tan skirt and white blouse with a pair of comfortable low-heeled shoes.

"You look nice," he said.

"I don't feel so nice."

"I spoke to Mike Franklin and Benetiz, that cop we met last night. It turns out New York and the Feds already have a joint task force working on this. We're all going to meet at Wilkerson's office at 11:00 a.m. to have a little chat with him. I called the number Wilkerson gave me for Yamaguchi's apartment and got the cleaning lady. She told me the roommate works for an ad agency on Forty-fourth and Second. I'm meeting her in a half-hour. You sure you don't want to tag along? I could help you with the research after."

"No. You go, John. I've got to get to the bottom of this. Research is one of my strengths and you'd just slow me down. Even so, I may come up with nothing."

"I understand." Delaney held her gaze for a moment before he went into his bedroom. He came out again a few seconds later, carrying a handgun.

"Have you ever used one of these?" he asked.

She took the weapon and examined it for a few seconds, then handed it back. It was a nickel-plated SIG-Sauer with a black handle.

"My ex collected them," she said. "I went to the shooting range with him a few times when we were married. I probably won't need it at the library . . . unless the librarians start giving me a hard time."

"It's not a joke, K.J. I want you to carry it. It'll fit in your purse with no problem."

He held the gun out to her again. From the look on his face, she could see that he was serious.

"I'm not even sure my license is up to date," she said. "Besides, it's from Georgia."

"Check. If it is, we can fax a copy over to the license division and get you a temporary permit. I've got a few friends down there."

"John—"

"*Check*, K.J."

Katherine took a deep breath and went to get her purse. She pulled out her wallet and began looking though it. Delaney watched as a pile of credit cards, bobby pins, and papers of varying sizes, colors, and shapes began to accumulate on his desk.

"Don't say a thing," she warned, glancing up at him. "Ah . . . here it is." Katherine held up a small plastic card.

Delaney looked at the pile, shook his head slightly, and took the card from her.

"November thirtieth, next year," he said. "Let me make a copy and I'll fax it over to the firearms license division."

"I'll carry it, but I really don't think—"

"We're not dealing with nice people here and there's been one attempt on your life already. So as long as I'm not around to protect you, I want you to have something that will."

Katherine was certain there were several good arguments she could come up with, but Delaney was so adamant she kept them to herself and simply said, "Yes, John."

He nodded once and went to his copy machine, laid her license on the glass, and pressed the START button.

Katherine poured another cup of coffee while he made his phone calls.

Less than thirty minutes later they got a return fax showing a replica of a temporary handgun permit.

FORTY-ONE

It took Katherine most of the day to find what she was looking for. Using the computers at Columbia's law school, the first thing she did was access New York's limited-partnership database and bring up a copy of the Farrington-Medlin Groups' certificate. It showed the company was owned by two other companies: a limited partnership in Maine, and a corporation out of Virginia, which had been formed eight years earlier. The information sheet filed along with the certificate indicated their registered agent was located at 927 Third Avenue. Katherine jotted down the number and stepped outside to call them. Other than acknowledging they represented Farrington-Medlin and that they were authorized to accept legal papers on their behalf, the agent refused to give out any other information about the company or its owners.

Another hour of searching turned up the names of the limited partners in Virginia. Katherine stared at the second name on the list and squeezed her eyes shut.

This wasn't supposed to happen. The words went around in her brain again. *Wasn't supposed to happen.*

Minutes turned into hours as her fingers moved automatically over the keyboard. More pieces of the puzzle fell into place. Katherine finally got up and went outside to get some fresh air. When she turned on her cell phone there were three messages waiting.

One was from Zach, checking to see how she was doing; one was from Alley, also checking on her; and one was from Delaney.

I have good kids, she thought, feeling her throat constrict. At the moment she very much wanted to be with them.

When the first two messages were finished, she played Delaney's.

Jamie Yamaguchi's roommate turned out to be a former teacher named Wendy Samson, who had had no word from her friend since the day she disappeared—something totally out of character for her, according to Samson. Her only communication had been a note telling her Jamie was getting married and would contact her when she returned from her honeymoon.

According to Delaney, Samson knew nothing about the man Yamaguchi was marrying, nor did Jamie's parents, who were worried and upset by the news. Delaney spoke with them from the roommate's workplace. They told him they had recently called the New Jersey Police to file a report. Jamie Yamaguchi had been missing for nearly three weeks now.

She tried calling him back but got his voice mail. She was about to leave a message when Beth Doliver beeped in.

"Hey, K. J., what'cha doin'?"

"I'm here at Columbia, doing some research. Where are you?"

"At the office. I came in to get Jack's mail and pick up some files for him. I have a question."

"What is it?"

"Didn't you say you went to see Ellis Stephens's boss yesterday?"

"Yeah, Warren Wilkerson. He's the dean of the department."

"Wilkerson, right," said Beth. "I'm not sure if it's the same man, but I just came across that name in our club newsletter. They have a section that announces the new members and upcoming events."

Katherine heard the sound of pages being turned.

"It says here, 'Warren and Marcia Wilkerson and family became members last week.' Do you think it's the same guy?"

"It might be," said Katherine. "It's a common name, but I'll check it out. Let me tell you what I found this morning."

Katherine quickly related her telephone conversation with Jacques Moussard and the fact that Wilkerson had lied to them. She also told Beth about Keith Haynes's sudden departure and Jamie Yamaguchi's disappearance. When she finished, there was a long pause before Beth spoke again.

"This is really scary, K. J. You think this whole thing is about money, right?"

"I do."

"Do you have any idea how much it costs to join the Stonebridge Country Club?"

"Not really. A bunch, I guess."

"It's a hundred and twenty-five grand *up front* and you don't get it back when you leave. That's pretty steep for the dean of a college, wouldn't you say?"

Katherine whistled through her teeth. She heard more pages turning on Beth's end of the line.

"It says here they've just bought a house on Garman Road and are relocating to Scarsdale from Yonkers."

"Is that near where you live?"

"About ten minutes away," Beth told her. "They're building new homes all along Garman and the property values there are going crazy. A new house probably runs in the one- to two-million-dollar range."

"Hmm. If I could check the real estate records at the courthouse, I might get a good idea what he paid for it, assuming it's the same person. John won't be back for a couple of hours yet. I tried to reach him on the cell phone, but got his voice mail."

"I could pick you up. I'm only twenty minutes from where you are. This way you won't have to take the trains."

"That would be wonderful—if you're free. I mean, I don't want to—"

"Oh, for the love of Pete, K. J."

Katherine stood under the library's portico and looked out across the campus for another minute. She drew a long breath and went back inside. Something Jacques Moussard had said during their conversation was sticking in her mind. She sat down in front of the computer screen once more and began to search the patents and trademark records on file in Washington.

It came as no surprise to learn that a patent for a new stem cell had been filed nine days ago. She dialed Delaney's phone again and left another message.

JOHN DELANEY cursed out loud when Katherine didn't answer his call. He and Mike Franklin were in the car. He tried her again a few minutes later.

"Pick up the phone, K. J.," he said, when it rang for a third time. "Fuck, I got her voice mail again."

"Do you think she's still at Columbia?"

"It's possible."

"You wanna run up there and have a look-see?"

Tight-lipped, Delaney nodded.

Franklin pulled the blue light out from under his seat, opened the window, and slapped it on the roof of the car.

Speeding uptown, they reached Columbia's campus in just under ten minutes.

A pretty coed at the reception desk told them a woman answering Katherine's description had been there most of the morning.

"Do you have any idea which way she went?" asked Delaney.

"No, I'm sorry."

"How long ago did she leave?" asked Franklin.

"A little less than an hour ago, I think."

John Delaney and his former partner walked down the steps together to their car. He tried Katherine's phone once more but without success.

"Any idea where your girlfriend ran off to?"

Delaney shook his head and tried to concentrate. The more time passed, the more worried he was getting. They were dealing with ruthless, cunning people who wouldn't hesitate to kill again. And his fear for Katherine's safety was making his stomach do flips.

"You want me to put out an APB on her?" Franklin asked, starting the engine.

"Not yet, Mike."

"Maybe she left a message on your home phone. What d'you think?"

"Let me check."

Delaney dialed his own number and punched in the code. There were three messages waiting for him; the last one was from Katherine.

FORTY-TWO

Katherine flipped through computer printouts of the previous month's real estate transactions while Beth watched over her shoulder. She quickly located Warren and Marcia Wilkerson's names under the grantee listings of the real estate index. The book referred them to another book, even larger than the first, where photocopies of the official documents were kept. Katherine opened it and turned to the correct page, then leaned back so Beth could see.

"What am I looking at?" asked Beth.

"This is a deed to secure debt."

"A what?"

"A mortgage. It was taken out ten days ago."

"Ten days?"

"Right. It seems our friend Mr. Wilkerson and his wife have just bought a home at 360 Garman Road for 2.4 million dollars."

"Damn."

"What's more, the mortgage is only for $1,680,000, and it's for fifteen years."

"They put down $720,000?" Beth asked, shaking her head.

"That's what it looks like."

"Maybe his wife has money, K. J."

"Yeah, maybe."

"Do you want to run by and take a look at it? Garman Road's only fifteen minutes from here."

"Good idea," said Katherine.

Katherine and Beth drove south from White Plains along Post Road and turned off at Palmer Avenue. They found Garman Road without difficulty. It was a tree-lined street containing a mixture of old brick homes, tall chimneys, and well-maintained lawns. Here and there, newer construction was beginning to replace the older, more dated homes.

A neighborhood in transition, Katherine thought, *going from rich to richer.*

Number 360 Garman was a French chateau complete with a slate roof and custom rock work around the entrance. An archway at the side of the house was also made of stone and led to a motor court and a four-car garage. There was a late-model Lexus parked in the driveway.

"All right, we've seen it. Now let's go," said Beth. "Someone's here."

Katherine said, "I think I'd like to go in and ask Mr. Wilkerson a couple of questions. A place like this is a lot of money to come up with, even if he is a dean, don't you think?"

"Yeah, it's a shitload of money," said Beth. "But he could have won it gambling or maybe he hit the lottery. He could have found it under a rock, for all we know. He's only going to tell you to fuck off and have us both arrested for trespassing. Now come on."

Katherine opened the door and started to get out. Beth grabbed her arm.

"*No,* K. J. If he's one of the bad guys, it could be dangerous. Just turn everything over to the police and let them deal with him."

Katherine considered doing just that for a second and was almost ready to agree when the image of several hundred dead bodies floating on the cold waters of the Atlantic Ocean and a burning ship came into her mind. Once before, a very long time ago, she'd escaped a horrific situation and others had died. It was time to end it, time to bury the ghosts.

"You wait here. I won't be long."

"*Katherine.*"

"I've got John's gun in my purse," she said, over her shoulder.

Beth watched her friend walk up the driveway and into the house. "Fuck," she said, and got out of the car as well.

Warren Wilkerson was seated in a large wingback chair in the family room. He didn't get up when Katherine entered. Nor did he answer when she spoke his name. When she heard the door close behind her, Katherine instinctively reached into her purse, but took her hand out a second later, realizing it was Beth. Without taking her eyes off Wilkerson, she set the purse down by the fireplace and took a few steps toward him. Even from where she was standing she could see he was dead. His eyes were open but they were staring at nothing.

Katherine studied his face for a several seconds. Wilkerson's right temple had a round black hole in it. He looked vaguely surprised, she thought. Her eyes passed over the rest of his body. A pistol was clutched in his right hand. Katherine started to move closer, when another sound stopped her. The sound of a gun's hammer being cocked. She turned slowly around to face Beth Doliver, who was standing in the middle of the room with a revolver aimed at her chest.

"*This wasn't supposed to happen.* Those were the words you used on the ship, weren't they, Beth? I didn't get it at the time."

"Step away from the body, K. J.," Beth said, motioning with her gun.

Katherine straightened and moved back a few steps.

"We've been friends for twenty-five years and you used me."

"Everybody uses everybody, Katherine. You get used to a certain lifestyle. Jack's company has been in trouble

for some time now, and the board was on the verge of fir-
ing him. I didn't have a choice."

"You didn't have a *choice?* You murdered people in
cold blood."

"Nobody was supposed to get killed. I swear to God.
Why couldn't you have let it alone?"

Katherine shook her head. "Right—just go home and
forget about the hundreds of people. Why? *Why?*"

"That was an accident. The problem with hiring terrorists
is they have their own agendas. All we wanted was Ellis's
research and for *you* to slow down Gotchal Biomedical. It
was just a matter of fingering Bennett Williams. And you
did exactly that. It couldn't have worked out any better."

"Slow them down?"

"That's right," Beth said. "We knew about your background, or at least I did. After a shipboard robbery and a
fire, who better to finger Williams than the attorney who
sent him to jail twenty years ago? It was all perfect."

"And you knew I'd go after him when I heard arson was
involved."

"I remembered how you went on and on about how the
callous prick had tried to burn people to death at the
clinic. You wanted to put him away for life. It was just a
matter of you making the right connection."

"But why kill poor Ellis?"

"Also an accident. It was never in the plan to kill
Stephens *or* to destroy that ship. Do you think I'm insane? Those Arab bastards did that on their own. We're
businesspeople."

"We're?"

"I have partners, K. J. Powerful people, with powerful
connections. I didn't manage this by myself, and Jack
could never have handled it."

"So you resorted to murder. That's beautiful."

"*All* they were supposed to do was to create a diversion . . . a small fire, nothing more. The *Marie Star* was waiting there to take our people off in the confusion. *That's it.*"

"And trying to have me killed in Portofino . . . that was part of your diversion too, right? Paul Marchefski, Keith Haynes, Jamie Yamaguchi . . . just more diversions, weren't they?"

"After things got mucked up, we had no choice," Beth explained. "That moron Cardwell gave Maharan his lighter. You were supposed to finish your vacation and go back home, but *no,* you and your playmate had to keep poking around."

"That farce with you and the car—that was all part of the charade, too?"

"Either the ignorant son of a bitch didn't understand English or he didn't care. Apparently it made no difference whether he took you out or took you and me out at the same time. A buck's a buck, right?"

Katherine nodded slowly. "I see."

"*No*, you don't see, K. J. That's why I got you here. I wanted to talk to you . . . to make you understand. I *had* no choice. I hope you believe that. Jack's nearly sixty and he has a bad heart. What's he going to do, start all over? I have this aversion to becoming a bag lady."

Katherine looked at her friend and shook her head sadly.

"The police already know everything, Beth. They're on their way here."

"Sure, they are," Beth said, glancing out the window. "I know you better than that. You're here because you want to tie things up in a neat little package. That's the way you are—one step at a time, Katherine. If you'll listen to reason, we can make a deal and everyone comes out ahead."

"Not likely."

"You're too close to the forest to see the trees. They're going to disbar you, K. J. It's just a matter of picking the right scapegoat . . . and *you're* it. We can help with that. We've got enough lawyers and resources to keep them tied up for the next twenty years. The same thing goes for Williams's stupid lawsuit."

"It's that simple?"

"It's that simple. Money makes the world go round. I learned that a long time ago. Ellis's research was the last piece we needed. When the clinical trials are over, Warwick Reed will get FDA approval. And I'm telling you, the economic return will be *unimaginable*. You could have anything you want—"

"Just as long as I keep my mouth shut and become your partner, right?" Katherine glanced at Warren Wilkerson's body. "Forgive me, but your track record with partners is somewhat depressing."

"The man was a fool. I told him to wait—to be patient. And what does he do? The imbecile goes out and joins a country club and buys a home he couldn't afford in his wildest dreams."

Katherine rubbed her face with her hands. Suddenly she felt very tired.

"How long do you think it's going to take them to figure out that Beth Doliver is one of the limited partners of the *Marie Star*? You think using your maiden name will hide it? I recognized Elizabeth *Medlin* immediately."

"So that was it."

"That, and your comment on the ship about this not being supposed to happen; the patent Warwick Reed just took out for a new stem cell; Pinky Marchefski's death; you name it. You're the only one I told about meeting him last night and what he was doing for us. You're not dealing with fools, Beth."

"Yes, I am. Everyone will listen to reason. Money has a way of doing that. And those who won't, well . . ."

"Yeah, what's a few more deaths, right?" Katherine said. "You make me sick."

Beth stared at Katherine for several seconds. "Where's the gun John gave you, K. J.?"

"In my purse."

Beth checked the room and saw the purse lying by the fireplace. Keeping her weapon trained on Katherine, she backed up, bent down, and picked it up. That was when she noticed Katherine's cell phone was open. It took another second before she realized there was a call in progress.

Beth opened her mouth in shock as Mike Franklin and John Delaney burst through the doors on either end of the room at the same time.

"Freeze," Franklin yelled.

FORTY-THREE

The first shot caught Delaney in the shoulder and spun him around. The second shot went wide as three bullets fired in rapid succession from Mike Franklin's gun sent Beth crashing backward into the wall. She was dead before she hit the ground. Keeping his weapon trained on her, Franklin walked over and kicked her gun away. He felt the pulse at her neck. After a few seconds he looked at Katherine and shook his head.

Within minutes, two uniformed police officers from the Scarsdale Police Department pulled up in their cruiser. They ran up the lawn, their service revolvers drawn.

Franklin met them at the front door and showed them his badge. He told one of the officers to call for an ambulance. His partner surveyed the scene and promptly radioed for backup.

Delaney was sitting up in a chair by the time Franklin came back. Katherine was by his side.

"How ya doin', buddy?" he asked, putting a hand on Delaney's good shoulder.

"I'm okay," Delaney answered, grimacing as he shifted positions.

"Don't move, John," said Katherine.

Delaney nodded and leaned his head back. "What a fuckin' mess," he said, looking at Beth and Wilkerson.

"I called for an ambulance," Franklin told them. "They should be here in a couple of minutes. You gonna hang in there?"

"Yeah."

"How about you, boat lady?" asked Franklin. "You still in one piece?"

"I'm fine. We have to get John to a doctor. He's bleeding."

"I can see that. Like I said, the ambulance is on the way."

"I promised to take her to a play," Delaney told him.

"You're not going anywhere, except maybe to a hospital," said Katherine.

"She's right. Let's get you cleaned up first, then we'll see how things go. Deal?"

"Deal."

When he finished checking Beth and Wilkerson, the Scarsdale police officer came over to join them.

"Somebody want to tell me what happened here?"

Franklin filled him in on the phone conversation he and Delaney had overheard while they were en route.

The officer took notes while Franklin was talking.

"This is Jack Doliver's wife?" he asked, indicating Beth.

"Right," said Katherine. She looked at Beth's body and thought that she should be feeling something.

"Brother, this is going to be a barrel of laughs," the officer said. "Her husband's a big shot around here. You know him?"

"I know him," said Katherine.

"So, let me get this straight—you and Mr. Delaney were on that cruise liner that sank, right?" the officer asked.

Katherine nodded.

"And you and Detective Franklin heard the deceased confess to killing this man and being involved with the ship going down?" he asked Delaney.

"K. J. turned her cell phone on when she and Beth got here," he explained. "It was pretty straightforward stuff."

The officer took a deep breath and flipped his notebook shut.

"You know you'll have to go through all this again when CID arrives. As soon as I get back to the station I'll type up my report and send each of you a copy. Okay?"

"That'll be fine," said Franklin. "You know where to reach me."

The reflection of a blue light outside turned everyone's head toward the window. The ambulance had arrived.

"Anything I can do for you?" asked the officer.

Delaney shook his head and gave him a tight-lipped smile.

"Hang in there, okay?" the officer said to Delaney. "Here come the paramedics."

The officer started toward the door, but then stopped and looked at Katherine. They held each other's gaze for a moment before he laughed once to himself and shook his head. Then he walked out.

FORTY-FOUR

Katherine Adams leaned back in the ambulance as it drove through the streets. Delaney was treated and released from White Plains Medical Center the following day. Mike Franklin managed to pull a few strings and got the ambulance company to transport them back to Manhattan that evening. By the time they reached the city most of the shops were closing down for the night. The sultry warmth of a New York summer night drifted in through the windows. The blue light was on, but not the siren. It was a clear night, free of smog and haze.

Katherine thought about Beth Doliver again and wondered why she felt so numb regarding her friend. Maybe the feelings would come later. She could still see her lying there. At the moment she felt nothing at all. The rain from two days ago had washed away the city's grit and grime, at least for a while, leaving an ink-black sky filled with a thousand lights. Katherine looked up. There were more stars out than she remembered seeing when she lived there.

Delaney was resting comfortably on the stretcher, his eyes closed. She watched his face for several seconds and felt his hand slide into hers. He squeezed and she squeezed back to let him know she was still there. A faint smile touched the corners of his mouth before the sedatives the doctors had given him took hold and he drifted off to sleep again.

A full, clear moon hung over the buildings on Manhattan's West Side, painting the waters of the Hudson River silver. In the trees, night birds called to one another, oblivious to the world outside Central Park. They would continue singing until morning came and a new day began.

Katherine listened to their songs, rested her head against the window, and smiled to herself.

EPILOGUE

In the weeks following Beth Doliver's funeral, a great deal of information about why the *Ocean Majestic* had been sunk and the parties responsible for it began to come out.

A federal judge sitting in New York issued an injunction against Warwick Reed Pharmaceuticals, enjoining them from disseminating or in any way using Ellis Stephens's research. Jack Doliver resigned as chairman of the board a month later, citing ill health.

The trustees of Columbia University, who had been following the case closely, immediately entered into a private settlement with Libby Stephens regarding ownership of her husband's work, the terms of which were not disclosed.

Keith Haynes's body was found in a remote Paris suburb. His throat had been cut and his wallet was missing. Initially, the Paris police wrote the crime off as a robbery, but the case was reopened after they spoke with agents of the FBI. Ellis's other assistant, Jamie Yamaguchi, was never heard from again.

The civil suit by Bennett Williams ended less spectacularly than it had begun. A national television network asked for and received permission to televise the trial. They set up cameras outside the courtroom and at the front gates of Katherine's home. Their expert analyst cast Williams in the role of an innocent who had been victimized by a vengeful former prosecutor for her own aggrandizement. This played well for nearly a week, until the trial judge dismissed the case against Katherine and the other defendants. His eight-page ruling held that Katherine had behaved in a proper manner and had done what any responsible citizen should have done under the circumstances. The opinion went on to state the United States Navy had the right to detain anyone suspected of terrorism and murder for a reasonable length of time while they conducted an inquiry. This was particularly true when such incidents took place on the high seas.

The State Bar of Georgia, cognizant of the good publicity Katherine was receiving, and not wishing to see themselves cast in the role of villains, rethought their original position and determined that her violation of the court order was only a *technical* one. A press conference was hurriedly convened. A spokesman for the Bar stated that *when balanced against the need to prevent a possible loss of life, they were in agreement with the federal trial judge*. In the end, they issued Katherine an informal letter of warning which amounted to less than a reprimand, and the case was closed.

Six weeks after John Delaney was shot, he traveled to Atlanta to attend a reception for the opening of Katherine Adams & Associates, P.C. During the trip he met all three of the Adams children. At one point at the reception party, after they had all sat down to eat, Alley Adams leaned around him and gave her mother a thumb's-up sign. The boys liked him as well.

Nearly a year later Katherine received an invitation to the unveiling of Beth Doliver's headstone at the Spring Lawn Cemetery in Scarsdale.

She declined to attend.

TOR

Award-winning authors
Compelling stories

Please join us at the website
below for more information
about this author and other great
Tor selections, and to sign up for
our monthly newsletter!